The Abandoned Daughter

8

Wood was born in Maidstone, Kent, and brought up
aybrooke, Leicestershire. Born one of fifteen children
middle-class mother and an East End barrow boy,
's family were poor but rich in love. This encouraged
 develop a natural empathy with the less fortunate and
ination with social history. In 1989 Mary was inspired
en her first novel and she is now a full-time novelist.

ary welcomes interaction with readers and invites you
 ubscribe to her website where you can contact her,
ive regular newsletters and follow links to meet her on
 book and Twitter: www.authormarywood.com

BY MARY WOOD

The Breckton series

To Catch a Dream
An Unbreakable Bond
Tomorrow Brings Sorrow
Time Passes Time

The Generation War saga

All I Have to Give
In Their Mother's Footsteps

The Girls Who Went to War series

The Forgotten Daughter
The Abandoned Daughter

Stand-alone novels

Proud of You
Brighter Days Ahead
The Street Orphans

The Abandoned Daughter

Mary Wood

PAN BOOKS

First published 2019 by Pan Books
an imprint of Pan Macmillan
20 New Wharf Road, London N1 9RR
Associated companies throughout the world
www.panmacmillan.com

ISBN 978-1-5098-5054-9

1 3 5 7 9 8 6 4 2

A CIP catalogue record for this book is available from the British Library.

Typeset in ITC Galliard Std by Palimpsest Book Production Ltd, Falkirk, Stirlingshire
Printed and bound by CPI Group (UK) Ltd, Croydon, CR0 4YY

*In memory of my darling friend, Sandra Moss Clements.
I cannot believe I will not be able to bring you my latest
book and see you smile with glee at the prospect of
reading it. You showed such pride in me and encouraged
me along the way from my very first book. You will
always be on my journey. Forever in my heart. Never
forgotten. Loved and cherished.*

PART ONE
France, Belgium and London, 1918

~

Ella and Paddy

A Desperate Situation

Chapter One

A cry of pain cut through the air as Ella and Jim walked past the tent-ward that stood on the edge of Field Hospital 16 in Dieppe, France. Ella heard these cries every day in her job as a Voluntary Aid nurse, but she never got used to it. A shudder trembled through her body. The war had raged for four long years and she wondered if all the young men she'd nursed during that time would be engraved forever on her mind.

Jim's hand tightened on hers, bringing her back to the present moment and causing her unease. Yes, she'd been attracted to him when they had first met, and he'd become a large part of her life, but her feelings had changed over the years and now she only wanted to be friends. She shouldn't have agreed to walk with him. She should have said her goodbyes amidst the comings and goings of the busy hospital, but Jim had been insistent. Now, as they headed away from the safety of being with other people, she feared he would try to make advances towards her, and she didn't want that. She wanted their parting to be a good one. *If only Jim would accept that I can't love him the way he wants me to.*

As an ambulance driver, Jim ferried the wounded to hospital from the battlefields. Tall and handsome, he had a cockney humour that endeared him to all who came across him, and he was one of the bravest men Ella knew. But as time went on, his advances had become a nuisance, and yet he'd been a constant in her life – a distraction from all the horror. Warding him off had become a part of their relationship. As had long chats and sharing jokes, and worrying about him when the fighting was heavy and Jim was in the thick of it. And yes, the feelings of happiness and relief when he showed up, grinning as if his smile was a permanent fixture, like one of those rag dolls with a sewn-on look of happiness.

'A penny for 'em, Ella.'

'Sorry, I was just thinking about my new placement.' It was a fib, but she couldn't share her true thoughts. 'I was wondering what Hospital 36 will be like and thinking what a coincidence it is that I should have started my war service in Belgium and am now returning there, for what looks like the end of the war.'

'It could well be. News is that the push forward is going well. But it will be dangerous and harrowing there. Not that I'm in the business of scaring yer, but Rousbrugge is very close to the front line.'

'Well, I'm used to that. I haven't forgotten what it was like when the fighting was a few fields away from here.'

'No, but at least we were together then. Now you will be far away from me – and that's cutting me in two.'

'Oh, Jim, I don't know what to say. You know that I can't . . . Well, let's not get into that. Besides, I will have others with me. The team that I work with are all going: the surgeons, Alan Mathews and Daniel Frazer, and Connie Knight, the senior theatre nurse.'

'That's summink then. But this is all so sudden. I feel as though 'alf of me is being torn from me.'

'Jim, I—'

'No, don't say it. We'll see, eh? Let's go to the clifftop and 'ave some time alone together before you go.'

Instinct saw Ella trying to wriggle out of this, as she reminded Jim that she had to get back to her duties.

'Just one more stroll there together, eh, girl? Go on, you know yer can't resist me.'

His wink, as he said this, made Ella laugh and she felt herself relax. She supposed there could be no harm in a last walk together to end their relationship, as that is what it would be – an end, because despite Jim having given her his home address, she knew she would never contact him again. This decision didn't sit easily with her, as she did value his friendship, but she knew it was the kindest thing she could do for him.

'Jim, you're incorrigible!'

'Don't you mean irresistible?'

Nerves clenched her stomach at the note she detected in his voice. But no, she was being silly. Yes, Jim wanted more than she could give, but he knew how she felt and he respected her. There was nothing to be afraid of. And although Ella knew her rejection of Jim hurt him, she also knew it was the right thing to do. One day he would meet someone who could love him as he deserved to be loved, and in the way that she could never love him – or any man, if it came to that, because she'd often wondered if she would ever give her heart fully to anyone.

Ella had never had much to do with men. Brought up by

her nanny and schooled at an all-girls school staffed solely by women, it was only when she went into nursing that she'd come into close contact with them. Since the outbreak of war she had mostly seen their vulnerable side – men who were maimed and broken – although she'd also seen how strong and resilient they could be.

She'd been shy at first when she'd found herself thrust into their world, perhaps because she couldn't remember a time with her own father. This thought nudged the ever-present ache she held in her heart at not knowing who her parents were or if they were still alive – or even if she had any family members.

The only information she had about herself was that her nanny had brought her from Poland to London as a child of three, and that an allowance was paid into her bank account, and a separate allowance was paid into Nanny's for their keep. Why this was so burned her soul with sadness and intense curiosity, but whenever she'd broached the subject, she'd sensed Nanny's hurt. Not wanting to be the cause of distress to the woman who was like a mother to her, and whom she loved dearly, Ella hadn't insisted that she be told the truth. Instead she'd drifted along and had reached the age of twenty-two without knowing about her past, but had never given up on her dream of wanting to find out. One day in the future she would.

When they reached the cliff edge they stood out of sight of the hospital, not talking, just gazing out to sea. The vastness of the endless water and the sound of the crashing waves held Ella in awe. Breathing in deeply, she noticed that the air, although fresh, was tinged by the smell of smoke from the cigarette Jim had lit.

Lifting her head, she allowed the mid-September sun to soothe her troubled thoughts. A kind of peace descended on her, but was shattered in seconds as Jim took her hand once more. His hold wasn't gentle. His look intensified the fear that she'd pushed to the back of her mind, as he discarded the butt of his cigarette and pulled her close. 'No! Jim, don't . . .'

'I have to, Ella. I have to make you mine.'

Clamped in his arms, Ella couldn't move. *Oh God, don't let this happen!* 'Let me go, Jim. You're hurting me!'

'Oh, Ella . . . Ella.' The hoarse sound of his voice heightened her fear. Jim had become a different being now.

'Don't – please. Please don't . . . No! We can forget this, if you stop now. Please, Jim.'

'Don't plead with me, Ella. Oh, Ella, I – I want you so badly.'

His lips kissed her face. Held as if moulded to his body, Ella could feel his need pressed against her. A sob caught in her throat. Jim's lust-filled eyes bored into hers and his breath fanned her face. The tang of the cigarette he'd smoked caught in her nostrils.

This was a Jim she didn't know – a powerful, animal-like man who cared nothing for her, only for his need of her.

'I love you, Ella. I 'ave to do this. I 'ave to make you mine.'

'This isn't love; this is you out of control. Stop it now, Jim! Please. I understand what is motivating you, but you don't have to give in to your feelings. Not like this. No—'

His movement toppled her, and the patch of grass they stood on didn't cushion her fall. Pain ricocheted through Ella's body. Her breath left her lungs with a force that made her think she would never be able to draw it back in again.

Jim's body pressed her into the earth. His weight was crushing her. He uttered something about being sorry, but didn't stop. His hands fumbled with her clothes and then kneaded the bare thigh above her stocking.

Despite being unable to breathe, she struggled against him, but his fingers reached inside her suspenders, then inside her knickers. His moan showed her the hopelessness of her situation. At last, drawing the breath back into her, she screamed out, 'Help me! Oh God, help me.' But her cry went into the wind and was drowned by the sounds of the sea below them. Despair engulfed her, as Jim pushed himself inside her knickers and entered her, causing pain of a different kind to sear through her. 'No! No. Oh God, help me!'

Droplets of sweat fell onto her face. Her name, spoken over and over again in a declaration of love, mocked her, as Jim pounded her unmercifully.

Disgust overcame all other feelings, turning Ella into a rag doll as she lay still beneath him, too hurt to fight, too humiliated to beg any longer. Her mind was tortured by the frailty that prevented her from being able stop this onslaught on her body – on her soul.

At last Jim stopped thrusting and stiffened. His moan became an animal-like grunting as he shot his seed into her. His gasping words taunted her. 'Now you're mine – mine, Ella. You belong to me. Marry me. Marry me, me darlin' girl.'

Taking advantage of the weakness that his release had brought upon him, Ella used what strength she had left to push him off her. Rolling over, she gave vent to the sobs that shook her body. Beside her, she felt Jim move. 'Don't touch me!'

'Oh, Ella, me darlin', I didn't mean to hurt yer. They say

it always hurts the first time. If you marry me, you can apply to stay near me, and then I'll show you what it really feels like. I love yer, Ella. I love yer so much.'

Sitting up, she turned to face him. 'You have no idea, have you? You pig-headed beast! I don't love you. I didn't want you to do that to me. I HATE YOU!'

For the first time, it seemed that the truth got through to Jim. Shock registered on his face as he stared at her. His mouth dropped open. 'But . . .'

'There is no "but". You're vile – vile!'

'And you're not, eh? Teasing me, giving me the run-around. Well, yer got what I should 'ave done a long time ago. You got what yer deserved.'

Gone was the Jim she'd known. This filthy being in front of her had a look that terrified her more than his lust did. Ella wanted to spit in his face.

'Don't look at me like that. Yer've always known how I've felt and yer played up to that. Yer nothing but a whore.'

'SHUT UP! STOP . . . STOP SPEAKING!'

Every limb of Ella's body trembled. For a moment she thought she would faint. Taking deep breaths, she adjusted her clothing. Jim didn't try to stop her as she turned and stumbled away.

When she came to the slope that would take her down to the sea, she began to run. Not stopping at the water's edge, she dived into a fierce, bitterly cold wave, wanting to be cleansed. The water took her into its depths, swirled her around, played with her. Then fear of a different kind gripped her, at the power the waves had over her. Fighting with all the strength she could muster, she felt her head surface above the water at last, only to look into Jim's evil eyes.

His hand reached for her. Terror filled her as a painful tug of her hair compelled her towards him. As he wrapped his legs around her, his weight pulled her down. His face, hideously distorted by the water, mocked her.

Fighting for all she was worth, Ella freed herself. She needed air! Desperation had her flapping her arms and this propelled her upwards. At last her head was out of the water.

Jim shot up beside her. 'Yer're not going to live to tell yer lies, whore!'

Grabbing her, he held her head under his arm. A wave crashed over them and the water engulfed her. Her lungs burned with the effort of holding her breath. As the water receded, Ella released the painful breath and gasped in another that filled her lungs. Jim forced her head under the water once more. Flailing her arms and legs didn't help. His strength was too much for her. The fear of death gripped her. *Oh God, save me – save me!*

Finding a strength she didn't know she possessed, Ella lifted her leg and kicked towards Jim's groin. He let her go. Kicking with all her might, she struggled against the force of the waves as they cut and bruised her and tossed her as if she were nothing. At last she emerged from the water. Jim was nowhere to be seen.

'Open your eyes, Ella. You're safe. Oh, Ella, what happened? Why – why did you go to the water's edge? You know how dangerous those waves are. They can take you in seconds.'

'Jim . . . he . . .' Shame stopped Ella finishing what she was going to say. She looked up into Matron's kindly eyes and read her trust. A trust that had seen Matron put her forward for extra training and had given her more responsibility than she'd given any other Voluntary Aid nurse. And she saw respect, too. That was there, along with concern. How could she break any of those feelings that Matron had for her by telling of the ugly, shameful thing that had happened?

'I'm sorry, Ella. Jim hasn't been found. The French coastal rescue workers are out in a boat looking for him, but haven't yet reported back to us. I'm so sorry. Such a lovely man.'

A sob released itself from Ella. A fearful, wrenching sob.

'We mustn't give up hope, Ella. You made it. And Jim will, too. Now, don't worry. You're bruised, but mostly around your thighs. You're suffering from cold and you're in shock, but you'll be all right. You can't move, because we have wrapped you up tightly in a blanket. Once you are warm, you can get a hot shower and see how you are then. I hope you will be all right to go with the others. You are sorely needed by Hospital 36. You're part of a very valuable team.'

Ella nodded. The misery she felt was embedded deep inside her, and she knew in that moment that she had to keep secret the terrible thing that had happened. Jim was dead, she was sure of it. She'd killed him. Yes, it was self-defence, but better that they all think it was an accident. She'd simply have to live with it, and immerse herself once more in the work of taking care of the wounded. She had so much more to give, and maybe in giving she could forget. Besides, she couldn't bear the shame of anyone knowing of the rape. Fingers would point at her. Many a time she'd been teased about Jim and she'd laughed it off, but everyone knew they were close. Hadn't most of them seen her go hand-in-hand with him to the clifftop? How could they believe that nice Jim, the lovable cockney, would do such a thing to her? She could hardly believe it herself.

11

As she lay back, her mind wandered to her friend, Flora, a volunteer with whom she'd formed a deep friendship at the beginning of the war. Ella, Flora and Mags had all been young, fresh-faced Voluntary Aid workers, or VADs, thrown together when they were shipped to Brussels in 1914.

When the Germans had invaded soon after their arrival, they'd found themselves stranded and alone. The friendship they formed then had helped them find the courage to cope.

Ella felt a new understanding dawn on her of what had motivated Flors, as she had called her, to come back to nursing, despite having given up after their escape from Brussels, in order to marry and have a child. Flors had needed to challenge herself beyond endurance, to help her forget. *And that's what I have to do. I have to cope with this.*

Ella remembered how Flors had been full of pain when she'd arrived in France two years ago. Cyrus, her beloved husband, had been captured and was in a prisoner-of-war camp – probably still was. And her much-loved half-brother Freddy was being sent here to fight. Flors had said she'd have gone mad if she'd spent her time waiting at home. But when Freddy had been killed in action, it had knocked the stuffing out of Flors and she'd left to go home to her child. How Ella wished Flors was here now.

Oh, Flors. War brought us together – will its end reunite us? But then, will it end? Yes, it must. It must. Jim said that the final push is going our way.

Ella's stomach lurched. The mere thought of Jim's name made her want to be sick.

'Nurse, fetch a vomit bowl, quickly.'

Ella felt as though she was heaving her heart out of her body, as wave after wave of sickness took her, but when at last the bout came to an end, a small part of her felt cleansed.

'There, that's better. Just some muck you must have swallowed. Drink this.' Matron held a mug of water to her lips.

Ella dutifully sipped and felt healed of the need to throw up. *But will I ever feel healed of the violation of my body and soul? Or of the betrayal of trust?* Because that's what Jim's vile act had done.

Well, now Jim was gone – Ella was certain of that. The kick she'd given him had found its mark. He would have gasped against the agony that assailed his body, but instead of taking in air, his lungs would have filled with water.

A tear trickled down her cheek as loneliness engulfed her. *Why – why did Jim, someone I took as a friend, do what he did?* No answer came.

Chapter Two

Paddy stood for a moment outside the makeshift ward of Hospital 36. Wiping the sweat from her brow, she welcomed the spots of rain hitting her face, because they hid the tears running down her cheeks. Tears shed for an unknown soldier, whose hand had gripped hers as he took his last agonizing breath. It was something that happened often, but it always got to her.

Explosions and gunfire assaulted her ears as an ambulance drew up, spraying muddy water over her feet. 'We've five inside for you, Paddy. It's hell out there, but we're winning, lass. This war is coming to an end.'

Taking a deep breath, Paddy nodded. 'How we're to cope with them is a matter for the Good Lord himself, Lou. Are they for being badly injured?'

'Naw. I reckon as you'll soon have them back in the firing line.' Lou laughed at his own joke, but Paddy couldn't join in. Oh, she knew the only way was to make light of it all, but not today. Today she was tired to the bones of her, and more than a bit down in spirits.

Lou passed by her as he guided the stretcher-bearers into

the ward, his smile lifting her a little. 'Perk up, lass. I heard there are reinforcements on the way for you.'

'Aye, it is that there's a team of Red Cross workers coming, and sorely needed they are, too.'

'You're reet there, lass. Our lads are not having an easy job of it.'

The lad on the stretcher chipped in. 'It's as bad as anything we experienced at the Somme.'

Forgetting her own sorrow, Paddy told him, 'Well, you're doing a good job, so you are. You're for nearly having it won. And it is that you're safe now.'

Safe, but for how long?

Shaking this thought away, Paddy straightened her body and wiped her face. She had been stationed in Hospital 36 for the last six months and during that time had visited the hell the soldiers had spoken of more than once.

She'd been surprised to be taken into Queen Alexandra's nursing service, but the rules had been altered, due to a shortage of nurses, and they no longer only took women from wealthy backgrounds, but welcomed all qualified nurses. A lot of Irish lasses were amongst the ranks. Oh, how she wished there were some of them here; she'd give anything to hear the lilt of the Irish tongue.

Leaving Lou to unload the men and show them to the receiving bay, Paddy walked away from tent-ward seven, where she had been working. Matron had given her a ten-minute break to collect herself, and she meant to take full advantage of it. Although Matron was a strict taskmaster, she had a sixth sense when it came to her nurses and often showed compassion, even though her usual maxim was that everything must carry on, no matter what.

Outside the perimeter of the hospital Paddy followed a

safe path away from the direction of the fighting. Huddled in her cloak against the onslaught of the rain, she felt an overwhelming sense of loneliness for her beloved Ireland engulf her.

She and her widowed father had been forced to flee to London. They had lived in the south of Ireland, not far from Dublin, on the estate of Lord Herringbone, an English gentleman – a good man, who had sponsored Paddy through her nurses' training. It had broken her heart when the Fenians had burned his house to the ground. She'd been glad that he and his family were away in England at the time. And glad, too, that her mammy hadn't lived to be part of her pappy taking to the drink, and of them living in squalor.

The war had saved Paddy, in a way. And her pappy, too, for he had joined up as a training-camp chef to the troops in England. It was a blessing to know that he was safe.

'You're a fast walker, Nurse. I'm out of breath trying to catch up with you.'

The voice made her jump. Turning, she saw Private Bobby Baker and her heart fluttered.

'What is it you are doing out here, Bobby? For sure you'll catch your death!'

'Oh? Quicker than I will when they send me back to the bloodbath, then?'

Bobby had been brought in with a broken ankle, sustained when he'd slid back into a trench and landed on a dead soldier's gun. He'd been traumatized to find the body was that of his friend, and hadn't felt the pain of his break until he'd tried to stand up. Now he was mended and would soon return to the front line. How would she bear that? For Bobby had snatched her heart from her the moment she'd

16

looked into his eyes. This thought had her lowering her head, as a blush crept up her cheeks.

'Don't be talking like that, Bobby. You are one of those who has nine lives, so you are. You'll come through. Is it not true that the war is almost over?'

'Aye, it is. But it isn't the war that I came after you to talk about. I – I, well, I was wondering, Paddy, if we could keep in touch?'

The flutter turned into a somersault as her heart leapt with joy. 'I'd be for liking that, Bobby, so I would.'

The silence between them held all the tension of their feelings. For Paddy, it was as if the dreams she'd had since first seeing Bobby were coming to life.

Bobby broke the stillness. 'You're beautiful, Paddy. I – I hope I'm not speaking out of turn, but, well, I would like us to be more than friends.' His hand reached out and touched her face.

'I'm for thinking we already are . . .'

Bobby's drawing of her into his arms stopped any further conversation. Paddy went willingly and lifted her head to him. His kiss was light at first, but deepened to one of intense desire, awakening deep feelings inside her.

'What do you think you are doing, Nurse Riley?'

The voice of Sister Price zinged fear through Paddy, and she jumped back and stood to attention. 'I – it's sorry, that I am, ma'am. I—'

'That may well be the case, but fraternizing with one of the patients, in such a manner, is a reportable offence.' Turning to Bobby, Sister Price pulled rank. 'Private Baker, stand to attention in the presence of a senior officer.'

Bobby stood straight and saluted. 'Permission to speak, ma'am.'

'I doubt you have anything to say that can excuse your behaviour. Report to the discharge clinic immediately. You have shown that you are more than ready to serve your country again.'

Bobby whispered, 'I'll get a message to you, my darling.'

Paddy started to protest that Bobby wasn't to blame, but Sister Price cut her off. 'Just get yourself back to the ward you are assigned to, Nurse Riley. We'll say no more about this. Private Baker will leave here tomorrow morning, and that should prevent any further such trysts between you. I do not condone your behaviour, but I do understand. However, these things have to be nipped in the bud.'

'Yes, ma'am, thank you.'

Wanting to shout that her love for Bobby would never be 'nipped in the bud', Paddy walked past the sister with her head held high.

When she reached the first tent, Bobby jumped out in front of her. Paddy swivelled round, but her fears were unfounded, for the sister must have carried on walking and wasn't following her. 'To be sure, Bobby, you gave me a fright.'

'Sorry, love, but I couldn't leave it there. I want to know your real name, and to tell you that I love you and, no matter what, I will find you.'

'Oh, Bobby, me name's Bernadette Riley and I live in Fenn Street, Cricklewood, in London, but I'll not be going back there, if I am for helping it. Me pappy will be there, though, and he will know where to find me. Can you be for remembering that?'

'It's written into my heart. As is the picture of your golden curls and beautiful Irish eyes. Here, I've written down me address at home.'

Taking the note, Paddy shoved it down the front of her apron. 'And I'll be for keeping your handsome face in me mind's eye, so I will, and your address close to me heart.' As she looked up into the eyes that she sometimes thought of as green and at other times as a light brown, she wanted to brush the raindrops off his face and hold it close to hers. To run her hands through the waves of his shiny black hair, which had grown quite long during his time here and now curled just above his ears.

Bobby reached for her, but she stepped back.

'We can't be touching each other – folk will see and we'll be up on a charge. Take care, my love, and keep safe. I'll be praying for you every day to the Good Lord.' She turned and almost ran away, her tears mingling once more with the rain.

'There you are, Nurse. That was a long ten minutes, but then I suppose you deserve it.'

'Yes, Matron. It's sorry that I am, but I walked further than I intended.'

'And got yourself soaked to the skin in the process. Take your wet cape off and dry yourself as best as you can. We need you. Hurry, now.'

Thrown once more into the gore of the incoming wounded, Paddy immersed herself in caring, soothing and administering to them, though her mind was singing with mixed emotions. Deep happiness vied with fear and sadness. But she would only let the happiness in. *Bobby loves me. Bobby loves me.*

19

Chapter Three

The journey across the border to Belgium wasn't easy. The open truck they were in increased Ella's discomfort with every yard it travelled. Roads that were originally tracks for farmers' traffic had taken a heavy toll with the vehicles of war and were now rutted and full of potholes.

Moving herself a little, Ella tried to ease the discomfort between her legs and the pain in her back. They were constant reminders of the horror she'd suffered; injuries that those who had tended her had thought were caused by the sea. Somehow, she knew, she must learn to live with her pain and the heavy feeling dragging her heart down. She was traumatized from her mind to her feet, but there was nothing to be done. It had happened and she couldn't undo it.

As a distraction, she looked out at what used to be green fields, but were now a churned-up monument to the bloody battles fought there. Trenches were still visible, and so too were many bodies, and body parts – limbs sticking hideously out of the mud; still hands, looking as though they reached for help; a leg, still in its boot, standing almost proudly on its own. Every so often a group of soldiers could be seen, carrying out the unenviable task of digging long lines of graves. How long would it take to get all the dead and body parts buried? And who would know who they were? Families would only know their men were killed in action, but not where or how, or where their remains lay. The pity of this brought tears to Ella's eyes. It seemed such a long time now that the world had been in turmoil. Some of her tears were for those who had come in and out of her life, some of whom she would never see again.

How she longed to be with Flors and Mags, who would hug her and make right again the small part of the world where she was. Was it the memories of what they'd been through that stopped them keeping in touch? Maybe, after a time, they would heal and reunite. Because what the three of them had shared could never be forgotten. The war had thrown them together and given them so much to contend with. At that moment Ella renewed her determination to get in touch one day with Flors and Mags.

Mags would be easy to find, for she lived with her family in Blackburn. Helping to run her father's mill, she was ready to take over one day, and it was all she wanted to do. Maybe Flors still lived in Stepney? *It would be so good to see them both.*

Trying not to long for home, Ella wiped a tear that had trickled down her cheek as her dear nanny came into her mind. How she missed her. A yearning to be held by Nanny and comforted overwhelmed her. How guilty she felt at leaving Nanny when she most needed her. She was in her late sixties now, and her infrequent letters broke Ella's heart, as Nanny wrote that she was 'just hanging on' to see Ella come home safely from the war.

Nanny had booked herself into a nursing home two months before the war was declared, because her chronic arthritis had rendered her unable to walk. Her hands were so gnarled that she could no longer care for herself, and she had refused to allow Ella to care for her: 'You have a life to lead, my dear Ella. And now that you are well again, you must follow your dream and continue with your nurse's training. It is your vocation.'

As war was imminent at the time and preparations were being made throughout the United Kingdom, Ella hadn't had enough time to complete her training to become a qualified nurse, which a mystery illness had interrupted. And so she had joined the Red Cross and become a volunteer nurse. Doing so had put purpose back into her life.

Her thoughts were interrupted as her travelling companion, senior theatre nurse Connie Knight, stirred. Even though they were squashed between boxes of supplies that dug into them as the truck rocked and jerked them about, Connie had managed to sleep most of the way. It was something nurses did whenever they got the chance, as Ella herself would have done, had she not felt so troubled.

A nice girl, but a bit of a closed book, Connie came across as being stand-offish at times, although Ella enjoyed working with her. She was a no-nonsense, get-the-job-done type, and that meant everything ran smoothly and efficiently in the operating theatre when Connie was in charge.

Stretching her limbs, Connie asked, 'How long have we been travelling? I hope I didn't snore. Sorry – I feel exhausted.'

'Only a little bit, a sort of snuffle really.'

'Oh?'

'Nothing, honestly. I – I wouldn't have said—'

To Ella's surprise, Connie burst out laughing. 'You goose. Are you all right, you look very peaky? I heard what happened this morning, and it must have been a great shock. I couldn't believe that Matron still sent you. Anything can develop from that experience – they say you nearly drowned.'

For a moment it had seemed as if Connie was referring to what Jim had done to her. 'I – I'm fine. Thank you. Just very tired, and yes, still suffering from the shock of it.'

'Thank goodness you were washed up onto the beach and that fisherman found you. Poor Jim, though. I wonder if they have found him. You must be out of your mind with worry for him.'

'Yes. I – I . . .' The words stuck in her throat. How could she say what was expected of her, when she wanted to scream out what he'd really done to her, and that she hoped he was never found? As if to give the lie to this, her eyes filled with tears again and her lips quivered.

This brought out a side of Connie that Ella had never experienced herself, though she'd witnessed it when Connie was dealing with patients. 'It's all right to show your emotions, old thing. Get it all out of your system, I say. You have been through a terrible ordeal. Look, I'm sorry to say it, but, Ella, I do think you have to prepare yourself. Here, I have a hanky.' Shaking her head, Connie added, 'It's horrific – just horrific.'

Unable to speak, Ella took the hanky. *Yes, it was horrific. So horrific.* With this thought, her tears flowed and sobs racked her. Somehow Connie managed to stand and come over to her. She didn't speak, but as best she could, with the motion of the truck swaying her, she placed one of her hands on Ella's shoulder and gently soothed her until she calmed.

'That's a good reaction, Ella. Now you will begin to come to terms with it. Hang on to the fact that you're safe. You could have died, but you didn't. You still have much to do, and the sooner you can come to a frame of mind where you can look on the positives, the better you will feel.'

Ella blew her nose. Although Connie knew only half the story, she was right. It was about coming to terms with it. But where she would find a positive to hang on to, she didn't know. 'Thank you, Connie. I do feel better now.' And, strangely, she did.

The truck halted, surprising them both. 'What a relief. Though why we're stopping, I don't know.' Connie looked at her watch. 'We're only two hours into our journey. But, hey-ho, let's stretch our legs. And don't worry – you look fine. If that had been me blubbing, I would look terrible, all puffed eyes and runny nose.'

Ella smiled for the first time. She'd never made any connection with Connie. She was one of those who accepted you when she was ready, but now Ella felt they could be friends. 'Maybe there is a positive to come out of what happened to me, as you and I have become closer.'

Connie looked embarrassed. 'I – I'm glad that has happened. I'd like to be friends. Sorry if I have come across as a bit offhand. I don't mean to. I don't find mixing easy. A childhood in the colonies didn't help – private tutor and interacting only with servants. Made me a bit gawky around others of my own age. Anyway, let's get off this damn truck, eh?'

Ella felt sad for Connie. There was everyone thinking she was a bit snobbish and hard to approach, when all the time she must have been very lonely. Impulsively she took Connie's hand and smiled at her. 'You've helped me more than you know, Connie. Thank you. Come on, let's jump down together and not wait for the steps to be unfolded.'

Jumping off the truck sounded a good idea, but poor

Connie, being taller than average, had to fold her body far more than Ella did.

Ella caught the expression of determination on Connie's rounded face as she prepared to leap. And as she took off, her straight hair, cut into a bob, flew into the air, but it was the action of her bosom that astonished Ella. Connie was a buxom girl, and her chest bounced as if it would never stop.

Ella leapt off the truck a second after Connie, but somehow they landed together, giggling like schoolgirls, only to look up and see Dr Mathews come round the corner of the truck. Ella had a moment of feeling foolish, and knew by the way she blushed that Connie did, too.

'Well, I thought I'd have to rescue you both. Are you all right?'

This seemed to be directed at Connie, as did the doctor's concerned look. Connie promptly retorted, 'Yes, but no thanks to your own and Dr Frazer's chivalry, which was very lacking.' A smile lit her face, taking the sting out of what she said.

'Sorry. We pulled rank and took the front seats for a reason. We may have to operate when we arrive, even if it will be gone midnight.'

'I forgive you.' This interaction between them suggested that Connie and Alan Mathews were rather more than friends. Ella was glad for them, though sad, too, because it was frowned upon for the medical staff to form attachments, and it had been known that one of an 'offending' pair found themselves posted elsewhere. To try to conduct a relationship under those constraints must be very difficult.

Having travelled for a further hour after their break, during which they drank hot tea made by their driver on a small paraffin stove, they transferred to a supply train. It was a lot more comfortable, and Ella was at last able to get off to sleep.

The deafening sound of explosions and gunfire woke her and she knew they must be nearing their destination. It surprised her how her stomach clenched in fear. She thought she was hardened to the sound of war, but their current situation heightened her awareness of it, as they had been warned that trains that carried food and other goods to the front line were a target for the enemy.

The train coming to a halt further alarmed Ella. Peering through the dim light, she saw that Connie was sitting up. 'Why have we stopped?'

'I don't know, but I don't like it; it could mean—'

A deafening explosion shook the carriage. Connie scrambled over a bale of clothing and was by Ella's side in seconds.

'Oh, Ella, I hate all of this.'

The trembling of Connie's body matched Ella's own. She went to give comfort, but then remembered something Flors had always said: *If someone is afraid, then showing your own fear often helps them more than trying to be the big, brave one.*

'Oh God, Connie. We're going to die!'

'We'll be fine. I – I didn't mean to startle you more than the damn war breaking out around us did. Keep hold of my hand.'

It had worked: Connie was back to being in charge.

After a few minutes the train chugged on again.

'Must have been a random attack nearby, which spooked the driver for a while. Phew! Thank goodness for that. For one moment there I thought we might be taken prisoner or, worse, blown up!'

Relief entered Ella, too. That was the nearest she'd ever been to the fighting, and it had scared her witless. It was the feeling of not knowing if this was the time a bullet had your name on it.

When they reached the hospital they had to trudge through ankle-deep mud leading to the receiving tent. There a horrific sight met them. Three nurses and a matron, along with one doctor, were coping with dozens of wounded, some of whom lay on a long tarpaulin spread out on the wooden floor of the tent and had not yet been attended to. The more seriously injured were on stretcher-type beds and were receiving attention.

Ella stared around her, taking in the sight of the blood that ran like a river and lay in pools on the floor. And how the walls of the tent, and the beleaguered staff, were splattered with it. Her nostrils were assailed with the smell of rotting flesh and vomit, and the wails and moans tugged at her heart.

Dr Mathews gave the impression that nothing was too much to cope with, as he spoke for them.

'Hello, Matron. We are Red Cross members, here to help. Tell us where our billets are and we'll get changed. I'm Dr Alan Mathews, a surgeon, as is Dr Daniel Frazer; and these are our nursing staff: theatre nurse Cornelia Knight and theatre assistant Marjella Wronski – we call them Connie and Ella.'

'We can introduce ourselves later. Nurse Riley, go with them and show them their billets. Hut B for the nurses, and G for the surgeons. But all of you, please change quickly and hurry back here.'

Dr Mathews looked taken aback at her abrupt tone. A

handsome man with dark eyes and dark hair greying at the temples – the only signs of his age, which Ella would put in his early fifties – he was used to commanding attention, not being dismissed.

Once out of the hearing of the matron, Nurse Riley spoke in a conspiratorial tone. 'For sure it is that you're very welcome. Don't you be minding Matron, she's a good old stick. It is with the pressure she is under that she was for coming over a bit snappy-sounding. For haven't we been asking for help this good while? We're at our wits' end, so we are. I'm Bernadette Riley, known as Paddy.'

Ella felt an immediate affinity with Paddy, and the feeling warmed her. It would be good to make a new friend who knew nothing about what happened at Dieppe.

After leaving the doctors at their hut, Paddy took Ella and Connie to their quarters. She smiled as she told them, 'I'm for having my bed in here too, so I am. Mine is the third one along. You are to be taking the fourth and fifth, and you'll find all you'll be needing on your beds. The bathroom is at the bottom end, behind that curtain. It's after being a bit primitive, but I expect you'll be used to that.'

The smile Paddy gave them lit up her face, and made her eyes appear even more blue and sparkly than the first impression Ella had had of them. *Irish eyes*, she thought to herself, remembering that she had heard the expression before. And she'd also heard that a lot of Irish colleens – as she believed single girls were called in Ireland – were known to have red hair. Well, Paddy kept to that tradition too, because although her hair was mainly covered by her nurse's veil, lots of ringlets escaped and shone a golden-red in the sunlight. The freckles on her face enhanced her prettiness, although the word 'cute' seemed to suit her more, because her teeth, though even and white, protruded a little, giving her a 'little girl' look.

'Right-o, we'll be as quick as we can.' With this from Connie, Paddy left them. Connie soon bagged her place. 'I'll take the fifth bunk, if that's all right with you, Ella? I can't bear the closed-in feeling of having a bed on each side of me.'

'That's fine. I'll be happy just to have somewhere to lay my head. I feel exhausted, but will be all right once we swill our faces. And donning my uniform always gets me in the mood for work.'

Ready, all but for her nurse's veil, Ella waited for Connie to finish with the mirror. When her turn came, she wasn't surprised to see the tired lines around her eyes. For a moment she studied her reflection. She'd never thought of herself as pretty. Yes, her hazel eyes were large and matched her brown hair, but her features were very precise, as her nanny's had been. Straight nose and defined lips – she wondered if it was her Polish heritage. Sometimes her features gave her a stern look. But they also came to her aid when she needed to assert herself, as being just under average height, she wasn't always taken seriously. This was why she chose to wear her long hair brushed off her face and coiled into a bun at the nape of her neck. Many a time, surprise was expressed when she let it fall loosely onto her shoulders, thick and awash with many shades of brown – chestnut and a light gold. She'd been told that her hair was beautiful and that wearing it down suited her. But then there weren't many occasions that called for her to do so.

Jim had uncoiled it and ruffled it with his fingers . . .

This memory made Ella's body tremble. Grabbing her hairbrush, she pulled it through her hair and tied it back so

tightly it hurt. But this was a better pain than the one that
visited her at the thought of Jim's hands touching her.

Within minutes of entering the receiving ward, Ella forgot
everything except what she was assigned to do by Matron.
'Nurse Wronski, was it?'

'Yes, Matron.'

'Right, I want you to assess all those patients lying on the
tarpaulin. Label them with these tags, Nurse. Tie the tags to
their feet where they can readily be seen. Red for those
needing urgent treatment; orange for "as soon as possible";
and green for minors.'

'Yes, Matron.'

Looking along the line of twenty or so men still to be
seen, Ella went first to the ones showing signs of great distress. She prayed this didn't mean she'd miss someone who
was too weak to cry out.

With eight red labels attached, she came to a man lying
on his side. Although he wasn't making a sound, something
about him worried her. Touching his shoulder, she spoke
gently to him. 'Are you in pain, sir?'

'Yes, I – I have pain in my . . . chest. It is hard to breathe.'
His French accent caressed her, even though his words were
hesitant.

Trying to turn him onto his back had him crying out.

'I'm so sorry. I need to assess you.'

'You're not English?'

'No, I'm Polish. I'm a nurse. Tell me what happened –
have you any open wounds?'

'I do not think so. I was caught in the blast of an explosion and thrown into a trench. The drop was about three
metres.'

Unused to this French term of measurement, Ella had to presume it was quite a way and act accordingly. It occurred to her that his back might be badly damaged. 'I'm going to put a red tag on your foot. This will ensure you're seen soonest.' Her worry increased as the soldier's breathing became more laboured while she carried out this task. 'Try to remain still; help will be with you very soon, I promise.' On a whim she told him, 'I'm Nurse Ella.'

'I'm Paulo Rennaise, an . . . officer in the French army. P – please face me, so that I can see you.'

Something compelled Ella to move closer, despite the other men waiting for her attention. 'Sorry. I stood behind you, hoping I could roll you onto your back.' Looking into his dark eyes caused Ella's heart to jolt. Without thinking, her hand reached out and stroked his curly black hair. 'You will be all right, Paulo. Don't worry.'

Somehow he managed a small smile. 'I – I think I will always be all right, now I have met you.'

'Ha! Haven't lost your French charm then?' Ella smiled. It was a manner she adopted with all the wounded, as she found that joking with them gave them the confidence to think they were going to make it. And she felt proud of herself for doing so now, as she'd thought she would never want to exchange a conversation with a man again, being afraid of giving out the wrong message.

But something about Paulo was different. It was as if he was a magnet to her, and she didn't want to leave his side. But then she wondered if he might not want to know her, if he knew she was soiled goods.

Shaking herself out of this strange feeling, she spoke gently. 'It is very important that you stay still, Paulo. Try not to move a limb. You're going to be fine, but you may have broken something, and moving will make it worse. I'll get someone to take a look at you.' With this, she ran to Matron. 'We have a lot of red cases – open, gaping wounds that may still hold bullets; and one who may lose his arm, but—'

'Oh dear, how did we miss him? I knew there were some serious cases, but didn't see an emergency of that nature. Where is he?'

'He is not the worst case, Matron. There is a French officer who cannot move without pain and has difficulty breathing. It is very worrying. He was blasted back into a trench by the force of an explosion.'

'Right. Run and fetch any of the surgeons who can come and see to the boy with the arm injury. Then get back to assessing the others – we mustn't miss any that need us to act quickly. I'll go to the officer with the back pain and check him myself, and arrange for the necessary treatment.'

After pointing out Paulo to Matron, Ella did as she was bid. But as she worked along the row of men in need of help, she couldn't get Paulo out of her mind and uttered silent prayers for him.

Matron's voice brought her out of her thoughts. 'How are you getting on, Nurse? You are needed in theatre, as a few of the cases that you red-tagged require urgent operations. Get cleaned up as quickly as you can. And well done – good job.'

Despite her mind being elsewhere, Ella finished assessing all the men and went over to report to Matron. 'There aren't any further emergencies. Mostly surface wounds that need cleaning and dressing. H – how is the French officer with the breathing problem?'

'We believe he has a slipped disc, but our immediate concern is his broken ribs, as one of them has punctured his lung, causing a collapse. Your Dr Frazer is a very special man. He re-inflated the lung, which lifted the immediate threat to the officer's life, but he is in theatre now, as he needed further repair. Poor man, his lungs show signs of damage from gas inhalation. The French were affected by the worst of the gas attacks. Now, go and get cleaned up, then present yourself to number-three theatre as soon as you can. Oh, and Nurse, do distance yourself emotionally from the patients, as they can break your heart, and we need you in one piece.'

Ella blushed. 'Yes, Matron.' Then, without knowing it would happen, her voice broke into a sob.

'Are you all right, Nurse? You look very peaky. You haven't a temperature, have you?'

Ella knew the matron would be looking out for flu symptoms. *Although it's a terrible thing for me to think, at this moment I wish it was that.* Exhaustion flooded through her. Had it only been this morning that the horror had happened to her?

'I – I'm just very tired. But I will carry on. Everything is overwhelming at times. I know it shouldn't be. I'm sorry, Matron.'

'I know the feeling, and I have been where you are. One out of a thousand of these men can touch something in you that makes you vulnerable. It passes, and it usually happens when you are at breaking point. Deep breaths, my dear. If I could send you to your bed, I would. But think about those who are dying, and whose lives you can save by putting the ramrod into your spine and carrying on. That's what I do.'

These words pulled Ella up. She smiled and thanked Matron, then walked in a determined manner in the direction of the accommodation hut. Yes, Paulo had been the one man who had touched something in her. How, or why, she didn't know. But she did know that she could, and would, carry on. And she also knew that what Paddy had said was true. Matron was a good stick.

Once outside, Ella lifted her long grey dress and ran to her billet, grabbed a clean uniform and set the shower in motion. The water was cold, and although she let it run for a while, it only reached a luke-warm temperature.

The sound of the water splashing into the enamel bowl reminded her of when she was just sixteen and had thrown a coin into a wishing well and made a wish. She'd watched the water spread out in ever-increasing ripples at the intrusion of her coin, and had wished that she would one day find her real family and have someone to love. Now she thought of those ripples as the ripples of her life, with many people coming in and out of it; but always she tried to focus on those who cared for her. Thinking of those who abandoned her or hurt her wouldn't make things better.

Would it ever happen that someone would come along and stay forever, and love her in a special way? Paulo's dark eyes, though filled with pain, had shown something in their depths – something that had drawn her to him. Could it possibly be him? *Please let it be so.*

With this thought, something lifted within her, for as silly as it seemed to have such a feeling after only a few moments' contact with Paulo, she knew he had taken precedence in her mind over the other occurrence today. No, she'd never think of that again – unless . . . But no, that wouldn't happen! She would pray, night and day, that God didn't allow it. *I couldn't cope with finding I'm pregnant . . . I couldn't.*

Chapter Four

Ella didn't feel refreshed as she reported for duty the next morning. She'd had a restless night, full of nightmares in which men with distorted faces tried to rape her. None of them had been Jim. She'd woken suddenly, crying out, and had found Paddy sitting up and asking if she was all right. She'd felt relief enter her, although she was mortified at having disturbed Paddy, but so grateful for having someone by her side. 'I'm for having dreams that disturb me as well, Ella, so don't you be worrying. Sure, I might be the one making you sit up in terror one of these nights.' This had made Ella smile and calmed some of the fear that was pounding in her heart.

Paddy had fetched her a drink of water and sat holding her hand, and this had comforted Ella, before the pair noticed Connie's gentle snores and started to giggle. 'Nothing wakes her; she even slept in the truck when we were being jolted about, though she did wake up quite frightened when we neared the battlefield and the explosions and gunfire were loud.'

'We all have a point of fear, so we do. Connie gives off an

air of being in control and not needing anyone, but it is that we all do need the comfort of others, so we must get past that and make sure she is for being all right.'

The warm feeling that Ella had felt earlier towards Paddy increased at this, and she told Paddy that her summing-up of Connie was right. Listening to Paddy helped to distance Ella from the horror of what had visited her in her dreams, and she managed to sleep peacefully for the rest of the night.

The briefing seemed to take forever, as Matron gave them their duties and the night-staff updated them on all the new intakes of the day before. When Paulo was mentioned, Ella felt a jolt in her heart. Now her mind was troubled once more, as she listened to the hand-over from the night-staff.

'Officer Rennaise is not well, and is on oxygen. Constant monitoring of his condition is required. He has several broken ribs and underwent an emergency operation. He is to be kept on traction. Pneumonia is an obvious concern.'

Although Ella felt for all the soldiers, hearing of Paulo's plight intensified this feeling to a painful dread. *Why? It's ridiculous. I've dealt with thousands of men, why should this one man have this effect on me?* Whatever the reason, she felt an urge to run to Paulo, comfort him and tell him that she would make him better. But she was assigned to the theatre and, listening to the operations to be carried out – from the amputation of limbs, because treated wounds had worsened, to an appendectomy for a young soldier brought in during the night in agony – she knew that visiting Paulo would be impossible until much later in the day. By then she might have managed to get her head straight and be able to put this impossible infatuation into some perspective.

What Matron was saying now brought Ella's attention back to the matter in hand. 'Now I am very sorry to have to tell you that we have another problem to contend with – influenza. We had a soldier brought in during the night suffering from the symptoms of this dreadful virus. A deadly strain is sweeping the trenches, but he has presented as our first case. All the other hospitals are full to capacity, so I have designated two nurses to care for him day and night. I have isolated part of tent three for this – and any other cases that come in. Nurse Evans on nights and Nurse Riley on days are to specialize in these cases. No one but them – and a doctor, if required – is to enter the isolation ward. And no one must try to make contact with either of these nurses during their working hours. I have put every precaution in place, so that they can shower and change before coming off-duty. From now on, shower room number two is for their use, and their use only.'

This shocked Ella, as she could see it did everyone. Looking around, she noticed that Paddy was nowhere to be seen. Matron must have collared her the moment she'd surfaced from the billet. Poor Paddy. She was the last one who needed to be in isolation. She was a chatterbox and someone who thrived on company. But then she was also a very caring person, and an excellent nurse, Ella was sure, so there were none better to take on this arduous task.

From their chat during the night Ella had learned a lot about Paddy, and now – as well as praying for Paulo – she would add Bobby Baker, the man Paddy loved, to her list of those she needed God to take care of. But at this moment she didn't feel she could pray; only berate God for the injustices that he piled on them. *Why – why, God? Why send us this devastating illness to deal with? Haven't we enough to put up with?*

Once in theatre, Ella forgot her worry about influenza being in such proximity to them. In the quiet and calm surroundings, case after case was attended to. She assisted wherever she was needed, passing instruments, counting them back onto trays. And she had to scrub-up time and time again, after fetching more supplies or making trips to sterilize batches of implements.

Most of their patients would go on to make a recovery, in body, if not in mind. Something much harder for them to do was coming to terms with all they had seen and experienced. But then Ella wondered if she herself would ever get to a peaceful state of mind.

By the end of her shift she'd somehow passed through the tiredness barrier and, after showering, she sought out Matron to ask permission to visit Paulo.

'I did warn you yesterday, Nurse Wronski, and I am disappointed at this request. However, I am considering granting you access, although why I'm allowing myself to, I do not know. I will ask the ward sister if your visit is unsettling to Officer Rennaise and, if so, then you are not to ask this of me again.'

Although it was a stern reply, Ella felt that Matron was on her side and that something of a romantic lay under the hard exterior she showed the world.

As Ella approached him, Paulo lay very still. His eyes were almost hidden from view by the oxygen mask, but he managed to open them when she called his name. 'I – I wanted to check on you. I have been in theatre all day. You're going to be all right. Have they told you about the damage you have suffered?'

Paulo nodded. He had the most expressive eyes she'd ever seen.

'Can I do anything for you?'

'St – stay . . .'

The word was distorted through the mask, but Ella understood. 'I can stay for a while. I won't ask you any more questions, as it is a strain on you. I've been thinking about you. Matron will let me visit you, as long as you don't show any distress at my doing so.'

His gaze held hers and this pleased Ella; but it also held something else, which she dared not put a name to. *I'm being silly. He can't possibly feel anything for me! What's the matter with me?*

'Are y – you . . . troubled?'

'No! I mean – well, all our lives are troubled. I'm fine. Just tired.'

'Tell me . . . about you.'

After a few minutes Ella realized she'd told Paulo everything – about her background, her life in London and her work. It had been so easy to talk to him. If only she could tell him . . . But no. She could never tell anyone that.

When she finished, she saw a movement and went to stop him, but his hand came out from under the covers. She took it in her own. A feeling zinged through her that left her feeling confused, as she had never felt this way before. Paulo's hand tightened on hers. 'I – I find you . . . very beautiful.'

Ella felt her heart would burst out of her chest, as a happiness like none she'd ever known filled her. She could only smile and look into his lovely eyes.

The patient in the next bed broke the beautiful moment

and brought her back to reality, as he called out: 'Hey, love-birds, you're not doing my temperature any good.'

Paulo laughed, but the pain this action caused saw his face creasing in a grimace.

'Nurse, you are causing a disruption. I think you had better leave.'

'Oh, Sister, I'm sorry. I didn't mean to.'

'No . . . st – stay.'

'Nurse Wronski has to go, I'm afraid. The other patients are getting restless. None of them have had a visitor, and it isn't fair for them to witness you two holding hands.' As Ella followed the sister out, she glanced back and gave a little wave, but her heart sank at the sister's words. 'I'm surprised at Matron allowing this. I will report that I was not happy with the reaction of the other men and think she should discourage any future visits.'

Ella wanted to cry out in protest, but thought it best to apologize once more and leave. She'd appeal to Matron and tell her that the sister had taken a joke from one man as signifying unrest; but if that failed, she would find out who was on night-duty in the officers' ward and beg them to help her sneak in after dark, when the sister was off-duty. One way or another, she would get to see Paulo again. She had to.

Once outside, she stood still for a moment. Yes, the end of her visit hadn't been what she'd wanted, but . . . *Oh, Paulo! Dare I believe that you feel something for me, as I do for you?* And she knew she dared. It was in his eyes, and the way he'd held her hand.

'Are you all right, Nurse? I'm sorry, I don't know your name.'

'Yes, thank you. Just daydreaming. I'm Nurse Wronski – Ella. I arrived yesterday.'

'Nice to meet you. I'm Belinda. I work on the officers' ward. Can't stop, as Sister is a stickler and these supplies are needed.'

'Oh, Belinda, do me a favour. Sorry to ask, but could you give a message to Officer Rennaise?'

Explaining what had happened, and asking Belinda to tell Paulo that she would come back after dark, Ella suddenly felt very silly and shy. 'Sorry, I shouldn't have asked this of you. What will you think of me?'

'Nothing. I understand. It happens to us all. The soldier I fell in love with is safely back at home. He lost a leg, but he has a loving family taking care of him. We write, but I would do anything to be with him. Of course I will tell Officer Rennaise, and I'll also tell him that I will arrange things. Wendy, the night-nurse, is my best friend. I'll have a word with her. Where are you billeted? I'll get a message to you, to tell you when is the best time to come back.'

'Oh, thank you. Thank you so much.' Ella could have kissed Belinda. As she turned away, her inner self was singing with joy. For now she knew that she was in love. Deeply in love with Paulo. Somehow, in letting this knowledge into her, she felt the first tentative healing. *I can overcome what happened. I can!*

Chapter Five

'Where are you going?'

A sleepy whisper came from Connie, stopping Ella in her tracks. She turned and saw Connie sitting up. 'I'm going to visit the man I love.'

'What?'

'Yes. I've fallen in love. It took me all of two days. He's a French officer in the officers' ward.'

'Is this wise, Ella, old thing? I mean, I know how you feel, but showing our feelings is frowned upon and could get us into serious trouble – let alone sneaking out during the night for a tête-à-tête.'

'I know, but I was banned from visiting in the day, so this is the only way. It's all arranged.'

'Good luck, then.' Yawning, Connie lay back down, muttering that she might try it, if Ella got away with it. Ella didn't have to guess who she would go and meet.

Once in the ward, all she could do was hold Paulo's hand, because talking would have disturbed the other patients. However, she had written a note for him and pressed this into his hand:

Paulo, my dear,

I know so little about you, but care very much for you. I will try to visit when I can, but know that I will be thinking of you. Once you are well again, you will leave here. If you feel the same way I do, please make sure that I have your address before you go, and then, once the war is over, I will come to you.

Love, Ella x

She knew this was forward of her, but having found him, she wasn't about to lose him. She'd waited all her life for that special love. And now that she knew she'd found it in Paulo, she wasn't about to let it pass by.

Rising to leave, Ella impulsively kissed Paulo's hand. He pulled hers to his heart and held it there for a few moments. A small gesture, but one that made her heart soar. Paulo loved her, she was sure of it.

'You look bright and breezy this morning – the best I've seen you look since before we left Dieppe. Being in love suits you.'

'Thank you, Connie. I do feel different; life feels like it's worth living.'

'Oh, it always is, but . . . Well, to tell the truth, I am very surprised at the turn of events. We all thought Jim was *the one*, and that you were so upset when he was lost.'

Ella froze. The spoon of porridge she was about to put into her mouth was suspended, and the chatter in the mess hut receded to a far-away mumble. Her nightmare crashed in on her.

'Ella? Ella, I'm sorry, did I say something wrong?'

Connie sat back, a look of concern on her face, but also

one of deep embarrassment. Paddy, who hadn't yet reported for duty in the isolation ward, leaned forward. 'What is it that troubles you, Ella? Oh, Ella, is that you crying?'

Sobs racked Ella's body – uncontrollable sobs that she had tried not to give in to.

'Come on, old thing. I'm so sorry, I didn't mean to upset you.'

'Connie, will you be getting in front of Ella? We must be for protecting her. The others are beginning to notice, so they are. Now, Ella, take me hanky and blow your nose. It is that you should stop yourself from showing this emotion. Me and Connie will walk each side of you. You are to hold your head up high, and we'll get outside without too much fuss.'

Ella nodded at Paddy.

Once outside, Ella took deep breaths and found some control. Inside, she felt a dread settle, as now she would have to tell the truth. It could be a secret no more. She prayed that Connie and Paddy would agree to keep it to themselves, for she couldn't face the consequences of what had happened being reported, and all that would entail. She hoped, too, that Connie believed her – and didn't believe that Ella had asked for it.

'Please, please don't tell anyone. I – I couldn't face the shame and the . . . well, people will point a finger at me and will think I am lying. A lot thought like you, Connie, that there was something going on between us. But there wasn't. Jim wanted there to be, but I never did.' Ella told them what had happened.

'Poor Ella. This is devastating. Jim raped you and tried to kill you! I'm shocked to my core. Look, you're right, we have to keep this between ourselves. There could be awkward questions, which you don't deserve. That wicked man. I know of another girl that Jim hurt. But I thought when he met you he'd changed, as you were close for years and never seemed troubled.'

'Oh? There was another girl?'

'Yes. She was a young VAD like you. Jim took a shine to her and tried it on with her, but she didn't want him. One night he forced her to kiss him – nothing more. He was reprimanded, but she was so upset, as she had a fiancé fighting in the war. In the end they shipped her out, to help her. We were all wary of Jim after that.'

This jolted a memory in Ella's mind. *Didn't Flors say that when Jim came across her, he'd made advances to her, and she'd had to fight him off while she was searching for her brother? His apology had been so genuine that she'd forgiven him.*

'He's for sounding like a menace to women, and a beast that the Lord Himself has stopped. You say Jim hasn't been found?'

'Not that we know of.'

'Well then, it is that he can hurt no other young girl and has got his just deserts. It is as you say: we need to keep this quiet. No one, or very few, believe there is such a thing as rape. It is that they say that the girl is always willing, then changes her mind, and that she is to blame for teasing the man beyond his point of no return. Ella, I'm only for knowing you this short while, but it is that I believe you don't deserve such a stigma.'

'Thank you. Thank you both.'

'Well now, you can be talking to us whenever you need to, for bottling it up can be very harmful. And now I'm going to do what me mammy would do and give you a hug.'

Finding herself in Paddy's arms felt good. Ella had so

wanted to be held. But she wasn't prepared for Connie joining in the hug, and the three of them clung to each other. When they parted, Connie and Paddy both had tears in their eyes.

Connie wiped hers. 'I haven't been held like that since Aadita, a servant who mothered me in India, held me.'

'To be sure, we are all lacking human contact. I was reminded of me mammy, and that choked me, so it did.'

'Thank you, I so needed a hug. And thank you for agreeing not to breathe a word.'

'I'm powerful sorry for you, Ella, and as I say, you can be talking to me whenever you need to. And if . . . well, if it comes to pass that you need help a few months down the line, I'll be there for you, so I will.'

'Oh, I – I never thought of that. Oh, Ella. What if that happened?'

'I know, Connie. I have thought of nothing else, and yet at the same time I have suppressed the thought.'

They were silent once more.

Connie broke the silence. 'I feel the same as Paddy. I'll always be ready to listen and I can offer help, too. I have a country pile in Surrey, which I inherited from the grandparents. If you need a refuge, you can come and stay there with me and I will look after you. None of us will see you go to one of those convents. And if you want to keep the baby, that will be easy – pass yourself off as a war widow.'

They made it all sound so simple, and yet Ella's mind screamed against the thought that she'd tried not to allow into her . . . What about Paulo? Would she have a chance with him, if she had another man's child? *Oh God.*

'We're for jumping the gun here. Sorry, Ella. I expect it is that you've tried not to face such a thing happening, and here we are giving you solutions.'

'No. It's all right, I know that I have to face the possibility. And what you have done between you has eased that, thank you. Thank you so much. I will always be grateful, and I will take you up on your offers if I need them. I just feel so sad as . . . well, I am in love with another man, and now that seems hopeless.'

'It isn't hopeless. Firstly, the worst may not have happened; and secondly, if he turns from you, then he wasn't worth having. Now, as much as we need to keep talking, we have to get to work. We'll chat some more tonight. There's two of us rooting for you now, Ella, so let that lighten the burden you have been carrying.'

A small smile came to Ella's lips. Connie had a way of instilling confidence in you that made you think you could cope with anything.

'Yes, I must away,' said Paddy. 'I'm to get on the special gown that Matron dug up from a crate. They are for being disposable. Our influenza cases are now numbering four! I'll be after seeing you both later.'

Although she had visited the possible consequences of the rape, Ella felt a sense of relief to have someone sharing her burden. As she stood threading needle after needle, for Dr Mathews to stitch the inside of a man's stomach from which he'd removed shrapnel, the sounds of fear – people screaming and shouting – filled the tent. Unnerved, Ella carried on without comment until the smell of burning permeated her nostrils. Turning her head, she saw tendrils of smoke seeping in below the tent flap to her right. 'Something's on fire, Alan.'

'I know, I smelt it. And the panic we can hear from outside suggests that it's something big. But I cannot stop now or my patient will bleed to death. Just keep the needles coming, Nurse Ella.'

Alan's calmness helped her. Passing him the needles he'd requested, she steadfastly continued threading others, in case he needed them.

Within minutes, flames were licking the far side of the tent. Smoke curled around them and then the worst happened: the lights flickered and died.

'Oh God, I'm nearly there. I must complete the repair.'

'I have a torch.' Taking hold of the torch on the tray, Ella shone it on the wound. 'How many more needles will you need?'

'One more. And I need it now!'

Ella coughed as the smoke rasped her throat. The nurse attending to the respiratory machine cried out, 'We have to leave. We . . .' Her voice dissolved into a fit of choking.

'There, that's the last. Now get this patient outside.'

Dr Mathews had hardly spoken before a shout came from another nurse. 'Get out – get out, quickly. The whole hospital is going up in flames. Four tents are alight and—'

Ella grabbed the hospital bed and, along with the respiratory nurse, pushed it outside.

For a moment they stood in shock, as around them lay a world of searing hell. Flames licked every tent, and smoke swirled in a fog that threatened to engulf them. All around them voices called out for help. Some were those of nurses trying to move patients, and others those of patients who were unable to move and were screaming the terror of their situation.

'Over here! We'll take care of your patient. He'll go on the first train.'

Leaving their patient in the care of the nurse who had

called out, they were told that an ambulance train with a doctor and nurses aboard was expected any minute. 'We were lucky it was on its way here, and we know it has left Hospital 19 already.'

Feeling relieved that help was at hand, Ella ran towards a burning tent where she knew bedridden patients were housed. Connie met her halfway. 'What happened, Connie? Dear God, is everybody safe?'

'I'm not sure. I was helping with an operation. But someone said the fire started in the officers' ward, where a lamp was knocked over. When I came out, there were only two tents burning, but it is spreading. Quickly, Ella, help me – I've just got one patient who could use crutches clear of tent nine, but there are dozens of others who are bedridden and trapped and are still in there.'

'Oh God, Paulo! Are all the officers out, Connie?'

'Yes, a nurse told me that one of them raised the alarm, and the rescue started there, as did the firefighting, although they couldn't contain it. We're going to lose the whole hospital at this rate.'

The fire scorched Ella's arms as she followed Connie into the tent.

'How are we going to shift the beds, Ella? We're not strong enough.'

Smoke burned Ella's throat as she shouted back, 'Grab the under-sheets and wrap them around the patients. Together we can drag them onto the floor and then pull them along.'

Their plan worked but, with the fifth patient through the burnt-out tent flap, Ella didn't know if she could carry on, as pain creased her back. She looked over at Connie and could see that she looked exhausted.

Burning pieces of canvas landed on them as they went in once more. Looking up, Ella saw the twisted iron frame of the tent silhouetted against the sky. The canvas had all burned away.

'The others will be safe now, as the fire has burned itself out. Let's go and see if we're needed elsewhere.' Shouting over to the dozen or so men left inside the empty shell of the tent that they must keep their sheets over their mouths to guard against the smoke, Ella turned to her fellow nurse. 'Oh, Connie, what are we going to do with everyone?'

A bell sounded at that moment and Matron's voice boomed out, 'Everyone to the stores. The men are all safe now. And there are more ambulances and trains on their way to ship them out. Medical supplies are in short supply everywhere, so save what you can.'

Exhausted, Ella trundled over to the stores, passing mangled shells of iron that had only this morning held tents in position, as protectors of the sick. She was amazed at how quickly a fire could destroy what man had built over many months.

With the last of the men put onto trains and ambulances, to be taken to various hospitals in the area, Ella climbed the steps of the train that had a makeshift operating theatre aboard. She had no idea where Paulo had been taken, and felt with a heavy heart that she would probably never see him again.

She and Connie were to continue assisting with the operations that were still to be carried out. These were only minor procedures and, once they were fixed, the patients would be taken aboard other trains or ambulances to be transferred to hospitals, ready to be shipped home, or sent back to the front line if they were judged fit enough to continue fighting.

'Does anyone know what is to happen to us?' Daniel Frazer asked, as they sat drinking cups of tea. With their shift finished, the train carrying them was about to reach Abbeville, where they would hand over the patients they had been operating on.

'I'm hoping our orders will be waiting for us at the hospital. Until then, I suppose, we will have to help out there, until we are contacted. It's all a mess. How can a whole hospital be destroyed, just like that?'

Ella was surprised to hear the shock in Alan Mathews's voice. He'd seemed so in control from the moment they'd first detected the smoke.

Connie looked up. 'Are you all right, Alan? I know – it was inconceivable, but at least no one was hurt by the fire, and we all got out.'

'Yes, I'm fine. You girls did a sterling job. How are you both?'

As Connie and Alan held each other's gaze, Ella looked over to Daniel and smiled, but any implication was lost on him. He lived in a world of his own.

When they reached Abbeville, Matron was waiting. As they'd learned in the brief time they had known her, she was unflappable and got everyone organized. Her voice boomed out, 'The Red Cross workers – where are they?'

'Here, Matron.'

'Right, Dr Mathews, you and your team are to stay on the train, as you are to join Australian Clearing Station number nineteen. It's one of the busiest stations, and the nearest to the front line. Good luck, and thank you for your help.'

Ella called after Matron, but she was met not with the

51

gentle person she knew existed under the cool exterior, but with the efficient, no-nonsense nurse. 'I know what you want to ask, but there is no time to pander to your infatuation. Do as you are told, Nurse Wronski.'

Feeling embarrassed, and with a heavy heart, Ella apologized.

'Come on, old thing. Let it go.'

'I wasn't only going to ask after Paulo, Connie. I haven't seen Paddy, either. I'm worried about her.'

'Me too, but no doubt she had to stay with the patients in isolation. I'm sure she will contact us when she can.'

Ella went back to their carriage. *Is that it, then? Oh, Paulo, I can't believe this is the end. No, something so beautiful – even if sudden – cannot end like this. I will find you, Paulo. I will.*

Chapter Six

It wasn't long before they arrived at the Clearing Station, where they found chaos that was worse than they had previously experienced. Not many casualties stayed here for long, just until they were well enough to be shipped out to other hospitals, home or back to the front line.

Ella thought nothing could shock her in caring for the wounded, but here, as they were shown around, she saw cases that she had never seen the like of. Some of these poor souls never even made it out, but left the Clearing Station in body bags.

'No time to settle you folk in. All hands are needed to start work as soon have you have washed up.'

Alan answered. 'Point us in the right direction and we'll be with you as soon as possible, Matron. We number two surgeons and two theatre staff.'

'Excellent. Exactly what we need. You're all very welcome, I'm only sorry it is the depths of hell that I'm welcoming you to.'

The matron was so different from the one they had just left. Her Australian way of speaking was jolly, and yet she exuded confidence in them. 'Any of you neurological? We could do with a brain surgeon.'

'No, but Dr Frazer was training in that field before volunteering for service out here.'

'I'll assess them as best I can, Matron, and I will attempt to save any of the men that I think I can.'

'That won't be many, Dr Frazer. You know, back in Australia we shoot badly injured animals, and I don't mind admitting that I've wished I could do the same for some of the poor buggers brought in here.'

Ella felt a giggle rise in her and knew that Connie did, too, as she heard her cough and saw her make a big pretence of covering her mouth. She had never heard a matron swear before, and doubted Connie had. And, by the look on both doctors' faces, they hadn't, either.

'Anyhow, it is what it is.'

'We've brought some supplies and we have some strong drugs, so we'll try to help as many as we can.'

'Good. Now, what did you say your name was?'

'I didn't. I'm Dr Alan Mathews, general surgeon, and I've already mentioned Dr Frazer. These are Nurses Wronski and Knight – theatre nurses.'

If Ella had been surprised at how Matron spoke, she was even more surprised by the formal way Dr Mathews had introduced them, but guessed the rebuff he'd had from their last matron had put him on his guard.

'You English. So bloody formal. Didn't your mother give you Christian names? Mine's Pollyanna, for my sins. Everyone calls me Matron Polly. I trained in Victoria and reached the status of sister. But recently I was elevated to matron when the poor woman we had in charge here was killed by a truck bringing the wounded in. She might have suited you better. Strait-laced she was. Mind, I'm for having everything done in an orderly fashion and by the book, but I don't stand on ceremony while I'm doing it. So you'll all have to get used to me. I'm too old to change.'

'I'm Alan, and this is Daniel, Connie and Ella. I'm sorry if I came across a bit on the stuffy side, but some matrons—'

'Right-o, no worries. Over there, we have a couple of tents of showers, and two with beds: A for men, and B for women. Accommodation is limited, as we up sticks and move forward or backwards depending on how the battles go. We could be moving any day, as the reports are that the Allies are advancing. I'd say this war is won – but for the shouting. Though the shouting is very intense, and we have our work cut out. Sort yourselves out quick as you can and report back to me. I'll have something fixed up for you all to get stuck into by then.'

'Thank you, Matron Polly.'

Ella thought she would burst, not only with amusement, but with pride in Alan. He'd handled everything so well and, as always, was ready to rise to the challenge.

As if the same had occurred to Connie, she giggled and linked arms with Ella, making her laugh out loud as she said, 'Did you pack your boomerang, woman?'

Once in the tent, Ella cringed for a moment at the over-crowded dormitory. Beds were lined up end-to-end, with very little space between them, although not all were made up, reflecting the shortage of staff.

She and Connie bagged two beds in the first row that had bare mattresses. Each had a pile of sheets, blankets and a pillow on it. 'These will do for us, though it looks like our things will have to stay in our rucksacks under our beds, as there doesn't appear to be anywhere to put them.'

'Yes, I'll take this one, Connie, then you can be on the

outside.' Ella shivered. The dampness of outside had crept into the inside of the hut, and she felt very cold. 'Let's hurry. I have a drawstring bag; we can take our clean clothes to the shower and put our dirty ones in the bag. I can throw it in here, to deal with later. I hope the water's hot.'

While drying and dressing, Connie surprised Ella with, 'What do you think of Alan?'

'I like him. And I have guessed you do, too – more than like, I would say.'

'Yes. Is it that obvious?'

'Well, you're both very discreet, and I never guessed before you and I became close. But yes, to me it is obvious how you feel about each other. I envy you being with your love all the time.'

'It isn't a piece of cake; we have to be so careful, in case we are found out. Alan's widowed, you know. He has two grown-up sons, both fighting, and he dreads every day that one of them may be brought in.'

'Oh no. I had no idea. I mean, I did wonder, as he is a lot older – not that it matters at all. I hope everything is fine with his sons, and that it all works out for you both.'

'Thanks. I'm glad you know. It's always easier when you can share things. And, Ella, I'm so sorry about everything . . . well, you know.'

'Thank you. Now that I have you and Paddy, wherever she is, I'll be fine. I have to get on with life as it is – it is the only way. But I so wish I hadn't been forced away from Paulo like this. How will I ever find him again?'

Returning to the wards was like a baptism of fire. Ella was assigned to assist Daniel Frazer in assessing the head injuries.

Her heart throbbed with the agony these men were experiencing. *How can a body live with just half a brain? How can a faceless man breathe and hold on to life?*

Her stomach churned at the sight of the fifth man they attended to. His eyes had gone, and their wide, gaping, blood-filled sockets were like gashes in his face. His left ear was missing, and his mouth was bleeding and toothless. She instinctively took hold of his hand.

Daniel leaned over him. 'We're here to help you; we're going to give you some pain relief, so that we can examine you.'

The boy tried to speak, but only a hissing sound came from his mouth. Blood sprayed over Ella.

Once he was sedated, the assessment wasn't good. In a quiet voice, Daniel expressed his frustration. 'If only we had something that could see deep inside the brain, but from what the surface X-ray tells us, there is a lot of debris embedded. Only going in can determine what and where, and that would be too dangerous. I must say that I agree with what Matron Polly said about mercy killing, at times like these. We can't even make this poor chap comfortable, and we haven't enough drugs to keep him free from pain until he dies, which is what will happen when infection sets in from the shrapnel . . . Dear God!'

Dr Frazer, a man in his thirties, took out a handkerchief and blew his nose. He turned his head, and Ella knew that he'd wiped a tear from his eyes. He needed a break – they all did. Daniel rarely engaged in conversation, and often, when they did have a respite, he had his head in a medical book, studying. His parents sent him any new ones they came across. Ella had considered him a lonely man, but maybe it was because he was often so deep in thought.

When he turned back to look at his patient, he put his hand out and took a phial from the tray that Ella had put on the side-table while she made notes. She'd prepared the tray at Daniel's instruction, after he'd assessed the wounded, patient by patient. Some phials of morphine had lesser doses than others, and some contained alternative pain-relief medicines.

Through his wire-framed spectacles he looked intently at her. She nodded. Then she held the boy's limp hand again, as Daniel administered a second, strong dose of morphine.

Neither of them spoke as she tucked the sheet around the boy, or as they turned to move on to the next patient. But when their round was done and they returned to the young man, Daniel pronounced him dead.

Ella saw the doctor's shoulders slump. Without thinking, she reached out and touched his hand. He looked up at her, but she wasn't sure he was really seeing her, until he nodded. Then his eyes cleared, as his unspilled tears dropped onto his cheeks.

'May he rest in peace – the peace that *we*, you and I, gave him.'

'Thank you, Ella. Never speak of this, will you?'

'Never, but we did this together. And I will always keep your compassion in my heart, and pray for the boy's soul and for his family.'

Together, they moved on to the next patient.

Chapter Seven

Six weeks later, Ella was startled when Connie burst into the ward where she was working. 'It's over! It's over!'

'What?' Ella looked up from the dressing she was administering. A cheer filled her ears, as men all around her expressed their joy. The feeling surged through her. *Can it really be over? Please God.*

Connie stood just inside the tent doing a jig, a piece of paper held aloft in her hand. 'A communication came through. Yesterday, at the eleventh hour of the eleventh day of the eleventh month, an armistice was signed between the Allies and Germany, in Compiègne. All hostilities are to cease. Oh, Ella . . . at last!'

Again the men cheered.

'But, Connie, I can still hear the guns and explosions.'

'I know. There are some German soldiers who won't give up. Foolish pride, which may cost even more unnecessary lives.'

'But how will they stop them? They must be made to stop. They must!'

'I'm sure our officers will find a way. But, Ella, it is

over – over.' Connie slumped down onto an empty bed and buried her head in her hands.

'Oh, Connie, I—' Ella couldn't finish what she was saying, as the young man whose arm she was dressing suddenly put his other arm around her and drew her down onto his knee, then planted a kiss on her cheek.

'Ha, I didn't expect that; you took advantage, Joshua Hardcastle!'

'Eeh, sorry, Nurse, forgive me, but I felt such a gush of happiness go through me that I wasn't responsible. I'm safe! I'm going home. By, me little lass is waiting for me, and me bairns, too. I'm so happy.'

Laughing with him, Ella realized that he had probably left home four years previously to do his bit for his country. Standing up, she told him, 'I salute you, Joshua Hardcastle, and thank you.'

'Naw, it's for us to thank you, and all the doctors – you saved our lives. And you fixed me broken bone up good and proper. I hope you've someone to go home to, Nurse.'

Ella simply smiled and moved over to Connie. 'I assume they are tears of joy, Connie?'

'A mixture, Ella. I am so glad it's all over, but will it mean parting with the man I love?'

'Why should it?'

'Oh, I'm being silly, but he has a family, and although I know Alan loves me, will he want to take it further, now that the time to part is upon us? Look at me, I'm a frump. Who would want to take me home with them?'

It was hard to hear Connie over all the cheering that was going on, both inside the tent and outside, but Ella had caught most of it. 'You're not a frump, and he does—'

An excited Alan came through the door. 'There you are,

Connie, I've been looking for you. Sorry, Ella, but I need to speak to Connie. There is something that convention, up till now, has prevented me from expressing.'

Ella's heart warmed at the look on Connie's face. 'She's all yours, Alan.' But then she was surprised as Alan grabbed her, and not Connie. 'Give me a hug first, dear girl. We've been through so much together.'

His arms held her tightly, but only for a moment, as he turned and grabbed Connie. 'Our hug needs to be in private, if we can find somewhere. Will you come with me, my darling Connie?'

The term 'catching flies' had never been more apt. Connie's mouth was wide open in shock. Ella could understand it, as she herself felt as though a sudden whirlwind had taken her and transported her to a world full of happiness that had drastically changed the people she knew, as this was a very different side of Alan that she was seeing.

It was four weeks before their work was done. Some of the happiness had been tarnished by ambulances bringing in the wounded from skirmishes that should never have taken place after the armistice, but at last they were heading home.

The train carrying them all came to a halt at a station near Calais. Alan stood up and pulled Connie to her feet. 'This is where I fell in love with you, darling, when we came over to France.'

Ella's heart warmed. Daniel looked up at her and his face blushed red.

'Oh, never mind them, Daniel – they deserve this time together. And, who knows, we may get an invite to the wedding!'

Daniel laughed. His laugh had a feminine sound, and Ella hoped, as she had done before about this young man she'd come to love like a brother, that he would find someone like himself to love, and would be safe in that love.

'Yes, you will, both of you. I am even going to ask you to be my bridesmaid, Ella. I hope you will agree.'

'Oh, I would love that. So you have popped the question then, Alan?' How quickly they had fallen into this relaxed way with each other, a lot of which could be put down to Matron Polly. Ella would never forget her.

'The moment I got the chance. All I need now is to hear that my boys are safe, and my world will be complete.'

There was a moment's silence. Connie broke it. 'Just as soon as we get to London we will contact the War Office. My father has some influential friends in government. We'll find out, darling. And I know the news will be good—'

'Is that yourself, Connie?'

The unmistakable voice made both Ella and Connie smile. 'Paddy! How lovely to see you.'

'And you, too. And before it is that we say any more, I have something for you, Ella.'

Ella stared at the letter that Paddy held out to her.

'It's from Officer Paulo Rennaise. I'm for thinking you made an impression on that young man. I am knowing that for a fact, as I helped him write this to you. Lucky you. He's for being the most handsome of all those I ever treated. I fell in love with him meself, so I did.'

'Oh?'

'Sure, I'm just kidding. But I have a feeling in me that you two fell head over heels in a split second of time. So romantic.'

'H – how is he? And where is he?'

'He's doing well, though his lungs are not recovering well. I'm powerful sorry, Ella. But as for where it is that he's at, I'm not for knowing. It was chaos, so it was. Most of those from Dieppe hospital, where I landed, were being shipped to England – French, Germans and English alike. The French hospitals had so little room and so few supplies. Now, how about all of you? How is it that you faired on the front line?'

After a hug, the girls sat down and chatted about where their roles had taken them, though Ella's mind was on the letter from Paulo. She longed to know where he was and only half-listened to what was being said, until Paddy spoke again.

'The cases of influenza sickened me. To think these lads had survived the trenches, and a virus was taking them down – it broke me heart.'

The silence that fell held all their anguish at this.

'To be sure, we had our successes, but be mindful to take care when you get home. For isn't it that the epidemic has hit England already?'

There were no words to express how Ella felt; it was as if some force was intent on killing them all.

When Paddy saw Alan and Connie holding hands, her cheer lifted them all and a spark of hope for their future was rekindled.

'Let's go and have a cup of tea to celebrate,' said Connie. 'That's if the canteen truck we are pulling has such a delicacy.'

Everyone agreed.

As they entered the canteen, Paddy took Ella's hand. 'How is it that you have been? I have thought of you often. And I wish it was that I could put your mind at rest, but I've told you all I know.'

'I have been all right. Keeping busy has helped, though everything visits me in the night.'

'So no sickness has visited your mornings, and it is that your monthly is on time?'

Ella blushed, but knew that Paddy was speaking out of concern for her. 'No sickness, but as for my monthlies, they've always been erratic, so I'm not sure. Most of my prayers are begging God not to let me be pregnant. Then I can put the whole thing behind me. I know that is the only way. But, Paddy, I'm more concerned for Paulo than for myself. When you say that his lungs are not healing, how bad is he?'

'Oh, Ella, I shouldn't have told you the truth of it, but I wasn't for realizing the depth of your feeling. For sure you only met for a wee while.'

'I know, but it was long enough to seal a lifetime's love. I know that sounds strange, but . . . well, I have known love at first sight to happen before.'

'So have I. Sure, didn't it be happening to meself? I fell for Bobby at first glance, and it's agony not having any news of him since he left to go back to the fighting.'

'I'm sorry, Paddy. It's a funny feeling, isn't it? It's as if you have an attachment to a complete stranger, but one you know better than anyone else in the world. I really hope your Bobby is all right.'

'I couldn't be for putting it better meself, though I did have more time than you had to get to know my Bobby. And I'm powerful sorry for you, as it is that I have no idea where they dispatched Paulo to. I only had time to write the letter, and to be putting his mind at rest that I would get it to you, though I did tell him how he could contact you. He tells you in his letter.'

'Oh, Paddy, that's wonderful. Thank you for thinking of that.'

'It is though that I can only give you bad news on his condition. Paulo may recover to enjoy some life, but he won't be for a long life. Not unless it is a miracle that happens. His lungs are damaged, to the extent that breathing is difficult for him. And his back gives him pain and prevents him from walking. I would say that he will be placed in one of the many convalescent homes for officers in England, until the time comes when he can be shipped back home to France.'

'Yes, as soon as I get a minute to myself, I'll read what he has to say. Oh, Paddy, I can't believe that love can strike so painfully. But my pain is twofold, with the separation and the news you have given me.'

'I know. To be sure, everything will be fine. Just look at Connie – everything has worked out for her. And it's glad I am that Matron didn't get a hint of anything between the two of them. She was a stickler, that one.'

'Oh, I don't know, she did have a soft centre at times. What happened to her?'

'I'm not for knowing, but if it was as she went to a hospital that already had a matron, sure I'd have liked to have seen the clash that would have taken place.'

They both laughed at this.

'Now, away into the lavatory to read your letter.'

Paulo's letter both warmed and saddened Ella. It was very short, and yet it held all she needed to know:

Dear Ella,

I hope you don't mind me writing, but I think you know why I am compelled to. At least I am hoping that you do.

Though it seems strange to admit it, after we only knew each other for a short time, I feel that I cannot live without you in my life. Is that possible? Are you feeling the same way about me? I ask myself that every hour.

I want to meet up with you after the war is over and I am well again . . .

Ella closed her eyes. *Poor Paulo, they couldn't have told him that he will not get well.* Her heart cried out in pain at the truth of this. *I must find him and take care of him.* The rest of the letter wasn't much help:

I cannot give you an address, because our village of Fleury-devant-Douaumont in north-east France suffered badly in many German attacks and is no more. It is with great sadness that I tell you that my family were all killed and there is nothing left of our house.

We weren't a rich family. My father was a farm labourer, and I, not wanting to follow in his footsteps, joined the army as a young boy. I rose through the ranks on merit, and not on commission. The war helped, as many of my standing were elevated far above the position they would have attained.

There is nothing left of my family's possessions for me to claim, and I feel that I will be pensioned out of the army, now that I am injured.

Nurse Paddy has told me that I will be able to contact you through the Red Cross in London. I will try to do that, once I know where I will be. I hope that, if I manage to, you will want to see me, as I cannot get you out of my mind.

I am yours, with love, Paulo Rennaise x

Holding the letter to her breast, Ella allowed the tears to tumble down her cheeks. *Yes, yes, yes! I do want to see you, my Paulo. And I cannot wait until your next letter arrives for me.*

Chapter Eight

Paddy's heart felt heavy. After a stormy crossing of the English Channel, and yet another train journey, they had reached London and she was about to say goodbye to her new-found friends.

Ella and Connie had made her feel that she belonged, and had accepted her like none of the army lot had. Discipline had come above everything else for Queen Alexandra's nursing service, and that maxim – and the other nurses she'd worked with having come from well-to-do backgrounds – hadn't made it easy for her to fit in. Ella and Connie had been different somehow.

'Wouldn't it be nice if it was that we could meet up for a proper goodbye? I'm for thinking that next week would be a good time, when it is that we will know our future. I am to have three weeks' leave, and then it is likely I'll be demobbed. So I'm for looking for another job and hope to secure something soon.'

'I'm sorry, Paddy, but until I know that my sons are safe, I don't think I can arrange anything. But if all is well with them, then Connie and I will be setting a date for our wedding. So if you all leave us your addresses, we would love to invite you all to that.'

'That would be grand, so it would. Thank you, Alan.'

With hugs and goodbyes said, and addresses exchanged, Paddy had left them and now stood on the platform of Willesden Green Tube Station. She'd vowed never to return to Cricklewood, but the reality was that she had nowhere else to go. Picking up her rucksack, she took a deep breath and marched towards the exit.

'Is that yourself home from the war, Bernadette? For sure, you are looking bonny.'

For all her dread at coming back, Paddy felt a warmth enter her at the sound of the Irish lilt and the familiar sight of Mrs Fitzpatrick. Familiar down to the blackened eye that the poor woman sported as she sucked on a fag, rolled so thin it drew her cheeks into the gap where her teeth used to be.

'It is that, Mrs Fitzpatrick. It is good to see you. Though it's evident that not much has changed. Why you put up with that husband of yours, I'll never be for knowing.'

'Me vows were me vows, and he ain't for being that bad, most of the time. Did you hear that he was wounded and returned in '16 with just the one arm?' Mrs Fitzpatrick stood on the step of the house that she and her family shared with one other family and with Paddy and her pappy.

'No. Me pappy wasn't for writing much. I've a lot to catch up on, but I'm sorry to be hearing such news. Now, you watch that you don't catch your death.' Secretly Paddy had the thought that it was a pity it wasn't both arms Brendan Fitzpatrick had lost, as then he'd not be able to beat his wife.

'I'll be for being right. I'm used to the cold. Your pappy's not home, by the way. Is it that he's expecting you? He was discharged a week ago and came back with his pockets full, so he did. Since then he's been giving nearly every penny to Gutteridge, the landlord of the Crown Hotel.'

Paddy couldn't find it in herself to answer this. Her disgust was so deep that she wanted to shout it out loud, and let her countrymen know what she thought of them and their ways. Not the womenfolk, for most of them struggled from one drunken beating to the next, their belly full of the next bairn, year in, year out; and in such poverty that it kept minimal flesh on their bones.

'Aye, well, it's of no matter, Mrs Fitzpatrick. I wouldn't have expected anything different.' The cry of a baby met Paddy as she passed Mrs Fitzpatrick and entered the cluttered hall. A pram and two bicycles made negotiating her way to the stairs difficult, but she was glad to see that one of the bikes – her own – looked in good condition, and rideable.

'The wee bairn exercising his lungs is mine. I've been delivered of two since you left: two boys, John and Mick, they've just eleven months between them. It's me eldest, Declan, who has kept your bike in order. You'll be after remembering him? He's been using your bike for his work. He got himself a paper round, and he helps the coalman once a week. I am sometimes at a loss to know what I would do, without what he fetches in.'

'Well, he's welcome, and I'm sure as we can come to an arrangement to share it. I'm glad to hear of him working, and to see me bike in one piece. Will you thank Declan for me? He's done a fine job, so he has.'

Six Fitzpatricks! And all in the one room. Jesus, it was hell before, but with six of them, and goodness knows the increase in the O'Leary family, in the room next to ours . . . I can't be bearing it, I can't.

The stench of the stale air, mingled with the nappies steeping in a bucket outside Mrs Fitzpatrick's room, and the dank odour of the dripping, mildewy walls, seemed at that moment to be worse than all the smells she'd endured in the tent hospital.

Once in her own and her dad's room, Paddy opened the window. Shivering against the cold blast of air this let in, she crossed over to the fire and lit the kindling that her pappy had laid for his return. At least the coal scuttle that stood next to the fire was full of coal.

When the fire jumped into life and she had the kettle on, a headline in the London *Evening Standard*, which had been discarded on her pappy's chair, caught Paddy's eye: 'Influenza sweeps Britain – Real danger that more lives will be lost than during the war.'

A shudder that was not prompted by the cold shook her whole body. She looked around the cramped room, which was shabby, but clean – her pappy always said that cleanliness was next to godliness, and that was evident in the threadbare rug placed between the two armchairs in front of the fire, which showed signs of being recently brushed, as the stiff yard broom had left trails. At the back of the room, opposite the fire, stood a table and chairs, and behind each fireside chair and against opposite walls stood the beds. Paddy smiled to see that they were both made up with clean sheets that had been ironed and looked crisp and white. *Pappy must have been expecting me then.*

But although her pappy had standards, not many of the others in the dwellings in the street did, and Paddy realized that the overcrowded conditions they lived in were rife for any virus to take root. The street was noted for sickness and diarrhoea outbreaks amongst the children. Any illness spread like wildfire amongst the folk of the area. There was nothing she could do about that, but she could get herself and her pappy out of here. Her pay had mounted up in the bank, and she was sure there was enough for them to rent something better.

Sipping her tea, she decided that once her pappy came home, she would discuss it with him. At that moment the sound of a series of sneezes heralded his return and instilled dread in Paddy.

'Me little darling, news travelled to me that it was that you were home.' Pappy stood as large as life in the doorway, his body swaying, though Paddy knew it wasn't with the drink he'd consumed.

'Pappy, come away in and get warm. Is something ailing you?'

'I have a powerful feeling that it does, me darling. I've a banging in me head as if the little people themselves have taken residence and are holding a concert.'

'Oh, Pappy . . . Pappy!'

Paddy's anguish deepened as her pappy looked as though he would pass out. She ran to him and helped him to his bed.

'How long have you felt ill, Pappy? To be sure, you should not have been going out. Not only for the sake of your own health, but also for the sake of others. I've a mind it is the influenza that is ailing you.'

'Is it that I'm going to die, me Bernadette?'

'Not if I have any say in it. Now, let me get you to bed.'

Her pappy didn't object as she stripped him down to his

long johns and vest. Although both were wet with his sweat, Paddy couldn't bring herself to remove them. She had to let her pappy keep his dignity.

'Have you some aspirin in the house, Pappy?'

There was no answer. It was as if the illness that had taken hold of her pappy suddenly wanted all of him. In no time it had escalated to uncontrollable shivering, as beads of sweat poured down his face.

Though Paddy did all she could, when she awoke during the night her pappy was lying lifeless, staring at the ceiling. 'No! Oh, Pappy, I only closed my eyes for a moment. I – I didn't say goodbye.'

Saying her goodbye to her pappy two days later, Paddy stood beside his grave and sobbed. For all that he was or wasn't, he was her pappy, and he was all she'd had in this world.

Picking up her suitcase, Paddy walked away from the graveside. This time she was never going to return to Fenn Street. She'd booked herself into a guesthouse. Tomorrow she would go to the address that Bobby had given her.

Please God, let him be safe.

Chapter Nine

The first-floor apartment in Wicklow Street, London, that Ella had shared with her nanny for as long as she could remember smelt musty. Stepping over the pile of letters, she crossed the hall and went into the living room and took in the dust sheets that covered the furniture. Opening the curtains, she unlatched a window and threw it wide open. Cold December air chilled her, but the low winter sun brought a little comfort.

She'd spent last night in a hotel, putting off coming here, where she knew the loneliness of her homecoming might overwhelm her. Busying herself was the answer, and soon the dust sheets were removed and a glowing fire crackled in welcome. Now she would light the fires in the three bedrooms and thoroughly air her bedding.

Looking around the rooms, it was difficult to keep her spirits high. Without Nanny giving the place the feel of a home, the rooms simply took on the mantle of the purpose for which they were designated. Shaking herself, Ella knew there was bound to be a sense of anti-climax about coming home, with no one to greet her. She'd known it would be so. *I'll just have to get on with life as it is, and not mourn the past.*

As soon as her grocery order arrived and was stashed away, she slipped her feet into her suede-and-leather boots and laced them up, before donning her coat. Not the regimental one she'd returned home in, but her favourite ankle-length, dark-green wool coat, with a luxurious, wide Hudson-seal trim to the collar, cuffs and hem. Pulling on her matching hat made entirely of Hudson-seal fur, with a domed crown and a drooping brim, Ella took a deep breath. *Oh, to wear such clothes again!* Yes, the coat and hat had a tinge of mothballs, but she didn't care.

Her spirits lifted with the feminine feel of her attire, prompting her to do a little twirl in front of the long mirror in the hall. She would hail a cab and go to the nursing home in Coventry Street. She was too tired to walk, even though it was only a couple of miles or so away. And besides, she couldn't wait to see Nanny.

'Miss Machalski is very poorly – I'm not sure if she will know you. However, in her lucid moments she does talk about you. She is very proud of you, as we all are.'

'Thank you, Matron. May I go through? I won't disturb her.'

'Of course. It is not our usual visiting hours, but for you I will make a special allowance.'

Ella's heart pounded to the rhythm of the squeak of her boots on the highly polished linoleum floors as she walked the corridors. But when she looked down at the shrunken figure of her nanny lying so still, with her breath coming in soft pants, the pounding became a thud, as sorrow and pain entered her. 'Nanny, it's me, Ella.'

Nanny's eyes didn't open, but her gnarled hand reached out. Taking it in hers, Ella sat down on the chair that Matron had put next to the bed for her. 'There, she knows who you are. How lovely. I'll leave you together. If you can, get her to sip some water. Stay as long as you like.'

'Thank you.' Once Matron had left, Ella spoke again to her nanny. 'It's been a long time, dear Nanny, but the war is over now and I am back. If you want to come home, I will take care of you.'

Nanny's eyes opened. The once-dark eyes had lightened and her pupils were now ringed with an almost blue, misty colour. Pain was etched in every line of Nanny's face, but so was happiness, as her eyes filled with tears. Her little smile told Ella they were tears of joy. But though Ella would fight hard to get her home, fear rested in her that Nanny wouldn't be around for long. The mystery of her own past always lay at the forefront of her mind. Time was running out and, with guilt in her heart, Ella asked, 'Can you talk, Nanny?'

Nanny nodded.

'Nanny, forgive me. I know my questions pain you, but I must know. Is Wronski my real name?'

'Y– yes.'

The tired eyes closed once more, but Nanny's hand held on to Ella's as if she would never let it go.

'Where am I from? Nanny, please don't leave me not knowing.' She waited, but there was no response to this. She sighed. 'Let me help you to take a sip of water, Nanny. Your lips are very dry.'

As she carried out this task, a little hope seeped into Ella. Not only because, at last, Nanny had answered one of her questions, but because Nanny was aware of what was being said, although she did worry about Nanny's cracked lips.

Surely someone should have tended to her need for them to be moistened? Not that she worried about Nanny's general welfare, as she could see that she was otherwise well cared for. But she realized, from the hustle and bustle going on in the place, that it was run by people who had to stretch their resources among many others.

Lifting Nanny into a sitting position, Ella could feel her poor, twisted bones. 'Nanny, I'm taking you home. I'll have to put some arrangements in place first and sort out my discharge from the Red Cross, but it will only take me a few days to do that. I'll buy a bath chair and take you for walks in the fresh air, and engage someone to care for you when I have to go out. Would you like that, Nanny?'

Taking a sip of the water Ella held for her, Nanny looked up. Her cloudy eyes sparkled with joy.

Laying Nanny down again, Ella kissed her forehead. 'Rest now, and I'll be back. I'll do everything as quickly as I can. I love you, Nanny.'

Nanny nodded and smiled. Ella knew she was doing the right thing. It wouldn't be easy, and she'd have to put her own plans to one side, but Nanny had devoted her life to caring for her. She'd left her own country to be with Ella, which must have been a wrench. She must have family back in Poland surely? What of them – did they know how Nanny was, or anything about her? And what of herself? *Do I have anyone there? What happened to cause Nanny to bring me to England and never speak of the past? Will I ever know?*

Telling Matron of her plans, was met with objections. 'Look, my dear, I know that your heart is in the right place, but you need to think this through very carefully. Your reaction is natural. You want to make everything as it was. But the reality is that your nanny cannot do anything for herself.

She needs a great deal of attention and help. There is a team of us dedicated to doing everything for her. On your own, you would never manage.'

'I will. I will engage some help. I can see that she hasn't got long. I need to care for her, in her last weeks or months. I have to do that for her.'

'Very well. There are, of course, some conditions to be met. Our fees are monthly, and we require a month's notice of termination of our agreement of care for a patient. The only exception occurs on the death of a client.'

'I will pay for that month, but I will not leave her here. It isn't anything to do with the home, or the care you give. It is a need within me to look after my nanny, as she has done for me all my life. I hope you understand.'

'Yes, of course I do. I just think that you are letting your heart rule your head. This isn't what you need to be doing, after what you must have been through, but I can see that you are determined. In that case you'd better make your arrangements, and we will prepare for Miss Machalski's departure.'

Ella had mixed emotions as she left the home. She'd not made any plans for the rest of her life, but she had wanted to seek out her friends, Flors and Mags, and she desperately wanted to find Paulo. Something told her that she might never do that now. Theirs was a tenuous connection, reliant on her being part of the Red Cross. She wouldn't be that any longer, but she hoped they would still forward mail to her.

Once outside the nursing home, Ella walked towards Piccadilly Circus Tube Station, intending to find a cab there, and was amazed to see a throng of people coming out from the station and walking in the direction of The Mall.

A young man leaning on a crutch stood outside the station, his back against the wall, and she could see that one of his legs was missing from the knee down. He looked tired and unshaven, and as if he hadn't eaten for days. His shabby clothes hung on his body and his cheeks were sunken onto his cheekbones, giving him a skeletal appearance. Ella felt compelled to ask him, 'Are you all right?'

The soldier looked at her, his eyes a blank stare.

'I'm sorry, I – I didn't mean to intrude, but you looked as though you might need help.'

'I'm sick of this lot. They're all eager to welcome Haig back as a hero.' He spat on the ground. 'To me, Haig and the rest of them are butchers, not heroes. They sent us over in droves, knowing that most of us wouldn't stand a chance. The real heroes are six foot under the fields of France and Belgium. Kids who've had no life. But then what would you know about it? Living in London, cosseted, with everything you need in life.'

It was then that Ella noticed his begging bowl on the pavement. Shock held her unable to speak for a moment. Here was a man who had been through hell for his country, reduced to having to beg to survive, and yet despite all the people passing him, his bowl was empty. 'I do know. I have been nursing in Belgium, then France and then Belgium again, since 1914. I have just returned.'

'Oh, I beg yer pardon, Miss. I—'

His body swayed. Ella jumped forward and caught hold of him. 'Let me help you – where do you live? I'll get you a cab, but first let me take you into that cafe across the road and get you something to eat. It may only be cakes, as I don't think they do much else, but at least it will put something inside you.'

'Ta, Miss, but I ain't got a home. Me and the missus were in a flat, but I couldn't pay the rent when they discharged me from the army. And I couldn't get a job. Not how I am, with me injuries. Me missus and kid live with her mother, but I'm not wanted there; never did get on with me ma-in-law.' A tear wound a shiny path through the grime on his face. 'I've nothing of me old life left.'

Ella had to swallow hard to prevent herself from crying. The injustice of his plight left her feeling helpless to know what to do. But suddenly something occurred to her. She propped the man up against the wall, told him to hang on and then, swallowing her pride and driven by indignation that this throng was ignoring someone who'd given his all for them, she grabbed his bowl. Without thinking of her usual shyness, she shouted, 'So, you all want to see a hero, do you? Well, you're walking by one right now! Spare a penny for him. He fought for you.'

A few people stopped in their tracks. A gentleman took out his wallet and drew out a one-pound note and shoved it at her, whilst muttering something about the pair of them being a disgrace – using his injury to beg, and at such a time, when they were all going to greet the man who had steered the country to victory. 'Take this, and be off with you. You are an insult to our proud nation!'

'I don't know this man, and I am not working a scam with him. It is you who are a disgrace. What did you do in the war? Here, take your pound. This valiant soldier doesn't want money from someone like you.'

Without taking the note back from her – something Ella was glad of, as it was a huge amount – the man hurried on, but another stopped and dropped a half-crown into the bowl. And then another man. In a short time the small change brimmed over, falling onto the floor, until Ella took off her hat and emptied it into that, to make room for all the money that those eager to give wanted to drop in the bowl.

By the time the crowd had passed, her hat was half-full and the bowl was nearing the top with coins. A lot of them were farthings, but it didn't matter. People had shown they were willing to help the man, and that had warmed her heart.

When she turned to him, he had slumped to the ground, pain grimacing across his face. 'Oh, I'm sorry I left you. Where's your crutch? Oh dear, I only wanted to help.'

'No, it's all right. I've got me crutch, I just find standing hard to do, especially on an empty belly.'

'Right. Well, stay there a moment. Now that the crowd has passed, I can see a hot-potato brazier along the road a little way. I'll go and get you one. Once you have eaten, you will feel stronger. We can get a cab to my home, and I'll take care of you till I can find somewhere for you to stay.'

As he ate, the soldier told her that his name was Reginald Pattison. 'I – I've never met anyone like you, Miss . . . I mean, there were a lot over in France, but then it was their job. I don't know what to say.'

'You don't have to say anything. I only want to help. I'm appalled to find you like this, and to think that those I nursed during the war may be in the same plight – it's hard to take in.'

'Aye, it is. And not what I expected. I fought with the First Essex Regiment, but copped for a bullet that smashed my kneecap. I lay for two days till someone found me, and by that time my wound had gone rotten, and the surgeon who operated had no choice but to amputate. I fought to stay alive. I kept thinking of me wife and me kid, but now I wish I'd given in and died.'

'Oh no, don't say that. Where's there's life, there's hope. We were always being told that in the field hospital; it made us do all we could to save young men like you.'

'What life have I? Me missus and I can't be together. I'm sleeping rough and begging for money to feed meself.'

'Does your wife bring you food and clothing?'

'She's under the thumb of her mother. That old witch never liked me. Joanie's all right – that's me wife – but she's easily bullied. Besides, we have no way of keeping in touch. Her mother has this bully of a husband, who has a lot of cronies. If I'm seen within a mile of the place, I'll be beaten up.'

'Oh dear, that's dreadful. I'll do all I can to help you, Reginald.'

How I will do that I have no idea, but I'll find a way. Her matron from the Dieppe hospital came to Ella's mind. She would say over and over again, 'Where there is a will, there is a way.' *I'll just have to hope she was right.*

By the time they reached Ella's apartment she knew that Reggie, as he preferred to be called, had been a dock worker in the London docks, shifting tobacco and tea from the cargo ships to the vast warehouses on the wharf before the war.

'It wasn't a well-paid job, but it kept me and me family with a roof over our heads, and fed and shod us. There weren't much left over for high days and holidays, but me and the wife enjoyed going to the pub for a sing-song once a week. It was a good life, and one that I mourn.'

Ella felt sadder by the minute as she listened to Reggie. 'Make yourself comfortable, I'll get you some hot tea.'

In the kitchen Ella filled more than the kettle, as she put three saucepans of water on the remaining gas rings. The fire she'd lit earlier was still going well and would have warmed the water, but not enough.

Over a hot cup of tea, she told Reggie that she was going to bath him. 'If it will make you feel better, I will don my nurse's uniform.'

Reggie didn't speak, but nodded his head.

Not being much of a cook, Ella had bought mainly cold meats and cheeses. She had learned how to fry potatoes, though, and thought they would make a meal with the ham and some thick slices of bread. What to give Reggie to wear posed a problem, and in the end she decided to take a sheet into the bathroom, for him to wrap around himself.

Wearing her uniform again brought memories flashing back. Reggie had mentioned that he was with the First Essex, and it brought Freddy, her friend Flora's brother, to mind. *I'll go to Flora's house, as soon as I have Reggie settled. Oh, Flors, I can't wait to hug you.*

With Reggie seated on a chair in the bathroom, Ella carried out the task of bathing him, with minimal fuss, but was appalled to see the state of his wound. 'This needs a doctor's attention, Reggie.'

'I can't pay no doctor. I 'aven't been given a war pension yet.'

'I'll clean it and dress it as best I can. Then I will see about getting a doctor to call.'

'I can't get over your kindness, Miss. You 'ave no need to do all of this for me.'

'I have every need, Reggie. You are a wounded soldier. I cannot believe you have been discarded like this.'

'There's not just me, Miss. There's loads of us, homeless and on the scrapheap.'

'I wonder if it is because there is nothing organized yet? The whole country has been focusing on the war.'

'You could be right, Miss, but it ain't 'ow it should be.'

Ella could say nothing to this, but decided that she would do her best for soldiers like Reggie. They deserved that, didn't they? The Red Cross would surely organize something, if they hadn't already done so. And Ella knew this was the kind of work she would like to do in future, caring for all those like Reggie.

With his bath done, Ella handed Reggie the sheet. 'I'll get you a meal now, such as it will be, as I'm no Mrs Beeton! Then I'll make a bed up for you, while you eat. Tomorrow's another day, and who knows what it will bring.'

His thanks came out with a sob, and Ella's heart felt heavy with sorrow that, after all he'd been through, he should come to this: relying on a total stranger to help him. She wasn't prepared for Reggie reaching out and taking hold of her hand, and she snatched it away from him as the memory of Jim flooded through her.

'Oh, Miss, I'm sorry. I – I didn't mean . . . I just—'

'No. No, I'm sorry, Reggie. Forgive me. I didn't think . . . I know you wouldn't. I – I . . . You made me jump, that's all. Please don't worry. Come on, I'll help you through to the sitting room.'

Feeling angry at herself for creating an atmosphere, and at Reggie for even thinking of making such a gesture towards her, Ella wondered if she would ever heal.

'Here, lean on me and take your crutch. Try not to put any weight on your leg.'

'I couldn't if I wanted to. The pain is creasing me, Miss.'

'Call me Ella. Look, about me jumping away from you. Please don't let that worry you. I really was simply taken unawares.'

'I shouldn't have. I just felt so grateful to you. I used to hold the hand of the nurse who took care of me, or rather she held mine, and it gave me comfort.'

'And of course if you feel the need of that comfort, I will sit and hold your hand. Let's forget it happened. I am your nurse, so perhaps it would help to call me Nurse Ella?'

'Aye, that would suit, as that's how I was thinking of you. I can understand your fear. It's a massive thing you've done taking me in. You don't know me from Adam.'

No. All I saw was someone needing help. Someone who knew nothing about me. What was I thinking? As for me learning to trust a male friend again, it is going to take a lot – let alone a stranger! But looking on this man as a patient will help.

By the time they reached the sofa, Reggie was exhausted. He put his head back and tears flowed down his cheeks. Ella's heart went out to him.

'Is the pain very bad, Reggie?'

'Aye. Unbearable.' His teeth gritted and a moan came from him.

'I'll go for the doctor right now. I can't see you suffering like this. I won't be long.'

'No. I couldn't bear being taken to hospital, not tonight. I'm done in. I'm used to the pain. I'll manage.'

'Well, I'll go to the chemist shop on the corner of the road. I know the pharmacist, he'll give me something for your pain.'

Reggie was in bed and sleeping soundly, after she had administered the phial of the pain-draught to him – she hadn't asked what it contained as she trusted Malic, the Greek owner of the chemist shop. He had a wonderful array of potions, in bottles of all colours and sizes. Most were his own concoctions, and all worked on the ailments that he had invented them for. Malic had told her to make sure her patient was in bed before she administered the drug, and had said that he would sleep like a baby. Ella was grateful to find that was so, as she watched Reggie, snoring gently, and thanked God he was now out of pain.

As she sat beside him, Ella knew that her immediate future was settled. She would get Nanny home, engage a nurse to help to care for her, and would approach the Red Cross. Perhaps they had plans to care for those who were returning wounded, and who could no longer work. She was sure they would have, and so she would volunteer her services to help. *For now, I know that if I'm to live with what happened to me – and without Paulo – then I will need to do more than stay at home with Nanny. I must keep busy, and channel all my energy into helping others like Reggie.*

Emerging from her bank on King's Cross Road a few days later, Ella was pleased to have found that financially she was secure for some time to come. Her allowance from her family – whoever they were – had been paid in for her each month of her absence, and her pay from the Red Cross was mostly untouched.

She stood for a moment, thinking of how quickly she'd burdened herself with concerns for others. For now, she had a lot pressing on her mind, when on first arriving home she'd stood in the empty flat, feeling the future stretching endlessly ahead.

'Ella, is that yourself?'

'Paddy, how wonderful! I thought you lived in Crickle-wood – what brings you here?'

Paddy's face dropped.

'What is it? Just a few days ago you were so full of hope.'

Paddy told Ella everything that had happened since she'd returned home.

'Oh, Paddy. I'm so sorry to hear of your loss. Is there anything I can do to help you?'

'It is that seeing you has helped me. I was for feeling so alone, I thought I would come to seek you out.'

'Oh, my dear.' Paddy came into Ella's open arms. For a moment they hugged. Paddy's body shuddered with sobs. People passing by stared, but didn't pass comment. Were they used to such scenes of despair?

'Paddy, I will do anything – anything – to help you. Where are you staying?'

Paddy straightened and blew her nose. 'I'm in a guest-house along the road. I set out to walk to your house, when it is I came across you in the street.'

'That must be awful; they are such impersonal places. Have you no friends living near to you?'

'No. Lots of acquaintances, but, Ella, if you were to see the area my home was in, you would be for understanding. I am still renting the room that my pappy lived in, as I'm for having a lot of things that I need to collect. But isn't it that I have been so cocooned in me grief that I cannot think straight, to begin to search for a flat. And I've no family left now. Not even in Ireland.'

'I'm so sorry. Why don't you come home with me, Paddy? You can stay as long as you like. That is, if you don't mind my other guest, Reggie; he is a wounded soldier and homeless.'

'Oh, Ella, can I? That would be lovely, so it would. And why is it I'm not surprised that you have already begun to collect waifs and strays. To be sure, I would be honoured to be your second.' Paddy controlled her crying and wiped her face, a smile lighting up her face.

'Ha! I didn't mean to. It just happened. I'll tell you what, let's go into that cafe over there and have a hot drink. It's bitterly cold.'

Paddy nodded and linked her arm through Ella's.

The warmth from a roaring fire made Ella's cheeks burn and tingle. She hadn't realized how cold she'd been.

As if to talk about anything but what was troubling her, Paddy said, 'I see you've been shopping. I'm in need of so much, too. I'll have to take meself along to the stores, so I will.'

'Oh, this. No, it's not for me, but for Reggie – the poor soul has nothing and he isn't well enough to get about.'

'Is it wise that you should have taken him into your home, Ella? He may be running off with your silver as we speak.'

'Poor man couldn't, if he tried.' Ella told Paddy about Reggie and how she was just about to go back to the doctor's house to get him to come and examine Reggie's wound again. 'I think he should be in hospital. I'm worried sick about him. But the doctor seemed to think that the pain relief and rest would do the trick, besides the food and warmth I'm providing.'

'Well, if you are worried, then it is that there is something to worry over. You should be insisting. But what if this Reginald is for staying with you and not going to the hospital? Is it sure that you have room for me as well?'

'Yes, of course I do. I have three bedrooms. You can have my room and I will sleep in my nanny's room.'

'You have a nanny!'

'It's a long story. I'll explain it all to you later. Do you have to give notice at your guesthouse?'

'No. I am for having it on a temporary basis, and it's only a short distance from here.'

'Perfect. You can collect your things while I go and see the doctor, as his surgery is just across the road, next to the bank. Then I only live round the corner.'

'Aye, I'm for knowing that. Oh, Ella, I'm that happy to have found you.'

'Me, too, Paddy. How's things with the army? I take it you're not on any duties at the moment?'

'No, I'm still on leave, pending my discharge. It is simply a matter of waiting for me papers, so it is. I'm for taking a break before I look for work.'

It occurred to Ella that Paddy would be able to help nurse Nanny, but now wasn't the time to discuss the subject. She didn't want Paddy to think she had a motive for asking her back to her home, as nothing was further from the truth. *Oh, but she could be the answer to my prayers.*

Taking on charity work had become important to Ella, because she needed a challenge if she was ever going to heal her mind of the nightmares that visited her. *And to help me to live without Paulo in my life . . . Can I do that?* At this moment she didn't think she could.

Chapter Ten

'This wound is not looking good, Ella. The bone is badly damaged at the point of the stump, and I think that a further amputation is needed.'

'No, Doctor. I couldn't face that again, I couldn't . . .'

Ella sought to comfort Reggie. 'It won't be anything like the operation you experienced in the field hospital, I promise. If you don't go ahead and infection sets in, you could end up dying from gangrene. I'm sure you saw that happen around you, Reggie. You wouldn't want that.'

'No, Miss, but amputation – I don't know if I can.'

'To be sure you can, Reggie. It is as Ella says; it is for being a different outcome in the hospital theatre.'

Reggie was quiet for a moment. Paddy had taken his hand and he clung on to it. After a moment, he nodded.

The doctor let out a sigh of relief. 'Very well. I will go along to the hospital and book you in myself. I'll send an ambulance to collect you. Now, if you nurses would be kind enough to prepare him, he doesn't want to arrive in his altogether.'

'Thank you, Doctor. I'll see you out and pay your bill. Which hospital will you take him to?'

'Great Portland Street, the Royal National. They take military personnel and those discharged from the services, but still needing treatment and care. It is an excellent orthopaedic hospital. King George visited recently, and they are expecting a visit soon from Queen Mary, so you may get lucky, Reggie, and be introduced to the great lady.'

Reggie gave a weak smile, but his eyes held fear.

Ella sought to comfort him. 'If you give me the address of your mother-in-law, Reggie, I'll make sure your wife knows where you are, and what is happening.'

'Ta, Miss. I don't know 'ow I can ever thank you.'

'You don't have to. I'll come to see you while you are in hospital. And I'll try to find accommodation for you, on your discharge. By then the war pensions may be sorted out and you should have an income.'

Following the doctor to the door, Ella settled his fee.

'I only require half the amount, thank you, Ella. What you have done for that young man is amazing, and humbling.'

'No, it was nothing. As long as he will be all right. That's all that matters.'

'I think he will be. He has been lucky that you came across him. There are so many out there like him. It is a tragedy. No one seems to have thought about the aftermath of war. The streets of London sometimes feel littered with beggars, as the returning wounded leave hospital and are unable to put their lives back together. But you cannot be helping them all in this way, my dear. Some are severely mentally damaged. It isn't safe.'

'I know.'

Ella told the doctor her thoughts about approaching the

Red Cross. 'Will it be enough, though? Will it be a permanent solution?'

He shook his head. 'We have lived through a time of horror, and those of you who took up the challenge and did your bit have had the worst of it, and there is bound to be fallout from it all for you. Take care of yourself, Ella. Give yourself a chance to heal.'

Ella nodded. Dr Grey had been her doctor for as long as she could remember. Not that she had needed to see him very often, as she had always known good health until she had been struck down with the mystery illness that laid her low. This he'd diagnosed as a virus that was not yet identified. But he'd brought her through it, and she'd regained the strength that had sapped from her.

As she closed the door on the doctor, Ella thought that knowing, as she did, that feeling of complete weakness and being unable to function had helped her in looking after others. She'd been able to understand when they couldn't lift a cup to their lips or, worse, take themselves to the bathroom; but, she thought, these were physical disabilities, which could be undertaken by anyone willing to help. *But what of mental disabilities, when fear and emotional instability are your hourly companions?* That must be the hardest to live with. And the hardest to heal. And she knew she was in that boat, with all those returning from the carnage of war. And on top of trying to forget all she'd seen, she had . . . *No! I must forget about it . . . I must! But how – how?*

Ella and Paddy sat together in the sitting room of her apartment later that evening. Reggie had gone off to hospital in an ambulance, and they had sorted out the room he'd been in and had made it ready for Paddy.

The fire crackled and spat, as if trying to make them feel that at long last they were home, but the feeling eluded Ella. And she was sure it eluded Paddy, too.

'Ella, you don't know what it is that you have done for me. I know we weren't for knowing each other long, but I'm for thinking we bonded very quickly. It is as if I have known you all me life, and yet am not knowing much about you at all.'

'Well, that makes two of us, as I know very little about who I am, too.'

Paddy listened to Ella's story without interrupting her. 'To be sure, that's a powerful tale of mystery. I can understand the need in you to know more. Your nanny should be telling you. It is unfair and cruel to leave you in the dark about your own family.'

'I don't blame Nanny. I think she has her reasons. I cannot think what they are, but she is a good person.'

'Will you be after trying to find out, in the future?'

'Yes. It is a burning need in me. But I don't know where to start. Nanny seems ready to tell me, but she isn't able to. I feel that my last chance is slipping away.'

'And what of Paulo?'

'I'm still hoping he will contact me, but it is early days. Have you heard anything from Bobby?'

'No. I've had no time, so I haven't. I'm not for knowing if he has returned home even. They say that those in the push forward to Germany may be a while returning, as the British have to be part of the occupation.'

'Oh, Paddy, suddenly the enormity of the aftermath of the war is upon us. Will life ever be the same as it was?'

'No, for sure the world has changed forever. But from

93

what they are saying, it is that it was a war to end all wars, so we have to be picking up the pieces as best we can.'

Ella knew she should feel a grain of hope in Paddy's words, but instead she felt a deep sadness descend on her as she remembered the doctor's comment: 'The streets of London sometimes feel littered with beggars.' *There are such a lot of pieces to pick up.*

'Ella, it is that you have been through so much more than any of us. I'm for admiring you and how you are coping. I have to be telling you that, as I sit here getting to know you, and realize that you have such a lot on your plate and yet give so much to others, I am inspired to see a way that I will get through the pain in me.'

'You will, dear Paddy. It isn't easy, and the pain you have is harder than any I have to live with. But it will ease. You will have your memories to help you – at least you will have, when visiting them doesn't hurt so much.'

'For you, it has been throwing yourself into work in the field hospital to blot out your pain that has helped, I can see that.'

'Yes. Especially since . . . well, you know. Dealing with those worse off than you is like a salve to your own hurt. As for my family mystery, that is pain of a different kind and one that I didn't really feel for years. I had never known any different, you see. My curiosity was aroused as a child, when friends I made asked me to visit and I began to understand what a real family should be like. But Nanny was a good replacement for that. It wasn't until I began to grow up that I realized my family made a choice to banish me from their lives.'

'It must be very difficult to come to terms with that. But it is that you have family, to a degree. I need to come to

94

terms with what has happened to me. My pappy was weak in many ways, but he was a loving father. I so wanted to come home to him and to be setting up a decent home for us both. I was for thinking that I wouldn't work for a long time, that I hadn't the heart for it, though how I was to manage, I didn't know or care. But now I can see that was the wrong path to take, so it was.'

'I think so. Carrying on is the only way.'

'Aye, I see that now . . . Ella, well, it is that you say you will be needing help with your nanny. Is it that you would consider me? I'm not for thinking that I could cope with nursing on a ward right now, but if I could take on the responsibility of caring for your nanny, it would be a start for me, in an environment that I'd feel happier in. I – I'm not meaning to be presumptuous . . . I mean, I would be for finding meself somewhere to live, but I really would like you to be considering me for the position.'

'Oh, Paddy, would you? It would be an answer to my prayers, to have you here helping me. That room is yours for as long as you need it. I was going to look for a live-in nurse, and for you to fill the role would be wonderful.'

'Really? Oh, Ella, it is glad I am that I sought you out. You've given me a lifeline, so you have. And in a while, when I have healed a little, I'll be glad to help you with the home-less, too.'

'I think we'll drink to that. I'll make some cocoa.'

'Cocoa? Is it nothing stronger that you have?'

Ella laughed. 'Of course – there's a drop of my nanny's night-medicine.' On Paddy turning her nose up at this, Ella laughed louder. 'It's a nice gin, if that will do you.'

'Well, now you're after talking the good talk. I don't mind if I do.'

As they clinked their glasses, some warmth entered Ella and seeped into her heart. She had Paddy, and Reggie was safe. Soon she would have Nanny home, and maybe – just maybe – Paulo would get in contact with her. Please God, let him do so. *Because whatever my future holds, I want it to hold Paulo.*

PART TWO

London, 1919

~

Ella and Paulo

Marred Happiness

Chapter Eleven

Ella climbed the steps to the Red Cross Headquarters in Moorfields, London. It had been two months now since her return from France and each week she'd made this vigil, hoping there would be a letter for her from Paulo.

The bitter, late-February wind cut into her as if she was naked, instead of being wrapped in her dark-green coat. If there was no letter today, she had decided she would begin to search for Paulo. She would start by writing to every officers' convalescent home in Britain, and if that was fruitless, then she would travel to France to the area of the lost village where Paulo was born and had lived until the war. Surely someone would know where he was? She had to know if he was all right. *But more than that, I want to see him – to be with him. I need to know if he will still want me, knowing . . .*

Ella pulled herself up. Admitting to herself that she was having a baby was so difficult to deal with. She hadn't even told Paddy.

Each month she'd begged her flow to start. But there

was nothing. And there were other signs, too. Her breasts had enlarged, her nipples had darkened and her stomach looked a little rounder, although she had been spared any morning sickness. *Maybe there is something else wrong with me? Please let it be so, as I can't bear it to be having Jim's baby.*

'I'm sorry, Miss, there is no post for you again.' The voice of the clerk seemed alien to Ella. In her anguish, she couldn't remember opening the door to enter the communication office and she hadn't spoken. But then she'd no need to. The clerk knew why it was that she came here.

'But there is a note for you to contact Miss Jane Embury. She said to tell you to call into her office as soon as you can.'

Ella nodded, then thanked the young girl. 'I could go there now. Can you check if she can see me?'

The girl came back saying that Miss Embury would receive Ella now. All very formal, as all dealings with the woman were. A middle-aged spinster, Miss Embury was a member of the governing board of the Red Cross. It was to her that Ella had written about carrying out work in a rehabilitation centre.

'Sit down, Ella. It is nice to see you again. Firstly, congratulations are in order. We received this.'

Ella took the certificate that Miss Embury handed to her, not knowing what it had to do with her.

'Read it.'

The smile on Miss Embury's face made Ella even more curious, but her curiosity turned to shock as she read:

100

*The KING has been pleased to award the Albert Medal
in recognition of gallantry displayed in saving life:*

MISS MARJELLA WRONSKI – VOLUNTARY AID
DETACHMENT

*1st October 1918 a fire broke out at No. 36 Casualty
Clearing Station at Rousbrugge, Belgium, and quickly
reached the operating theatre, where the surgeon was performing an abdominal operation. The lights went out, and
the theatre was quickly filled with smoke and flames, but
the operation was continued by the light of an electric
torch, Miss Wronski continuing her work of handing
instruments and threading needles with steadfast calmness, thereby enabling the surgeon to complete the operation.
Miss Wronski afterwards did splendid work in helping to
carry men from the burning wards to places of safety.*

'Oh, but I . . . What about the others? There were so
many of us.'

'They have all been recognized, my dear, and we will be
contacting them. We are arranging a ceremony for every Red
Cross worker who was involved. We are very proud of you
all. You will receive your medal at the ceremony, and we will
contact you all soon to arrange it.'

'Thank you. I'm so undeserving, but feel very honoured.
Have you the list of all those honoured? I mean, do you
know if any of the Queen Alexandra nurses are to receive
recognition?'

'No, but I understand that each and every person involved
in the evacuation of the patients is to receive recognition.
Did you have someone in mind?'

101

'Yes, Bernadette Riley. She is helping me with my nanny, who needs constant care. Bernadette was bereaved when she came home, and so she's staying with me.'

'Well, if she has informed the army of her new address, I am sure she will receive her honour. Is that everything?'

'I wanted to ask you about the rehabilitation centres?'

'Yes, I did want to discuss that with you, as we have joined with the Salvation Army. That is, we have offered them our help and some resources. They have an excellent system in place for feeding, clothing and generally helping the homeless. I understand you want to channel your spare time into this work?'

'I do. Very much so.'

'Then here is the address of our contact. You will go as a Red Cross worker, as you haven't left our service, only taken a break – something that I was pleased to see. Go along and see Charles Wormington, who will give you further instructions.'

'Thank you. He does know that I only have limited hours?'

'Yes, but you can discuss all of that with him. Now I'm afraid I am very busy, Miss Wronski, so if there's nothing else, I'll say goodbye for now and will look forward to seeing you at the ceremony. We are hoping to get our chief to come along to present you all with your medals.'

It's now or never. I'll never get this chance again. Miss Embury rarely gives interviews regarding personal staff problems. But there is no one better to help me than her.

'Th – there is something. I'm sorry to take up your time, but I'm looking for a French officer. I – I, well, we met at Hospital 36. He was a patient and was evacuated from the fire. He would have needed further intense treatment—'

'I do know something of this, but you know it is not encouraged that you make alliances, Miss Wronski.'

'I – I know, but we didn't mean to. It just happened. He wrote to me. He said he would write here when he was settled, but nothing has arrived. I – I'm sorry, I shouldn't have mentioned it . . .'

There was a long silence. Ella didn't know whether to rise and leave or carry on sitting there. Eventually she stood.

'I may seem to you like an over-the-hill spinster, but something similar happened to me during the Boer War. My young man was killed. We met on the ward of a field hospital and fell instantly in love. He recovered enough to go back to the front line. I never saw him again.'

During the pause that followed, Ella could only say that she was sorry.

'No, don't be. I have come to terms with my loss. I just wanted you to know that I do understand. I must have come across as heartless, giving you the official line. But rules don't take into account human emotions. Give me all the information you have and I will see if I can trace your young man. Now, I really must get on.'

This last was said rather abruptly, but Ella knew, from Miss Embury's reddened cheeks, that she was covering the embarrassment she felt at sharing something so personal.

Saying her goodbyes, Ella left the office feeling full of hope. There must be records of where every soldier was sent that day of the fire – and afterwards. Miss Embury would have access to those.

Within an hour Ella was sitting opposite Charles Wormington, the coordinator of the charitable operations run by the

Salvation Army. In his fifties, he was small and balding and had an air of importance about him.

'We will be glad of your help, Miss Wronski. There is much to do. Especially for those displaced by the war. We have many nationalities waiting for transport home. Canadians, Australians and those from other Commonwealth countries. It is a challenging task.'

'What will you expect of me, Mr Wormington?'

'Whatever you can give. Time, of course, to help where needed. We supply meals to the many homeless, and medical care on a small scale, and with the help of local doctors who can give their time and expertise to us. But a lot of work is needed to keep those men who are displaced looked after, until they are shipped home. It is all work the government should be tackling, but doesn't seem able to. We most need help in the soup kitchens, and distributing clothing. We have only a few hostels, so placements in them are limited, but each person needs assessing for those. That's medical, more than anything, and I fear we are helping to spread the flu virus by giving aid to all and sundry, and yet . . .'

'You cannot refuse help. I understand. But I agree that an assessment of health should be carried out on each applicant. Some sort of isolation for those with the virus maybe?'

'Yes, that's exactly it. Help for all, but channelled correctly, so that we don't end up killing everyone.'

'That is where I could help the most. I'm not a qualified nurse, but I have a great deal of training and experience that would enable me to assess each applicant. But where would I send those in need of medical help?'

'That's where the Red Cross will come in. They are running several clinics and helping out at hospitals. I will contact Miss Embury, and will organize something with them. Can you start tomorrow?'

With the arrangements in place, Ella began her walk home. The threat of the virus was so frightening that she avoided all public transport. Even taxi cabs didn't feel safe. The biggest threat would come when she returned the next day to help assess those needing assistance, but at least then she would have her uniform on and would wear a mask, besides having sterilization equipment to hand.

But should she be taking such a risk, knowing what she knew about her condition?

Calling out that she was home, Ella was surprised not to be greeted. A cold fear seized her as she remembered how pale Paddy had looked this morning.

'Paddy?'

Still no reaction.

Discarding her coat, Ella rushed through the empty living room to her nanny's bedroom. 'Paddy. Oh, Paddy, what's happened?'

Paddy lay on the floor next to Nanny's bed. Her body was trembling.

'I – I had a – a sudden attack of dizziness.'

'Oh, Paddy, you're sweating.'

'I'm so c – cold.'

Dread entered Ella's heart. 'Let me help you up. Is Nanny all right?'

'Yes . . .'

Getting Paddy up took all of Ella's strength. Pain creased her back as she finally got Paddy to the sofa in the living room. Exhausted, she slumped down into a chair, just as Paddy threw up.

Unable to move as the pain in her back increased, Ella tried to soothe her friend. 'Don't worry, Paddy, it might not be influenza. I'll get my breath back and then I'll clean you up and fetch the doctor.'

Paddy didn't answer, but laid her head back. Her face had a deathly pallor.

Making a huge effort, Ella got out of the chair and fetched a bowl of water. Never had the smell of vomit made her feel sick, but before long she was using the bowl herself. *Oh, dear God, no!*

'Oh, Ella, I'm sorry. Let me help. It is that I'm for feeling better now.'

Judging by how Paddy looked and how difficult it was for her to get across the room without holding on to things, Ella thought she must have felt rotten before. Dear Paddy was making an extreme effort. 'No. Come and sit back down. I'm all right now. I – I, well, I have a reason why things that I usually take in my stride now upset my stomach.'

Paddy had reached the table in the corner. She clung on to it and turned to stare at Ella. 'No! No – not that . . . Holy Mary, Mother of God!'

Ella couldn't hold her tears back.

'D – don't, Ella . . . don't. There's worse things. And we said that if it happens, we will deal with it. Well, we will. We'll get ourselves through this, so we will. And – and we'll be after loving the child.'

'Oh yes. No matter how it was conceived, it is my child and I will love it. But I didn't want to be having a baby. I didn't.'

'Me poor wee Ella. This shouldn't be happening to you, of all people.'

Paddy had made it back to the sofa, stepping over the

mess as she went. Sitting down, she reached over and took Ella's hand. For a split second the action made Ella afraid and she nearly snatched her hand away, but then scolded herself. *Don't be silly. If the influenza virus is in this house, then I'll more than likely catch it anyway.* She clung tightly to Paddy.

After a moment Paddy said, 'Will you look at us? Sitting here crying. For the love of Jesus, there's an awful smell in here.'

Ella felt a giggle coming on and, when she let it out, it was a full laugh. 'Oh, Paddy, Paddy.'

'What? Here's me taking to me sickbed and all you can do is laugh!'

'I know. I'll soon have you sorted. Let me help you to the bathroom. I'll bring you a nightie and you can get into bed. Then I'll clean this mess up.'

Once Paddy was in bed, a little colour came back to her, although that worried Ella, as it consisted of two spots, high up on her cheeks.

'Paddy. How are you feeling? Do you have aches in your limbs? A sore throat? Shivers?'

'Y – yes.'

'Well, I think we both know what this is. Now you're to stay in this room at all times. I have a jerry-pot somewhere – you can use that to go to the toilet in. I'll bring a screen in from my room, so you can have privacy while you use it. I'm sorry, love, but I must go back into medical mode. I will wear my uniform and keep changing my apron and gloves, and I'll wear a mask while I am in here. Is that all right with you?'

'It's for being fine, and for the best. Do it right away, this very minute, Ella. Scrub everything I've been for touching.

And let us hope that the Good Lord is merciful and doesn't let you come down with it.'

For the next twelve hours Ella rested for only five minutes at a time, between dousing Paddy's hot, sweaty, trembling body with cold water, in a desperate attempt to reduce her temperature, and changing her and her bedding, to try and keep her comfortable.

Her supply of clean sheets and nightwear was running out, so she resorted to ripping in half the clean linen that was left and using the strips as draw sheets, but the task of keeping Paddy in a dry bed was proving too difficult.

During a respite of ten minutes, when Paddy was less distressed, Ella managed to fill and light the copper and dunk the soiled bedclothes into it to boil.

Nanny slept through most of it, as she was doing most of the time now. But just after two in the morning, her voice became stronger than Ella had heard it since coming home. 'Ella . . . Ella!'

Ripping off her apron and gloves and donning clean ones, Ella removed her mask. 'I'm coming, Nanny. I won't be a moment.'

Rushing into the bathroom, Ella scrubbed her face and hands, before entering Nanny's bedroom. Nanny had pushed her bedclothes off and had sat up. Her expression was one of dazed unawareness.

'Oh, Nanny, what's to do? Is there something the matter?'
'Ella. I . . . I can't remember.'
'Lie down, dear. Don't get cold. There, that's better. Here, take a sip of water, Nanny.' Taking the glass of water at the side of Nanny's bed, Ella held it to her lips while she drank. 'Were you dreaming, Nanny?'

'What, dear? Oh, I didn't know you were a nurse, Mona.'

'Who's Mona, Nanny? I'm Ella, remember?'

'Yes. I have an Ella – Marjella. Ella is her new name, given to her during the war. I like it. I call my Marjella "Ella" now.'

'That's right. That's me, dear. I'm Ella.'

'How's Momma, Mona? Is she well? I haven't seen her for a long time. I had to leave. I had a child. I had no business having a child.' Nanny began to cry.

'It's all right, Nanny. Ella's here.'

'No . . . no, Ella's *his* child, not mine! But I love her. I hate *him*! He – he made me, Mona. I – I'm sorry. Tell Momma I'm sorry.'

Shock, on hearing this, stilled Ella. But Nanny's heart-rending sobs brought her back to what was required. 'Nanny, it's Ella, not Mona. You're all right, Nanny darling. I'm taking care of you.'

'My child died, Mona. H – he died. Little Aleksy, he was beautiful . . . beautiful.'

'Oh, Nanny. I'm sorry. Dear Nanny, try to forget. Rest now.'

'I'll never forget him, ever. His blue eyes and curly brown hair. Oh, Aleksy . . . Aleksy.'

Ella held Nanny's hand. It seemed that no matter what she said, Nanny was in this other world, where these people she'd never before spoken of lived.

'Ella must never know, Mona . . . never! Promise you won't tell her.'

'It's all right, Nanny. I'm here. It's Ella, Nanny. There's no Mona here.'

'Mona, stop mentioning Ella. It must be our secret, she must never know. The Wronskis are devils. Spiteful! Not Mrs

Wronski; she was an angel. She died giving birth to Ella. Oh, how she would have loved her. But I have loved Ella for her. I tried to be with Ella how I knew Kasienka would have been, if she had lived. I never told Ella of her hateful, lying, cheating father. He got rid of Ella, you know, Mona. He banished me and made me take Ella with me. That new wife of his didn't want us around. Well, she was welcome to him. Though he did keep paying the money to us, so he hadn't forgotten us altogether.'

'Nanny, where do they live? Where in Poland?'

'I can't tell you that, Mona. I can't. No one must know who might tell my Ella.'

Against all that she believed she should do, Ella pretended that she was Mona. 'I won't tell her, Nanny, nor will I tell Momma.'

'Momma knows. She got me the position there.'

'Where? And who made you have a baby?'

'That pig. That Wronski. He – he didn't help me. The man came to visit. I was a maid, just a maid. I waited on them at table, and Wronski's friend took a shine to me. They – they played cards. I served them drinks . . . Oh, Mona, they played one of the games with *me* as the prize. Whoever won, they would . . . I begged, Mona. I screamed and kicked, but they took me to a bedroom – and Wronski watched. He watched!'

'Oh, Nanny. Nanny.' This was too much. To hear that her dear nanny had been through such an ordeal. And to hear so much information, at last, about her own parents – terrible things. *My father was a monster, but my mother was a good person. Oh, Mama, I'm so sorry that my birth killed you. So sorry . . .*

'There, there, don't cry, Ella. Are you hurt? Nanny kiss you better.'

'Oh, my dear Nanny, I love you.' As she said this, Ella lowered herself to accept the hug that Nanny's open arms promised. It felt good to be held by her, and to have her back in the real world.

'I'm tired, Ella. So tired.'

'Rest now, dear. I'll sit by your side. I'm all better now. Look, I'm not crying.' *But am I better? Will I ever feel better again? The past is now one of the ripples of my life – a persistent ripple. The biggest ripple of them all.*

Chapter Twelve

On the third day of Paddy's illness, Ella knew that she too was coming down with the dreaded virus. As she listened to the hacking cough and moans of pain coming from Paddy, a sudden dizziness seized her. Leaning forward, she rested her head on Paddy's bed. How long she'd been sitting next to her, she couldn't remember, but now her body didn't want to sit, but cried out to be allowed to lie down. Every limb felt heavy, and her head pounded with pain. When she lifted it, the room spun.

But how could she be ill? Who would take care of Nanny and Paddy? Somehow she had to beat this. Trying to stand up brought on a feeling of nausea. Grabbing the bucket that she'd placed next to the bed for Paddy to use, she retched her heart out.

'Ella? Ella, what's wrong? Oh . . . no, Ella. No.'

Wiping her mouth, Ella patted Paddy's hand. 'Pregnancy sickness – that's all.' But she knew that wasn't all, because surely such a condition didn't make every part of you shiver and yet feel as though you were burning up?

Paddy lifted herself onto her elbow. 'Ella, y – you're shaking. Is it that you don't you feel well?'

'I – I feel very unwell. Oh dear, Paddy, what are we going to do?'

'Get yourself on the bed and lie down. It – it's early, yet. We'll think of something.'

'I'll . . . take the bucket out. I can't leave it.'

Holding on to the bed and then the chair, Ella made it to the door with the bucket. Once there, her legs gave way. Somehow she managed to keep the bucket upright. But she bruised her leg as she caught it on the doorframe. Waiting a moment for the stinging pain to subside, she lay down and tried rolling over to move herself, but she couldn't. A weakness, like none she'd ever known, had overcome her whole body.

'Ella . . . Oh, Ella.'

A blanket came over her. 'I – I'm not able to lift you, but it is that I can fetch a pillow for you and be for making you comfortable.'

A swirling mist swamped Ella. As parts of it cleared, faces came at her – the hateful Jim, grinning at her, taunting her. She tried to slap him, but her arms were too heavy. Then another face: one that she knew, and yet didn't know. He had a beard and dark, twinkly eyes. She giggled. She was a child. The man tickled her tummy and called her his beautiful little Marjella. He was speaking in Polish.

'*Tatuś*?' The word for 'Daddy' came so easily to her. This was her *Tatuś*. She remembered him . . . but he was going. He was leaving her. '*Nie idź, Tatuś* . . . No, don't go, Daddy . . . *Tatuś*. Noooo!'

Pain tightened her chest. She couldn't breathe. It was so hot, and yet she felt cold. Icy cold. Again she tried to move,

113

but every part of her body hurt. Nothing worked as it should. It felt as if a great weight was on her, holding her down. Her head screamed with agony. But then the swirling began again, only this time it dragged her towards a black hole. She tried to fight, but couldn't. The hole sucked her into its depths.

'Miss Wronski, come on now. Take a drink. That's right. One sip at a time.'

The water was cold. It soothed Ella's burning throat. But who was giving her the drink? She hadn't heard the voice before.

'There, that's better. You're looking a lot brighter today. I think you have turned a corner.'

'Who . . . ?' The word rasped her throat. She couldn't say any more.

'I'm Nurse Flemming. You're in hospital. Your friend is in the bed next to you. She has almost fully recovered now.'

'Nan – ny?'

'It's all right, Ella. It is that your nanny is back in the nursing home.'

'Paddy? Oh, Paddy, h – how?'

'I was for managing to get to the door and called out to a passing stranger. Thank the Good Lord, he happened to be a kindly gentleman. I asked him to go for your doctor and to tell him to get to us as quickly as he could.'

'My . . . my baby?'

'I'm heart-sorry, Ella, it is that you—'

'It – it's gone?'

'Yes.' The voice of the nurse again. 'You miscarried. This flu virus does that to some pregnant women. I'm very sorry.

Although, given your unwed state, I expect you will be pleased.'

Pleased? No. Not pleased. A deep sadness overcame Ella. The depth of it surprised her, as she hadn't wanted Jim's baby, and yet somehow she'd bonded with the tiny spec inside her, and part of her had been looking forward to welcoming her child. A tear slid a cold trail down her hot cheek.

'I'm sure you will come to look on this as a blessing, *Miss* Wronski. Now, it won't do you any good to get upset. You are verging on being very ill, and you must put your mind to good thoughts and to getting better.'

As the nurse walked away, Ella wondered if she had ever sounded like that to any of her patients. Had her encouragement come across as so cold-hearted? She hoped not.

'Ella, now don't be taking any notice of her. It is . . . judgemental that she is. But oh, Ella, it is good to see you are awake, so it is—' A fit of coughing overcame Paddy.

Ella turned her head, afraid at the hacking, chesty sound. 'Ooh, my neck!'

'I know, it is that the pain is everywhere. But keep willing yourself well – it is for being the only way. We knew that, when we were nursing, we could be doing all the right things and still suffer the loss of our patient, if they were not for having that will to get better.'

'M – my baby . . .'

'It is sad, I know, Ella—' Again the coughing.

'Paddy, your chest sounds bad. Don't talk. I'm sorry, I will be all right.'

'Call . . . on your wee one's soul to help you.'

Weakness seized Ella once more. She couldn't answer Paddy. Closing her eyes, she tried to think good thoughts,

115

ones that would give her the will to live. But the haze that was never far away took her and she went into a deep sleep.

The nurse woke her. 'Miss Wronski, a note has been delivered for you. Do you want me to read it to you?'

'Y – yes. Thank you.'

The sound of the note being opened seemed magnified a thousandfold, rasping the throbbing pain in Ella's head.

'Oh, it's from Miss Embury, one of the directors of the Red Cross.'

Ella's heart jolted. 'How d – does she know I'm here?'

'It says here that your doctor reported it to her. Are you a Red Cross worker, too?'

'Yes, I worked in field hospitals from 1914.'

'Oh, I beg your pardon, Nurse Wronski. I – I shouldn't have—'

'It – it doesn't matter.'

'It is that it does . . . matter, Ella. I was overhearing the tone in your voice, Nurse Flemming. You are not for knowing a patient's circumstances, so you should not be standing . . . in judgement.'

Ella's concern for Paddy increased. She looked over at her. Paddy was gasping for breath.

'You're right, of course.' The nurse leaned heavily on the bedstead. 'I'm just tired and not thinking straight. I'm . . . It's no excuse, but we are so stretched. I've been on duty for fourteen hours already, with not a minute to sit down or have a cup of tea.'

'I know how that feels. Please don't worry.'

'Thank you. Anyway, your note:

Dear Nurse Wronski,

'We are very sad to hear of your own and Nurse Riley's plight, and wish you both a speedy and excellent recovery.

'I have decided to get this message to you in the hope that the news I have for you will spur you on to fight through the effects of the virus. It can be done. And if you do so, then I know you will help Nurse Riley, too.

'Well, to my news. I have located Officer Rennaise. Permission has been sought from him to allow us to give you some information, and he readily agreed. Though I am sorry to say that all my news is not good. However, weighing everything up, I still think you will want to know.

'Officer Rennaise was in a hostel run by the Salvation Army for displaced soldiers. How he came to be there and not in hospital, I do not know, but our resources are all stretched to the limit. Not that I see that as an excuse. It is inexcusable that such a sick man was not sent immediately to hospital, or at the very least to a convalescent home for officers. I can only say that everything was chaotic when the fire occurred in Hospital 36.

'Please rest assured, Ella, that a place is being sought for Officer Rennaise as soon as possible.

'My report says that he was in poor health, but that attempts to get him into hospital had failed due to him not having the financial means to support his stay, and to delays in getting assurances from the French authorities that they would foot the bill. A sorry state of affairs. I am doing all I can to rectify the situation and

will keep you informed. I urge you to get well soon, so
that you can be reunited with Officer Rennaise.

'I also want to make sure that you see the positives in
what I have told you. You now know where Officer
Rennaise is. You know that he wants to be in contact
with you. You know that everything that can be done for
him is being done. I have already arranged for him to
see a doctor and, although in poor health, he is being
cared for very well at the hostel.

'I look forward to hearing a much better report on
your progress, and to you returning to full health very
quickly.

'Yours sincerely . . .'

'Now, isn't that for being good news?' Paddy going into
a spasm of coughing prevented Ella from answering. Her
concern for Paddy overrode any other feeling, as she caught
sight of the muck that Paddy spat into a bowl.

'Nurse, she . . . she should be on oxygen.'

'I know, but we haven't any.'

'Then a steam tent. Do something!'

The nurse scurried away.

'Paddy, lie back. Please don't talk. Don't exert yourself.
Please.'

As Paddy closed her eyes, the sound of her breathing –
though still rasping – slowed. Ella willed the nurse to hurry.
Surely they had something that would help Paddy. Even a
bowl of steaming water would give her a little relief.

As she rested back herself, Ella's mind wandered to the
contents of the letter. As Miss Embury said, there were a
lot of positives, but oh, her heart ached for Paulo. What
discomfort he must be in. *Dear God, I must get better – I*

must! Paddy needs me, and so does Nanny. And my Paulo. Her lost child came to her mind and increased the soreness of her heart. *I never knew you, little one, but I will always think of you. It wasn't your fault that you were conceived as you were. I know I would have loved you, despite that.*

Although she fought against it, wanting to keep her eye on Paddy, sleep took Ella into its depths. Her mind became a swirl of dreams. From time to time the sound of Paddy coughing drifted into those dreams, but she couldn't untangle the web of slumber to offer any comfort.

When finally she opened her eyes, Ella noticed the silence. Feeling stronger, she lifted her head. Paddy's bed was empty! Her cry came out as a moan. 'Nurse . . .'

'Now, now, what are you doing? Rest back, Miss Wronski.'

'W – where's Paddy?'

'Do you mean Miss Riley?'

'Yes.'

'She was rushed to primary care, as her breathing got worse. I'm sorry, but she is very poorly.'

'Oh no!'

'Now, you be careful – getting in despair invites unwelcome infections. Miss Riley is being taken care of, so you just rest and stop worrying.'

Rest? How can I rest? My baby is gone. Paulo and Paddy are very ill. Nanny is back in the nursing home. And I feel so lifeless and full of pain that I can't do anything to help them.

Chapter Thirteen

Ella stared into the fire as it spat and crackled. Her eyes concentrated on the sparks that formed a pattern on the back of the grate, before disappearing and having others take their place. She had never felt so lonely in her life as she had these last two weeks. Had it already been that long since Paddy had died?

Ella shuddered and exhaled a long sigh. Today was the funeral, delayed this long because there were so many funerals that the undertakers couldn't cope. Miss Embury had sorted out everything and would be here at any moment to pick up Ella and take her to the church.

How she was going to find the strength to endure the ordeal of saying goodbye to Paddy, she didn't know. Weakness was her constant companion, although she had been declared clear of the influenza virus now.

Her tears threatened to overspill once more, as the last spark of the fire went out. It seemed to symbolize the final part of the young woman she'd been, when she had come home from war. Strong, healthy and ready to take on the aftermath and put everything right with the world, she now found it difficult to get out of bed in the morning.

The doctor had said this was to be expected, after what she'd been through. He'd been embarrassed to find out that she'd been pregnant. But he gave her his condolences on losing the child.

Condolences hadn't helped. Nothing could. She had cried so many times, but hadn't found any release from the grief that engulfed her waking hours. *If only I could hear further news of Paulo, that would help. Or feel strong enough to have Nanny home and care for her.*

Nanny's words visited Ella again. She felt certain that Mona was Nanny's sister, but would a name be enough to go on, in order to find the woman – even supposing she was still alive? Nanny was sixty. Was her sister older? And the child that Nanny had conceived must have been when she was in her thirties, as she had indicated she had been banished not long after conceiving and had to take Ella with her. But no, none of that fitted. The timing was all wrong. *If I was three when we left Poland and I'm twenty-three now, then we only left twenty years ago. Nanny would have been forty – not impossible to have had a child then, but . . . Oh, I don't know, it is all so confusing.*

A knock on the door gave some relief, as thinking things through increased the pain that was a constant in Ella's head.

On opening the door, Ella found Miss Embury standing there, looking striking in black. Her small hat was veiled, covering her eyes. She wore a pencil-slim skirt to her calves and a flowing jacket with an astrakhan collar.

'Hello, Ella, it's a sad day, my dear. Are you all right? No, I can see that you're not. Well, in all the sadness, I have good news. Come along and get into my cab and we can discuss it on the way.'

A small hope rose in Ella. She picked up her coat from where she'd placed it over a chair in the hall and wrapped it around her.

'Here, let me help you. You will need your coat on. And have you a wrap that you can wear, too? I have both in the cab for myself.'

'Yes, I have a fox fur. I'll get it.'

Once they were on the way, Miss Embury told Ella how sorry she was that they had this duty to do today. 'And to think there are no relatives to mourn Paddy – just you and me, the friends you told me about and a devastated young man.'

This shocked Ella. 'Is the young man called Bobby?'

'Yes. He came to the office. It was a coincidence really, though we do have so many people calling in to try and find friends and relatives – it is very sad. Anyway, he told us that he was looking for Bernadette and that he'd been to her home address, but neighbours had told him she had left there. He didn't know where else to go, so he came to us.'

'Oh, that is so sad. Paddy had tried to find Bobby, but had assumed he was in Germany. And then I was so locked up in my own troubles . . . Poor Paddy. I – I should have—'

'There is always room for "should haves", but they are an encumbrance we don't need. None of us can be perfect, and I gather that you had a lot more on your mind than we all knew about. Was your child Officer Rennaise's?'

Ella gasped, but then realized that of course the report that went to Miss Embury would have mentioned her condition. 'No. I – I was raped. It happened a few months before we came home.'

'Oh? Was that anything to do with you being found in the sea?'

'Yes – everything, but I didn't want to tell anyone. He was a friend, so no one would have believed me. I would have had fingers pointed at me. I just couldn't deal with the disgrace.'

'I understand that. Well, from what I read, he got what he deserved.'

Ella didn't speak; she didn't want to visit the memory of it all today.

'And I agree, sometimes these things are best left alone. You have been through so much, Ella. And I won't say I am pleased that you lost your baby. A life is a life.'

'Thank you.' Relief flooded through Ella.

Her thoughts were a turmoil concerning how she was to get through today, how she was to deal with Bobby, and a longing to find out how Paulo was – and, more than that, where he was.

'Let's talk of other things, Ella. You will be pleased to know that I have managed to get news of your Reginald Pattison. He has had an operation that went well. Of course he is still quite poorly and has a long way to go, but if you hadn't helped him when you did, then he would have died. And probably in the streets, with no one around. That was very kind of you. His case is being used as an example of what we should be doing to help our desolate soldiers. He knows that you are not well, and what has happened to Paddy, so he isn't expecting a visit from you. And we have taken on finding him a place to live. Not our usual remit, but we did it. I will give you all the details when I have them. His wife and child are moving in with him.'

'Oh, that's wonderful. I can't tell you how that makes me feel.'

'I know. It is one of our better outcomes. Now, while we are on the subject of assisting others, you are not to worry about helping out the Salvation Army. I have contacted Mr Wormington and he says you are welcome back when you are well enough, but I warned him that you may not be available even then. And that is because of my next, and most important, news . . . Officer Rennaise.'

Ella held her breath.

'I saved this till last as I wanted to give you something to hang on to today. I have been informed that he has been moved to a convalescent home for officers – the Manor of Lockleys. It is near Welwyn in Hertfordshire, and is being run for Australian and New Zealand Army Corps officers, but they have agreed to take Officer Rennaise.'

'Oh, that's such good news. I can't believe it, thank you. How is he?'

'Initial reports on his health are very good. The hostel had kept him in traction, and that has made a difference. He is beginning to walk a little, and enjoys trips around the grounds – partly in a wheelchair, but often hopping out and pushing the chair, rather than sitting in it. I think you have a determined young man there, my dear. Here, I have the address for you in my bag. I hope you will visit as soon as you can. I so want a good outcome for you both. A much different and happier outcome than I had, and something to help you through all you are facing.'

Ella's heart sang and she hoped that Paddy would be rejoicing with her, if she could.

'I can't thank you enough, Miss Embury. You have done so much for me.'

'And you for me, but . . . well, anyway, I'm glad it looks as though it will all turn out well for you both.'

In the smile Miss Embury gave her, Ella knew that going against her own nature to help to find Paulo was like a salve to the older woman, and helped to make up for her own loss. Ella was glad of that.

At the graveside the bitter wind whipped around them. Bobby stood next to Ella. Never had she seen a face so devastated. Connie and Alan stood on her other side, and Daniel next to Alan. It was so good to see them. They had been contacted by Miss Embury, after Ella had told her about the friendship they had all formed.

Connie's hand found hers as the coffin was lowered. Ella held on to it for all she was worth, as memories of the lovely Paddy assailed her. It was so cruel that she should be taken, but Ella hoped that Paddy was now reunited with her parents. Another cold hand came into hers, and she looked up at Bobby. Tears were streaming down his face. All Ella could do was grip his hand tightly. She needed his strength, as the knot inside her was almost harder to bear than the tears had been, but she couldn't cry any more. She went through the motions, as required of her, to keep from showing how weak she felt.

Afterwards they were gathered in Miss Embury's office, drinking hot tea and nibbling on a biscuit, when Connie asked how she was.

'I don't know how to begin to tell you, Connie. This has been such a blow to me, on top of being ill – it has taken all my stuffing from me.'

'My poor Ella. We were so sorry to hear about Paddy and that you haven't been well. And Miss Embury told us about Officer Rennaise. We would like to take you down to him, if you will accept? We are hoping to marry as soon as we can. Both of Alan's sons are safe – Ronald and Patrick, they're called. Patrick will be home in two weeks, as he has been discharged, but Ronald was with the conquering forces that went into Germany and it could be months before he comes home, as there is much to be done there.'

'Oh dear, I'm sorry. And yes, I would love to accept your offer, thank you. I'd like to go very soon, if that's all right? Have you both got jobs? Are you able to go at the weekend?'

'I haven't. I was exhausted, but both Alan and Daniel are working. In different hospitals, although Daniel has signed up for neurological surgical training, so he will be going back to college. He'll probably tell you about it later. You know, I still want you to be my bridesmaid. I hope you are willing. I haven't any sisters, and my cousins are all boys. I have one other friend I am going to ask. What do you think?'

'I would love to, thank you.'

'What are you two arranging?' Miss Embury came over to them. 'I hope it doesn't clash with my plans. I have managed to get the award-ceremony evening sorted. It is to be on Monday. Oh, I know: celebrating anything is the last thing on your minds, but we should. We cannot let the bravery you all showed go unmarked. And there's something I haven't told you yet. I have been in contact with the officer who was in charge of Paddy – Bernadette – in Queen Alexandra's nursing service. She is coming along to present Bernadette's medal, as she feels it is fitting that it is done on

126

the same evening, with all her friends receiving theirs. It has been the consensus that we want to ask you, Ella, to accept Bernadette's medal. I have sought and been granted permission for this from the officer of Queen Alexandra's.'

Ella didn't know what to say. It would be lovely to have something of Paddy's, but she wished Miss Embury had thought to have the medal buried with her.

'I know what you are thinking, but if Bernadette had taken her medal with her to the grave, who would know of her bravery in the future?'

'I think you are absolutely right, Miss Embury, and I think Ella should accept. What do you say, Ella?'

'I say thank you, but no. I think Bobby should have it and should accept it on Paddy's behalf.'

Bobby looked across at her. He hadn't spoken much, but had stayed close to Ella. 'Thank you, I would be honoured. I mean, if none of you object.'

'That's a very nice gesture, Ella, and I think that ultimately it is up to you. However, you will have to accept the medal, as it is all arranged now. But what you do with the medal is up to you.'

Bobby nodded at her and Ella accepted, but she became aware of how the room was beginning to feel very stuffy. 'May I sit down, please? I'm still feeling very weak.'

For the next few minutes they fussed over her until she felt like screaming, but she didn't. They didn't deserve that of her.

Before they all left for home, it was confirmed that they would attend on Monday evening. The ceremony was to take place in a small room of the Plaza Hotel, which was just a few minutes from the Red Cross Headquarters. Ella was already dreading it. But before that, she would be seeing Paulo, and the excitement and joy of that overrode everything else.

Ella's nerves clenched in her stomach as she alighted from Alan's car and looked up at the Manor of Lockleys – an imposing square building made up of many windows.

'We'll let you go in on your own. Will you be all right?'

'I will, Connie. I can't thank you enough.'

'No thanks needed. You're very special to me, Ella. Now, we will go and find somewhere to stay. Alan and I will pick you up at six, so you have three hours with your Paulo. Then you can have another couple of hours in the morning, before we head back to London.'

'That will be wonderful. I feel very nervous, but excited and happy, all at the same time.'

'That sounds good. I know the feeling. The nervousness is part of not believing that such a good thing as love can happen to you. Especially not as suddenly as it did for you, Ella. But ours were exceptional circumstances. Death and loss surrounded us. Life seemed so tenuous, and our emotions were on a different level. But that doesn't mean that sudden love cannot be lasting. I believe it can.' Without her knowing it was going to happen, Ella found herself in Connie's arms. 'That goes for friendship love, too. And I'm so glad we found that, Ella.'

Ella held Connie close. 'I am, too.' The words came out on a choking sound, as the love and friendship she'd shared with Paddy revisited her. How painful it was to love. How very painful.

'Go on, then. You're getting me all soppy. Have a lovely time, darling Ella.'

As she neared the house, a voice that she had kept inside her head reached her. 'Ella!'

Looking to her left, she saw him – her Paulo. Sitting in a wheelchair with a blanket around him, the low winter sun shining on him, his beautiful face smiling, his arms held out.

'Paulo. Oh, Paulo.' She ran to him, but then shyness overcame her, and slowed her step and increased her nervous state.

'Ella. Oh, Ella, I have dreamed of this moment.'

The shyness passed and she was bent over and, for the first time, being held in Paulo's arms. They clung together. Nothing marred the moment. It was as if they had known each other all their lives, and yet it contained the excitement of a new love.

When Ella came out of his arms, Paulo indicated that she should sit on his knee. The instant rapport they had found on first meeting was back.

'Is that an honourable thing to ask a lady, Officer?'

'No. It is very dishonourable, and what is more, it has dishonourable intentions, so be warned.'

Ella laughed out loud, something she had thought she would never do again. But then she felt a moment's worry, as Paulo's laugh ended abruptly in a fit of coughing.

'Oh, Paulo – oh dear, we shouldn't have joked. Are you all right?'

His reply came in short gasps. 'I have to live with what's happening to me. But never stop making me laugh; it is what I love about you . . .' The words hung in the air between them. His hand pulled her to his knee, and his eyes sought hers. 'I do love you, Ella.'

Did someone open the gate to heaven? Because the feeling that overcame Ella, on hearing this, seemed as divine as if the ultimate happiness had been showered on her. 'Oh, Paulo, my Paulo, I love you, too.'

The way he held her had showed surprising strength. She clung to him as his arms pulled her close. After a moment Paulo eased her away, so that her face was looking into his. 'Kiss me, Ella darling. Kiss me.'

Had she thought heaven had opened to her with his words? Now she knew the true feeling and depth of happiness, as their lips met. A tender touch at first, but one that deepened into a passionate drinking-in of each other.

'Will you marry me, Ella?'

'Yes.'

'I haven't much to offer, as I told you in my letter, but I will have a small pension. We will manage.'

'I don't care about all that. I have an allowance we can live on, and a flat in London. We will be all right. I just know that we need to be together.'

Once more Paulo held her to him.

The sound of footsteps drew them apart. A nurse approached. 'Paulo, there you are. I have your medicine ready for you on your bedside table.'

'Thank you, but I have all the medicine I need. This is my fiancée, Ella.'

'Pleased to meet you, Ella. You are taking on a handful, with this one. He will never do as he is told.'

Ella laughed. 'One of the things I love about him, his independent spirit.'

'You can say that again. I have the devil's own job getting his medication down him.'

'But it makes me so drowsy. I promise I will take the next dose, but I would rather feel my pain and know that I am alive than be in a non-state.'

'Right-o, it's your decision. Look, I'll keep the medicine to hand, and if you feel that you can't cope, you can take it then. Enjoy your day.'

With this, the nurse left. But the episode had worried Ella. Paulo must be on morphine or something similar, for it to have the effect of making him so drowsy. The realization of just how ill he was came to her, and she looked at him in an intense way. *Oh, Paulo, my love, my love.*

Chapter Fourteen

The cold seeped into Ella now, when she hadn't felt it before. She shivered.

'Let's go inside, darling.'

Was this really happening? Paulo loved her, and that was what she would hang on to. She'd banish all thoughts of future doom. 'Is there somewhere we can talk?'

'Yes, there is a little sitting room where the officers take their guests. We can have tea served in there. Cook is so kind and bakes delicious cakes.'

'That sounds wonderful.'

Once inside, the warmth tingled Ella's cheeks. The reception hall had an air of grandeur that seemed out of place, as the broken men housed in the manor wandered around aimlessly.

'Most congregate here. I don't know why. Probably because, being near the door, they don't feel so trapped in. Poor beggars are a long way from home.'

'That's sad. Their loved ones are on the other side of the world, when they most need them; and many won't have seen them for three to four years, as it is. My heart goes out to them.'

'Yes, and yet, most of the time, they are a jolly lot. Something about Australians in particular makes you feel good.'

'I know, we had an Australian matron in our last posting, and she was full of fun.'

'Here, this is the room. You go in, there's usually a fire burning. I'll ask for some tea for us.'

The room had an air of comfort in every piece of its furniture. Two large sofas, styled with straight backs and arms, but with plumped-up feather cushions that invited you to snuggle into them, and a coffee table with arched legs formed the main features of the room. The blue-and-gold decor gave an air of grandeur: the sofas were in a dark blue, and the carpet squares were in swirls of blue and gold. The walls were cream and housed many family photos, and the ornate border of the ceiling was picked out in gold. A large window, framed with dark-blue velvet curtains, looked out over the most beautiful landscaped gardens, with hedges neatly cut into many shapes.

When Paulo came into the room he had discarded his coat and scarf, giving Ella her first real view of how thin he had become. He wheeled his chair in, but now he stood and she realized this was the first time she'd seen him do so. 'Oh, you look so tall.' The words were said in surprise, but why she hadn't expected him to be tall, she couldn't imagine.

'It is you who is so tiny. Tiny and beautiful. I want to take care of you.'

His walk towards her was unsteady. She went to him and held his hand. For a moment he stood gazing down at her. 'I'm going to have to bend to kiss you, but I may cry out.'

'Oh no, don't do that. Sit down first.'

'You will let me kiss you again then?'

'Well, yes, I thought I would, seeing as how I enjoyed the first one.'

'Ha! And I haven't practised much, either.'

'Nor me.' An image of Jim wetting her face with his kisses shuddered through her. Ella banished it and covered her discomfort by joking. 'But I intend to. I intend to kiss you all afternoon, so I will be a professional by the time I leave.'

Paulo laughed out loud – a laugh that once again had him gasping for breath. But this time Ella didn't apologize. Paulo was right: they should laugh together. Laughter was healing, and they both needed that.

'Paulo . . . I – I, well, when you asked me to marry you, when were you thinking of? I mean, I was wondering if you would consider coming to live with me in my flat? I have room, and I could take care of you. I have an excellent doctor. I . . .'

Paulo was silent, but his face held wonderment. 'You really would care for me?'

'Of course. I can help you to get better. I know I can.'

Again he was silent.

'Paulo?'

'Ella, you have to know that the doctors don't give much for my chances. They have said that . . . my lungs, you see. They are damaged. I – I can't get better.'

A tear plopped onto his cheek. Ella stared at his despair and found it unbearable. She wanted to lift it and replace it with hope. 'That is now, darling, but medicine is advancing all the time. Let me take care of you. We will be happy. Your illness won't be the biggest feature in our lives – our love will. We'll find a way of doing everything all young couples do. We'll go to the theatre, and for walks; and yes, we'll travel. We'll live, not die.'

'Oh, Ella. That is what I want to do. I want to live the life that I have. And I want to live it with you.'

'Will you come home with me tomorrow?'

'What? How? I mean . . .'

'My friends will take us. We can have your things brought to us later. Just bring a change of clothing.'

'That is all I have.'

'Oh? Well, no matter, we will sort that out. And I can buy a wheelchair for you. I live on the ground floor and there's only a few steps to get in – can you manage those?'

'Yes, yes, but . . . do you mean it?'

'I do. I don't want to miss another moment with you.'

'Then yes, I will come, and thank you. Thank you, Ella, my darling.' Another tear found the trail of the last, and more followed.

Ella stood and held Paulo's head to her breast. 'Everything is going to be all right, Paulo darling. How can it not be, when we are together? We will marry as soon as we can. But if you will have me, I will be yours from this moment forward.'

'I will, Ella. You are a light in my darkness.'

Connie and Alan didn't raise any objections to her plan. 'We're happy for you, Ella.'

'Thank you, Alan. I know it is unconventional, but I must do this. I am so worried about Paulo. Any exertion has him gasping for breath, and when we laugh, he . . . It is frightening. But I love him and I need to care for him myself.'

'We will help you all we can. That is, while we are here. We have some news we haven't shared.'

'Oh? What is it, Connie?'

'Well, we have plans to go to America. We didn't say, as we still had things to discuss. We have done that today. America is crying out for doctors, and they are so much more advanced than we are. I am interested in medical research and want to explore the possibilities of that field. I can do that there.'

'But that is wonderful. How do you know about America? When will you go?'

'We have decided to get married soon. Then we will go. We were going to wait for my son's return, but we don't know when that will be. Ronald knows about our plans, as we wrote to him. You see, I have an aunt who married an American. She met him through my uncle, her brother. The chap was over here at university with my uncle, and he went to their home during term breaks. When she wrote to my mother, my aunt mentioned that I should finish my career over there – in the land of opportunity and money.'

'You're not that old, Alan. You have such a lot to give. I know, because as your nurse in theatre I witnessed your talent. So, no talk of finishing your career . . . you will be just beginning it!'

'Yes, I think of it like that, but I temper my enthusiasm in case others think I am over the hill.'

Ella understood this. 'But what about your sons, will they go, too?'

'They will make their own minds up. They have a lot of catching up to do in their own careers. Patrick is an engineer. He is considering coming out, once we are settled. And Ronald, poor chap, could be in Germany for two to three years. He has written to say that he has accepted his lot, and that we are to get on with our lives. He is still very young,

136

and will need to take up a university place when the army finally releases him. If we can, we will get a travel pass to visit him before we go.'

'It is tragic that all those who were in the victory push have to stay in Germany. It seems so unfair, but they are in the army and they are needed, so that is that.'

'Well, I wish you both all the luck in the world, and I cannot thank you enough for helping me to get Paulo to my home. I will be arranging our wedding, too, just as soon as I can, so we will have a lot to celebrate.'

'Good for you. We lost so much of our young lives, so we shouldn't stand on our laurels and waste another minute.'

'I agree, Connie.'

'And so do I. I think I'll order some champagne and we will drink to that. What say you, Ella?'

'A great idea, Alan – one of your best ones!'

By the time they arrived at her home, Ella felt exhausted. The weakness that dogged her consumed every ounce of her strength, and Alan and Connie had to help her and Paulo into the flat.

'You'll feel better once you have eaten. What have you got in the cupboards? I'll cook you something. No . . . no objections. You're not well, Ella. This has been a big move for you.'

'Ella, please listen to Connie. I'm very worried about you.'

'I will, Paulo. I have no choice. But I know I will be fine after a rest. There is so much to do.'

'I shouldn't have let you persuade me to come. We should have waited.'

'None of that. I think you have done the right thing. The

influenza and losing Paddy have taken it out of Ella, that's all. She'll bounce back. You can help each other, but I don't think you should be apart for a moment longer.'

'Your turn to listen to Connie, Paulo.'

Paulo grinned. They had such an easy way with each other, which Ella couldn't help but marvel at.

Connie was right; once they'd eaten the delicious omelette she made from whatever she found in the cupboards, Ella felt her strength coming back to her.

'We'll be fine now. You must both be whacked. Thank you for everything.'

'Well, that sounds like you are throwing us out! But I don't blame you.'

'No, Connie . . . I—'

'Ha, I'm only teasing. I'm ready to go, and I know Alan is. We've been so busy planning, we stayed up half the night.' Connie blushed as she said this, but Ella didn't comment, she just smiled. She had seen Connie slip out of the room they had shared at the hotel, when she thought Ella was asleep. Ella had smiled and turned over, glad that Connie had found happiness.

'I – I mean . . .'

'There's no covering up now, darling. And by the look on Ella's face, she already knew what you got up to last night.'

'Alan!'

They all laughed. After a moment an embarrassed Connie joined in.

When they left, a sudden shyness came over Ella. Everything had happened so suddenly, she'd not dreamed she'd be sitting in her home with Paulo, and now she didn't know what to do next. Paulo looked as tired as she felt, and yet she was shy of suggesting that they retire. Paulo saved her from this as he said, 'I don't know about you, darling, but I'm ready for my bed.'

Embarrassed, Ella was unsure what Paulo might expect of her. She had planned to settle Paulo in Nanny's bed, which she'd put fresh linen on. But Paulo's next words changed this. 'If you have a big enough bed, I would love to be welcomed into it. Just snuggling up to you would be all I ask . . . Well, all I could manage, I think, my darling. But I understand if you want me to sleep in a bed of my own.'

This made up Ella's mind, but she made a joke of it to cover her earlier hesitation. 'And what kind of girl do you think I am, Officer Rennaise?'

'Oh, I – I . . .'

'Well, I'll tell you. I'm your girl, and I would like nothing more than to snuggle up with you.'

'Ha. You minx, you had me worried then.'

'Sorry. I was worried myself, and not sure what we should do. But tomorrow we will see about getting married at the earliest opportunity, so what does it matter? It's only a bit of paper – it can't make us feel any different. We don't need anyone's permission to take our love further.'

'Mmm, very French thinking.'

Once Ella had helped Paulo into bed, she went to leave the room to get ready herself.

'Don't leave, darling. Let me watch you.'

Ella's breath caught in her lungs. Feelings started up inside her that she'd never experienced before. Slowly she removed her frock and then her shift. When she went to tackle her corset, Paulo called her over to him.

'Come here and let me unlace you.'

As she sat on the bed and turned to Paulo, he ran his

fingers over her breasts. The tingle this caused zinged through her. His eyes held so much promise and love.

'My Ella.'

She sank into his arms and looked up at him. His look was full of honesty, and at that moment she felt acutely aware of her deceit. Would he see signs of what she'd been through? He hadn't seemed to notice that her nipples were dark and larger than usual. But then maybe he didn't know of the changes that happen to a woman's body after conceiving a child.

'You look sad, darling. If you don't want to – I mean, nothing will happen; not fully, I – I . . .'

'No, it isn't that. I am sad that we are both so unwell and may not be able to give of ourselves fully to each other.' *Yes, I must lie. I cannot hurt Paulo with the truth.*

'But if nothing happens, then just to lie with you, to see you, to touch you and feel your body on mine will be enough for now. When we get stronger – and we will – then more will come, I know it will.'

With this, she turned on her back and let Paulo unlace her corset. The strength of her feelings for him coursed through her, but she would be patient. It would be enough to enjoy having him next to her; something she had never dreamed would happen.

Snuggled into Paulo, Ella marvelled at his strong body. Holding him as they lay, she couldn't visualize how ill he was, but listening to the effort he had to make to breathe, which increased as he moved towards her and caressed her, she was reminded and her heart felt heavy.

'Hold me, my darling. Hold me close.'

'Always, my Paulo. Always.'

'We'll find a way. We must. I want you so much.' As he

said this, he moved closer and she could feel how urgent his need was.

'Teach me, Paulo. Tell me what to do.' He guided her hand. Thrill zinged through her at the feel of him. 'I love you, Paulo, and I love your body.'

'Come to me, *mon amour*.' As he pulled her gently, Ella realized what he was asking. Though tainted by Jim, she knew nothing about the different ways that men and women made love, and this way hadn't occurred to her. But now, as she let him guide her, she knew the extreme pleasure of lowering herself onto her man.

Paulo sobbed his joy, crying out her name as her body moved on his. Her tears joined his, as feelings that she never thought to experience racked her body. And then it happened. A crescendo of sensations built, until she felt as though something had exploded inside her. She stiffened and her cries filled the room. 'Oh, Paulo. Paulo!'

He clung to her, his own hollers joining hers. When at last the feeling faded, Ella slumped down on his chest and knew the joy of them having become one. Wiping his tears with her fingers, she kissed every part of his face as she eased herself off him.

After a moment, his breathing slowed. His hand curled tendrils of her hair around his fingers and she told him joyfully, 'We found a way, darling. Thank you for teaching me. I love you.'

Paulo was silent for a moment. When he spoke, fear coursed through Ella. 'And it didn't hurt you, darling? I – I thought it would. I was afraid, as I couldn't be in charge and treat you very gently. I had to leave it to you. But . . .'

'Oh, Paulo, don't ask me. You'll hate me – I couldn't help

it . . . it was awful. I don't want to taint what just happened.'

'Did something bad happen to you, my darling? You can tell me.'

As she told him, the pain of the rape and the loss of her child racked her soul. Paulo held her throughout. 'No! No, how could that happen to you, my Ella. My lovely Ella.'

He isn't condemning me. Oh, thank God.

Ella clung to him, both taking comfort and trying to give it, as their sobs joined in a desperate crying. Not only for the rape, but for all they had been through and seen. For the hell they had visited, which had left its mark upon them, and for all those they had lost.

Paulo cried out '*Ma mère et mon père*' for his lost mamma and papa. Ella cried for Paddy, and for her unborn child; for her sick nanny, and for the family who didn't want her.

When they came to a calmness, they vowed that they would never hurt each other and would never leave each other.

With these vows sealing their love, and with their souls cleansed of their hurt, they fell asleep holding hands.

Chapter Fifteen

Attending the Plaza Hotel on Monday evening for the medal presentation was something Ella had been dreading, but it went surprisingly well. Instead of feeling the sadness of Paddy's loss, she felt extreme pride at collecting Paddy's medal as well as her own.

Paulo managed to attend alongside her, and Connie and Alan helped them both to get ready and drove them to the ceremony. Bobby was already there waiting for them, and he stood to attention and saluted at their arrival.

'Dear Bobby, you don't have to stand on ceremony. We are no longer in service. Take a seat next to me. This is my fiancé, Paulo.'

'Pleased to meet you.'

Paulo was gracious in his reply. 'Ella told me about you, Bobby. I am very sorry about Paddy. I only met her for a short time. She was a courageous nurse.'

Bobby relaxed and sat down, as they all did.

After the presentation, Ella went over to Bobby and pinned Paddy's medal to him. He didn't speak; he didn't need to, as his eyes filled with tears.

As she took her place beside Paulo, with her medal pinned to her frock, Paulo leaned closer to her. 'That was a horrible day – the day of the fire, Ella. I was so afraid. The lamp that fell wasn't far from my bed, and the smoke engulfed me. If I hadn't have met you, I would have taken large gulps of it into my lungs and would have let that be the end of me, but I already knew that I had a lot to live for. I feel so grateful to you, my darling, and so proud that you have been honoured in this way.'

Ella could only squeeze his hand.

They both clapped as loudly as they could when Alan and Connie collected their medals, and then it was the turn of Daniel. His commendation was very moving. Unbeknown to Ella, Daniel had continued with the operation that he was engaged in for a lot longer than she and Alan had, even though the medical tent was burning around him. He'd organized the two nurses who were helping him to cover him and the patient, leave him with a torch and then save themselves. Even the wooden floor he stood on was burning, before he left with his operation complete and his patient saved. For this he was awarded the Distinguished Service Cross.

A cheer went up that nearly deafened Ella. Daniel's face shone with pride. He'd always been such a retiring fellow, so it was good to see him enjoying the limelight.

With his medal being the last presentation, Miss Embury approached Ella. 'Well now, is this your young man?'

'Yes, may I present Paulo.'

'I can see why she fell for you in an instant. How do you do?'

Paulo looked taken aback, but recovered well. 'Much

144

better than I did last week. Thank you, Madame, for reuniting us. I am most grateful.'

'Well, I expect Ella told you my motivation. I hope you will both be very happy, and that you recover your health very soon.'

'*Merci*, Madame. And I am sorry for what happened to you.'

'Thank you. Now I understand, Paulo, that you need a wheelchair? I know where there is one, and you can borrow it until you are able to get another.'

'Oh, that would be wonderful, thank you.'

'It is made of wicker, with two back wheels as opposed to the one wheel most chairs have, which are sometimes difficult to steer. I think you will manage this one very well. It will give you a chance to get out and about. There's nothing like fresh air to cure, or at least relieve, lung problems.'

Connie immediately offered to collect the chair and deliver it the next day. The kindness of Ella's friends overwhelmed her, and she wondered what she would do without them. Miss Embury was showing another side of herself, which continued to amaze and delight both Ella and Paulo.

For Ella, life had never been happier, but that feeling was constantly marred by Paulo's suffering. His back pain often extended down his legs, and he constantly struggled to get enough oxygen into his lungs. But he took it all in his stride and remained cheerful.

A week had passed since Paulo had arrived at her home, and in that time they hadn't made love again. Ella felt there was a resistance in Paulo that was far greater than his poor health justified. She knew, in her heart, that the revelation of what Jim had done had cut deeply into Paulo.

They were sipping their cocoa in front of a roaring fire, both ready for bed, when she felt compelled to broach the subject. Paulo was staring into the flames, his mind far away; only his wheeze was audible beyond the crackling of the logs, which spat out sparks angrily. Ella had often thought that becoming fuel to warm a house was an undignified end for what was once part of a magnificent tree, giving oxygen to the world. How she wished she could perform such a feat and give oxygen to her beloved Paulo.

'Darling, are you all right? I feel there is something between us, which I cannot make better.'

'*Non, mon amour*, it is nothing.'

'Please be honest with me, darling.' Ella had slipped off her chair and placed herself on the rug at Paulo's feet. She gazed up at him, but he averted his eyes. 'I understand. I – I feel violated, so I know that, to you, it must be like buying something you thought was new, and finding it has already been used.'

'Oh, Ella. I find it difficult to think about it, let alone talk it through. That such a thing should happen to you is an abomination. We can only hope that man did die, and was sent to hell. Then there would be some justice.'

Relief that he wasn't blaming her helped Ella, but she wanted him to put it behind him. Revisiting it all was so painful.

'Oh, my Ella, don't cry. Forgive me. I promised we would forget, but I am struggling to do so.'

'As I am, my darling. But having you by my side and you loving me, despite everything, has helped me. I can't bear to think that you are suffering because of it. What can I do to help you? I can't undo it. It happened to me – but I didn't want it to. Oh, Paulo, I didn't want anything to spoil our love. I . . . please forgive me.'

'*Non*, Ella, *non*. My darling, this will be an end to it. I will show you.'

Lying in his arms after making love, Ella acknowledged that the pain in her heart had been right: her attack had hung between them and prevented Paulo from showing his love for her. She could only hope that he meant what he said now, about having put it out of his mind, but she knew from her own experience how difficult that was. *If only I hadn't told him.*

It was two days later that Ella felt well enough to take Paulo out in the wheelchair, which Connie had delivered. The first signs of spring were all around them, as daffodils stood proudly in front gardens, and birds tweeted their declaration of having found a partner, or something they could furnish their nest with. Whatever had them chirping, they sounded full of promise of a new beginning.

Today was going to be a fresh start for Ella and Paulo, as they were to apply to the church to put up their banns for their wedding, which they planned would take place in three weeks from now.

After they had visited St Patrick's Church in Soho Square, Ella felt an urge to go and see her nanny. They were so near the nursing home, and what with her illness and losing Paddy, she hadn't been for what seemed like an age. Messages from the home spoke of Nanny being peaceful, and this had kept Ella's mind at rest.

Paulo was happy to go along with her, and Ella hoped with all her heart that Nanny was less confused than she had been, and would recognize her and be able to understand about Paulo.

Sadly, there were only a few lucid moments, during which Nanny said that she liked Paulo and hoped he would get better. 'I need someone to take care of my Ella, young man, so you must get yourself strong.'

Paulo laughed and said he would do his best. But Nanny had given him a look of pity and, for a moment, the atmosphere had dampened.

'Nanny, it is good to see you so well. You know, if you want to come home in a few weeks' time, when I am a lot stronger, we would love you to.'

'We haven't got a home, Mona.'

Oh no! How quickly Nanny could revert to this other world she lived in. Paulo's hand gave comfort as he took hold of Ella's. She'd explained to him that these episodes could happen, and how painful they were to her.

'Nanny, Mona isn't here; it's Ella and Paulo.'

'Yes, it was Ella's father – that beast of a man – who set up the flat for us. He said we could live there rent-free for the rest of our lives, but he wouldn't give me that in writing, and I don't trust him.'

Ella looked over at Paulo. This shocked her. She'd always thought the flat belonged to Nanny. Remembering Nanny's name, which she'd only learned the last time Nanny had gone back into the past, she thought she would again try the tactic of pretending to be Mona. 'Lonia, how can I contact Ella's father? I must make sure Ella can live in the flat for as long as she needs to.'

'It's all written down for her, Mona. And all with my solicitor, Banks and Partridge; they have an office around the corner from our flat. When I pass on, will you take her there? But take care of her, as there are things she will find out that will upset her. I've never been able to tell her everything that happened, and about her beast of a father, but it's all there in my diary. I want her to know who she is, but not to think she is anything like them. She's my darling girl and has made up for all that I suffered.'

'That's good to know, Lonia. And I'm sure Ella knows that, too.'

Nanny closed her eyes then, and Ella knew it was time for them to leave. She wondered about waking Nanny and trying to make her aware that she was there, but decided it was better that she got some rest.

As they prepared to leave, Ella felt a mixture of emotions: joy at knowing all she wanted to find out about herself was written down for her, but also a deep sadness at how she would soon face losing Nanny.

When they were outside, Paulo's breathing became laboured, as often happened when he was taken from one atmosphere to another.

'I shouldn't have brought you, my darling. I should have taken you home.' Ella tucked a blanket around him. The grey pallor of his beloved face frightened her. 'We'll soon be home, darling, and I will help you to bed. You need a rest.'

Paulo couldn't answer her, as his body went into a spasm of coughing. Ella held him to her until it passed.

She wished she could hail a cab to get him home quickly, but that was impossible, as the chair would never fit in. With this thought came an idea that she should buy a car and learn to drive. Yes, that would be perfect. There were a few models that she thought big enough to take the chair, but if not, she could park close to wherever their destination was and Paulo could walk a few steps. As the idea took hold, it developed and she warmed to the thought of how she could not only take Paulo wherever they needed to go, but on outings, too – drives out into the country, and maybe even as far as Brighton to get some sea air.

Excitement seized her as it seemed a real possibility now, and she headed homewards finding new strength with which to push Paulo, and feeling full of hope for a better future. But her enthusiasm faded when they reached home and she saw the weariness in Paulo's beloved face, and how his lips had a tinge of blueness to them.

For a moment she wondered if it would all be worth it, but then she knew it would. She had to make every moment she spent with Paulo a happy one – filled with adventure, love and laughter.

Chapter Sixteen

Two months had passed since Ella had first introduced Paulo to Nanny. She and Paulo were now man and wife, as were Connie and Alan.

Their own wedding had been a quiet affair. She'd worn a simple cream suit, and Paulo had looked so handsome in a dark suit with a gleaming white shirt and black tie. A nurse had brought Nanny along in a bath chair, and Connie and Alan had also attended. Daniel hadn't been able to get away from college, but something in Ella had been glad about that, as she had a feeling that the time was upon her and Daniel to part company. Though she loved him dearly as a friend and would always be there for him, he was a difficult character to engage with, and as their lives were now so far apart, they found little common ground, other than the memories they shared. One particular memory was probably more likely to drive a wedge through their friendship than it was to bind them close. But she would always know that her own and Daniel's action had been an act of kindness and love, when they helped that poor soldier to pass over. For all that, it hung in the air between them.

They'd all gone to dinner after the wedding service, and Nanny had been like her old self, chatting away to Paulo. Though this pleased Ella, and she felt pride in the way that Paulo and Nanny got on so well, she was also a little jealous of how Nanny was more lucid in his presence than in her own, and she had talked this over with him.

'You are a source of deep love and concern to her, darling. I think, with me, there is no past – nothing to worry her. But she feels great heartache for the fact that she can no longer take care of you, and that she holds so many secrets that will affect your life. I think it is this that sends her into the safety of the past, where she can vent her anger at her sister, Mona.'

'Quite the psychiatrist, darling,' she'd told Paulo, but in a teasing way, as his theory had given an answer as to why Nanny behaved as she did around her, and an acceptable one that lessened her hurt.

Connie and Alan's wedding had been a wonderful affair, and Ella had loved being a bridesmaid. She'd felt so special, in the long lilac frock made of the finest silk. Paulo had been in awe when he saw her. It was at this event that Ella felt she'd been right about Daniel. He'd been awkward in her company and avoided her whenever he could. She hoped that he wasn't letting the memory haunt him and wished that she could broach the subject, but instinctively she knew that would be a disastrous thing to do.

'That was a big sigh, *chérie* – what are you thinking about?'

They were sitting in the small yard at the back of the apartment, enjoying the June sun, and Ella thought to take this opportunity, not to say what had really been passing through her mind, but to broach the subject of the house-hunting she had been doing. 'How I think it is time to tell you that I've found our perfect home.'

'Oh, when did this happen? A new car, and now a new home?'

'Well, I've been thinking lately that this place isn't secure for us – not with the apartment being a favour of my father towards Nanny. And dear Nanny is failing fast. I don't know if the favour dies with her or not. I have visited the solicitor who deals with Nanny's business, but they can't – or won't – help me. They say that while Nanny is alive, it is up to her what she tells me. They have their instructions, but none of them come into being until after Nanny's death.'

'So now we are to up-sticks? Can we afford to? I – I mean, can you afford to?'

'We can, darling. And that is "we", not "I", for whatever I have is yours. This will make a massive hole in what savings we have, but with your pension and my allowance, we will do very well. Besides, I'm thinking of taking up a few hours' work at the hospital, and I also want to help the Salvation Army now and again, as I promised I would.'

'Oh? So all these decisions you have taken on your own. You say it is "we", not "I", and yet you don't consult me on major decisions like a new home and a car, and a proposal to return to work. I believe that indicates you are still very much thinking independently.'

'Oh, I'm sorry, darling. I – I've always been used to doing so. It's a habit. And I don't like to concern you. I just thought if I got on with things, then you will have nothing to worry about.'

'I *want* to worry, I want to be involved. Not doing so is like not living. It's like being a child who has to have everything done for them. I'm your husband, Ella, not your baby.'

These words stung her. Not least because they held the ring of truth.

'So is it also a fait accompli, what will happen to this place?'

'I'm so sorry; forgive me, Paulo. I have made a huge mistake. In trying to protect you, I have taken so much from you. I – I had the best intentions. I so want to keep you from anything that might cause you stress, but in doing so, I've caused you even more. How can I make that up to you?'

'By treating me as your husband, and not your patient. I know your heart is in the right place, Ella darling, but even when we make love, you are caring for me and not giving of your all to me.'

'Oh? I didn't . . . I mean . . . Oh, darling, I've tried to help you, but in doing so I have smothered you. I can see that now. I'm so sorry, my darling, so very sorry. I can change. The new flat hasn't been finalized; we'll go together to view it, and it will be your decision whether or not we go ahead. As for this place, Nanny won't be coming back to it. And I don't like being here, now that I know who it belongs to and what the motivation behind it is. It has taken on the mantle of being the prison I was sent to, to get me out of sight of my father and his new wife.'

'*Mon amour* – don't. I do forgive you, because I know you acted out of love. And yes, I would like to see this new place before a final decision is made. But you must hang on to the scant image you have of your father. From that snippet of memory that came to you when you were delirious, I think you can draw a conclusion that he *did* love you. You don't really know the circumstances in which he felt it best to give you up, but he has taken care of you, and not abandoned you.'

'You're right, of course, but I feel strongly that this place could be taken from us, once Nanny passes away. I want to be ready, and independent. I don't mind taking the allowance – I feel he owes me that; but even that may not last forever. Oh, it's the not knowing that is so frustrating. Is that money there for my whole lifetime? I just don't know, and I have to think of you and me. In our own place we will have a security that I feel we lack here and—'

'*We* have to think of you and me. You haven't shared any of this with me before. But now that you have, you don't have to shoulder it all on your own. We'll start by looking at the place you have found, and then weigh up together what the financial implications of buying it will be and act accordingly. How does that sound?'

'Like someone has taken a weight off my shoulders. Oh, darling, I've been an idiot.'

'Yes, but you're *my* idiot. Now drop the nurse's mantle, right now. Come here.'

Diving into the arms of this new, masterful husband thrilled Ella. For once, she allowed Paulo to take the lead. He struggled to get to the bedroom holding her hand, but she didn't offer him any help; instead she played the game, begging him kindly not to use her so.

By the time they reached their bed, Paulo was exhausted, but Ella ignored this and kept up the act of the little woman having to do her husband's bidding, by asking what it was that he desired of her.

Recovering, Paulo pulled her down onto the bed and told her he would show her, rather than tell her, and that she was to be a good girl while he did so.

What followed eclipsed all they'd had before. Paulo found a strength she didn't know him capable of, as he made love to her.

Afterwards she lay in his arms. 'My man. My darling, I love you.'

Paulo held her close. Though she knew he was drained, she also knew it was one of the very best ways that he could feel. He was his own man, and he had done what they had first promised each other: he'd lived and acted, despite his illness – not because of it. She had stifled that for a while, but not any more. From now on, they truly were a couple.

Seeing Connie and Alan off was a low point of the following week, but Ella and Paulo tempered their sadness by viewing the flat that Ella thought of as their dream home. In a large house converted into two flats, the ground-floor flat, which Ella thought ideal for them, had a large private garden, which had been the main attraction for her, as she hoped Paulo would develop an interest in tending the garden and, with her help, would maybe turn part of it into a patch for growing vegetables. French windows led directly into the garden from the sitting room, and would give Paulo easy access whenever he wished to go out there. Paulo loved it.

Within six weeks they had moved into their new home, which was only a couple of streets away from Wicklow Street, meaning they weren't far from all that Ella knew in the area and were still near Nanny, whose health lately had been improving. Ella was happier than she'd ever been. She didn't give a thought to how long this happiness would last, but lived each day as it came.

August brought more of the fine weather they had enjoyed in June, making sitting in the garden of their new home a pleasure. 'It's so lovely out here,' Ella exclaimed.

'Mmm, and it has meant a lot to me to be able to come out into the garden whenever I want to. It's a haven. I've been planning what I want to do with the vegetable patch.'

Listening to Paulo, Ella filled with hope. Surely someone who had such plans for the future couldn't be dying?

'So, what do you think about that patch over there? It will be difficult to do much with it, as it is laid with bricks and probably has a base underneath it.'

Ella looked over to the part of the garden that had an old bench standing on a bricked area, with many weeds growing in the cracks and moss lying on its surface. 'I have the very idea for that. Our child will need a play area, and that will do nicely. It only needs cleaning up.'

Paulo fell silent.

'Paulo? Did you hear what I said?'

A huge sigh shuddered through his body. 'Ella, my darling, you have to accept that maybe—'

The grin on her face stopped him mid-sentence.

'What? No! Ella . . . really? Oh, *mon Dieu! Mon amour* – a baby! We are going to have *un bébé*. But how? I mean . . . Oh, that's wonderful news. Thank you.'

Ella had been nodding throughout, and now she was in Paulo's arms and still he couldn't take it in. 'Are you sure, my darling?'

'Yes. I went to see my very disapproving doctor. He has been that way with me since I fell from grace in his eyes, when he found out I had been carrying a child out of wedlock. He knew nothing of the circumstances. And now, just

157

a short time after, I present as pregnant again! But he said he was a lot happier about my situation this time, and that a pregnancy can happen quite quickly after a miscarriage. He also said that I can now look on the fate of my lost child as a blessing. I wanted to hit him, but I—'

Something in Paulo's face stopped her from going on. She stared at him. His look held disdain.

'Paulo? Don't look at me like that. My baby had nothing to do with how he or she was conceived. I loved it. It was mine just as much as our child is. And that will never change. I thought you understood? I don't want never to mention my lost child again; it helps me to remember.'

'It's just that it rakes up the hurt again – for you, mainly. And I didn't want to have the moment I heard I was to be a father to be tainted . . . Ella! Ella, where are you going?'

'As far away from you as I can get. If you love me, you love *all* of me. I'm not a part-person; I'm me, and that includes all that has happened to me. My lost child happened, and he or she can never taint anything – except my heart, which broke when I miscarried.'

'Oh, Ella. I'm sorry. Come back. Please. I haven't the strength to run after you. I'm so sorry. I simply want to forget.'

Ella came back and sat down. 'I don't want you to forget; I want you to accept. That way, I will be free from the shackles that bind me to silence, even when I am hurting.'

'You are right – if only it was that simple to do. But I will try. I promise. Now, can I thank you for giving me such a wonderful gift? A child, Ella. Our very own child!'

Ella couldn't help but be caught up in Paulo's joy, but a small part of her remembered – and would always remember – the bundle of promised joy that she had lost. And in the greatness of all she had, Paulo's struggle to come to terms with how she felt was a small cross to bear, and only slightly marred the happiness of the moment.

PART THREE
London, 1920

~

Ella and Paulo

Falling Apart

Chapter Seventeen

'There, it's all over, you have a lovely little boy.'

Ella could hardly hear the midwife over the wails of her son. Her heart swelled, all memory of the dreadful pain she'd been in fading, and she was filled with a feeling of such deep, consuming love for the tiny bundle in her arms that tears of joy flowed down her cheeks.

'That's a sight for sore eyes. Now, let me take him and sort him out, then I'll see to you. After that, I will let your husband in. He's pestered the life out of me every time I put my head out of the door.'

Ella smiled. Paulo had been in a state of anxiety lately. With her time getting nearer, he'd gone from being a happy, carefree father-to-be to a nervous wreck, wondering if he was up to the job of being a parent and worrying constantly about her. She'd laughed at him most of the time, but his health had concerned her, and she hadn't felt able to give him the support he needed.

Now she would soon recover, and everything would get back to normal. *Their* normal, anyway, as poor Paulo had been more or less stuck in the house, with Ella being unable to push his chair or drive her car. More than once she'd felt glad of the garden, for at least he'd been able to get some air and occupy himself for short periods of time.

'Was it the gas that your husband suffered? I've been worried about him for the last few hours. What treatment is he having?'

'Very little. Our doctor has the theory that only fresh air can help. And yes, Paulo was in a gas attack.'

'I think he needs a little more than fresh air. There's a doctor I worked with during the war, before I took up district midwifery. I met him again recently, and he told me he'd gone on to specialize in respiratory illnesses. I think he might be able to help your husband. He has a private practice, as well as working in the hospital. A very clever man and a lovely person. I'll leave you his address.'

A small kernel of hope was planted in Ella, tempered with the knowledge that there was little that could be done – other than a miracle. But if this doctor could give Paulo some relief from his pain, and help him to breathe more easily, that would be enough.

When Paulo came into the room, her heart dropped. The stress he'd been through during her labour had taken its toll on him. The nurse wheeled him in in his chair, which was an indication of the weakness of his body, because she knew that if he could, he would have walked in to greet his son. Trying to keep the concern out of her voice, she welcomed him. 'Darling, we have a son! A son, can you believe it?'

'I – I'm so proud of you, *mon amour*. *Merci*, you have made me a happy man, my darling.'

Ella's smile widened as the nurse put their little boy into Paulo's lap. When Paulo looked up, his face was lit with joy, and yet wet with tears. '*Mon fils* – my son.' He quickly handed the baby back to Ella, as his stick-thin body bent over and was convulsed with hacking coughs that racked him.

The nurse ran out of the room and came back a few minutes later with a small bottle of oxygen. 'I carry this with me. It will help him.' As she said this, she placed the mask over Paulo's nose and mouth, and within a short time he relaxed back. 'There, that's better, sir. I think you should have an oxygen cylinder in the house, Mrs Rennaise. But if you go and see Dr Warner – the doctor I mentioned just now – I'm sure he will sort that out for you.'

'Thank you, Nurse, thank you. Would you be kind enough to push Paulo near me?'

'I will, love. There you go. Now that all's well here, I've to see a lady around the corner, so I'll come back in about twenty minutes. In the meantime keep the mask on, sir, and you'll feel a lot better.'

Paulo nodded. His breathing was far less laboured now. When the nurse reached the door, she turned and gave them a pitying smile. Reality crashed into Ella. The complacency that had settled in her of late, and her acceptance of everything as her lot, dissolved. She'd even kidded herself that the happiness they had, despite their difficulties, could go on for a long time; that they would manage somehow. Now, she looked at her failing Paulo and wondered what the future had in store for them?

She'd brushed these thoughts away before and had made the most of everything. Well, that's what she would do now. *I have to . . . yes, I have to. I have to make this a happy, living home, not a dying one.*

With this thought, she smiled through her tears. 'Oh, Paulo, I can't believe it . . . We have a son! What shall we call him? Somehow the names we discussed don't suit him. Look at him: a shock of black hair like yours, and your nose. He needs a dashing name to go with his good looks.'

Through the mask Paulo's voice was muted, but she could hear the tone of amusement as he said, 'A – a dashing name? What is this?'

'Ha, it's a name like Romeo, or Casanova!'

Paulo's laugh made him cough, but the sound of it was a salve to her pain.

She laughed with him. 'Well, they are a bit much, but it gives you an idea of the name he needs. He's not a plain Joe.'

'Oh, my Ella, you are funny. A dashing name it is, then. But not those you have suggested! Ha, you'll have him laughed at when he attends school. Ella, I – I may not be here then, I—'

'No, Paulo! We have never spoken like that, and we mustn't start now. There is a doctor who may be able to help. As soon as I am up and about, we'll go and see him. Now, a name for our son. How about a French name? They always conjure up dashing, handsome men.'

Paulo laughed again and this time, to Ella's relief, he didn't cough. It was a sign that he wasn't short of oxygen in his body. *I don't care about convention; in a couple of days I'm out of this bed and going to see this doctor, no matter what anyone says.* With this decided, Ella turned her mind back to choosing a name.

'Christophe. I would love him to be called that. It was the name of *mon père*.'

'Oh, that's perfect, Paulo – it suits him and is very dashing. One day you will have to tell me more about our baby's grandparents, as he will need to know.' As if Christophe

166

agreed, he made a gurgling sound. They both laughed and Ella was glad, as it softened the fact that she'd unwittingly referred to a time when Paulo might no longer be with them.

Dr Warner sat, tugging his long ginger beard. His eyes were a piercing blue, which made you feel that he could see into your soul.

'I have to tell you that any intervention I make may not prolong the time you have, Paulo' – the doctor had insisted on first names – 'but I can make you more comfortable, and even possibly more active. Your main problem is lack of oxygen, but also that your body isn't using what little it is getting to best advantage. I would recommend that you have an oxygen tank at home, and that you use it most of the time. I also have had a great deal of success with patients who take on certain exercises, and with an oil-based ointment that I have concocted. This oil, rubbed directly into your chest wall twice a day, will give you relief of the tightness you feel, and will, after a time, allow you to expand your lungs more. However, some of the ingredients are very difficult to get hold of, and so they come at a premium, I'm afraid.'

'We'll take it and will do everything you suggest, Doctor, won't we, Paulo?'

Paulo smiled. The effort of getting here, and the examination and tests he'd endured, had taken their toll on him.

'Right. Oxygen is to be fitted, now. I have some straps on my tanks, and an extra-long tube from the tank to the mask. This is to allow the tank to be fitted onto your chair. I see that you have a shelf under your seat – no doubt very useful for shopping, but I think that's an excellent place to rest the tank. I'll get my assistant to fetch me the equipment and fit it for you. The oil, I have here.' He reached into a drawer of a cabinet that contained many small drawers and brought out a jar. 'This will last you a week. Now, as for the exercises, I will make an appointment for you next week, when you should be feeling a lot better. You will need to come in here for these, in the first instance. But the two of you could probably manage them at home after that.'

Once outside, Ella was reeling from shock at the amount she'd had to write on the cheque, to cover the doctor's bill. Could they afford this treatment? But then a more pressing worry took precedence in her mind, as the weight of the chair with the oxygen attached was taking all the strength she had.

Christophe had slept right through the consultation, but now he decided it was his turn to seek attention. Paulo held him on his lap, but struggled to soothe him.

Sweat poured from Ella, as she desperately made for a park that she knew was nearby. Finding a bench, she sat for a moment, trying to get her breath. When she did, she laughed out loud. 'What a pair! Oh, Paulo, we sit gasping for breath together. Not many couples do that as a hobby.'

Paulo pulled his mask down and smiled, but it was a smile that soon disappeared. 'Ella, my darling. There are to be no more walks out – not with the oxygen tank. What was the doctor thinking of? How are we to get home?'

'We will, but first I will have to put little Christophe inside my coat and feed him. We'll just have to hope that no one comes by and sees me, or we may find ourselves in the police station.'

Keeping her humour up was becoming more and more difficult for Ella. As she wrapped Christophe into her coat, the chilly spring air crept inside with him. She shivered. Everything had become too much for her. She needed help. She needed someone to talk to. Her mind went to Flors and Mags. She hadn't thought of them for a long time. *How come more than a year has passed since the war ended and I haven't looked them up? But then, what a year! How I've survived this far, I don't know. More ripples have happened. Paddy has gone from my life, and Connie, Alan and Daniel . . .*

She looked over at Paulo; his head was leaning to one side, his eyes had closed and his face looked sunken. Ella's worries piled in on her.

Nanny, too, was failing. And recently the nursing home had increased its costs. Not to mention the cost of having a midwife attend the childbirth, another expense; and now this. The doctor had charged the huge sum of thirty pounds! And she would need to pay more for the future visits they had planned, and for further supplies of oxygen and oil. *How am I to manage?*

Christophe became detached and yelled out at that moment. Ella knew that her distress was filtering through to him. She reattached him to her breast and decided not to worry. The next day she would go to the bank, and then find her way to Flora's. She still had her address somewhere. It was in Stepney, she was sure of that.

Feeling better, Ella finished feeding Christophe and, keeping him wrapped up against the March wind, gave his back a few rubs. She was rewarded with a loud burp. Smiling, she said, 'Time to get going, darling.'

Paulo shivered. 'It's very cold, Ella.'

Only just feeling the cold herself, as the exertion of pushing Paulo had made her sweat, Ella pulled his blanket up with her free hand and wrapped it round him. 'You only need one free arm, darling, to hold Christophe – can you manage that?'

The effort it took for Paulo to do this was devastating to Ella. She drew in a deep breath. No matter what it took, she would find the money for his treatment. She had to.

Chapter Eighteen

Ella stood in the bank and stared down at her bank balance. The four hundred pounds she'd had on her return from France had dwindled to ninety. Buying the car for eighty pounds and the apartment for two hundred and ten, and only able to add a little to her savings now and again, was the reason. What she had left would, under normal circumstances – with her allowance and Paulo's pension – keep them going for quite some time, but their situation wasn't normal, as they had crippling medical bills to pay.

Getting a job was now out of the question, as Paulo couldn't take care of Christophe. Or himself, if it came to that. Though he tried very hard to do as much as he could, exhaustion often defeated him. *There's only one thing for it. I will have to sell the car.*

This thought dampened Ella's spirits even further. Their dependence on her second-hand Morris car had increased, but it guzzled petrol, which wasn't always easy to come by; and, if they had to, they could take a cab on journeys that were too far to walk.

Outside in the early sunshine, Ella's head cleared a little

as she walked towards where she'd parked, leaving Paulo and Christophe in the car, and she decided to put on a cheerful face. The sun's warmth, and seeing it reflect off the gleaming green paintwork of her car, gave her an idea. Paulo was having a good day so far, and she always tried to make the most of those. Well, today would be no exception; she had a full tank of petrol, so what was there to stop them from going for a drive?

Canvey Island came to mind. Nanny had taken her there as a child, and Ella had loved the walk along the bank top, and tiptoeing on the pebbles to dip her toes in the sea. And sitting on a blanket spread out on the grass, eating jam sandwiches and drinking lemonade.

Excitement built in her. She could almost feel the salty wind brushing her cheeks and smell the fish-tainted air of the sea.

Turning away from the car, she walked towards the row of shops. She would buy a loaf of bread, a wedge of cheese and, best of all, the Jewish shop on the corner sold lemonade in a corked brown bottle. And she would need a map. Not that she knew how to read one, but Paulo would, she was sure. Anyway what would it matter? They would find somewhere to spread the rug they had in the car and enjoy a picnic. A smile crossed her face. At least she didn't have to worry about food for Christophe, for she carried that around on tap for him.

Paulo was mystified when she returned to the car. 'That's a lovely smile. Did you find that we are rich?'

'Yes, we are! We're the richest couple in the world. Ha, so rich we're going for a picnic.'

Paulo laughed out loud, a good sound. 'How did that happen? You never cease to amaze me, my Ella. You left me,

172

afraid of what you would find out; and you return, full of joy and a mad plan to take me off somewhere.'

Ella laughed with him. It filled her with happiness to see his face expressing laughter and not pain. And the effect of the oxygen, which was his constant companion, meant that he didn't go into a fit of coughing afterwards. Nor did he raise any objections to her suggestion. A free spirit like herself, Paulo was always ready for any new challenge, despite everything. She loved that about him.

It wasn't until they were almost there that Paulo said, 'We're not exactly dressed for the seaside, are we?'

Ella smiled. 'No. I didn't think of that. We will probably get some funny looks: you in your suit and tie, and me in this business-like costume, which is old-fashioned to say the least, with its ankle-length skirt. Every young woman we have passed is wearing much shorter clothes now. I can't get used to it.'

'You look lovely; you always do, darling, and blue suits you. We can always take off our shoes, and I'll help you to take off your stockings, if you like.'

'In broad daylight? Monsieur Rennaise, you are being very forward.'

They collapsed into a fit of giggles. Happiness filled Ella, pushing her fears and worries into a small corner of her, where she paid them no attention. Christophe, who had been snuggled into Paulo, gave a gurgle at that moment. This increased their giggles, giving Ella the feeling that her happiness was complete. Her troubles seemed almost non-existent.

'What a perfect day, darling. *Merci, mon amour.*'

Ella turned her head and looked into Paulo's eyes. They

lay on the blanket, the sun basking them in warmth. Paulo was propped up on his elbow, looking down at her. Children's laughter rang in the air, to the background sound of the rolling waves breaking on the pebbles. Remnants of the bread they had torn chunks off, and the ragged-looking cheese they had unceremoniously broken pieces from, lay between them.

'You're welcome, Monsieur. Oh, Paulo, I never want to forget this day. With the sun framing you, you look so handsome.'

A look crossed his face that Ella knew and loved. It tingled feelings right through her. His voice, when he spoke, was deep and husky. 'I want to kiss you and make love to you right here, my Ella. I love you so much.'

'You are in England, my love. Such a gesture would start a second war! Ha, we would end up in prison.'

'We should live in France. There I could take you in my arms, as I long to do.'

There was more than a hint of wistfulness in Paulo's tone. Sadness entered Ella. Paulo rarely spoke of his loss, and never about how it was for him to live in a foreign country; and she hadn't given it a thought, in her struggle to give them as normal a life as possible. Suddenly she felt very selfish. The money she'd spent on a whim, buying a flat and a car, she could have saved. The flat owned by her father stood empty, and they could have remained there. If they had, maybe she could have taken Paulo back to his home. Even though it didn't exist any longer, it might have given him a feeling of closure, seeing how it was now.

'I'm sorry, Paulo, my love. I – I should have taken you back to France. Forgive me.'

'No, no. I am only missing the carefree attitude of my

people; well, besides my family of course. But we cannot bring them back. I just find all the stuffiness of your countrymen very limiting. Here I am, on a beautiful day, in a beautiful spot with my beautiful wife, and longing to hold her close to me and kiss every part of her, but in the eyes of the people around us, that would be a crime. I am not used to that.'

Changing the subject, Ella smiled. 'Come on. Let's go for a paddle that will cool your ardour. Do you think you could make it to the water's edge, if you hold on to me? Christophe is sleeping soundly, and we will be able to see him from down the slope.'

'Only if you let me help you take your stockings off.'

They both laughed and the tension that had crept in lifted. 'You can jolly well turn the other way. Any gentleman would.'

'Not this one. I will watch your every move, and wish it was me taking them off you.'

Ella laughed so loudly that two women passing by tutted their disapproval. It was a gesture that didn't help, but simply exacerbated the situation. Paulo had to lie back, he was laughing so much.

Ella's whole body filled with joy. They could be like other couples. Illness didn't have to dominate their lives.

Having wriggled out of her stockings in a most unconventional way, amidst much teasing and laughter, she stood up. 'Come on. You haven't taken your socks off yet!' Making a play of it, she bent down to help him to roll up his trouser legs, knowing that even such a small task could bring exhaustion on him. She so wanted Paulo to have enough energy to make it to the water with her.

Checking on baby Christophe and finding him sleeping

peacefully, snuggled up in his shawl, lying on the blanket, Ella waited, holding her breath. Paulo was struggling, she could hear that. Glancing towards him, she saw him roll onto his side and try to push himself up. Fear clenched her. *What if he can't get up? Oh God!* Looking around her, she saw a group of young men playing football, whom she hadn't noticed before. All the sounds around her had merged, beyond the world of happiness that had cocooned her. The sight of the men gave her some relief, as they would be able to help, and she was sure they would if she asked them.

But Paulo eventually managed, just needing Ella to steady him as he made the final effort to stand. Not mentioning his effort, Ella took his hand.

'I might need my stick, darling.'

'Yes, that would be a good idea. Hold on to the car, darling.'

Digging out his walking stick, Ella worried whether she was doing the right thing in encouraging Paulo. Access to the water's edge was down a slope of pebbled ground. The able-bodied found the going precarious, let alone someone with a weakness, who struggled to breathe. But when she returned to Paulo, he was standing tall and looked ready for the challenge.

Though their progress was slow, they made it. Once more, joy filled Ella and lit her soul. To be doing something with Paulo that everyone else took for granted was a dream come true for her.

They giggled as the water tingled their toes. Then Ella squealed, as Paulo swung his foot and splashed her with water. He almost fell over in the process, but she clung on to him. And what did it matter that the salt would ruin her skirt? Who cared; it was only a bit of material. Put that against the memory of this precious moment with Paulo, which she would take with her through the rest of her life, and it paled into insignificance.

The note waiting for Ella, when they returned home, sent her into a panic:

> *We called today to ask you to attend the Miller Nursing Home. We are very sorry to tell you that Miss Machalski has suddenly become very ill. We think that you should visit as soon as you can.*

On the envelope there was a time of delivery: 4 p.m. *Oh no, that was two hours ago!*

'I have to go, Paulo, will you be okay?'

'I will come, darling. They have bath chairs there. I can use one of those to help me to Nanny's bedside. And I can hold Christophe.'

'Yes, I would love to have you with me. Let me just change Christophe – poor thing feels soaked through. He's such a good baby, aren't you, darling? Never murmurs, always content. Ooh, I love you, my little one, Mummy loves you.'

'And Daddy does, even though you have soaked me through, too, my son.'

'Right, let's all have a quick change of clothes and then we will go. I'm so worried that we won't be in time. I can't bear to think that would happen.'

Christophe gurgled and made no protest when Ella hurriedly swabbed him down and changed his clothes. A sense of something she had experienced a few times niggled Ella. Why was that? Wouldn't most babies bring the house down when wet through, as he was? And why wasn't he showing any signs of wanting to sit up, when she held his hands and gently pulled him? Surely at four months he should be doing this, but he was always floppy and didn't resist her doing whatever she wanted. He didn't even kick his legs about. Sighing, Ella completed the task of changing Christophe and then left him lying on the sofa while she went to give Paulo a hand. Her worries were compounded when she entered the bedroom, as Paulo was lying on the bed and gasping for breath.

'I'll fetch your oxygen, darling – hang on.'

'No, leave it in the . . . car. I – I'm just catching my breath. I'm ready, you get . . . yourself together, darling.'

'Oh, Paulo, you should have waited.'

Trying not to dwell on all that she faced, Ella didn't bother to wash, but simply donned clean stockings and a change of clothing. Thinking it didn't matter what she wore, she opened her wardrobe and immediately spotted the white blouse with lavender flowers adorning it. Nanny had always loved her in that blouse. *The outfit might lift my spirits, too. If ever they can be lifted again. Why? Why are we sent so much to bear – and today of all days, which has been so special?*

Chapter Nineteen

The next night, when Paulo had taken Christophe to bed and had said he would lie down himself for a while, Ella sat in the quiet of the still house, clutching Nanny's diary. Nanny's solicitor had handed it to her after she'd taken the death certificate to him. He'd known how important it was to her, and told her he would see to any other of Nanny's requests in the next few days. *Oh, Nanny, I cannot believe that you have gone.*

Ella couldn't ever remember seeing the diary before: an old and tattered notebook with a piece of ribbon keeping its green, leather cover around its aged, brown, dog-eared pages. Where it had been when she was a child, Ella didn't know. Or perhaps it was something she had never noticed.

Sighing deeply, she wondered if the diary contained any answers to what Nanny had unwittingly told her, in her confused moments when she thought she was talking to Mona. But then none of that gave the whole picture.

Opening the notebook, Ella saw something she had longed to know. On the first page, she read:

*This diary is my account of what happened to me
while in the employ of Pan Wronski of Pedzichow 20,
Krakow.*

*At last, an address. But what to do with it? Dare I write to
it?* No, something told Ella that wouldn't help. After all, her
father knew exactly where she was, or at least he believed her
to be in his apartment in London, so if he had wanted to
write to her, he could have done. He never did.

*I must visit. But how? Paulo isn't strong enough to go with
me. If only I had someone to help me . . . Flors!* Yes, Flors
would help, Ella felt sure of that. She would go tomorrow
to the address she had for Flors. It would be so lovely to see
her, even if she could not do anything to help; just to be
hugged by her, and to catch up on old times and introduce
her to Paulo, and Christophe . . . *Oh, it will be amazing. I
can't wait!*

Turning another leaf, Ella found that the diary began in
November 1899. Her eyes scanned words that only increased
her sorrow:

*I bought this book today to help relieve me of my pain.
By writing down what has happened in the house of Pan
Wronski – and to me at his hands – I hope I will find
some release.*

*I am on a train with my beloved charge, Marjella,
daughter of Pan Wronski and Kasienka, his beautiful
late-wife.*

Ella read on for a while and learned nothing new, only
a more detailed account of the rape of her dear nanny. It
agonized her to read the shocking revelation that her father

and his friend had taunted Nanny about being a woman of forty-one and still a virgin:

I had just turned forty-one and was of single state, as my fiancé had been killed in an accident. As I never wanted to look at another man, my mother found a position with a family of three children. When they had all grown, I moved to the Wronski household, in preparation for their expected child . . .

What followed was an account of how Ella's mother had died from a haemorrhage. Ella's face flooded with tears.

When she closed the book, she was wiser only about the address of her father; everything else was simply a confirmation of what she already knew. Ella still felt confused as to why Nanny had been distressed about her own mother, when she implied that her mother sent her away; it seemed that her parents and her sister, Mona, were already deceased by the time all of this happened. *Poor Nanny, how difficult it must have been for you, with all your memories fused and distorted in your mind.*

With this thought, peace came to Ella. Nanny deserved her eternal rest. It was selfish to want her back.

At the back of the diary there was a business card for Banks and Partridge, Solicitors. Ella made up her mind that she would visit them once more. Maybe they had further information they could give her about the money her mother had left her, now that Nanny had passed on.

A few days later, leaving Paulo and Christophe in the car, Ella walked across the road to the address that she now had for Flora. When she found that Flora no longer lived in Stepney, a neighbour told Ella where she had moved to and that a woman called Rowena had moved with her.

Ella felt ridiculously light-hearted, considering her worries, which had been compounded this morning, where Christophe was concerned. Try as she might, she hadn't been able to get her child to eat the light oats she'd prepared for him, nor would he suckle at her breast. But then she had to let in the truth – it wasn't so much that he wouldn't, but he didn't seem able to.

Shaking this silly notion from her head, Ella walked faster, convincing herself that Christophe maybe had the beginnings of a summer cold and was just off his food.

Anticipation zinged through her as she rapped the shiny brass knocker.

Maybe she'd rapped it too hard, as she heard what sounded like an African woman's accent. 'Lordie, is there a need to knock me door down? I'm coming as fast as me legs will carry me.'

When the door opened, a profusion of colour stood before Ella. The woman who answered it had her huge body wrapped in a daffodil-yellow robe with white daisies printed all over it, and a red silk cummerbund around her waist. Her head was swaddled in the same silk, in a turban that made her appear six feet tall.

'I'm sorry to disturb you, but I believe that my friend, Flora, lives here.'

'Yous a friend of Flora's? What's your name then, girl?'

'I'm Ella. Flora and I were Voluntary Aid workers together.'

'Lordie! Come on in, girl. I'm Rowena. And this here is Flora's house, but she's not living here – I am. But I do have something for you. A letter. I have instructions that if ever you called, I was to give it to you, along with Flora's new address.'

'Oh? Does she live near here?'

'No, Missy, she lives in France, with her husband and Freddy, her baby. They've been gone a few months.'

'France? Oh, I . . . I needed her help. I – I mean, well, I . . .'

'Now don't you be all embarrassed, I know the way of it. We lose touch with those we love, and keep meaning to contact them, then one day we are forced to. Now, tell me what it is you need help with.'

Ella explained how she needed to go to Poland, but couldn't leave her husband and child. 'And – and, on top of that, my nanny died.'

Blurting this out brought the tears that Ella had fought against all morning.

'There, there, honey child. There's a lot for you to cry about, but at the moment it sounds like you need to be strong. I'll help you, girl. Yous a friend of Flora's, so that makes you mine, too. Is that your car across the road?' At Ella's nod, Rowena told her to bring her family inside. 'They can stay with me while you visit this solicitor and make the other arrangements for your departed nanny.'

'Oh no, I couldn't impose on you.'

'It will be a pleasure. I've been a lonely woman since me friend Pru died and Flora left.'

'Pru was Flors's aunt, wasn't she? And what of Flors's child – a little girl? You only mentioned a baby.'

Listening to the troubles that had beset Flors after she returned from nursing in Dieppe, leaving Ella behind in the field hospital, Ella felt a veil of deep sadness envelop her.

'Now, don't you be feeling sorry for Flora; she's a strong girl and has found happiness. Her letters tell of how settled they all are, and how they are learning to live with their sorrow – and their past. They are having an exciting time building up a vineyard, and will be producing their first bottles of wine very soon.'

'That's good to know. No doubt Flora's letter to me will give me more details. And yes, if I can, I would like to accept your offer of help. I – I can pay you a little.'

'No, I won't take no payment for kindness – you're a friend of my dear Flora.'

'I'm sorry, I didn't mean to offend.'

'No offence taken. Now bring your family in and introduce me.'

Entering the house again, Ella took in her surroundings. The furniture was conventional and of the sort that she imagined Flors would choose: not expensive, more functional and in muted colours. Every chair had been brought alive with colour, though, the unmistakable touch of Rowena. There was no dominating hue, but a rainbow of cushions and beautiful fabrics draped over the backs and arms of the furniture and covering the table. It created an atmosphere of happiness, if it was possible for a room to give off such an air.

Rowena greeted Paulo in such a manner that Ella feared he would fall over, but the strong hug held him upright. 'A brave soldier, you are, and I thank you. We all should go on our knees to thank you. And to these girls. Now, sit yourself down and make yourself comfortable . . . Ah, a beautiful babby.'

When Rowena took Christophe, her face clouded. She looked over in a questioning way towards Ella. Ella shook her head and hoped this would stop Rowena voicing what she knew the woman had detected, and what Ella feared – that there was something wrong with her son.

As Rowena cradled him to her, Christophe's free arm hung down and his head rolled back. At that moment Ella let in what she had feared: that Christophe had floppy baby syndrome, something for which there was no known cure, but which a child could grow out of. So little was known about the condition; some children gradually grew stronger, while others . . . *Oh God, I cannot bear to think that – please don't let that happen.*

Rowena didn't remark on Christophe's health, but instead proceeded to help Paulo to relax. 'Now then, young man, I would love you and Christophe to stay with me while Ella attends to her business. I make a delicious tea, and me rum buns are second to none, made with me own home-made rum. I would give you a tipple, if it wasn't so early in the day. But I will pack you some to take with you. If that doesn't make your pain go away, then nothing will. You are very welcome here.' Her laughter filled the room and it was impossible not to join in with her.

The office of Banks and Partridge, Solicitors was in a Victorian building on King's Cross Road, the road where she and Nanny had done most of their banking and shopping, being within walking distance from their home, and it was still close to Ella's new home. The building gave off an air of having been there for centuries, with its dark-green paint and unkempt exterior. There were many places where the cladding had come away from the outside walls and had not been repaired.

Inside, it was stuffy and furnished with big, old, polished furniture. The chairs in the waiting room were of brown leather and had seen better days. Always, when visiting here, Ella felt intimidated, and that was so today.

John Partridge looked over his glasses. His long face, with its drooping jowls, had an almost sinister aura and sent a shiver through Ella.

'As solicitors to Miss Machalski, it is our duty to discharge her wishes, upon her death. Unfortunately, the amount of money she wanted to leave to you, Miss Wronski, has greatly diminished with the need to pay the expensive fees for her care – something she always thought you would undertake.'

'I – I couldn't. I – I . . .' Taking a deep breath, Ella composed herself. 'It may have escaped your notice, tucked up here in your plush office, Mr Partridge, but there was a war on. My dear nanny was perfectly well, when I left to do my duty in France. And although I tried to care for her when I returned, I was struck down with influenza. I then had the care of my husband, who, before the war that I am reminding you of, was a fit and healthy young man, but unfortunately – whilst fighting for the freedom of the likes of you – was badly injured and now needs full-time care.' Feeling her lips begin to quiver, Ella swallowed hard and stared at the astonished solicitor.

'I'm sorry. Forgive me. I didn't realize. I only saw this dear client of ours being cared for in a home, when she wanted to be taken care of by you. Shall we press on?'

'Yes, I think we should.'

'As I say, Miss Machalski's assets have diminished, but she was a frugal woman and saved most of her allowance. She leaves you all that she owns, plus any money left in her account. I believe this will be in the region of four hundred pounds. The exact amount will be calculated when her estate is finalized and all outstanding payments have been made.'

The relief that surged through Ella was short-lived.

'I'm afraid there is other news that isn't so good, where

your finances are concerned. We act on behalf of a solicitor in Poland. His clients, who are directly concerned with our transactions, are your family. There has been a sudden change of circumstances. Sadly, my news coincides with the demise of Miss Machalski, though it isn't in any way related to her passing.'

Ella tensed. Her heart began to beat rapidly, sending fear coursing through her.

'I am charged with telling you that you will receive no further allowance, and that the apartment you live in is not available to you after the end of the month. I'm very sorry.'

'What? No! Why?'

'We can give you no information, as we do not know anything about your family. We have only been charged with administering to Miss Machalski's needs, and to yours after her death. I know nothing of your family, except that they are clients of the solicitor in Poland, on whose behalf we act. We are paid a fee, which will now cease, for administering your own and Miss Machalski's affairs. We have paid all dues on the apartment, as per our instructions, and have asked no questions. I can tell you nothing, as I don't know anything. I'm very sorry.' Seeing the devastation on Ella's face prompted him to ask, 'Would you like a drink of water?'

'Yes. Yes, please. This has been a complete shock. I don't live in the apartment, so that part of your news doesn't affect me, but I do rely on my allowance.'

As she sipped the cold water, Ella began to feel in charge of her senses once more. And they overwhelmed her with despair. 'So you are saying that you know nothing about my family, and yet Nanny always said you would give me the information I seek about them.'

'I think she referred to a diary that she left with us, which you collected. Didn't that give you what you want to know?'

'Yes, I have learned quite a bit, but I was hoping there would be more.'

'I'm sorry. You are in an unenviable position. What the reason for this is, I cannot imagine. It all seems very cruel.'

The impression Ella had formed of this man being a sour-faced individual with no feeling changed, at this. 'Thank you. I think I will have to go to Poland to find out more. The money Nanny has left me will pay for that. You see, Nanny has written that I was left a fortune by my mother, who died at my birth. And that my father married again. Is there any way his new wife and family – if they had one – can take my inheritance from me?'

'I see. Well, that is a difficult question. Polish law will be different from ours. Here, I would say, it is possible. There are old laws which state that all a woman owns becomes the property of her husband, on her marriage. And so a claim – even if it was in a will – could be voided by that husband, if the legacy was made by his wife. I imagine there is some-thing similar in Poland. But I must caution you. The news from Poland, as you must know, is of a great deal of unrest.'

'Oh? No, I haven't kept abreast of current affairs abroad. What is happening there?' Ella felt an intense desire to know. Poland was her birthplace and that of her parents, and being brought up in England didn't detract from the feelings she had for the country.

'Well, having gained its status as an independent state in 1918, Poland is now under threat from the Soviet Union, which seeks to spread communism to the West. It would be a dangerous venture to go there. Let me try to resolve your dilemma through communication with the solicitor that I am in touch with.'

Not agreeing to this, as she felt it would alert her family, Ella left feeling determined that she would travel to Poland. The fact that there was a prospect of war there didn't deter her. Her only concern was how she was going to be able to leave Paulo and Christophe behind.

Though distressed by all she had heard, Ella found much to cheer her when she arrived back at Rowena's home, as the sound of laughter met her.

'Oh, *mon amour*, Rowena is a tonic. And the best news is that she has agreed to be a nanny to our little Christophe and to help me, whenever I need it. This means that you will be free to carry out anything that doesn't require me and, most importantly, to be able to rest more.'

'That's wonderful. Thank you so much, Rowena.'

This news helped to settle Ella's heart, as now she would carry out her wish to go to Poland, no matter what was happening there. And she could do so knowing that Paulo and Christophe would be cared for. For although she hadn't yet had time to read Flora's letter, she knew this woman must mean a lot to Flors, for her to entrust her house to Rowena.

Well, I already like Rowena very much and, as a friend of Flora's, she is a friend of mine. And God knows I am in need of a friend.

Chapter Twenty

It was almost teatime by the time Ella arrived home and had a moment to read Flora's letter:

Dearest Ella,

Forgive me for not writing to you before. I lost your full address, and only knew the area that you lived in. I should have sent this to the Red Cross, but so much has happened to me that I find myself ready to go off to France with my husband, Cyrus, before I have any time to make proper arrangements.

I cannot write everything here, as most of it is still very raw inside me and I cannot face putting it down on paper. My resolve to move forward and get on with my life will be broken, if I do.

But I have never forgotten our friendship, or you, and I so want us to be in touch.

Mags is soon to be my sister-in-law, as I write this, but as you know the circumstances of my family, you will realize this will drive a wedge between me and her, which saddens me, as she has been very good to me. I

hope you will look her up and tell her that I will always
be a friend to her.

I have to rush now, my dear friend, but what I am
rushing to is happiness. I will send my address to
Rowena as soon as I know it, and I have left
instructions with her that if you ask for it, she is to give
it to you. Then you can make your own mind up as to
whether you want to contact me. I trust that you will,
because if you are reading this, it will mean that you
called at my house to see me.

I remain your loving friend, Flora.

As Ella lowered the letter to her knee, she wondered what had befallen Flors that it would cause her too much pain to relate it in a letter. And how it had come about that Mags was going to marry the horrid Harold, Flora's brother. She was sure it must be him. Flora's other brother was a timid soul, and was not well in his mind. Harold had been very taken with Mags when he and Flors had visited Mags in Blackburn.

Harold often made business trips there, as he had a part-ownership in a mill very near to the one owned by Mags's family. Flors had asked Harold to take her and Ella up with him, so that they could meet up with Mags. It had been an amazing day. Mags's home was beautiful and in a stunning setting, and her parents had made them very welcome. It had been at dinner that evening, when Harold had joined them, that she'd noticed how attracted to one another Harold and Mags were. Much to Flors's consternation, as her brother was a monster. *Poor Mags. I must try and contact her. It would be good to catch up with her again.*

Sitting back on the bench, Ella lifted her face to the sun. The aromas from her rose garden calmed her. *What a good job Paulo has done with the rosebed. It will always be a precious place for me, somewhere to sit and think of him.*

That thought jolted through Ella. Sitting up straight, she wondered how she could feel such a calm acceptance flow over her. Paulo must not die, he must not! The anguish in her lifted her body. Standing now, she walked back through the French windows. Inside, the house was quiet. Paulo sat on a chair next to the fireplace, his eyes closed. Christophe, as always, lay still in his cot under the window, gazing into nothing.

As she looked down on his angelic face, her anguish increased. His arms were by his side, his legs straight out, relaxed. No part of his body moved. Not even his head, which she would expect to turn her way when she approached.

'Christophe, Mama is here, darling.'

He gurgled, but still didn't respond by moving or looking over to her. Paulo's voice from behind her, had Ella turning round, as he said, 'Ah, you're in from the garden. Are you all right, my darling?'

'Y . . . es, but . . .'

'What is it? Are you having a sad moment?'

'For Nanny? No. My heart is heavy with her loss, but I am glad she is at peace.'

'What, then?'

Moving over to Paulo's side, Ella bent and kissed his head. 'I have many worries. I'll sit next to you and tell you them all.' Beginning with what the solicitor had told her, Ella found that Paulo was in agreement that she needed to go to Poland to find out the truth about her past, and

192

what happened to her legacy. 'But not yet, darling. Poland is – as the solicitor has told you – a dangerous place. The Russians have reached Warsaw, I read about it in my paper today.'

'It has to be now, darling. Everything is right for it to be now. Besides, Krakow is a long way from Warsaw. Going now may be my only chance. If the Soviets win the battles that are raging, they may close the borders.'

'I really don't want you to go, my darling. Please listen to me. I have tried not to tell you, but I am feeling weaker by the day.'

'Oh, my darling, I know. I – I don't know how to help you more than we are doing already. I'll go and see Dr Warner again and will see if he will call.'

'But the cost—'

'I know his potions are expensive, but we will get by. Maybe it won't be too long before Nanny's money is made available to me. And, Paulo, now that we have found Rowena, why don't I go back out to work? And we could sell the car, too.'

'But you aren't strong, my darling. I don't want—' Another fit of coughing seized Paulo. His body was racked with the effort of trying to breathe.

'Oh, my darling, my darling.' Paulo collapsed back, his face a deathly, drained image of a death mask. 'No! No, no, no. Paulo!'

Rushing to the bedroom, Ella dragged the cylinder of oxygen through to the lounge. Her breath came in short pants, and her heart banged against her chest. 'Paulo – Paulo, breathe; breathe, my darling.'

After a few moments Paulo made a small noise. His face, tinged with blue veins, relaxed. 'Paulo!' Shaking him, Ella called his name over and over again. Gradually, the blue began to turn pink and the steady sound of the oxygen being taken in overcame Ella's fear and helped her to cope.

She didn't speak to Paulo again, but just laid him down, lifted his feet onto the end of the sofa and knelt beside him. Holding his hand, she stroked the raised veins and prayed.

With aches locking her joints, Ella woke a few hours later. Paulo was still breathing spasmodically and was sound asleep. Stretching herself to release the aches in her legs and arms, she rose stiffly and went to look into the cot. Christophe was sound asleep. Going back towards Paulo, she dragged some cushions onto the floor and lay down.

Weary almost beyond endurance, she tried to close her eyes, but her worries crowded in on her. *How am I going to cope? With no allowance, the money I have will only pay for one visit and for the medicines that Dr Warner prescribes, besides keeping us for one month. Paulo's pension is so small, it won't stretch to keeping us. Yes, a job would help, but how would Rowena cope with episodes like tonight? And what of Christophe? He needs to see a doctor. Why? Why – with all that I have to contend with – do I have to have this extra worry over my son?*

The morning brought no relief. Paulo was weakened by his experience, and Christophe didn't respond to his feed. He simply lay in Ella's arms, looking into her eyes.

As her arms held her son to her, she sensed that she was going to lose him, too. 'Oh God, help me. Help me!'

'W – what . . . is it . . . d – darling?'

Ashamed at having spoken aloud, Ella tried to cover it up. 'Oh, nothing. I'm tired, and Christophe won't suckle.

That's all. He mustn't be hungry. I suppose we cannot force him.'

'C – come here, d – darling.'

Taking Christophe over to where Paulo lay, Ella looked down at him and tried to smile. His words stopped her and showed her a truth she did not want to face.

'What is wrong with our . . . our son? Ella? There is something.'

'Oh, Paulo. I didn't want to tell you, but I think he has floppy baby syndrome.'

'What is that?'

'It means his muscles are weak. Babies can grow out of it and become quite strong and lead normal lives, but it depends on what causes it. No one knows, but . . . well, some babies don't— Oh, Paulo. I can't bear it.'

'Take him – take him to the doctor. Never . . . mind about me. Use what money we have for Christophe.'

'I will. I didn't want to, because I didn't want to believe it. He seems so happy and content, I thought I had imagined it. But then I did the test. Watch. If I hold him with my hand under his stomach, everything about him just hangs there. There is no resistance. No trying to save himself by straining and protesting.' Bringing Christophe close to her once more, Ella cradled him. 'My baby. My son.'

Paulo gasped for breath. The sound of his rattling chest almost undid Ella. But then a new strength entered her. She had to be strong for her boys. She had to.

A week later, Ella had the worst day of her life.

A visit that morning to the doctor had confirmed her fears concerning Christophe. 'I am sorry, my dear, but your child does show signs of having the worst possible form of floppy baby syndrome. He must have an underlying cause, but we don't know enough about it to determine what treatment is best. The fact that he cannot use his mouth to suckle or to eat solids, as the muscles that he needs are not working properly, means there is very little hope. I just don't know what to say.'

Shaking with the shock and realization of her deepest fears, Ella had somehow gathered the strength to attend Nanny's funeral. Rowena had agreed to come to her home to take care of Paulo and Christophe, as neither was well enough to make the journey to her house.

And now as she stood by the grave, Ella's heart screamed with pain, but not only for her loss. At a time when she should be able to recall memories of Nanny, her mind was a raging hell of fear, despair and agony for the future and what it held.

As the mourners moved away from the graveside, each one had a word with her. Matron from the home and a couple of the staff spoke kindly of their joy in having looked after Nanny, and what a gracious lady she was. An old neighbour, Mr Flynn, told her of how her nanny had been the kindest soul to him when he'd lost his wife. And a lady whom Ella found familiar, but couldn't say why, told her that she and Nanny used to play cards together in their younger days. 'But I moved away and we lost touch. I heard she had died and found out about today. I wished I had looked her up while she was alive.'

Ella tried to show compassion and patience to each person, but her emotions were so turbulent that what they said didn't register properly.

In a daze she looked over at Mr Partridge as he approached her. His face looked even longer, greyer and more forlorn than she remembered. 'My dear, do you think you could accompany me to my office? I have further news for you.'

She nodded, praying that what he had to say was good news.

As she sat opposite Mr Partridge in his office, she knew the news wasn't good. His clearing of his throat resounded around the room, making Ella want to scream, *'Don't tell me!'* But she sat quietly, waiting.

'There has been a development. I'm sorry, but it isn't good news.'

Ella stiffened, trying to brace herself against another onslaught.

'The son of Miss Machalski's sister has been in touch. It appears that he found some papers amongst his mother's effects, after she died. On them was our office address. And a letter telling him that he was the sole descendant of his Aunt Lonia. He has filed a claim on her estate.'

'Oh? Can he do that?'

'Yes, I am afraid so. Technically, Miss Machalski can leave her money and effects to whomever she wishes, but this young man is saying that his mother told him that she intended to leave everything to him. He is contesting the validity of the will, given that your nanny, as you call her, was unstable at the end.'

'But wasn't her will in place a long time ago?'

'Yes, it was. But he will argue that she might have changed it in his favour, had she not become ill. It appears he visited her, while stationed here during the war. You were away. Then, when he was deployed, he wrote often to her. The matron of the home let him know about his aunt's passing. He is unable to leave Poland at the moment.'

It felt to Ella as if someone had pulled the plug on her last hope. The money that she thought Nanny had left her had become a lifeline to the future for her. Their medical bills had escalated this last week. Money was draining from her like a river that has been released from its dam.

'I just don't know what I am going to do.'

'Oh, my dear. I am so sorry. Here.'

Taking the large white hanky that Mr Partridge offered, Ella blew her nose loudly. 'I'm sorry, you see . . .' Why she blurted out all of her troubles, Ella didn't know, but when she finally calmed down, Mr Partridge was looking at her in a kindly, concerned way.

'I am so very sorry. That is more than anyone – let alone a young woman, as you are – should have to contend with. I wish that I could help. Have you tried some of the free hospitals, to see if they know of a doctor who would help you? There must be something out there.'

Regaining her dignity, Ella straightened. 'No. But I will. Thank you.'

As she rose, Mr Partridge said, 'Please try not to worry, but at the same time keep in mind that you may lose any case you put up against this young man. The courts often favour family and, well, men against women.'

'I know. I won't be contesting it. Please allow Nanny's nephew to have whatever there is. He can take the money and any possessions, but he can never take the beautiful memories that Nanny gave me. Good day, Mr Partridge. And thank you.'

Sitting in her car, Ella wondered if it was feasible that she could go back to work. And if she did, how many hours could she do, and how much money would she bring in?

Nurses were paid a pittance, as it was. And she wasn't fully qualified. Could she pick up her training once more? But that would mean more expense, as books had to be paid for, and paper and pens, not to mention tuition fees. And what other work could she turn her hand to? Nothing. She knew nothing of office work or shop work. Maybe she could be a tutor. But often they were live-in positions in the country, where the children didn't have access to good day-schools.

Getting into the car, she slumped over the wheel. It was no use. She needed money now. This minute. The car would have to go.

At least when Ella opened the door to her home, the same lovely atmosphere greeted her as there had been when she'd left Paulo and Christophe in her home with Rowena.

Rowena's infectious laughter rang out and bounced off the walls. Paulo, too, was giggling, between coughs and gasps for air.

'Missy Ella. Hello, girl. We were beginning to think you would never return. Not that it matters. I found some stewing meat on the cold slab in the pantry, and some veg, and I have a casserole on the go. And these boys have behaved well . . . Oh, honey child, come on – you cry all the tears you need to. Rowena won't be leaving you. I'll see to the dinner and clear up afterwards. You sit down with your lovely Paulo, girl.'

'I – I've sold the car. I . . . there's nothing coming from Nanny. And . . . and our child is going to die! Christophe will die . . .'

The room fell silent. A ringing started up in Ella's ears.

Her eyes blurred and then her vision went altogether, as she allowed herself to sink into the blessed peace and relief of the black hole that had opened up and swallowed her.

'Come on, child, come on. Open your eyes.'

'What happened?'

'You fainted. You told us all this bad stuff, and then you went out like a light. And I'm not surprised, Missy Ella. That is more than any girl can be asked to bear. I'm sad for you, honey child.'

'Paulo?'

'I – I'm here, darling. Oh, Ella, come to me. My legs won't work.'

In Paulo's arms, Ella found some comfort. Nothing could really comfort her, but to know that she wasn't alone helped.

'We'll get through this, my darling Ella. I'll be there for you. I feel stronger today.'

Ella could only nod. Everything was falling apart, but they still had their love. They still had each other.

'I will get Dr Warner to you tomorrow, darling. I will have enough from what the car fetched.'

'Who did you sell it to, darling, and how much did they pay you? And why is there nothing to come from Nanny?'

She told him about the will being contested and then said, 'As for the car, I called into the dealer that I bought it from, and he gave me a very generous seventy-five pounds.'

'Maybe you shouldn't have been so hasty, as the car was so valuable to us.'

'We are desperate. We have so little left.'

The silence between them held all their worries.

Ella broke it. 'I only have one chance, and I have to take it. I need to use some of that money to take me to Poland. I need to speak to my father – he has to help me.'

Paulo didn't object.

Chapter Twenty-One

Ella watched as Rowena held the banana-shaped bottle, which contained milk expressed from Ella's breast, to Christophe's mouth.

Her heart tore in two as she saw her child make no sucking movement. His head flopped back on his shoulders. His eyes looked huge in their sunken sockets, and his skin hung loosely on his wasted body, exposing his ribs.

'Oh, Rowena, if only we could get food inside him. He would gain strength then.'

Rowena looked up. Her eyes were full of tears. 'It's God's will, Missy Ella. There are children that belong to Him and, no matter what we do, we cannot hold on to them.'

'No! No, I won't accept that. There must be a way of feeding my darling child. *Please*, God, show us a way.'

Rowena shook her head. 'Help him, Missy Ella. Help him to take his last journey. He needs you to let him go.'

A gasp from behind her had Ella turning. Paulo stood, supported by his two walking sticks. 'Rowena is right.

Darling, y – you . . . we gave him life, now we have to help him p – pass.'

On hearing this, everything drained from Ella.

The last week, since Ella had sold the car, had seen her world crumble around her. Some of the money she'd spent on a visit from Dr Warner. The potion he'd brought with him, which she was to rub on Paulo's chest, had helped him greatly, and a new oxygen cylinder had meant that he could spend longer getting relief from his struggle to breathe. They had been trying to make the old one last longer, and limiting his time using it. Now, with this new regime, Paulo was so much better. But her beloved son had deteriorated and they had been told by the doctor that he only had days to live.

Standing as if turned to a statue, Ella stared at her child; something told her that once she held him, she would lose him. *Help me, Lord, to do what I must do . . . Help me.*

A feeling of strength filled her as her prayer died, and she moved forward. Gently taking Christophe from Rowena, Ella sat down on the sofa and cradled him to her. Paulo sat down next to her. His hand found hers under the blanket that was wrapped around their child.

The click of the door leading to the kitchen was hardly discernible, but Ella knew that Rowena had left them alone.

'My son, we . . . M – Mama and Papa . . . understand that you have to go.'

Ella wanted to scream against Paulo's words, but she didn't. She found Christophe's tiny hand and curled it around her finger. 'Papa's right, m – my darling, we . . . we know that you have to go, but you will always be in our hearts. We love you.' Her tears fell onto Christophe's dear little face. He closed his eyes. His chest expanded one more time. And he was gone.

Agony clutched at Ella's heart. 'My baby, my beautiful baby.' Her moans burned her chest and rasped her throat. Paulo clung on to her, his own sobs trembling through her. His arms were holding her, his love trying to shield her, but nothing could do that. Her world had slipped into a gulf of nothingness.

Three weeks of silence had descended on their home, ever since the burial of little Christophe. Nothing of the outside world could penetrate the grief that was clothing the very walls around them. Hours were spent just sitting, holding hands, staring into a void.

Today, Rowena had called round. Mechanically Ella had opened the door to her and Rowena had walked in. Now she was busy. Curtains that had remained closed were opened, and windows slid up on their sashes, making a noise that grated on Ella.

The sound of a carpet sweeper, and then of a brush, went on around them. They remained in their place of nothingness.

'Lordie, Missy Ella, how long yous going to sit there? Master Christophe wouldn't want his ma and pa to carry on in this way.'

Hearing *His* name curled Ella's insides into a tight, agonizing knot, but Rowena was right. Dear Rowena, what a friend she'd turned out to be, visiting them every couple of days, even though it was a bus ride and a fair walk for her. Each time she'd cleaned around them and cooked them a meal and then left them to themselves, but today was different; today she seemed determined to disturb them.

'Missy Ella, yous got to snap out of this. I'm afraid for you both. 'Tis doing you no good. No good at all.'

'She's right, *mon amour*. Let's go for a walk today. Let's visit Christophe.'

Ella nodded. Rising, she crossed over to the bedroom. 'I'll get your chair and oxygen.'

'Lord, ain't this a good day. After today you will both begin to live a little, once more. Now hurry yourselves – yous are in me way.'

Without thinking, Ella smiled. She never thought she would ever smile again, but a warmth entered her as she did so.

The noise was the first thing Ella noticed in the outside world: horses' hooves rhythmically tapping the cobbled road; the screeching wheels of the carriages they pulled; but above this was the heavy sound of motorized vehicles, which far outnumbered the horse-drawn ones, and added a smell that was worse than horse-dung, as they puffed out dirty fumes from their exhausts.

Clutching the handles of the wicker bath chair, Ella stared straight ahead. The cemetery was only a short distance away, but it was far enough for her to push the chair, with the added weight of the oxygen.

Seeing the tiny mound of earth sliced pain through Ella. She sought and found Paulo's hand. He pulled her round to him and sat her on his knee. Together they sat, saying nothing, letting the breeze that rustled through the trees, and the birds singing out, be the only sounds. It was surprisingly therapeutic, and a peace descended that Ella hadn't experienced since Christophe left them.

Paulo's arms tightened around her. His lips nuzzled her neck. 'I love you, my darling – *mon amour*.'

Inside, Ella felt as if she was awakening from a dream, one that had encased and held her in its nightmarish grasp. Being able to feel anything at all had been difficult, because pain overrode all other emotions. But other emotions were now seeping into her. Love for Paulo. Thrill at his touch. A tingling that crept over her and clenched her muscles in anticipation.

Paulo felt it, too. It was as if life itself was breathing back into them. How this could happen, when the source of their pain lay at their feet, Ella did not know. She turned and smiled at Paulo, a watery smile that dripped with her tears. His eyes glistened with his heartache, but also with a love that she felt she could taste. When her lips met his, she tasted love. Salty tears spilled over, bittersweet with their shared pain – and yet it was all she needed.

'Put our flowers on our little one's grave, darling. We need to go home, to give comfort and receive it, knowing that we have Christophe's blessing to go forward.'

'I felt that, too. Almost as if he spoke to us. I know for certain that our darling boy wants us to be happy.'

Rowena had already left when they arrived home. She'd scribbled a note, telling them that her heart remained with them, but that her husband would be coming in to find no tea, if she didn't get home. She'd left a stew on the stove. Most of the message was misspelled, which made Ella giggle – 'I left a meet stow on the cocker, make sure yous eat it. It will give you strength.'

'What a lovely sound.'

'What?'

'You giggling, *mon amour*.'

Turning, Ella saw that Paulo was out of his chair and was

standing, strong and tall. *What a difference the oxygen and the chest rub are having on his health.* 'You look beautiful,' she told him.

'I want to make love to you, my beautiful.'

Ella caught her breath with the intensity of feeling that zinged through her veins.

She wasn't sure how she came to be in his arms, feeling his breath on her cheek and then on her chest, as he lowered his head and kissed the mound of her breast, now rising and falling as she gasped in air and expelled it.

His touch was light, brushing the delicate skin that lay exposed in the deep neckline of her blouse. Ella shuddered.

'Come.' Taking her hand, Paulo led her to their bedroom. The heady smell of roses mingled with wax polish met them. Rowena must have been in here – what a wonder she was! Perhaps she had a sixth sense that they would come alive again, once they had taken that step to visit Christophe?

'They're from our rose garden. How thoughtful of Rowena.'

'Yes, darling, she is a wise lady. The roses speak of the love that I have for you.' Paulo's voice held a deep, husky sound.

As they helped each other out of their clothing, it was as if there was nothing wrong with Paulo. For this moment in time he was whole. Strong. Her lover.

Though Ella felt an urgency, there was no haste to give themselves to one another. They dedicated time to delicious coaxing, caressing, kissing and sensuous words, whispered, breathed, sighed.

When finally they joined, it was as if it was the first time. Ella felt in touch with a deeper inner self, heightened to sensation. Within moments of feeling Paulo enter her, she exploded. She was the Catherine wheel she'd seen during the celebrations at the end of the war, spitting out a kaleido-scope of coloured sparks in a joyous swirl of pleasure. A pleasure that built as Paulo's movements became stronger, and his ardour had him sucking on her nipples, her skin and nipping her lips in gentle sensual bites.

They reached their climax together, their gasps and hollers joining, their grip on each other tightening as if they would never let go.

It was then that they folded in tears. Joy mingled with sorrow. Their bodies remained entwined, their arms seeking to comfort and to love.

Chapter Twenty-Two

The letter that had plopped through the letter box had the bank's insignia on the envelope. Ella stared down at it – she could no longer avoid the truth.

As she bent to pick up the brown envelope, nausea came over her, confirming what she feared – her monthly was three weeks overdue. Leaving the letter on the cork mat, she dashed outside, only just making it before projectile vomiting left her gasping for breath.

When the spasm passed, she leaned against the wall. *Oh no. Not now. How will we cope?*

It was almost two months now since Christophe had died, and each day, with the new medicines, Paulo had become stronger in his body, and they had both become stronger in mind and emotions. They'd talked of getting jobs. Paulo felt sure he could manage a desk job and they had contacted Miss Embury, who had promised to help.

Ella had thought to try the local shops to see if they had a vacancy, and had even talked to Miss Embury about volunteering at the Salvation Army. Miss Embury had given them an update on Reginald. He continued to make progress, and he and his family were happy. They still had support, food and milk distributed to them by the Sallies. Ella had hoped to be involved with them once more, if she was accepted as a volunteer. Now most of what they had planned would be thwarted.

But it wasn't only that. Fear rested in her. What if their second child had the same affliction as Christophe? She couldn't bear to lose another child; she couldn't.

Besides all this, they were already overdrawn at the bank, she knew that, without reading the sinister letter in the frightening brown envelope that she'd left on the mat; but she feared what repayment demands the bank manager had laid down in its contents.

After throwing buckets of water to clean down the slabs, Ella went inside to face the dreaded news.

It was worse than she thought. Their account was suspended! And she'd already issued cheques to the grocer for the last month's deliveries and to the baker for a week's bread delivery. *Oh God! What am I going to do?*

Three hours later, Ella left Banks and Partridge, Solicitors, having procured their services in mortgaging her apartment to the bank – a condition laid down as the only way the bank would allow any further credit.

What Paulo would say, she didn't know, and how would she tell him? The bank manager had made it clear that one missed payment on the outstanding debt would mean that he would foreclose. The thought was unbearable. But at least for the moment they had funds and the cheques she had written would be cleared. It was a relief to know, too, that Dr Warner could be paid for the medicines and oxygen that were to be delivered later today.

As she neared home, Ella made up her mind not to tell Paulo just yet. Let him get established in a job first, and then there would be time enough to tell him everything. She would also keep quiet about her pregnancy, too. If she told him, he would stop her getting a job, and there could be months when she could work without any problems. After all, when she carried Christophe, no one really knew she was pregnant, right up to the seventh month.

With this settled in her mind, Ella strolled along, feeling increasingly nervous about their situation, mixed with relief that her immediate problems were taken care of. Her thoughts turned to Poland. If there was a way of making a claim on her mother's money, she needed to go there in person. *I must go to Poland, and soon. Maybe it is more important to do so than to look for work?*

The news in the papers was a little better. The Polish army was winning its defence of Warsaw, and none of the fighting had reached Krakow, although some unrest had spread there. *Surely I would be safe?*

The excitement on Paulo's face, when a week later he was ready to leave their home for a week's trial in the Red Cross 'distribution of aid' office, was a picture to see.

'Have you got everything, darling?'

'Yes. I'm ready, *mon amour*. I just hope the taxi is on time. Oh, I wish I could get there by other means, as the cost of the journey each morning and evening is going to take a lot of my pay.'

'It'll work out, you'll see. And, darling, I'm so proud of you. I know they will give you the job. Thank goodness for Miss Embury.'

Ella could detect nervousness in Paulo when he kissed

her. She wanted to hold him to her and tell him not to go, but they were so desperately in need of income.

The office was on the ground floor, as it was attached to the stores, and Paulo would be booking out every item that left the premises, and reordering stock as it was needed. 'Not a massively busy job,' Miss Embury had said, 'and one that will be so suitable for Paulo. I will personally see that he has a comfortable chair, and we have positioned his desk so that the toilets and little kitchenette are right next him, so with his sticks, he'll manage well. And we are happy for him to have an oxygen cylinder there, for emergency use. He'll be fine.'

Buying a second cylinder of oxygen, so that Paulo didn't have to lug one backwards and forwards, was what had put them in financial jeopardy. When Ella had steeled herself and visited the bank, she'd found they were already twenty pounds in the red, before she'd paid Dr Warner's last bill. All in all, she was in debt to sixty pounds – an enormous sum – and now, with what the bank had debited from her account, coupled with the interest they had charged, she had nearly double that tied up in a mortgage on the house.

Ella hoped, with all her heart, that Paulo would be fine. It was a miracle in itself that he was even well enough to think of holding down a job, let alone actually securing one and setting off on his first day. And they so needed his wage, which was to be in the region of one hundred and thirty pounds a year. Not a princely sum, but one that would enable Ella to meet the payments the bank was going to charge her and, together with Paulo's pension, would be enough for them to live on, albeit frugally. If she was able to get a job, too, that would be a bonus.

The house seemed empty, once Ella shut the door on

Paulo. Being alone wasn't a comfortable feeling. Too much time to think – and worry. Thank goodness he was only going to be doing half-days at the beginning.

Going to the bureau that stood under the window, Ella set about the task of writing her long-overdue letters. The first was to Flors, which was so difficult. She wouldn't tell her all that had happened – not her financial worries, of course, for these were not to be shared with anyone, but she penned everything else. It was cathartic to tell Flors about her time in France, meeting and marrying Paulo, and his health issues; and about her lovely friendship with Paddy. Tears fell from her eyes as she wrote about losing Paddy, then Nanny, and making friends with dear Rowena. Finally she could no longer avoid the most painful topic of all, and she wrote about her son and losing him, and how she was certain that she was pregnant again.

By the time she'd finished, Ella felt drained, her head too heavy to hold up. Resting her arms on the drop-down desk-top of the bureau, she laid her head on them and let her body sob out her anguish and her pain. *Oh, Flors, I'm in despair – complete and utter despair.*

The front door closed with a bang and Rowena called out, 'It's only me, honey. I thought you might be in need of some company— Oh, my sweet child,' which had Ella rising and running towards her.

It felt good to be encased in Rowena's arms. To feel like a child again, and that someone was going to take care of her. Rowena smelt of the spices she used in her cooking, and which permeated her home. Her huge, soft, squidgy body oozed love and cushioned Ella's pain.

'I don't have to ask, honey child, what this is all about. You get it all out of your system, Missy Ella.'

Between sobs, Ella told Rowena that it wasn't all about one thing. 'It's about the ripples of my life – the ebb and flow of loving people and having them taken from me, or getting on with their lives without me, as my family have done. No one has ever stayed and been there for me, and I cannot even look forward to that happening with Paulo. Dr Warner has warned me that Paulo's new-found health is solely due to his treatment, but eventually it won't work any more. His lung condition is so bad that the strain on his heart, and the lack of oxygen to his organs, will mean . . . Oh, Rowena, I can't bear it, I can't.'

'The Good Lord only sends us what we can bear, child, though he seems to think some of us can stand more than others. But it is as my ma used to say, that a lot of what happens to us does so because of our own actions.'

Ella could see that, although forces outside her control had contributed to the course of her life. If that nineteen-year-old young man hadn't assassinated Archduke Franz Ferdinand on a sunny Sunday morning in Sarajevo, she would probably never have set foot in Belgium or France. The war had completely shaped her life.

'Tell me about your life, Rowena. Do you have other family?'

'Me da brought me and me ma to this country in a huge ship. "We're going to make our fortune in the Motherland, girl," he told me, but instead he died of the cold, and me ma of the coughing sickness, leaving me in an orphanage. More of my folk came over and got me out of that place. I have a big family here now, though only three cousins live nearby. And we all take care of each other. They still live around Stepney; it's a way from Brixton, where Flora and Pru ended up, and me and my old man now live, but they

214

come and visit and we have big parties, and the menfolk all have jobs. Them's only cleaning jobs and kitchen work, but them's jobs all the same. My old man works in the kitchens of the Savoy Hotel, and he brings home a wage that would keep us for a year back home in Jamaica.'

'Oh, you're Jamaican!'

'Yes, I'm from lovely Jamaica, where everyone is happy, though a mite poor. Where singing and dancing go on, no matter what we are doing, and where the world is colourful – the clothes we wear, and our houses, all are splashes of lovely colour. The sun always shines – ha, except for the rainy season; and the sea is blue as it caresses the white-as-salt sand. Palm trees sway to the music, and children squeal with delight as the men play the tin drums with a rhythm that gets your heart beating.'

The wistfulness in Rowena's voice made Ella feel sad. She knew what it was to be living in a country that wasn't your own. 'What do you miss most about Jamaica, Rowena?'

'I miss everything, but when my family come a-calling, we sing till the sun rises, though me neighbours can be a bit huffy about it. I used to sing all the time when I lived in Stepney. Them folk around there are all in the same boat – poor and downtrodden – but we used to party. Sometimes I would sit on me step at night and just sing me heart out. No one tut-tutted, as me neighbours do now. It's one thing I have learned in life: being poor can bring you happiness, if you are among your own. For they pull together and make a community – a place where they can all feel safe and help each other. Where I live now there is kindness, but it isn't the same.'

'Oh, Rowena, I'm sorry. I bet Flors thought she was doing the right thing for you, by moving you to her house.'

'And she did. I'm warm and cosy, me roof doesn't leak and, as we live rent-free, we have plenty of money to live on. But you folk as have been brought up proper don't seem to know how to have fun. Spontaneous fun, where you throw all caution to the wind and spend next week's rent on a crate of rum, and sing and dance as if you were a rich person.'

Ella laughed. But with irony, as Rowena hadn't a clue just how poor she was, and how she too worried about how she was going to find enough money to live on. Even to the point of sending her sick husband out to work.

'Now you're doing it again, honey child. Yous looking all solemn. We should have a sing-song. I'd like to bet that there piano in the corner has never had its lid opened. Do you play?'

'I do; not very well, and I haven't done for ages, so I'm rusty.'

'Well, come on, let's sing some songs. Let's get rehearsed, so that when Paulo comes home from his first day at work we can lighten his load by performing for him.'

Ella couldn't believe what happened next. She found herself at the piano, playing what she called 'honky-tonk music', with Rowena banging out a tune on the dustbin lid with two metal serving spoons. The music filled her with joy, as did the song that Rowena sang, a kind of poem that was more chanted than sung:

'Oh, we take our cares to the river dam
And there we washes our lovely yam
For we are to make a curry hot
So as to feed our hungry lot.'

Before she'd finished, Ella was in fits of laughter. 'Oh, Rowena, you made that up as you went along.'

'No, honey child, that be one of the songs we sang. But our mas did make them up. They sang about life. A life that was hard, and poor, and often meant their bellies were empty, but they didn't mope, they sang.'

At this, she burst into song again:

'*Oh, we watch how the river flows*
Rippling and shimmering as it goes
Bringing life to our community
And even watches us as we pee . . .'

'Oh, Rowena, you didn't sing that! Oh, my stomach hurts – stop it . . .' Tears that were different from those she'd shed in anguish tumbled down Ella's face. She doubled over with laughter.

Rowena's own laughter filled the room, a huge sound that was accompanied by a little snort as she took a breath. This made Ella laugh all the more.

'Oh, Rowena, I love you.' And she knew she did. She loved this jolly, soulful woman with all her heart and knew that, in her, she had found a precious friend. 'Why don't we have a party? A party to celebrate all that is good in our life.' Ella laughed again at this as she added, 'I'm sure we can find something that's good.'

'We can. We have our health, our dear ones, a roof over our head and, to top that, Missy Ella, we have the wolves at the door!'

This set Ella off again. When she calmed down, she looked at Rowena. 'What a wonderful way you have of seeing the world, Rowena: counting your blessings, not your woes. I'm going to try to be like you. I am. You have made me see that, no matter how bad things get, there is always something to be thankful for.'

'There is, Missy Ella. Even the saddest things that happen to us happen because we have known love. Things that are bad are only so because something we had that was good has gone wrong, but we did have the good in the first place.'

'Yes, I can see that. I had so much love and good things with Nanny, and my friend Paddy. And I had goodness beyond measure with my little Christophe. That's a lovely way of looking at life, and I'm going to make sure that, from now on, I appreciate what I have while I have it.'

Her thoughts turned to Paulo. Yes, he was goodness itself in her life, and while she had him, she would make sure he was happy and she would start by arranging a party to celebrate all they had had, and still had.

'We will have that party, Rowena. Tonight. I'll get Paulo to rest when he comes home, so that he can cope with it. You go and invite all of your family – it will be wonderful.'

'I don't think your neighbours will think so, Missy Ella.'

'I'll invite them. It's a lovely late-summer day, and we'll have it in the garden – all welcome. Oh, let's do it, Rowena. I so want to have the memory of a party with my Paulo . . .'

For a moment they were silent. And Ella felt a dread descend on her. Yes, she needed to build memories; memories she could keep and that would make her smile. Like the day at the seaside, and her wedding day. Lovely memories, and the building of them would fill her days more than she would allow her pain and fears to.

Chapter Twenty-Three

To Ella's surprise, all of her near-neighbours agreed to come to her impromptu party. She and Rowena had spent time, before Rowena left, preparing jerk chicken with rice and peas. And now Ella was putting the finishing touches to the table, adding serviettes and drinking glasses. This was to be a proper Jamaican party.

Paulo was still resting. He had been jubilant when he'd come home, telling her how well he'd managed, and how he loved what he was learning to do. His explanation of the listing of every item used that he was tasked to do had Ella saying, 'Oh, very Miss Embury!' They had both laughed at this. And Ella added, 'She even channels people where she thinks they should be. Look how she worked tirelessly to reunite us.'

At this, Paulo had taken her in his arms and kissed her. 'How very glad I am that she did, *mon amour*.'

He'd wanted Ella to lie with him then, and she had done. No matter that she had a million things to do, this was the new her. From now on, she would take every chance to savour all that was good.

Despite how tired he was feeling, Paulo had made love to her. Not in the earth-shattering way he had done, the afternoon they had returned from visiting Christophe's grave – the time she was convinced their new child was planted in her; but in a gentle, slow way that had taken her to a calm place, filled with love and happiness.

The September evening was balmy. And although dusk had fallen, the gas mantles inside the house threw enough light through the window for it still to be possible for everyone to mill around the garden.

Ella chatted away to a neighbour that she'd only passed the time of day with previously; and other neighbours were all enjoying each other's company when a silence descended. Turning, Ella saw that Rowena and her family had arrived.

Shocked at the tension this caused, and at how her neighbours turned themselves away and now talked in hushed tones to one another, Ella felt a moment of embarrassment and discomfort descend. Bounding towards Rowena, she greeted her in a loud, cheerful voice, before giving her a hug.

'Listen, everyone, this is my wonderful friend Rowena, and her family. They are from a British colony – Jamaica, no less – and her cousins here fought in the war, as did many of their fellow countrymen.' Turning back to Rowena, Ella held her at arm's length. 'You look beautiful, Rowena, absolutely beautiful.'

Dressed in a long, wraparound silk frock in vivid orange with a print of small bunches of colourful flowers all over it, and a matching turban on her head, Rowena looked the picture of joy and loveliness. A picture enhanced by her lovely smile.

'This here is me husband, Tobias, and his brother . . .' The introductions went on and on, accompanied by a hug for Ella and a jolly handshake for Paulo. The atmosphere gradually relaxed and became positively jolly, as Rowena distributed copious amounts of her home-made rum.

'Time for a sing-song, everyone.'

This was met with a feeling of uncertainty, as if everyone was thinking that perhaps they shouldn't have accepted this invitation after all. But soon everyone was laughing out loud, as Rowena began to tell of her former life through song.

Paulo looked exhausted by the time the last guest left. 'This evening showed that we can live again – despite all we have been through. It . . . was . . . wonderful, darling.'

A small worry reared up in Ella as she heard how Paulo was struggling with his breathing, but she brushed it aside, dismissing it as him being tired; that was all. Half an hour on his oxygen would sort him out, as would a good night's sleep.

Only a few days later, this proved not to be enough. Ella was busy at home with the laundry when a knock on the door interrupted her.

'Miss Embury, how nice . . . Oh, is there something wrong?'

'I'm sorry, my dear, but Paulo collapsed at work. He has been taken to St Mary's Hospital. I have come to take you.'

'St Mary's?' Fear overwhelmed Ella. Her first thought was that it was the obvious place for her darling Paulo, but the second – that St Mary's was an expensive hospital to receive treatment in – compounded her panic. 'What happened

221

exactly? How is he? Is he . . . will he . . . Oh God!' As she spoke, Ella removed her wraparound pinny and ran her fingers through her hair.

'You'll do – now come along, I have a taxi waiting; we can talk on the way.'

Miss Embury told her that Paulo had been working and seemed all right, when he'd suddenly become very short of breath. His colleagues had helped him to his oxygen, but it didn't ease him. Within minutes he turned very blue and fell to the floor.

'One of the men working with Paulo said that Paulo had told him his doctor had worked miracles for him, and had said, in conversation, that the doctor's name was Dr Walker. So I sent for him immediately. It was Dr Walker who ordered an ambulance to take Paulo to St Mary's.'

Ella sat back. Her body trembled. *Please God let Paulo be all right.*

'Try not to worry. By the time Dr Walker had administered some medicine and massaged Paulo's chest, Paulo was responding and the colour was coming back to his face. I'm sure the hospital was just a precaution.'

'Thank you.' *My poor, dear Paulo. Please, please let him get well.* But her prayers were not all for Paulo. *If only I could stop thinking about the cost. How on earth am I going to pay Dr Walker, let alone an ambulance and the hospital fees. Please help me, dear God – help me.*

When they arrived at the hospital they were met by Dr Walker. 'My dear, it isn't good news. Paulo has suffered a heart attack. He is very poorly.'

Shock rendered Ella unable to speak.

'Follow me. He is in a special unit. Please be as quiet as

you can, because the patients in this ward are all extremely ill and are dying. Peace is part of their treatment.'

Oh God, Paulo is in a ward for the dying!

The man lying in the hospital bed didn't look like her Paulo. His cheeks were sunken, his eyes closed and set deep in their sockets, his lips a purplish-blue.

'Paulo, darling, it's me – Ella.' Her lips were close to his ear as she whispered the words. Paulo didn't respond. For a moment Ella watched as his shallow breathing took in oxygen. She willed it to help him. Then, turning to the doctor, she asked, 'What are his chances? Can I take him home and nurse him there?'

Dr Walker shook his head. 'Not good. I'm sorry, Ella, but you have been prepared for this. Paulo is very weak and could suffer another heart attack at any time. He wouldn't be able to recover from such an incident. But there is nothing we can do to prevent that happening. We can treat him and hope he recovers, but that is all.'

'Then I will take him home. It is the very best place for him. I can nurse him. I have the equipment that you have here: the oxygen and the medication.'

'I agree. Yes, maybe that would be the best thing. You are a nurse, all but for the papers that state you are qualified, I know that. And yes, although there are now extra medicines that Paulo will need, you do have most of them, and you administer them. But do you have help? You will need someone to help you to turn him, and so on.'

'Yes, I have a friend who will help me.'

'Very well.'

'But surely not, Doctor,' Miss Embury said. 'If you do this, you are saying that Paulo is going home to die. Surely he needs the care of the hospital.'

223

'I'm sorry, Miss Embury, but as Ella has already realized, that is what is happening, and I am a great believer that everyone deserves to die at home. I will order the ambulance for later today, Ella. That will give you time to put some preparations in place.'

Ella couldn't answer him. His words about Paulo dying had hit her hard. Yes, she had always known she wouldn't have him for long, but to think he might die at any moment . . . *No, no, that can't happen. It won't happen!*

'Oh, my dear, how are you going to manage? What possessed you to want to have Paulo home? Surely you can see that he would be better off in hospital?'

They were on their way back to Ella's home. 'No, Miss Embury. I know exactly what you are thinking, but no. If Paulo is going to die, then it has to be at home, with me. Not in some clinical room with strangers around him.'

'Yes, I can see that. Look, I can offer you some help. Just let me know whenever you need it. I can come round after I finish work, on occasions, and help you to bathe Paulo.'

'Thank you for all you have done for us, and continue to do. Yes, I would like that. I also have a friend who can come during the day, every day. She will help me, I am sure. It will all work out.'

A month later, with Paulo a little improved in his health and waiting in a taxi, to follow all of their worldly goods – what was left of them, as Ella had sold most to pay for his medicine – Ella locked the front door of their lovely home for the last time.

Unable to pay the hospital fees, she had been before the debtors' court. The court had demanded that the bank pay the fees, as there was enough collateral in Ella's apartment. After doing so, the bank had immediately foreclosed on her, repossessing her apartment. She had been given three weeks to leave.

With her income solely coming from Paulo's pension, she'd looked for the cheapest accommodation she could find. She'd found a room to rent in Cricklewood, in the same street that Paddy had lived in.

'D – don't cry, *mon . . . amour.*'

'I'm not, darling; it's the rain. Right, driver, we're all done. Follow that van in front, please.' As the taxi pulled away, Ella smiled at Paulo. 'What does it matter, as long as we are together? Now, don't worry about a thing; everything will turn out. Rowena has all her menfolk travelling to our new home. They did a sterling job of packing everything and loading it on the van.'

'Yes. We are lucky to – to have such fr – friends.'

'Don't talk, my love. Save all your energy. You have made such wonderful progress. Dr Walker says that you are a miracle.'

'Y – you are *my* miracle.'

Paulo's eyes closed. Although he'd come this far and was a lot stronger than he had been, his heart was now damaged. It was only a matter of time. But that time could be extended with the supply of expensive drugs. Somehow she would find the money for them. *I have to.* To this end, Ella knew in her heart there was one thing she needed to do – had to do. *I must find the money to go to Poland, I must. Surely my father will help me, when he knows the position I am in? And it is only there that I can hope to try and claim my inheritance.*

So far, God had answered her prayers in keeping Paulo

alive, and in his improvement. Ella now prayed fervently to Him to make it possible that she could go to her homeland.

Suddenly, Paulo woke. 'D – did you . . . let Miss Embury know that we are moving?'

Telling a little white lie, Ella said that she had. But how could she? How could she face the shame of her position? Not face-to-face anyway. So she'd taken the coward's way out and had left a note at the office:

> *Sorry that I haven't been in touch. I have been*
> *extremely busy. Paulo is improving. To help that, we are*
> *moving to warmer climes. I will write when we are*
> *settled. Thank you for all you have done for us. I will*
> *always be in your debt.*
> *Ella Rennaise x*

By taking this way out, Ella knew she hadn't avoided shame. It was a shameful way to treat someone as good as Miss Embury had been to her and Paulo. *But it is for the best, and at the end of the day I had no choice. It was either that or admit the disgrace of our position. I could not do that.*

As the car wove its way through the damp streets of London, Ella's tears matched the raindrops tumbling down the windows. They were silent tears. Tears that she couldn't stop, but tears she kept hidden from her darling Paulo, who had once more closed his eyes.

PART FOUR
London and Poland, 1921

~

Ella and Paulo

Loss Is Twofold

Chapter Twenty-Four

Ella shivered as she pulled her coat around her and trudged through the snow. Life in Cricklewood was a million miles from anything she'd ever known. Their home consisted of just one room in a four-roomed house – one of which was a shared kitchen. Cold was their constant companion, and it was having an adverse effect on Paulo's health.

Christmas had come and gone, without much to mark it from any other time of the year, except that it had been the mildest weather conditions for a long time and they had managed to keep warm, and enjoy a nice meal, which Ella had scraped and saved for. Now the bleakness of January was upon them, and very little cheer surrounded them.

The other occupants of the house were nice, but very poor; by their standards, Ella felt rich, even if the conditions they lived in were appalling. The walls of their room were black with mildew, and their solitary window was cracked and refused to shut completely, allowing a draught to whip around the room. The fireplace served as a cooker and oven, but gave out little heat. The floors were bare of carpets, save for a rug that Ella had brought with her. Other than that, she'd managed to hold on to their bed and two chairs and a table. Everything else she had sold.

Paulo's pension went mainly on paying for his medicines, and Ella managed to earn a little by using her nursing skills. One of the women in the house had asked her about herself and she'd mentioned being a nurse. From that moment, her skills had been called upon, even though she had told everyone that she wasn't qualified. 'Ach, you looked after men in the trenches, so you did, and that's good enough for us, who can't afford the likes of a doctor.'

Ella loved the Irish lilt that abounded in these quarters, and had even spoken to a woman who had known Paddy and her pappy. It had been during one of Ella's first nursing jobs, delivering a baby to a sixteen-year-old. The expectant girl's mother had been a friend of Paddy's and they'd chatted for hours while the labour progressed. Paddy had come alive again for Ella, in the tales of mischief that the woman said the pair had got up to together.

Leaving Paulo alone at these times was a worry for Ella, but this was eased by the help offered to her, as she had discovered the meaning of community. For all those in the house – and in the street, for that matter – rallied around, when needed. There was always someone calling in on Paulo, taking him a cup of tea or a bowl of soup, or just sitting with him and telling him some funny Irish tales.

All in all, their life wasn't too bad, considering how vastly it had changed. Making ends meet was a constant struggle, because often those Ella attended paid in kind – a pot of home-made jam, a knitted cardigan for her expected baby, and even a sack of coal was once delivered to her, a very welcome gift.

Whatever she managed to bring home from her labours,

Ella found that she enjoyed the feeling of being needed and valued by these people. It fulfilled the need in her to help others whenever she could.

Mostly her work consisted of helping at births, but the woman she was on her way to see now had a deep ulcer on her leg, which needed daily attention. Ella's heart held dread as she neared the house of her patient, Mrs McMahon, as she and her son, Shamus, were notorious landlords and money-lenders and were feared by all. Most of the residents in Cricklewood were in debt to them and were terrified of the heavy-handed tactics that Shamus and his cronies used if they fell behind with their rent, or with payments on their debts.

Ella prayed that Shamus wouldn't be in when she arrived – a giant of a man, he had an eye for her and had tried many times to express his desire for her. He didn't care that she was married, and hadn't noticed that she was pregnant. Not that you could tell, unless you knew. As when she was carrying Christophe, at four-and-a-half months her stomach was only slightly rounded, and the increase in size of her breasts only served to give her an hourglass figure.

Paulo had been shocked, and yet overwhelmed, when she'd broken the news to him that they were to have another child. They had both cried, but not for long and not with any depth. They dared not give in to tears. They had made a pact to make the best of their situation, and that's what they had done.

Sometimes they went without food so that they could pay for the extra medication. Dr Walker was good to them and often slipped in a few extra tablets, which he prescribed for Paulo's heart condition. Ella was to go there after this visit – a journey on the Underground that she hated, but which

231

was the quickest way to get to west London. Each visit there broke her heart, when she saw the way they used to live.

Her rap on the door was answered by Shamus, and Ella's heart sank. He leered at her. 'To be sure, it's me pretty wee nurse. Come away in.'

The trepidation she'd felt turned to fear. Something seemed different. Shamus had never greeted her so boldly in the past. When he closed the door after her, there was an empty echo that suggested they were the only ones in the house. 'What has happened – is your mother not in?'

'They were after taking me mammy to the hospital just this morning, as she took with a pain in her chest during the night. So we're all on our own, me wee lass. Isn't that what we've wanted this good while?'

'No, *I* haven't. I will leave immediately. I'm sorry about your mother, and I hope that she recovers. Please contact me if you need me to attend her again in the future.'

'You'll not be wanting to be going without your payment, now will you? Mammy said to be sure I gave it to you, as you would need it. Is it strapped for cash that you are, me wee one?'

'That's none of your business, Shamus. Please give me the payment that your mother left, and I will be on my way.' Though she sounded brave, Ella didn't feel it. Terror gripped her now.

'I think it is that you have to be earning your payment.' With this, Shamus grabbed her and pulled her to him.

'Stop it, Shamus. I am with child, and you are hurting me.'

Shamus hesitated. But then he laughed. 'So, it is that you are trying to convince me that your weedy man can be after planting a babby in you – ha! I wasn't born of the little people, you know. It takes a man to make a woman have her belly up.'

The insult to Paulo spurred Ella into action. She swung her bag. The blow caught Shamus on the side of the face and made him loosen his grip. Rushing towards the door, Ella had just made it, when Shamus grabbed her arm.

'It is that you would do well to cooperate with me, pretty nurse, for isn't it that I can be doing you – and that excuse for a man of yours – a lot of harm?'

'Let go of me. There's nothing that you can do to me. I owe you nothing.'

'Ah, but you're forgetting that it is me who owns the property in which you live. I can evict you at any time, so I can.'

'Please, Shamus. I am telling the truth when I say that I am with child; please don't harm me. And if you put me out, I'll have nowhere to go. I – I have nothing.'

Shamus loosened his grip and stood looking at Ella. His Irish blue eyes reminded her of Paddy's and were his only good feature, although, with his dark curly hair, she thought he might have been handsome, if he hadn't developed huge muscles in his neck. But then his ugly personality would have marred him.

'Like what you see, pretty nurse?'

Ella didn't answer this. 'I need to leave now. I have to fetch medicines for my husband.'

'So that's where your money goes, on keeping him alive. But for how long is it that you hope to be doing that? Sure it is that everyone knows he's on his last legs.'

'Don't! Don't speak of my husband – he is worthy of more than being on your filthy lips.'

Shamus lifted his fist, but then lowered it. 'It is class that you are, and not for being taught a lesson by the fist. But, my pretty nurse, cross me and you will be for regretting it. Treat me right, and I can be the answer to your dreams. Now, come away with you and get yourself into me car. I'll take you to where it is that this doctor has his surgery.'

'No! I – I won't be beholden to you. Just get out of my way.'

His face came near and his breath wafted over her face as he snarled, 'It is that I can take you here and now, and fuck you till I'm a contented man, but that isn't what I want from you. I want you to be having some respect for me. As one day – mark me words – you will be mine. I'll be for taking you properly as me bride, for I have a powerful feeling for you, pretty nurse. And if you are not for knowing it now, you will soon find out that what Shamus McMahon wants, Shamus McMahon gets.'

The fear came back into Ella and intensified.

'I see that it is that you have my meaning. Good. Well, I have the power to carry out all of me threats, so we walk out of here and you get yourself into me car, or you and that husband of yours will know the consequences.'

'Why? Why would you punish me for not wanting a lift with you?'

'Because I am after needing your respect. I have offered you a lift. I am not for giving out favours. But for you, it is that I will do anything.'

His voice softened with this last, and his eyes bored into hers. Ella knew in that moment that to make an enemy of this man would bring a hell worse than anything she'd been through. She nodded her head.

It was while they were driving into London, and Shamus's attention was taken up with concentrating on the mayhem of the roads, that it came to Ella that he could be of use to her. She could get the help she needed by stringing him along, making promises that she had no intention of keeping. Yes, it was a form of blackmail, but she didn't care.

Shamus could be her ticket to Poland.

'There *is* something that you can do for me, Shamus. Something that will make me very grateful to you.'

He smiled. 'Those words are for being music to me ears. Anything, pretty nurse, anything. Though it is that I need to call you by your name. I know it is Ella. Have you an objection to that?'

Although she knew that by agreeing she was taking a step towards a deeper intimacy with Shamus, Ella told him that he could use her name, and as she did so, determination entered her. She could do this – she could let him think he had a chance. And in doing so, she could save Paulo. *If I can get to Poland and confront my family, I feel certain my problems will be over. I just need enough money to be able to seek further treatment for Paulo.* Without more medical help, Paulo would continue to fade fast.

'So, what is it that I can do for you, me darling?'

Ella spun a lie about how her father was dying. 'He is Polish, and he lives in Poland. I need to go and see him, but I cannot afford to.'

'So this is you seeking to sell yourself to me, is it?'

'No! I – I . . .'

'Ha, it is of no matter. I would pay all the money there is in the world to have you as my girl.'

Oh God! His girl? What have I done?

'Shamus, I – I didn't mean . . . You must understand that I can't be your girl. I'm married. I simply meant that we can be friendly.'

'Friendly isn't enough, Ella. I have a burning need for you.'

Horror settled in Ella, as Jim came to her mind. Shamus was showing the same obsession as Jim had.

'Let's be honest here, shall we? It is that I want you. You are for having a dying husband. From what I hear, he isn't long for this world. I can see that you have principles, and I am liking that. When it is that you become my wife, I will want loyalty – and you have that, and everything that I am needing in a wife. I'm for thinking that I won't spoil that. All I need from you, me little darling Ella, is that you promise me that when the Good Lord makes you free, then you will take me on.'

Shocked, Ella remained silent. Shamus had told her the stark truth. Yes, she would soon lose Paulo . . . But no, she wouldn't accept that. She knew there were treatments for the lung condition that Paulo had. Going somewhere where the air was pure, and held more oxygen, was one. Somewhere like Switzerland. Oh, if only she'd taken him there in the beginning. But it could still work. She just needed the money. For one thing was sure: if she didn't get Paulo out of that damp room, and soon, then he would die. This last thought prompted her to answer as she did.

'I cannot think of the time when I have to say goodbye to my husband. I love him beyond words, but . . . well, to know there is someone willing to take care of me – that gives me comfort. You ask too much of me, Shamus, to agree to marry you in such circumstances, but I would value your friendship, and then we would see.'

Shamus was quiet for a while. Ella imagined that his mentality didn't allow for compromises; he had what he wanted at all times, and there were no maybes. She prayed that he would accept what she had to offer.

'You're for being unlike anyone I've ever been knowing, Ella, and I find that fascinating. Part of me wants to bully and threaten you, as is me way, but I'm for thinking that I would spoil something I want, and that could be mine. You have courage, so you do. Not many stand up to me and live to tell of it. But you are different. And it is that the more you stand up to me, the more I have a longing to have you as me own.'

Ella didn't know what to say. In her mind, she knew she was never going to give herself to this man, but she was seeing a different side to him. A side that showed he was a thinking man and could be managed. Somehow she had to be clever enough to do that. Clever enough to manipulate him, so that she got what she wanted, without giving in to his demands. Was she seeing a new side to herself, too?

'I'll tell you how it is going to be.'

'Hold on a moment, Shamus – that's the street that we need. There, the second on the left. That's where Dr Warner lives.'

Shamus looked around. 'Nice. I'm not one for coming up west. So this is how you used to live?'

'Yes. We lived in this area.'

Shamus pulled the car up outside the house Ella pointed to. As she went to get out of the car, he caught hold of her arm. 'I've something I have to say. I'll be for paying your way to Poland, and in return we'll have this friendship that you are for wanting. I'll see to it that your man is taken care of. But I'm for thinking you could show me things that I've only dreamed of doing. Like going to the theatre. You lot, from this end of London, are for doing that, and dining in posh places. I am for having the money, but not the experience of these things, or how it is that I am to dress and behave. You can show me, and I will be for loving that I am with you. I'll not be making any demands on you. I'll be for respecting you.'

Ella knew that for a man like Shamus to say such things was a rarity, and she realized in that moment just how highly he must think of her. Something in her hated the deception she meant to carry out, but she had to, if she was to stand a chance of saving Paulo, for now the idea of taking him to Switzerland was taking root. 'I – I would like that. And thank you. Affording me respect is something I never expected, but it has already made me begin to like you.'

Shamus looked shocked, but didn't speak until she was out of the car, then he called out to her. 'Ella, I'm for thinking you need to get extra supplies of the medicine that your man needs. Here, will that cover it?'

Ella couldn't believe Shamus handing her three guineas, in the form of three pound notes and three shilling coins. It wasn't just the money, but the fact that he had realized the medicine would be priced in guineas. Nevertheless, she had to tell him it wasn't enough. 'That is the cost of one week's supply. I'll need three times that, because with the time it takes to travel to Poland, I will be away for at least a month.'

'What? Is it that you have been finding all this money yourself? How?'

Ella wouldn't normally share her business with others, but with Shamus as astute as he was, he wasn't one to fob off. 'I have, and it isn't easy. I have sold nearly everything we owned. We have Paulo's war pension and what I can earn, which isn't much. And I still have some jewellery to sell. We manage.'

238

'Me poor darling. Well, that will change now, for it is that you have Shamus on your side, and that's a promise, so it is.'

As he said this, he dug out more notes and coins and handed them to her. Ella felt as if she was nothing better than a prostitute – worse, in fact, because she had no intention of delivering what Shamus was paying for.

Oh, Paulo, my darling, what will you think of me? I pray that you will understand. But this thought had hardly entered her head when she knew that Paulo wouldn't have the chance to agree or not, because she wouldn't tell him. Not the truth, she wouldn't. She would say that she went to the moneylender, as a last chance to get them out of the hovel they lived in, and to save his life. She would ask Rowena to take Paulo in, while she was away. At least he would be in a safe place, a warm dry place.

Rowena had begged them to move in with her, once their house was taken away, but neither of them had wanted to. No matter how lowly, they wanted a place of their own. *Not that I could have found anywhere worse than where we are. Please God, let my trip to my family be worth it.*

In her heart, Ella didn't want to go. She didn't want to leave Paulo, but she had no alternative.

Chapter Twenty-Five

'Darling, I can't b – bear . . . that you are . . . going tomorrow.'

'Hush, don't talk. I know all that is in your heart, because it is in mine, too, Paulo. But I also know that I must make this trip. You have to be in Switzerland. I have read so much about their treatments for lung conditions and their success rates. I will be sure to come home with enough money from my father to pay for it all. He cannot refuse me.'

'But you are nearly five . . . months pregnant. The – the journey alone is—'

A fit of coughing consumed Paulo.

'Please, darling, relax. Keep calm about it. Look at this trip as a way to make it possible for us to have a future with our child. I am strong. As when carrying our darling Christophe, I am doing fine. I promise I will do nothing that will put a strain on our baby. I have arranged transport to London Victoria Station, and once I reach Dover I only have a couple of hours before I board the boat to Calais. I know the route so well; I travelled it a few times during my war service. And the train service within France is easy, so my onward journey will only take me three days, which means that in less than a week I will be in Krakow. I'll be home before you know it.'

Ella's words came back to haunt her the next day, as she cradled Paulo to her to say her goodbyes, for a month away from him now seemed like an eternity and her heart was breaking.

Rowena stood behind Paulo, her hands on his shoulders. 'Now don't you be worrying, Missy Ella. Him'll be fine with me. I'll look after him as one of me own, cos that's what he is.'

'I know, Rowena. Thank you. Now you're sure that you understand all the medication? The times and the amounts? Because Paulo hasn't got a clue, he just takes what I give him.'

'I have it all in me head, honey child. Now you go, or you will miss your train.'

One last hug and Ella left. Once in the car, she gave vent to her tears. Shamus didn't say anything until she'd calmed. 'Sure it is that the time will soon pass. Have you had word about your pappy – is he worse?'

This threw Ella for a moment. She'd forgotten the lie she'd told Shamus about her father dying and needing her. 'No, no word, which is good news, as I would have had a telegram otherwise.'

'Are you sure that fifty pounds is going to be enough? I'm for worrying over you.'

'More than enough. And I will pay you back every penny, I promise.'

'I'll be paid back when it is that you come to me. But it

is patient that I am, as knowing that will happen in the future is enough for now.'

Ella felt a twinge of guilt. Shamus had been a different person towards her since that first day, over a week ago, when he'd declared himself to her. He was polite and attentive on the couple of times she had seen him.

Changing the subject, she asked after his mother.

'Sure, Mammy is in the right place. St Mary's is taking good care of her, so they are. Though they say that her heart is failing and she's not likely to get a lot better.'

Ella wondered just how rich Shamus was. She knew, from experience, that St Mary's cost the earth.

At the station she alighted as quickly as she could. 'There's no need to come into the station. I'll be fine. Goodbye, Shamus, and thank you for everything.'

Shamus skirted around the car. Grabbing her hand, he stared down at her. 'Ella, it is that I need you to promise me that you will be me wife. I can be for carrying on then.'

'How can I do that, when I am already married? I told you that I will be a friend. I will need friends more and more, as it comes time for my baby to be born, and if . . . well, if Paulo doesn't get better.'

'I need more than that. I'm needing you to promise.' The ugly, evil Shamus that she'd seen in the beginning surfaced. His eyes glared with it.

Ella shivered. 'You're scaring me and hurting my hand. I don't like these bullying tactics, Shamus, and I won't stand for it.'

As had happened once before when she challenged him, Shamus immediately backed down. 'It's sorry I am, but me feeling for you is so deep that I cannot sleep for wanting you.'

242

Ella felt relief in her at the change in his mood. 'Well, I have to go. I will see you when I come home. And thank you again for making this trip possible.'

Turning, she attracted the attention of a porter, praying that he would come over quickly.

'Ella, I'm needing to tell you—'

'Madam, you need a porter?'

'Yes, I have two cases. I am on the route to Dover, thank you. Well, goodbye, Shamus, and thank you again. I hope your mother is soon well.' With these words, Ella followed the porter and disappeared into the station. Her heart seemed suspended from beating as she prayed that Shamus wouldn't follow her. Only when she arrived on the platform did she dare to look back and then breathe a sigh of relief.

Krakow, with its beautiful buildings and wide streets, seemed immediately familiar to Ella, and the feeling that settled in her was one of being home. Not that she had any memory of the city, but it was as if it was in her make-up to be here.

A happy sensation descended on her as she left her hotel on the fourth morning after leaving London and inhaled a breath of cold, crisp air. The feeling was nudged by her longing for Paulo, but with each step in the direction of Pedzichow 20, she told herself that this mission was worth the pain of separation. The street where her father lived was just two streets away from where she was staying. She'd asked the driver of the cab to take her to a hotel as near there as possible, and he'd told her how to get to Pedzichow from there.

Treading carefully in the snow, Ella was aware of a cramp in her left side – something that had started during the night, and which she thought had been the result of sitting for so long on trains and on the boat. Taking off her glove, she massaged the spot and instinctively knew that the lump she could feel was a tiny foot. *Oh, little one, shift yourself, you're hurting Mama.* As if her child had heard her, the pressure released and Ella felt the movement. She giggled at the experience, then patted her tummy and said, 'Thank you, little one, that's much more comfortable.'

It was an interaction that filled her with warmth and even more determination to succeed on this mission. She did not want her child to grow up in the hovel they now lived in. But most of all, she wanted it to grow up knowing Paulo's love. These thoughts overrode the trepidation that almost sank her resolve.

Pedzichow 20 was a magnificent grey-cladded building in a row of similar ones, some with the lower half having a white cladding. They stood at various heights. Number twenty had three storeys, a huge thick wooden door and windows that looked as if they were framed by the white bricks that surrounded them.

Ella's hand shook as she pulled the bell of apartment three. Her nerves were heightened as she waited, causing sweat to break out all over her body.

When the door opened, a young woman appeared, and her look held astonishment, which was mirrored by Ella. For the woman looked so much like herself, although her hair was a darker brown and her eyes were blue, not hazel like Ella's.

'Who are you?'

Ella understood the greeting and didn't consider it rude, as she had felt like blurting out the same thing.

In Polish she answered, 'I am Marjella, the daughter of Pan Wronski.'

'What? Don't be so ridiculous. I am – was – Pan Wronski's only daughter!'

'Was?'

'Yes, my father died just over a year ago. And my mother last month.'

Ella's world went into a spin, and she leaned heavily against the wall. 'No. No!'

'Look, you had better come in. Are you ill?'

'No, it was the shock, but I am pregnant and I need to sit down.'

The woman turned and called out, 'Abram.'

A handsome man whom Ella would put in his late twenties appeared. Dark-haired, and good-looking in a clean-cut way, as his features showed high, protruding cheekbones and startling blue eyes. 'What is it, darling?'

'We have a caller, and she needs help. Will you assist her into the living room?'

Abram had the same shocked look on his face, when he came to the door and saw Ella. She knew he'd seen the resemblance in her to his wife. He took Ella's arm and guided her into the hall and through an open door on the right.

Ella looked around the plush living room. Her feet sunk into the cream-and-blue carpet. Everything she saw spoke of wealth, from the glass chandelier hanging from the high ceiling to the sumptuous suite, which consisted of two deep-blue sofas and two matching wing-backed armchairs. Other furniture – occasional tables, a bureau and an elegant side-board – were of a deep mahogany inlaid with gold-leaf patterns of birds of prey. It was all beautiful.

Abram ushered her to a chair and she sank into the comfort it offered. Standing looking down at her, Abram spoke for the first time. 'May I ask who you are?'

'She says her name is Marjella, and that she is the daughter of my papa. It cannot be so, Abram, as I am the only child. Papa would have told me if he had another child. I know that Mama was his second wife, but there was never any mention of him having had a child with his first wife.' The woman's voice had risen to a high pitch with this last sentence.

'Calm down, Calek, there must be a mistake. Miss . . . Marjella, why are you making this outrageous claim?'

After telling them her story – missing out the mistreatment of Nanny by their father, because this girl, whom Ella had realized was her half-sister, didn't deserve to hear that of her papa – Ella said, 'I know my mother left me a fortune, and I have come to claim it. I have a diary, in which my nanny wrote that she was witness to a will that my mama made while she was carrying me, and that my mama instructed her that if anything happened to her, Nanny was to see that the will was implemented.'

'Then why didn't she?'

'She couldn't because of the circumstances, but she wrote in her diary that, as far as she knew, my father put the legacy in trust for me. But she didn't know who the solicitor was, as she said that my father took over the administration of my affairs and didn't give her any details. When I was banished, by order of your mother, Nanny wrote to ask what would happen to my legacy – Nanny was bold in that way, and she was told that everything would be taken care of. She was given the address of a solicitor in London, who would be dealing with my own and her affairs.' Ella went on to tell them how she had been caused great hardship by her allowance ceasing, and by the counter-claim by a nephew on her nanny's will.

246

'So you thought to come here and take from us, in much the same way? Well, it won't work.'

Ella stared at Calek.

'Calek! Let us discuss this in a rational manner. I don't know if you have realized, but this is your half-sister.'

'Oh, I have realized. That's if her story is true. I can accept that she is family, but she may be a cousin who is making a wild claim, as the only people who could validate her story are dead.'

Ella kept calm, knowing this was a massive shock to Calek. 'Are the solicitors Babić and Company still in existence?'

'Yes, they are. And they seem a good place to begin to unravel all of this. I will go and telephone them now, Calek, and I suggest that you offer our guest some refreshment and a little kindness.'

Calek turned to her husband. Fury crossed her face, but she kept quiet and watched his retreating back until the door closed on him. 'You won't get away with this, Marjella.'

'Ella, call me Ella. And for my part, I am delighted to know that I have a sister and hope that we will become friends. I'm sure my legacy is in trust for me, and so it won't interfere with anything that you have been left by our papa.'

'There is no trust. Nothing of that nature showed up during the winding-up of Papa's affairs. Yes, the payments to a solicitor in London did show, but they were stopped immediately on my instructions, as the sole benefactor. I wasn't a party to what they were for, but they had no legal validity. You say they were to you and your nanny, but that doesn't make you who you say you are – you could still be a distant relative to whom Papa felt obligated.'

'I understand that. Though wouldn't it have been kinder

to try and find out who was receiving the payments and why, instead of cutting them off? However, that is done now, and I would like us to forget it and be friends, because none of what has happened is our doing. We are the innocents in it all. I have suffered enough, through knowing that my father didn't want me.'

Calek didn't answer, but for a moment Ella thought she saw her expression soften.

'In my memory, Calek, which is very vague, Papa did love me and played with me. My nanny wrote in her diary that your mother didn't want anything to do with me, but I don't put the blame on her shoulders. If that was so, then my father was weak. He should have helped her to accept me, to see that I wasn't a rival for his affections, and that he loved me in a different way from how he loved her. He is to blame.'

Calek came and sat down next to Ella. 'I'm sorry; you frightened me by turning up on the doorstep out of the blue. Of course I realized immediately that you were telling the truth about who you are, but I feared you might be entitled to take all that I have. I couldn't bear that.'

'No, I wouldn't do that. And I don't think I am entitled to what you have. All I want is what my mother left me. I am destitute and had to borrow from a moneylender to get here.'

Ella went on to tell Calek about Paulo and his illness, and how she lived in London and finally about dear Christophe. Somehow, the sharing bonded them, and Calek held out her arms to Ella.

'I am so sorry. It is unbearable, and I am shocked that my papa allowed such a thing to happen.'

'He didn't, as I now know. It all happened after he died.

And neither are you to blame, for it is natural that you would instruct your solicitor to cease the payments, as you didn't know what they were for.'

'I know you said it would have been kinder to find out, but I took the word of my solicitor when he told me the payments were no longer valid and I should stop them. I believed him. I had no reason not to.'

When Abram came back into the room, Calek stood up and every sinew of her seemed tense. 'Well?'

'I'm afraid it isn't good news for you, Marjella.'

'Oh? I . . . What happened – is there no legacy?'

'No. I rang Babić and he told me that, yes, there was a daughter from the first marriage; and that, yes, there was a will in her favour; but that after Pan Wronski's second marriage, all of the Wronski affairs were moved to our present solicitor. So I rang them, and it appears that your father put in a claim after his second marriage on the whole of your mother's estate. As the widower, he was entitled to claim that what had been his spouse's became his, on his remarriage. There were no surviving grandparents and no other family to contest this, and so his claim was validated.'

'Oh God!'

'I'm sorry. I – we – will do what we can to help, won't we, Calek?'

'We will have to discuss it with our solicitor first, Abram. I am sure Ella understands that. How long are you staying in Poland, Ella?'

'I only have a few days. I won't be able to stay longer, because with the time the journey takes, it will mean that I am away from home too long. I am in the fifth month of my pregnancy, and soon it will be too difficult for me to travel.'

A look passed over Calek's face that was indiscernible,

before she faced her husband and raised her brows. He didn't seem to get the implication of whatever she was trying to convey, and simply smiled at her. But the look made Ella feel unsure.

'And our father left me nothing? Not even an indication that my allowance should continue for life?'

'No, but don't be too hard on him; he lost his mind towards the end of his life and didn't know what day it was or who we were. He—'

'Abram! I don't think Ella needed to know that.'

Again, with the feeling that Calek had an agenda, Ella's concern deepened, but hearing that her father hadn't been in his right mind at the end helped her. 'I am relieved to hear about this, although sad, too, of course. But it provides a reason other than my own conclusion, which was that my father didn't care about me. The fact that, at some point, he told your solicitor never to let you know about me, and to pass off the payments he was making as an investment, means that he was trying to save his wife from finding out that he had always taken care of me and Nanny. It was a kind act on his behalf, for his wife and you, but one that has left me destitute. I – I wonder if you would consider reinstating it, now that you know that it was our father's wish?'

Abram went to speak, but Calek jumped in. 'As I say, we need to consult our solicitor, so please give us time to do that.'

'Calek, I don't see why we cannot make that decision. After all, it is *our* money and we have more than enough to help your half-sister. She has been dealt an injustice, and we can put that right.'

Calek shot a look of utter disdain towards her husband, before turning and making as if to leave the room. Opening the door, she looked back. 'Please give the address of where you are staying to my husband, and allow us time to absorb what we have learned and to come to an agreement on the way forward. My husband is always hasty to make decisions. Goodbye, Marjella.'

Abram started to protest, but Calek's look stopped him. Ella rose and went out the door. 'For my part, Calek, I am happy to have a sister and a family. I hope you will consider welcoming me, my husband and my child as your relations. Yes, we need help now, but we won't always be an encumbrance on you, and I only want what is rightfully mine.'

A cold feeling seeped inside Ella, which wasn't down to the icy wind that whipped up the street as she stepped out of the house. From what she knew of Calek's mother, it seemed that Calek had many of the same traits in her own personality. And Ella knew that just as her father's new wife had cast her out, so too would the daughter.

Please don't let that happen. Let Abram be strong enough to stand up to Calek, for in him I saw a fair and kind man.

Chapter Twenty-Six

Abram stood in the hall of the boarding house and looked up at Ella as she descended the stairs towards him. Two days had passed without a word, but now, at last, Ella would know their decision.

Keeping her eyes on him, Ella could see that he was growing more uncomfortable by the minute, and the dread that she had lived with since leaving his home clutched at her.

'I take it there is to be no help for me?'

'It isn't straightforward. I'm sorry, Ella, but I have come to take you to my home, where we will have a meeting. Once we have come to a decision, our solicitor will attend and make it a legal agreement.'

'Oh, I didn't get any indication of that, from the way you looked. Thank you. I am so grateful to you both.'

'I think you should wait until you hear the terms of our offer before you show gratitude. I will only say that the plan is not something I agree with, but Calek is a very determined woman. And I realize that her plan, if you agree to it, will bring us great happiness and will give you the money that you need immediately to sort out your life, and security for the rest of it, so I am happy to go along with the plan as long as you are.'

Ella couldn't think what the terms were that would bring Calek and Abram happiness. Unless it was that she should never encroach upon them again, and would sign away any further claim to their estate. *It must be that.*

Getting into the carriage beside Abram, Ella's heart lifted. Those terms would be easy to comply with, as long as the settlement was sufficient for her plans. And she would fight for it to be. After all, she never even knew Calek existed until a couple of days ago and hadn't felt any immediate attachment to her. Not seeing her ever again wouldn't be a hardship.

Ella cast her thoughts aside, settled back into the plush velvet seat of the carriage and enjoyed the sensation of being transported by horses once more. It was something she missed, now that motor cars clogged the London roads.

The sights of Krakow passed slowly by the window: the beautiful Vistula River and the majestic buildings. And yet nothing stirred in her memory, although she felt a sense of belonging. There was hope in her heart, too, that her problems were about to end, and at last it might be possible for her to take her beloved Paulo to Switzerland.

Nothing had prepared her for what Calek had in mind.

'Ella, I am not going to go around the trees, but will get straight to the point. You turning up was a huge shock for me. As was the threat that I assumed you posed to what is mine and Abram's, and to our future as we had planned it. However, I have now found out that you have very little chance of winning a claim against us in a court of law. The money that has been paid to you since your third birthday – and to your nanny for the care of you – more than covers what you would have inherited from your mother. Your only claim would be to what it might be reasonably assumed that your father would have left you, had you continued to live in his household as his daughter. However, he left only a small legacy to me, for the bulk of his estate went to his wife, my mother. And it is from her that I received my legacy. The court might consider that Papa's decision-making was jeopardized by his mental condition towards the end of his life, but as he never rescinded his instructions to his solicitor that you were to be kept hidden from our knowledge, this indicates that he did not intend to have your existence known to us, by including you in his will.'

'I see. So what is your intention? Are you planning to do right by me, now that you do know I exist?'

'Yes, but there is a condition and, without your agreement to it, nothing will be forthcoming from us.'

'If it is that you want me out of your life and never to contact you again, I am very willing to do that, for I cannot see a time when we could be friends, Calek. You are so different from me, and have shown me very little friendship and have not welcomed me.'

'That is part of it, but not all. I am unable to have children, and Abram and I long to have a child—'

'No!'

'In that case, we wash our hands of you, and we have every right to do so.'

Ella's legs wobbled. 'Please may I sit down?'

'There is no need for you to do so. You will be shown to the door and taken back to your boarding house.'

'Calek, how can you be so cruel? Please sit down, Ella. I will have some water brought in for you. I am sorry. This has been a shock to you. I'm very sorry.'

After Abram pulled the cord and instructed that water should be brought to the room, Ella said, 'So this is what you meant by the terms bringing you both happiness, Abram?'

'Yes, it is. Our dearest wish is to have a child, and although I didn't agree with Calek, I have come to think that her idea isn't a bad one. Your child will be related to us, and needs us. Without us, what kind of life will the child have? Living in squalor? With no proper education? Maybe not even enough food, and – I am sorry to remind you – but possibly without one of his or her parents. So why would you not sacrifice yourself and your own feelings, for the good of your child? We will offer love, and every material need a child could possibly want. We would bring him or her up as if they were our own. In return, we will make a settlement on you that will mean that you are set up for life.'

Ella's heart was breaking. 'I cannot give up my child. I cannot. Please, please help me.' Never had she felt as degraded as she did at this moment. She had suffered so much at the hands of Jim, and had sold her soul to Shamus, but to sit here and beg her own kin for money stripped her of every ounce of dignity.

'We have told you the terms under which we will extend our generosity to you, and we are not about to change our minds; that is for you to do.'

'I won't change my mind, but somehow I will raise the money to challenge my father's will. I was at least entitled to what you had.'

'A stupid quest, because it was very little. Court fees and travelling backwards and forwards to Poland would eat up more money than you would benefit from. What we are offering is not only the best chance in life that your child could have, but a lifetime of security for you, and a chance for your husband to recover sufficiently to live longer. I think you are being very stubborn – and selfish beyond words. Get her out of my sight. I want to forget you even exist.'

Tears streamed down Ella's face as the door to the house closed behind her. *What have I done? I thought that by coming here I would end my troubles, but I have doubled them, as now I am deeply in debt to Shamus, with no prospect of paying him back.* She shuddered at what this would mean. Shamus now had a hold over her.

Arriving back in England, Ella's worries paled into insignificance as she found Paulo had deteriorated.

'Oh, Missy Ella, am I glad to see you. As soon as you left, Paulo became sicker. He has been coughing up blood. Big clots of it, and some have threatened to choke him. I went to that doctor you told me about . . . I'm sorry, Missy Ella, but he said there was no more he could do. That it was just a matter of time.'

Ella collapsed into Rowena's arms. This time she found no comfort in the soft feel of the fleshy body, or in the smell of spices that had permeated Rowena's clothes. Her sobs heaved her chest in painful spasms that tore at her heart.

'Now, now, honey child, you must take the courage that I know you have and grasp it, to get you and Paulo through this. He deserves your help in his passing.'

'I can't bear it, Rowena. Oh, why did I go – why?'

'I take it that you didn't get the outcome you needed, Missy Ella?'

'No. I met the most vicious person I have ever come

256

across, and to think that she is my own flesh and blood. But I will tell you later. I'm composed now. I'll go and see Paulo.'

As had happened once before, the man Ella saw lying in the bed bore little resemblance to her Paulo, but whereas that time she had been able to nurse him back to health, this time she knew the despair of not being able to.

Taking his hand, she whispered his name. His eyes opened. If ever Ella had known love, she knew it to be tenfold now. Paulo's look told her of his beautiful love for her. His hand tightened on hers, then loosened. His eyes closed as a sigh left his body. A stillness enclosed him and took him from her.

'No . . . NO. Nooo!'

Ella sank to the floor. Her body crumpled as the gates to complete her misery were flung open. Her screams were pitiful, and full of anguish and loss. It was as if her soul was being ripped from her. She was nothing. The ripples of her life were winning, and she could no longer fight the tide of them, as they claimed yet another of her loved ones. Her thoughts were that she wanted to die. To go with Paulo, and not have to stand losing anyone else.

'Missy Ella. Honey child, come to me. Let me hold you.'

Once more in Rowena's arms, Ella let her body empty itself of her anguish.

'Think of your unborn child, Missy Ella. That be a gift that you have, and a reason to carry on. We will help you. Come on through and sit down, I'll make you a hot tea. You have to look after yourself, honey child.'

'No, I can't leave Paulo. I'll be all right if you can bring me a chair. I don't think that I can drink anything. I would be sick.'

When Rowena brought a chair through for her, Ella sat and took Paulo's unresponsive hand in hers. His features had fallen into a waxy mask. Leaning forward, she closed his unseeing eyes and his slack mouth. Rowena took her pinny off, rolled it up and wedged it under Paulo's chin. 'That will help him keep his mouth closed. There, look – in death, his youth and his time free of pain are coming back to him. That soothes me heart.'

Yes. Ella could see what Rowena was seeing. Without the lines of pain, Paulo did look younger and, more importantly, at peace. A feeling came over her that even if she could do so, she would not wake him to suffer again. 'Go, my darling. Fly high and find our little Christophe and take care of each other. You will always live in my heart.'

With this, some comfort came to her.

How Ella got through the next few days, she didn't know. Nor could she remember most of them.

Paulo was laid to rest next to Christophe. Ella used the last of the fifty pounds she'd borrowed from Shamus to pay for the burial, and Rowena had catered for the wake. Not that there were many people there, but all of Rowena's family attended and, to her surprise, turned the later part of the afternoon into a Jamaican send-off, with music and singing and plenty of rum. But even more surprising to Ella was the fact that she joined in and enjoyed herself. She knew Paulo would have loved it, and would want her to give him such a send-off.

Now she sat in her empty room back in Cricklewood, with Paulo's empty chair and a deep loneliness as her only companion.

Rowena had begged her to stay longer, but Ella had

known that she had to try and make sense of her life, and to sort out what she could do to keep herself going and make a life for her child.

Paulo's pension would now stop. There had been three cheques waiting for her that had taken her up to his death, and another had come since, which she had returned, with a letter giving them the details of his demise. The money from the cheques that had not been cashed while she was away was keeping her going, and would for another two weeks, as she had no medicines to buy now. But after that, she did not know. Pictures of the workhouse loomed large in her mind. Always when she thought of that prospect, her body trembled with fear. But she knew it might be the only way of surviving.

A knock on the door startled her. She'd heard the front door open, but had thought it was one of the other tenants coming in.

Getting up from the chair, Ella felt the extra weight of her body, which was so noticeable now. It was as if in the last month her baby had doubled in size, leaving her feeling drained of energy.

When she opened the door to find Shamus standing there, her heart dropped.

'I heard of your plight, Ella, me darling. I wanted you to know that I'm thinking about you and am ready for you whenever you feel the time is right.'

'Ready?'

'Have you forgotten your promise to me? Or was it that you were stringing me along to get your hands on me money?'

'N – no, I – I . . . Look Shamus, I cannot think of our

arrangement yet. I'm racked with grief for Paulo. Please give me time.'

'If it's time as you are wanting, then I am willing to give you that, but it is that you made a promise to me, and I want to know you intend to keep it.'

Ella just looked at him. She could find no words. That he should come demanding that she keep her word, mere days after her darling Paulo had died, beggared belief.

'Cat got your tongue, eh? Well, what happened in Poland? Did your father die? I don't see that he gave you any money, as you're not being forthcoming in paying me back, like you said you would. So, with your man gone now, I see only a future of hardship for you. Well, I can be changing that, as I promised.'

'Shamus, don't you see the pain I am in? Can't you understand that I haven't the heart or the stomach to discuss this yet? I'm only three months off having a child. My beloved husband is gone. My father is dead and left nothing to me.' It was a truth that she could hold up her head and tell. 'And I have no income. I'm cold and very worried. The last thing I want to think about is giving myself to another man. I have no feeling in me – only a deep, empty void. Please, just leave me alone, at least until my child is born.'

Shamus coughed and his cheeks reddened. It seemed she could always reason with him, if she took him to task.

'Aye, well, it is as you say: it is early days for you. But I don't see that giving me hope, by confirming that it was that you meant your words, can hurt you. Because to hear you say so would settle me.'

'I don't know.'

'Well, you'd better be thinking on. I'm not a man to be

messed with. You promised. And on that promise, I haven't come to ask for me back-rent that you've missed while you went gallivanting; nor is it that I am asking for repayment of the loan I made you. But if you are going back on your promise, then I'm here demanding both, or you will face the consequences.'

'And what consequences are those? Because there is little that you could do to me that will top what I am going through.'

'Eviction. Your arse would find itself on the street this night. And confiscation of everything you have, to pay me debt back. Is it that you think you can stand a night on the street, in your condition, then?'

'I have friends that I can go to.'

'Is it that black lot you're talking of? Go to them, and they will think they are back in their own country, as they will feel the heat of the burning of their house.'

This shocked Ella more than any threat Shamus had ever made. And, worse, she knew him capable of carrying it out. *Oh, why did I ever get him to take me there and expose them to his wrath?*

'N – no, it isn't them; they have no room for me, or I would be there now.'

'Well, I don't see you going to any other friends for help, this long while that you've needed it. Ella, I can be your friend. I can be taking care of you. All I need is for you to say that your promise was meant and, one day soon, you will be me wife.'

Defeated, Ella nodded. 'But I want nothing to happen until after my child is born. Nothing.'

'You have me word. But I'm thinking that we can discuss

261

things further. I have some conditions of me own, which I want you to know about.'

'Not now.'

'Yes, now.' With this, Shamus pushed by her, sending her reeling backwards. He jumped forward and caught her from falling. Holding her unbalanced, with a strength she had never known any man to possess, his lips came down on hers.

Ella struggled, managing to twist her head away from him, but his grip tightened as he straightened her and pulled her in close to his body, at the same time closing the door with a backward kick of his foot.

Having no time to think of her situation, Ella fought wildly, but he was too strong for her. He crushed her swollen belly against him. Now, as she felt the hardness of him pressing against her, terror engulfed her. 'No . . . I p – promise, when I am ready, I promise, but not yet. Not like this.'

If there was any respect she could ever give to this man, it was at this moment, as Shamus released her and turned from her. In this action she saw an ounce of decency in him. He could have taken her and she wouldn't have been able to do anything about it. But he hadn't. Instead he was fighting for control.

'Thank you. Thank . . . you.' Her second time of saying it came out on a huge sob. She sank down onto the chair behind her. Paulo's chair. Holding the arms of it, she tried to imagine that he was holding her and protecting her. *Oh, Paulo, my Paulo.*

Shamus stood for a while with his back to her, his shoulders hunched. 'Whisht your crying, woman. No harm has come to you.'

Ella wiped her face on her sleeve and swallowed hard.

'If it is that you mean what you say about being me wife, why is it that you refuse me a kiss? You drive me wild, woman.'

'I can't, not yet. You once said that what you liked about me was my loyalty. Well, I still have that for Paulo.'

'He's gone. He's not for feeling your loyalty, or anything else about you.' Shamus sat down on the chair opposite hers. A thought came to her that she was glad she was in Paulo's favourite chair, as she would hate Shamus to sit in it. 'You have your conditions; well, it is that I have mine, too. I'm not for bringing up another man's child. You're to get it adopted.'

'What? Are you mad? Leave my house at once. How dare you make such demands of me! I wouldn't even entertain your proposal, but for your threats, which I'm powerless against. What kind of man are you? You threaten my friends, you even threatened to do things to my dying husband while he was alive; and now you threaten that I must part with my child. You're disgusting!'

Shamus's face turned purple with rage, as he held his breath and clamped his mouth into a hard line. But Ella no longer felt fear. She didn't care. The worst he could do to her was kill her, and she would welcome that.

But Shamus stood and turned from her. Striding across the room, he didn't stop until he opened the door, and then he looked back at her. 'Think on. That's all I'm saying. Everything I've said has been said in truth, so it has. I'm not for making idle threats. The decisions are yours.'

With this, he slammed the door behind him, leaving Ella trembling from head to foot.

Oh God, what possessed me to get in this deep? I thought I had all the answers. That I would come home from Poland with enough money, and take my Paulo to Switzerland, where Shamus would never find us. Now I'm destitute, and oh, so alone . . .

Chapter Twenty-Seven

'No, honey child, you can't do it. *The workhouse?* No! I'll see meself dead first. You move in here. You'll be welcome. More than welcome.'

'I know. But there is something I haven't told you, and it could mean you are in danger if you help me. You see, I have been a fool, I . . .'

When Ella had finished telling Rowena how she'd duped Shamus out of the money she needed, she was mortified to see the look of fear on her dear friend's face.

'I'm sorry. So sorry, Rowena. I didn't mean to put you and your family in danger. I only wanted to try and get what was owed to me from my family, and Shamus was my only hope. I wanted to get Paulo better and . . . Oh, Rowena. What else can I do, other than go into the workhouse? If I agree to marry Shamus, I will save us all; but if I don't, and I come here, I will put you in danger. I can't keep myself until my baby is born – I have no income. He can't touch me if I am in the workhouse. And he can't blame you for my escape from him. Oh, why did I do it? Why did I leave my poor darling Paulo?'

The tears that had seemed like a dry bed of sand in her chest since Paulo's funeral, and hadn't freed her from their grip when she had cried with fear of Shamus, now released themselves. Ella sank into Rowena's arms.

'There, honey child, let it all out.'

When Ella finally lifted her head, she saw tears glistening in Rowena's eyes and felt her love. Her guilt was compounded. That she should bring trouble to the door of this lovely lady and her family. *The workhouse is a fitting place for me.*

'And tell me, honey child: your sister wouldn't help you?'

Ella had mentioned finding a sister, but had only said there was no legacy for her. Now she told Rowena the horrifying condition that her sister had placed on helping her out.

Rowena was quiet for a moment.

'You ain't going to like what I'm going to say, Missy Ella, but I would take that offer of your sister's. For your child's sake, I would.'

'No, I can't bear to do it. I cannot be without Paulo's and my child. It would be like selling him or her, to save my soul. I can't believe you think I should do that.'

'No, it wouldn't. Look at it from the child's point of view. What life will it have in a workhouse? Cos I hear tell that once yous in there, they never lets yous out. Children die of disease every day in there.'

'I have no choice. I cannot do what you say.'

'Well then I will write to Flora and ask her to help you. She'll send you some money, I'm sure. And I'll visit you and sneak in some food for you. And if you'll let me, I'll take in your child. I'll bring it up for you, but will bring him or her to visit you whenever I can.'

'Thank you, Rowena, that is something that I will consider, but if it is possible, I will keep my child with me. And we will get out of there somehow.'

Leaving Rowena's house, Ella made her way back to Cricklewood. Her head ached and her bones held a weariness that made her feel they wouldn't carry her for much longer, but at least the spring day had some warmth to offer.

She decided there was no time like the present. There was nothing she could do about her possessions, and she was afraid to go back to the house, in case Shamus was waiting for her. And so she made for the vicarage.

As she stood on the step of the vicarage and tapped on the light oak door, her resolve began to waver.

Though a Catholic, she hadn't been a churchgoer and couldn't imagine the Catholic priests helping her. They wouldn't understand – how could they? Having never married or had children, or known the problems that brings, they didn't seem to live in the real world.

A woman opened the door to her. 'What can I do for yer, Missus?'

'I'm homeless. I wanted to ask the vicar for help.'

'I see. And I see you have your belly full an' all. Are yer married?'

'Widowed.'

'Hmm, that's what they all say.'

'I have my marriage certificate and my husband's death certificate in my bag.'

'Beg your pardon then. Though I must say, you aren't the usual type we get at the door. You have a foreign sound to your voice, and you talk well. Like moneyed folk does.'

'I – I . . .' Ella's body swayed.

'Here, are you ill? Come inside and sit down, I'll call the vicar's wife, she'll know what to do.'

The vicar's wife introduced herself as Mrs Paine and then instructed the woman who had opened the door. 'Betty, go and get a drink of water for . . . ?'

'My name's . . . Ella. Ella Rennaise.'

The woman scurried off.

'Betty is our housekeeper, and she tells me that you are homeless. Once you have had a sip of water and feel better, please tell me how this sorry state of affairs came about.'

A tall woman, with a way of talking that was kindly but intimidating, Mrs Paine sat down on one of the other chairs next to Ella. There were six chairs altogether, lined up in the large hallway at the bottom of a wide, red-carpeted stair-case. The smell of wax polish, and the squeak of shoes on the shiny wooden floor of the hall, reminded Ella of her schooldays.

After hearing as much of her story as Ella was prepared to tell, peppered with fibs, Mrs Paine did something Ella wouldn't have expected of her; she put out her hand and covered Ella's tightly clasped ones. 'How shocking. And how sad. So you have no family that you know of in Poland, and now that your poor husband has died, no pension coming in. And being so heavily with child, you cannot work. Nor will you be able to, once your child is born, as it will need caring for. Well, I have the very place in mind.'

Ella held her breath, all the while praying it wasn't the workhouse. She'd prefer a correction convent to that, but had made her mind up that if it was to be the workhouse, then she would just have to get on with it. Anything was better than being forced to marry Shamus.

'This place is where my husband and I had a parish,

before we were moved here. It is in Lexden, near Colchester. It houses the homeless and those too poor to manage. My husband is still on the board and attends their meetings. He will have to propose you, as you haven't been committed there. But he does have a meeting there tomorrow, as it happens. We will take you there with us, as I know they do have vacancies and, with your background, once your baby is born you can help in the infirmary. They are very short-staffed and are desperate for experienced people.'

'Thank you. Thank you so very much.' Ella swallowed hard. She didn't want to cry. Crying brought her low and weakened her resolve.

'Tonight you will have to throw yourself on the mercy of the Salvation Army. They may give you a bed, but if they are all taken, then at least a chair for the night. Have you eaten?'

'Not since twelve noon today.'

'I'll get Betty to make you a sandwich. You can sit here and eat it. And be back here by nine in the morning, as we have quite a journey to undertake.'

The sandwich was delicious, two slices of bread filled with mashed boiled egg. While she ate, Ella thought over what to do for the night and decided she'd have to take the chance and go back to her room. She needed to wash and change her clothes. If Mrs Paine noticed anything tomorrow, she would say that she had left a change of clothing at a friend's home. But that the friend couldn't put her up, as she only had the one room, and four of them lived in it. *How easy it is to weave a web of lies, when needs must.*

Ella stood out of sight and peeped round the corner of her street. She'd sat on a low wall near to a park for over an hour, waiting for night to fall. When it had, she'd made her way towards her home. She'd dreaded seeing Shamus waiting for her, but the street was clear of vehicles.

As quickly as she could, she made her way to the house and slipped into her room. She'd left the curtains closed. Sinking into Paulo's chair, she pulled around her the blanket that she used to tuck around Paulo and let his comfort surround her. She dared not light the gas mantle. She'd wait for first light to get washed and change, and could hopefully slip out without being noticed.

'So, where is it that you have been then?'

Ella froze.

A movement, and then the sound of a match being struck, which lit Shamus's face, showed Ella that he was standing next to the mantle that hung from the wall just inside the door. The hiss of gas told of his intention, as he held the flame to the mantle. It exploded into life and began to spread light around the rest of the room.

Shocked to her core, Ella couldn't feel any emotion. She stared at Shamus, who seemed to have taken on gigantic proportions.

'I've been waiting here for two hours, so I have.'

'I – I didn't see your car.'

'I parked around the corner, so that you wouldn't. And then I let meself in and sat waiting. I know it is that you have been avoiding me. Well, it won't work; nothing works in trying to get a trick over Shamus McMahon.'

Shamus walked towards her as he spoke, his voice menacing, his anger reddening his face. When he reached her chair, he leaned over her, his face close to hers. His breath had a tinge of alcohol. 'It is that I am for taking you back to my house tonight. I have your things packed. Get yourself up, out of this chair. The promise you made me is about to come true.'

'No, Shamus, that's kidnap. A criminal offence.'

'I'm not for caring what it's called – it's happening. And you can be making it easy on yourself by coming willingly, or I'll take you by force. I'm not caring, either way. But I'm not leaving without you, and that's for sure.'

Defeated, Ella rose.

'That's good. Now, listen to me. It is that you will walk along the street to me car, without protest, and sure it is that no problems will befall your black friends; but one peep out of you and, I tell you, it'll be curtains for the woman. And each one will be seen to in turn, each time you cross me, so they will.'

Ella felt too tired and afraid to protest. Accepting her fate, she walked the street without a murmur.

As always, Shamus's house was warm and cosy. A welcoming place, even if she was forced to go there. Fitted with everything that the houses he owned lacked, it even had a bathroom with running hot water, something rarely found in this area.

A fire in the grate was soon brought back to life, as Shamus added kindling and a log to it. Ella sat on the sofa. None of the warmth of the place, or the heat that the fire gave out, could touch the coldness inside her. It was as if she'd closed herself down.

'Are you not well, Ella?'

Ella didn't give a reply.

'Come on now, me little darling, it is that you will be comfortable and well looked after. You'll have everything it is that you need, so you will. All I ask is that you are for being a good wife to me.'

'Not to mention that I have to give my baby away.'

'God love the spirit of you. It does me good, for sure, you're like me mammy in that way.'

'How is your mother?'

'She's not long for this world, and she worries about me. It would do her good to know that I have you by my side when she passes.'

'Shamus, you are a mystery to me. It is as if you have two personalities: the rough and vicious you, and this soft side. I don't know where I am with you.'

'I would always be using me soft side with you, if only you would stand by the promise you made.'

'I won't ever be a wife to you, in the way you want me to be. I will do as you say, because of your threats, and what you are capable of doing to those I love if I don't.'

'Well, I'll have to settle for that then.'

Despair entered Ella. She had no way of beating this man. If she escaped when he was asleep, then Rowena . . . No, she couldn't think about it. She had to accept that her life was mapped out for her. A life as a wife to Shamus. But she would never give up. Never.

'You've gone quiet. What is it that's going around your pretty head?'

'I only have thoughts of my baby.'

'I've told you my feelings on that. But if you won't give it away willingly, then I'll be making the arrangements, so I will.'

'No, please. Please, Shamus.'

'Och, don't be crying. I'm not to be moved on this. I couldn't have another man's child in me house. I want you to bear me children. Fine sons, who will follow in me footsteps and take on me business when they're old enough. And then you and me will take off to Ireland and live out our time in peace together.'

'You have it all mapped out, don't you? You don't care about me and my life.'

'I am for telling you that you are part of me. I can never rid meself of you. And you will never get me out of your life – never.'

Leaning back, Ella closed her eyes. Her baby moved inside her at that moment. Placing her hand on her stomach, she vowed to her child that one day they would be free, and together. The enormity of what this thought meant jolted through her. And with the jolt she realized that, without knowing where her baby was, she might never get the chance of having it with her. Unless . . .

'Shamus. There is somewhere that I can take my baby.'

Ella's already-broken heart tore into shreds as she told Shamus about her sister. Leaving out that her sister was rich and would give her money enough to care for herself, she told him that Calek loved her, but could do nothing for her, although she could take care of her child for her.

'But that would mean you having to travel to Poland, and I'm not for trusting you to come back, so I'm not.'

'I would do nothing that would bring harm on Rowena.'

'Well then, I'm for thinking it could be a good plan.'

'They would want me to give birth to the baby there.'

'And why is it they would make such a demand? The journey would be too much for you, so it would.'

'Not if you paid for me to go first-class and take Rowena with me, to care for me.'

'Ha, are you thinking that I was born with the little people?'

Thinking quickly, Ella tried to come up with something that would convince Shamus to let her go. 'It makes sense. I go and have my child, then I come back to you and we marry. None of your cronies would even have to know that I had children before I met you.'

'Children, is it? And what happened to others that you've had?'

Ella told him about Christophe, but not about her miscarried child. Though still painful to her and thought of as a lost child, she didn't want to discuss Jim and what he'd done to her.

'It is a powerful lot of bad luck that you've been having – and you giving your young life to the saving of others, too. I'm sorry for you, Ella, me darling, and sorry to add to your heartache, but I cannot find it in me to relent on the keeping of your child.'

Ella never ceased to be amazed at the many sides Shamus had. If his mind wasn't so warped, he wouldn't be a bad man.

'Now, here is what will happen. But before I'm telling you, tell me how long it is that you have before your babby is born?'

'Six to nine weeks at the most, I would say. But I'm not sure, as I haven't had any medical care. I can only count forward from . . . well, from when I am sure it happened.'

Shamus was quiet once more. His face showed many emotions. When he spoke, the main one came to the fore.

'I want you never to speak of lying with that husband of yours, do you hear me?'

Exhausted, afraid and fearful for her child, Ella nodded.

'You will be taking yourself to Poland, but I will choose the one to go with you.'

'No! I won't go as a prisoner. You have to trust me. If I can't take Rowena, then I will go alone. I have told you I won't do anything that will harm my friend. I will come back.'

Ella was desperate not to have Shamus find out that her sister was very wealthy. If she could get the money her sister promised, she might stand a chance of getting herself and Rowena, and her family, out of Shamus's clutches. And then she could reclaim her child. It was the only way out of her dilemma that she could see.

'You will marry me first, so you will. I'll fix up one of those special licences tomorrow, and we'll marry in three days. Now, it is hungry that I am. I've a stew on the stove in the kitchen, which me daily helper left ready. Though now you are here, I will not be needing her. Are you up to doing your first duty as me proposed wife and getting me supper on the table?'

Ella rose. Every limb, muscle and sinew of her screamed against doing so, but she did it with dignity and went towards the kitchen. She knew where it was and its layout, as she had made tea for Shamus's mother when visiting her to dress her ulcer.

If the circumstances had been different, Ella would be pleased to live in a house such as this. The furniture wasn't in the fashionable Edwardian style, but it was of good quality. The kitchen was fitted out well, with a dresser displaying the best china, and cupboards containing the everyday chinaware. The light oak dresser had roses carved into a lip adjoining each shelf, and ornate doors. The floor of the kitchen was quarry-tiled, and the tiles were red-leaded until they shone. The deep pot-sink had a pretty curtain around it that matched the one at the window. Bright yellow with a daisy pattern, the curtains lifted the room. The large table in the centre was covered in a yellow oilcloth and added to the feel of the airy brightness of the kitchen. To the side of the gas stove there was a wood-burning stove, which Ella knew was constantly alight and was the source of the hot water, as a boiler was housed behind it.

Lighting the gas, Ella moved the stew over the flame. As she stood stirring the liquid, it was not only her body that screamed with pain, but her heart did, too. *How did I come to this? How is it fair that so much should be put on my shoulders?* Sighing, she cut some large chunks off the loaf of bread that she'd found on the cold slab of the pantry, and called out to Shamus that supper was ready. *I can do this. For the sake of my child, and for the safety of Rowena and her family, I can and I will.* She didn't let in the thought that she might never get out of Shamus's clutches. That was too unbearable.

Chapter Twenty-Eight

Ella lay awake. Shamus's mother's bed offered deep comfort, with its feather mattress, but although tired to the bones, she couldn't sleep.

A creek of floorboards had her sitting up in terror.

The door opened and the flicker of candlelight lit the room. 'What do you want, Shamus?'

'I think it is you know the answer to that.'

Ella felt her world leave her. This was the beginning of yet another different life. One she couldn't fight on her own, destitute and under threat as she was.

'Come into me bed, Ella. It is a double one that I have.'

Throwing the covers back, Ella found it difficult to shift her bulk from the soft mattress. Shamus came forward and helped her. His actions were gentle, emboldening her to say, 'I'm not sure that I can . . . I mean, well, it . . .' Embarrassment overcame her and she couldn't go on.

'It will be enough to lie with you, so it will.'

But that didn't prove to be so, once they were in Shamus's bed. His hands wandered over her body, even stroking the

277

mound of her stomach, and then finding and caressing her most private part. His lips kissed hers, his tongue probed her mouth and licked her neck. Ella lay still, and nothing of her inner self responded. But afraid to do anything else, she moaned as if she was receiving pleasure.

'Oh, Ella, I'm for wanting to make you mine. I have to. Turn yourself on your side, me little darling.'

A silent scream filled her as she did as he bade and she felt him lift her nightie and press himself into her. It wasn't that it was painful, but that it took from her everything she had been. And it took her darling Paulo even further from her, for now he wasn't even the last man to have done this to her.

It didn't last long. Though Shamus was gentle in his movements, he quickened and thrust deeper into her within minutes, and then gasped his release. 'Oh, Ella. Ella, me love.'

Feeling dirty and ashamed, Ella curled up into a ball as best she could. Shamus curled around her, asking her if she was all right; had he hurt her, did she like it, and so on? Each time she reassured him, and was thankful when he finally fell asleep.

The morning came as a shock. Ella hadn't thought she would fall asleep, but suddenly it was light, and a weak sun was shining through the windows. The curtains were open and Shamus was no longer beside her. As she rubbed her eyes, the sounds of the day came to her. Birds chirping, the odd vehicle passing by and the sound of someone moving about downstairs. Her heart dropped as memory tapped her fully awake. *Oh God. Why? Why?*

'So it is awake that you are, me darling. And pretty that you look, with your hair hung loose. Sure, didn't I love running me fingers through the softness of it last night. Here, I've brought you a cup of tea. And while it is that you drink it, I will run you a bath. The water's piping, so it is.'

Ella looked at him. His bulk filled a large space of the room. He was a giant of a man, who could defy all reason and be so different when dealing with her. As long as she jumped to his tune. The man he was then would be easy to love, but having seen the other side of him, which was never far from the surface, Ella was too afraid of Shamus to feel anything other than loathing.

The tea was welcome, and as she sipped it she tried to make a plan, without giving her mind to what Shamus had done to her in the night, or how she knew her nights would be filled as long as she was with him, for she knew that would undo her. Instead she tried to work out how she would manage to make everyone safe, and yet get away from Shamus's clutches. It came to her then that she would need help. She could go and see Mr Partridge, the solicitor, but then he would want to do everything legally, and that would mean Shamus would know . . . No, she couldn't risk it. She had to protect Rowena. Going to the police would be dangerous, as she'd heard many say that the police were paid to do the bidding of Shamus and his mother.

She was trapped.

On the morning of the wedding they travelled to north London. 'I'm not for wanting anyone seeing us; we will have a proper wedding, and tell the world, when you come home. For now, I just need you to be tied to me in an unbreakable way. I need to know that when you go, you are me wife.'

The ceremony was carried out without ceremony. Words

were said, and the registrar – a legal requirement in a Catholic church, as this was – witnessed them signing his book. Once it was done, Shamus gave a roll of notes to him and to the priest and tapped his nose. 'As arranged, we'll have nothing said about this. Thank you both for your services.'

Both the priest and the registrar bowed their heads; neither said a word, but both pocketed the money.

That night Shamus wasn't as gentle with her as he had been, and was demanding of her to do more for him. Ella ended up in tears, and was sore and in pain as she curled up once more, as if to protect herself and her baby. Shamus became angry at this. 'It is as if you are rejecting me, even though you have been a willing partner. You're not giving fully of yourself. I'll excuse this as being a symptom of your condition, but I will be expecting more when you return.'

With this, he turned his back on her and fell asleep. Ella lay awake for a long time. Tomorrow she would leave for Dover. Part of her was dreading the journey, but part of her welcomed the chance to be away from Shamus.

Worn out, Ella stepped from the carriage and went once more into the small hotel in Krakow where she had stayed before. With the heartache that she was suffering, she didn't feel the same peace that coming 'home' had given her the first time.

It was still very early in the morning, so she lay down on the soft bed in the small room that she was allocated. Since Paulo had died, she hadn't ever felt as desolate and alone as she did at this moment, and although she tried not to cry, her tears flowed as she thought of her reason for being here.

Hours later, she woke from a fitful sleep and went along

to the bathroom. It was still only midday, so she made up her mind that she would go to Calek and Abram after having something to eat.

Splashing her swollen face in cold water didn't help. Her eyes had crusted and were sore. Her hair hung lank and refused even to be tied neatly into a bun. In the end she left a few strands hanging, as her arms ached with the effort it took to try and tame it.

Before going to her sister's apartment, Ella called in at the bank. In her bag she had details of the account that had been opened for her when she was a child, which she had found amongst Nanny's papers, but to which she hadn't paid any attention until now.

After completing her business, Ella directed the driver of the carriage to continue to her sister's address. This time, while making the journey, she didn't gaze out of the windows at the Vistula River or enjoy the sights of the busy roads. Instead she clasped her hands in prayer that Calek and Abram would have a change of heart and would help her out of her desperate situation.

There was no such help forthcoming.

'So, you have come to your senses then? You have put your child and your sick husband before yourself. That is good news.'

'There is no sick husband now. Paulo passed away on my return. I am alone and destitute. My only option is to go into a workhouse – a kind of poor house where I would receive food in exchange for work, and probably never get out again. I didn't want that for my child.'

'Nor for yourself, I shouldn't wonder. Well, it is of no matter. You will move in here and receive medical attention until you are fit to travel back. Then a sum of money will be made over to you—'

'I beg your pardon, Calek. You may think you are the one to say how things will be, but you are not. I want a cheque to deposit into my account. I have a Polish bank account. It has been open since I was a child. Today I have presented the bank with all my credentials and had my name changed on the account. Once the cheque is cleared, they will transfer the money to my English bank. That is the only way I am going to conduct this arrangement with you. And I want the cheque to be for at least the equivalent of five thousand pounds. With inflation running absolutely wild here at the moment, that is at least three hundred thousand Polish marka.'

'That is not possible. With the way our economy has been failing, we shifted the majority of our money into overseas banks and shares, before the worst of the slump. There is a large portion of it in the British bank that used to handle your allowance. I can instruct them to pay the amount you ask into the account they still hold open for you. My solicitor has checked these things out for me, as I wanted to be ready for when you arrived.'

'You knew I would come back, then?'

'No. We guessed you would and wanted to be prepared.'

'Very well. But I want proof that you have transferred the money before I continue with any plans that you have for me.'

'Just tell me one thing: how did you manage to get over here again?'

'I went to a moneylender, as I did the last time. Not that it is any of your business.'

Abram walked into the room at that moment. His surprise

at seeing her changed his expression from one of extreme worry to pleasure. 'I hope this means you have come to your senses, Sister-in-law?'

'It means that I have no choice but to sell my baby to you, although I do so with a deep loathing of myself and of you both.'

'You have spirit, I will give you that. But, my dear, this is a sacrifice that is as right for you as it is for us and your baby. Your life will change. But don't expect riches, as everything is going haywire here.' Turning to Calek, Abram said, 'We are to lose money again, darling. The marka is losing ground every second. There is talk of bringing back the old zloty and starting the economy afresh.'

'We won't discuss our financial business in front of Ella. She has already made her demand, and it is a sum that we can easily afford from our English holdings. I am in agreement, as the deal is beneficial to us, and it means that Ella won't have the financial means to stay here in Poland.'

When Calek told Abram the amount, he looked very relieved. Ella wished she had asked for more now, but as it was, she had asked for a small fortune, and one that would allow her to carry out the plans that she had. With this amount, she was sure she would be richer than Shamus, and that would give her power.

Ella didn't let the thought enter her mind that she would not have her child with her, or her resolve would weaken. She would hang on to the hope that one day she would come and reclaim her child, no matter how long it took.

Calek broke into her thoughts. 'Abram and I have talked about how we would handle everything, if you returned, and have come up with a plan. We are going to tell our friends, and Abram's family and mine, that you have been diagnosed with a terminal illness and that you have asked us to take care of you in the last weeks of your pregnancy and to look after your child as our own. After the child is born, the story will be that you have gone into a clinic, to spend the last days of your life.'

Ella gasped. The cunning of this half-sister of hers, and the lack of feeling she showed, were incomprehensible to her. But she could see that it was a way of stopping tongues wagging.

Life in her sister's home, though comfortable, was lonely. Ella had been assigned a room just off the nursery, which would be occupied by a nanny when the baby arrived. Her meals were served to her in a small sitting room adjacent to this. She did not attempt to go into the nursery, as it would have been too painful. For exercise, she wandered around the streets and tried to remember something about her surroundings, but nothing presented itself as familiar, although the feeling of belonging persisted.

As she walked outside, a week after her arrival, intending to get a carriage to the cafe that she'd seen opposite the Vistula River, Ella was stopped by a lady who had come out of the apartment next door.

'Oh! You must be Kasienka's little girl. Where did you go to? My husband and I knew your mother – she was a distant relation of mine.'

Ella was overwhelmed. 'Y – yes, I am. I was brought up by my nanny in England.'

'Lonia? How is she? I knew her well; she was nanny to me, you know.'

'I'm sorry, but she is no longer with us.' Ella told the lady what happened to Nanny.

'Oh, that is sad. I'm Janah. It is lovely to see you; my friends and I, we have often spoken about you over the years.' Lowering her voice, she continued, 'We always thought that woman who became your father's wife was a nasty piece of work, and when you disappeared, we knew it for a fact.'

As a woman in around her early forties, Janah must have been just a teenager when Ella left for England, and yet she remembered her.

'Now let me see, you are called Marjella, is that right? You look so like your mother, I would have known you anywhere. I have a picture of her somewhere. Is your husband over with you?'

For the first time Ella had to tell the lie that Calek had conjured up, and she felt as though she was betraying her mother, and her child.

Janah took her hand. 'I am so sorry. So very sorry.'

'Thank you. I – I think I will have to go back in, I'm not feeling well enough to walk out after all.'

'You get back inside then. And I'll look out those pictures and post them through the door for you tonight.'

'Thank you. Thank you so much.'

Turning and leaving Janah standing on the pavement, Ella made it inside and shut the door, leaning on it to compose herself before going back into the apartment. Her body felt clammy with sweat. *Oh God, to see a picture of my mother. That would be so wonderful and would make her real to me.*

When the pictures arrived, Calek was annoyed, to say the least.

'You needn't worry, Calek, I have told your lie, so the news of me being here, of my terminal illness and of your wonderful sisterly act in taking my baby will be common knowledge before long.'

Taking the envelope to her room, Ella opened it carefully. The image of the beautiful young woman undid her. Tears flowed down her cheeks: for her mother, who was lost to her; for all that had happened in her life; for her lost child and her unborn child; and for Paulo, and her nanny and Paddy. Her body drained of tears and pain, and she was left feeling cold and empty once more.

Twice Calek had called out her name and begged to be let in, but this had been a private time for Ella, and one during which she came to a certain acceptance. There were only two avenues open to her. One was to end her life; the other was to go forward and try to make the best life she could for herself. Neither would be easy, but she chose the second option. That way, she would stand some chance of being reunited with her child – sometime in the future.

On 16th June, and two weeks later than her own calculations, Ella gave birth to a son.

To her great shock, she wasn't allowed to see him. He was taken from her the moment he was born. A wet-nurse had been engaged to feed him, and the next day Ella was taken by ambulance to a private hospital. They were kind to her there, but nothing they did could help her. Her heart was splintered.

It would always be so.

Somehow, two weeks after entering the hospital she made the journey back to England, and the first place she went to was to her bank.

The money was all accounted for. As she left, she looked straight ahead. It might be blood-money, but it would be the saving of her and would secure Rowena's safety, and her family's, too. That's what she had to hang on to. That and the thought that, one day, she would fetch her little Paulo, because in her heart that is what Ella had named her lost son.

PART FIVE
London and Poland, 1921

~

Ella and Shamus

At What Cost Achieving a Dream?

Chapter Twenty-Nine

Ella walked along the pavement, her nerves on edge, her heart pounding. She had to see Rowena, make sure she was all right and beg her to leave her house.

By the time she'd arrived home, seven weeks ago, Ella had completely recovered from the birth, and Shamus took advantage of that, making her his in a way that he had been restricted from doing so previously. Ella dreaded each night that they went to the marriage bed. It wasn't that he was rough, not in his love-making, but she was repulsed by him and felt dirty and used, in a way that tainted the memory of her beloved Paulo.

She was a prisoner – nothing else. She hated Shamus, his attitude to life, his treatment of others, and how his possessiveness of her and his threats kept her bound to do his will. But most of all, she hated what he had made her do.

Her heart bled for her son, her little Paulo; and for her Paulo, her darling husband.

But despite everything, she drew on all her courage and tried to make the best of her lot, with the constant reminder that if she didn't, or if she crossed Shamus, Rowena would suffer.

Ella hadn't seen Rowena since the night she'd told her that she was going into the workhouse, but today she was going to visit her.

Today was different, because Shamus had been called to his mother's side. They had warned him that she had only hours to live. Before going, he had shown his grief and fear of losing his mother, and had told Ella that he would stay with her until she died. This Ella took to mean that she had a lot more time than she usually did.

Any trip outdoors was met with questions and accusations, and had once ended in Shamus hitting her. He had been mortified afterwards, but to Ella it had been worth it to have achieved what she had, on that outing.

Always planning how she could make Rowena safe, and escape herself, she had plotted to visit her bank and had drawn out some money. With this, she had gone to a shop that handled overseas transactions, the cashing of cheques and hiring of mailboxes. To make her plan work, she had to have a way of receiving messages from Rowena. At first she thought she would write a letter and give Rowena the information about the mailbox that she now had, but then she'd had second thoughts.

What Rowena didn't know, she couldn't reveal, if ever Shamus paid her a visit. So Ella had decided to wait until everything was in place, and to visit Rowena and put her in the picture.

As soon as Shamus left the house to go and visit his mother, Ella did, too. At last she had enough time to put her plan into action.

A fearful-looking Rowena opened the door. 'No, honey

292

child, what are you doing here? You must go. He will kill us all.'

Shock zinged through Ella. 'Shamus? Has he been here?'

Rowena stepped onto the top stair and looked up and down the street, her movements jerky. Fear lit her darting eyes. 'Come in. Come in quickly.'

Once inside, Rowena hugged Ella, but as she did so, Ella could feel the trembling of her body. 'Tell me, Rowena, has Shamus been here?'

'Yes. He say that if we try to contact you, or assist you in any way, he will burn our home to the ground, with us in it! Oh, Missy Ella, I am so afraid.'

'I'm sorry, I didn't know. I can't believe he'd dare come here himself and threaten you! I'm so sorry. And now I have added to your fear. But I thought you imagined me in a workhouse, and I had to come and let you know what has happened to me.'

'I know that you are the wife of that beast, and I know it isn't because you are willing. But I'm afraid for us. Oh, honey child . . .'

'I have a plan, Rowena, my dear friend, but it will mean you and your family moving away. Maybe even from London.'

'But where will we go, and how?'

'There is a lot of industry in Birmingham. I have money . . .' Ella told her everything.

'Oh, Missy Ella. How do you bear it all?'

'I don't know. But what keeps me going now is that I have the means of saving you and getting away from Shamus myself, and one day I will find a way of getting my little Paulo back.'

'I will have to talk to Tobias. I'm not sure he will agree.

He thinks he and his cousins should tackle Shamus and then take him to the police.'

'Don't let him do that, please, Rowena; the police are in Shamus's pay. They will only serve to bring the wrath of Shamus down on you all. He is a wicked man.'

'Then us leaving is the only way to free us of him, and of freeing you, too. I will speak to Tobias and make him see. How can I get messages to you, Missy Ella?'

Ella gave her the address of the mailbox she had rented. 'I will write to you. I daren't visit again. I'll let you know what you need to do, the moment I hear from you. I'll buy two houses in Birmingham, for you and your family, and make sure you have plenty of money to keep you going till you can all get work.'

Rowena looked ill.

'I'm so sorry, my dear Rowena, so very sorry. I wish I had never met Shamus. I don't want to be married to him and, once he can't touch you, I will leave him.'

'But where will you go, Missy Ella?'

'To Flora in France.'

'Oh, I forgot. Flora did send a letter in reply to mine. She said she will help us all she can, but they aren't properly established yet. They were sold some diseased vines and have to start all over again. She said it is difficult at the moment. But the good news is that she now has three children and – my, oh my – the Good Lord is to bless her with a fourth, although we mustn't be forgetting little Alice, God rest her soul; so it's her fifth really.'

A pain gripped Ella's heart. *No, we can never forget those who left us. Whether they were born or not.*

'Are you all right, honey child? I shouldn't have told you, when here you are, with none of your children around you.'

'Yes, I'm happy for Flora, really. I just had a moment. What are the names of the children?'

'Freddy, Randolph and Marjella.'

'Oh! That's my name. Dear Flors. How lovely that she has named her daughter after me. Ella is the short form of Marjella.'

'Well, amidst all the bad, we have some good news to hang on to then.'

'Yes, now I must go. Try to message me as soon as you can, Rowena. I'll get to my mailbox as often as I can. I still have to go to the solicitor, and I'm not sure how long I can be out.'

Rowena didn't answer this, but her pitying look said it all. And her hug soothed Ella.

As she sat across from Mr Partridge, he seemed changed, more distant. 'And what is it that you think we can do for you, Mrs Rennaise?'

Ella didn't correct him, for she never wanted to acknowledge being Mrs McMahon. 'My circumstances have changed.'

'Oh, I know that. I was involved in the sordid business of you selling your child.'

This stung Ella. But she held her head high. 'I didn't. Well, not willingly. Things happened over which I had no control. I – it was my only option.'

'Yes, I know that your husband died, and I am sorry. But—'

'There is no "but", and I cannot explain everything to you. I will just say that some friends of mine are in grave danger. I need to help them move to Birmingham. To this end, I will need to purchase two dwellings, each to have

295

three bedrooms and, if possible, sanitary arrangements that are indoors. The other thing I need you to keep in mind is that these friends are Jamaican, so please choose an area that isn't a slum area, but where they would be accepted and made welcome.'

'I see. They haven't done anything illegal, have they?'

'No, nothing; they are decent citizens and good Christians. However, I have seen them shunned before, because of their colour, and I don't want that to happen to them again.'

'This is all very mysterious. I'm not sure it is something we can handle.'

'Can you recommend someone who can? It may not all happen yet, but I need a solicitor to handle this, whom I can contact when I am ready to go ahead and who can transfer the money as I need it. Someone I can trust. I would very much like that to be you.'

Mr Partridge was quiet for a moment. When he spoke, he leaned forward. 'I have known you for a long time. I know that we didn't have a lot to do with each other, but my dealings required me to keep an eye on you, and I liked what I saw. All that has happened to you, since you gave your services in the war, is tragic. I admire your determination and your desire to help others. I don't like that you cannot tell me what this is all about, and what really motivated you to sell your child, but something inside me tells me to trust you and help you. Where can I write to you?'

'Again I am going to have to ask you to bear with me and write to a mailbox address. There is someone I have to keep all this from, for the safety of my friends.'

For a moment Ella thought Mr Partridge was going to

change his mind once more, but he just nodded, then took down the address.

'Thank you. Please excuse me now – I have to dash. I will be in touch.'

Mr Partridge stood. His eyes seemed to pierce her soul, but to her relief, he didn't ask any further questions.

'Where is it that you have been?'

A simple question, but asked with so much malice that Ella swallowed hard. Taking a deep breath, she asked, 'Your mother? Has she . . . ?'

'As if you are for caring? I come home in need of comfort, and I find a cold and empty house, and sit here for an hour or more alone with me grief. Tell me: what is it that you have been up to?'

'Nothing, just walking. What can I get up to . . . No!'

Her jacket tightened around her neck as Shamus grabbed it and pulled her to him. 'Don't lie! Isn't it that I drove around everywhere that you could walk and had no sight of you?' His grip tightened, his face now inches from hers. 'Where have you been?'

'I – I went to the doctor's. I have an infection. A – and I needed to talk to him. You seem to forget that so little time has gone by since I lost my husband, and then I had to part with my son. I haven't been allowed to grieve. I needed to talk to someone who knew me and who understood.'

Shamus let her go. His eyes held hers. Evil glittered in the dark depths of them, but she could see that he faltered, unsure. How she'd thought up the lie, Ella didn't know, but then she was a different person from the one she had been; now she had to plot and scheme and lie her way through life.

'There's something about you, so there is. Something I'm not for putting me finger on. You're clever. Aye, and it is that you have courage, but I'm not sure of you. It is your own fault that I threaten you.'

Shamus let go of her collar. But his stance still held fear for Ella. She didn't let this deter her. 'No, it is your fault. All of it is your fault.' Something happened then that rarely happened to her: her temper flared. 'You are the cause of all my pain. You are a bully, a kidnapper, a vile, hateful beast and I loathe you!'

His hand shot out. Ella dodged the blow, but wielded one of her own as she swung her bag. Shamus caught it. It was then that she saw something dawn on him. 'Ah, it is the precious bag that I have in me possession now, so it is. The bag of secrets, which you're not for letting out of your sight. Now it is that I will know the truth.'

Ella sprang at him. Where this cat-like person that she'd turned into came from, she didn't know. Driven by desperation, she clawed at Shamus. Thumped him, kicked him, all the while screaming abuse at him.

'Get off me – it is an animal that you are.' As he crouched under the attack, Ella saw her bag drop to the floor. Grabbing it gave Shamus time to stand up, but the demon in Ella wasn't going to give in. Lifting her foot, she drove it into his groin.

While he writhed and moaned, she went to the fire and emptied the contents of her bag onto it. It didn't matter that she was burning receipts, and the agreement for the mailbox; all could be replaced, but none should ever get into Shamus's hands. She'd been a fool not to leave them in her mailbox. When she felt the key to it, she hesitated, her mind aflame with desperation as she sought for a solution. Then it came to her. With her back to Shamus, she dropped the keys onto the rug and, with her foot, manoeuvred them under his heavy armchair, before turning to face him.

He was still bent double, but he had lifted his face, which bulged and was red, and his tears mingled with his snot. But it was his expression that penetrated Ella's shield of anger and had her crumbling. Sinking into his chair, she resigned herself to her fate.

Recovering enough to move, Shamus came towards her as if he was the beast she thought of him as. His breathing hissed through his clenched teeth. He lumbered rather than walked.

Ella cringed backwards, her protest a whimper. But nothing stopped his progress. When he stood over her, excruciating pain zinged through her head, as clumps of her hair came out in his vicious grabbing and tugging of it.

'Stop, let me go. Noooo!'

But there was no reasoning with the animal that was Shamus.

'What is it you are hiding, bitch? Why burn all of that? Tell me. Tell me!'

'Nothing. Don't . . .' A scream filled the space around them as Ella's body was propelled from the chair by her hair and flung onto the floor. Her scream didn't stop him, as his fist sank into her stomach. Unable to breathe and gasping in pain, Ella stared up at this monster she was tied to. His fist blocked out his face. The punch knocked her head backwards. The room spun. The walls came in towards her. She sank into deep unconsciousness.

Chapter Thirty

Ella's head pounded. Her eyes felt as though something heavy was lying across them. She tried to lift her head, but couldn't.

Gradually she became aware of her surroundings and knew that she was lying in a bed. But not her own bed. She tried to speak. Wanted to call out and ask where she was, but only a croak came out of her lips.

'Don't try to talk, dear, you are in hospital. Your husband brought you in. You had an accident. A car knocked you over, and you are very badly bruised. But no real injuries that we can detect, so your husband will collect you later and take you home. Aren't you the lucky one, married to such a handsome man with lovely Irish eyes, eh?'

Ella closed her eyes. *Lucky?* That wasn't a phrase she would use about much of her life. Tentatively feeling her face, she found that her lips were twice the size they were normally. Her tongue felt sore, and her eyes, she could feel, were swollen to the size of ping-pong balls. As the memory of what happened trickled back to her, dread came with it.

Shamus wouldn't forget; he would get his revenge

somehow. Why had she been so stupid as to carry evidence in her handbag of what she planned to do?

Realizing that she had to be much more cunning, she let her mind wander to her plan, and how she would be able to get to the mailbox after this. *I'll have to find a way – I'll have to.*

'So it is that you are awake? Sure you gave me a fright there, so you did.'

Through the slit that was all she could see through, Ella looked at Shamus. She wanted to claw him to death.

'Come on. They say it is that you are well enough to recover at home. I'm glad of that, as this place costs a fortune. It's two days that you have been here already.'

Two days! I shouldn't be moved. Two days is a long time to be unconscious!

Once more she tried to speak, but her tongue stuck to the roof of her mouth and her lips wouldn't move.

A moan came from her as Shamus lifted her. Every part of her body gave her pain.

'Come on now, it is that you will have to walk. I'll help you.'

Once off the bed, Ella made an extreme effort. She was going to find it difficult to do anything to help her situation, once back in Shamus's house, but impossible while she was here. She had to get back to the house and work out how she could contact Rowena.

'That's right. You're fine, so you are. You're bound to be a bit on the shaky side, isn't that right, Nurse?'

'It is. You've had a good knock and been sleeping most of the time since you came in.'

Just sleeping? Then I will be fine. But how come I can't remember anything of my time in here? But then she could remember every detail of the fight she and Shamus had, and he bore some of the scars on his face and neck. Ella allowed herself to feel pleased about this, though the pleasure was tainted with guilt. She'd never willingly be violent; always she'd been the one wanting to heal others. Now, for a second time, she'd lashed out. This shuddered through her, as she thought of kicking out at Jim. *No, no, I mustn't think of that.*

The nurse helped her to dress, and Ella found that, as she did so, apart from her head, she had no pain elsewhere, even though she remembered that she'd taken punches to her stomach.

As she stepped outside, after a slow but surprisingly easy walk from the ward, the cool late-September air sent a shiver through her.

'Come on, me darling – me car's parked at the pavement over there. We'll soon have you home.'

When they sat in the car, Shamus tried to take her hand, but Ella snatched it away.

'We'll not be for having that attitude now, will we? I'm an inch off showing you that I mean my threats, as I'm sure that whatever it was you were up to involved that black lot.'

Ella sat still and made no further objection to Shamus ministering to her. He tucked a blanket around her knees and stroked her hair. 'I've been for missing you.'

Repulsion at what his tone suggested shuddered through her. *I have to get away, I have to.*

'I've been busy arranging things for me mammy. She's to be buried on Friday. It's been difficult for me, so it has. I'm hoping it is that you are well by then, me darling.'

Ella tried to work out what day it was now. If she'd been in hospital for two days, then it was Monday now, as she'd gone to Rowena on Friday. That gave her four more days. If she could possibly get strong enough by Friday, she would, but she wouldn't let Shamus know. She'd take a chance on slipping out of the house again, to see if Rowena had written. If she had, thought Ella, then she'd need to go to her bank and arrange the money transfer to the solicitor. *Please God, it all works out.*

When they reached home, Shamus helped her upstairs. When he tried to undress her, Ella shook him off.

'Wasn't I for saying that we'll have none of that now? We were for having a fight, as all married couples do. We have to be putting it behind us and carry on. You deserved what you got. It was a fair fisticuffs, so it was. You have a left hook that I'm proud of, though you played dirty with that kick.'

His manner was gentle. Ella guessed why. And she didn't have to wait long to be proven right. As Shamus undid her blouse, she finally found her voice. 'I'm not up to it.'

'Sure, you have nothing to do. I'll be gentle. It's right that we should make up in this way. I need to, so I do. Just lie back and let me undress you.'

'Please, Shamus. I – I can't.'

'Is it that you are refusing me, your husband that I am? Well, I'm telling you that I'm going to be having you, so stop your protests and lie back.'

The note in his voice, which she'd heard many times, made her do as he bade. He kissed her bruises, and hurt her lips as he pressed his against them – mistaking her moans of pain for those of pleasure. 'That's right, me darling, it is that you're wanting it, too. Oh, me Ella, I love you, and I'll not be hurting you again.'

Feeling defeated, Ella allowed him to have his way with

her. It was as if she was dead inside, since Paulo had last made love to her; but, afraid to do anything other than show pleasure, she went through the motions, hoping it would soon be over.

When it was, Shamus's attitude changed. 'You will be telling me what it was that you burned, Ella. There's nothing as sure as that. I need to know.'

'It was nothing. You made me angry, so I wanted to taunt you. It was only shopping lists, and bits of notes I'd made as to what we might need. A letter from a friend, that's all.'

'And what friend would that be then?'

'A girl that I met, who was also nursing during the war. She lives in . . . in Belgium.' Just in time, Ella changed her mind about being truthful. She didn't want Shamus to know too much about anyone she loved.

He was quiet for a moment. His eyes scrutinized her, but Ella was practised at lying now, and showed no sign that would make him suspect her.

Thinking she'd got away with convincing him, Ella relaxed as Shamus left the bed. She averted her eyes as, still naked, he walked round to her side of the bed. 'If I'm for finding that you're lying, I'll see that you regret it.'

As he left the room, Ella placed her weary, painful head back on the pillow. And though she tried not to cry, a cold tear traced a path down her cheek.

By Thursday morning Ella knew that getting out of going to the funeral was impossible. Though her eyes were not swollen, they were bloodshot and her right one was surrounded by a purplish-black bruise, but they no longer smarted. Her lips were back to normal, and in herself she felt almost as strong as she did before the attack, although she still suffered from a persistent headache, which – thank goodness – had lessened in intensity.

Shamus had brought home a black hat for her, which had a veil attached that covered her face. He said he'd seen it in a shop window and had asked one of his lady tenants to buy it for him. It was a beautiful hat, and one that Ella would have chosen herself and felt proud to wear, but at this moment it represented part of the shackles that held her to Shamus's bidding.

Yesterday he had returned to work, as he called it, collecting rents and money due to him, which Ella looked on as extorting money from many who could ill afford to pay. She was left alone, though not knowing for how long, because Shamus always called back at the house to drop off what he'd collected, but he'd done so much more frequently recently, making her feel even more of a prisoner.

Restlessly she wandered around the house. Everywhere there was the distinct, unpleasant smell of death hanging in the air, as Shamus had had his mother's body brought home earlier this morning. Her open coffin lay under the window of the back parlour, a room seldom used, and which housed the very best furniture and was carpeted with a thick Persian rug that almost reached the walls. Mourners, and those who were afraid not to show their faces, would come later to pay their respects, and all would attend the funeral the next day.

Ella finally settled down at the table in the front room. Shamus had told her to begin the job of counting his money and logging the sums into the ledgers, something that usually took place in the evenings, but which he wanted out of the way before the callers began to arrive. As she piled the coins into easily counted amounts, she tried not to think of

305

the people who had been threatened or even beaten up in order to gather it all in.

She'd met some of the desperate people who called at the house frequently, asking for loans; and some begging to be given a little extra time to pay the money back. Unless they came while Shamus was out, Ella wasn't allowed any interaction with them; and if she did deal with them, she was under strict instructions about what to say. Not that she could ever threaten anyone, let alone the destitute. Instead she would ask them to do all they could to pay at least some small amount back, each time Shamus called. And counsel them that it would be possible to do so, if they would only take one less drink and put less tobacco in their rolled-up cigarettes.

Just as she had most of the coins piled up, a knock on the door startled her. All callers – as they were only of the kind who were connected to Shamus's business – knew that they had to use the back door. This was a knock on the front door.

Unsure what to do for a moment, Ella rose. The front door led straight into this room and she dared not let anyone in here, with the table covered with piles of money. The knock came again, only more persistent this time. Calling out that she wouldn't be a moment, Ella rushed to the dresser, grabbed a tablecloth from one of the drawers and covered the money with it.

On opening the door, she was surprised to see a young man of around her own age standing on the step. Tall, with his hair parted in the middle and sleeked down with hair oil, which didn't disguise that he was blond, he had surprisingly dark eyebrows and brown eyes that usually went with much darker hair. Handsome in a rakish kind of way, he was smartly dressed, which marked him out as different from the usual customer. His voice, when he spoke, told of a well-educated man, as he asked if this was the residence of Shamus McMahon.

'It is. But he isn't at home at present. Who shall I say called?'

'Forgive me, ma'am, but have you been in an accident?'

The unexpected question threw Ella for a moment. It seemed such a bold thing for a stranger to ask, but made the lie of having been hit by a vehicle as she crossed the road easier to tell than having him stare at her, and her stammering to explain.

'I'm very sorry to hear that, although the injuries you have do not detract from your beauty.'

Ella was even more flummoxed by this. 'P – please, just state your business, and leave me your name and how you can be contacted, and Mr McMahon will get back to you.'

'Oh, I was hoping that you might be able to help me. You see, my plight is rather urgent. I owe money to a bounder who fleeced me at cards last night. He said he was returning to collect tonight, and if I didn't have the money, he would set his cronies onto me – I have been told that he is deadly serious. I don't have the money to pay him. I've never come across this before. I usually write an IOU and honour it as soon as I can, but I don't mind telling you, I'm scared out of my wits.'

There was something about him that Ella liked and this emboldened her to reprimand him. 'Well, perhaps you will think better of gambling in the future. Tell me, how did you come to knock on my door? You are not my husband's usual type of customer.'

'I was desperate, so I asked around and was told that a moneylender by the name of Shamus McMahon lived here.'

'Well, you would be better served facing your fate with the hustler than getting into the clutches of Shamus McMahon. I think you should turn around and go back to where you came from.'

'Please, ma'am. These men are not to be tangled with. I was told that they killed one young man.'

Ella could see that he was genuinely afraid as he said this. And out of the blue, an idea came to her that she could help him; and maybe, just maybe, he could help her, too. 'What is your name?'

'Arnold Smith-Palmer. Though everyone calls me Arnie. I'm a law student, in my final year of six long years of study. Years that were interrupted by me having to go to war. I have a monthly allowance from my father, which I have drawn on rather heavily, and Father has clamped down on me drawing from it again this month. He is making me wait until next month, and I daren't go to him and plead my case. He has threatened to take me out of college and make me work in his shoe factory, if I don't knuckle down. I can think of nothing more appalling. And yet if he withdraws his support for me, I will have no choice but to do so. So you see, you must help me.'

Ella wanted to laugh, something she hadn't felt like doing for a long time. 'Are you trustworthy, Arnie? I mean in a general way, because obviously you're not when it comes to handling money and obeying your father's wishes.'

She couldn't believe how she was engaging with him, but oh, it felt so good to do so.

'I am, ma'am. And for you, I would go to the ends of the earth, but what is it you want to entrust me with?'

Looking up and down the street and finding it empty, Ella invited him in. Nerves clenched her stomach as she did so.

'I have a proposition to put to you – a way of earning the money you need, rather than owing it. But you will have to promise me not to breathe a word of it to anyone.'

For a moment Arnie looked nonplussed. His eyes scanned the room before falling on the bulge under the tablecloth. At the same time he took his handkerchief from his pocket and held it over his nose.

'It's all right, don't worry. I'm not going to ask you to murder anyone. The smell is that of my mother-in-law's dead body – she's lying in the parlour.'

'What? Good God!' The look that passed over Arnie's face released the laughter that had been bubbling up inside Ella.

'Oh, I'm sorry. But you did look funny, as if you thought that any minute I was going to kill you.'

Arnie relaxed as she told him that having the body of a loved one in your house the night before they were buried was a widespread practice of the Irish. 'They will have a wake tonight, with lots of drinking and frivolity, and anecdotes about the deceased. Anyway, what I'm asking of you is to be a kind of courier for me. I'm in need of help. I cannot tell you why, but I need someone to go to a mailbox that I have and bring the contents to me. But all must be done in great secrecy, especially from my husband.'

'Oh? Well, I can do that, ma'am. That is, as long as it is nothing illegal. Despite what my father thinks, I do take my studies seriously and very much want to become a lawyer. Being involved in anything criminal will thwart that.'

Ella loved the way he spoke; it was as if he had been left over from another era – a time before the Great War.

'No, it's nothing illegal, merely messages between me and a friend, and between me and my solicitor. You will be doing me a great service.' On a whim, Ella told him why. 'You see, I am here against my will, and these messages will help me to get away.'

'But that's terrible. Why can't you just walk out and leave?'

Ella explained a little; not wanting to frighten Arnie, she told him that she had married in haste, after being smitten by the handsome looks and Irish charm of Shamus, but now she was deeply unhappy and desperate to get away. 'He would hound me, so I need to leave the country. For that, I have to have everything in place. My solicitor and a friend are helping me, and I have a friend abroad to go to.' Why she was trusting this young man with this information, she did not know. It was simply the feeling that at last a chance had opened up for her, when she had been so sure that all was lost.

'Does he treat you badly? You really don't seem the kind of lady to be married to a moneylender. And, well, your injuries look—'

'Arnie, I have no time to talk. He may be home any minute. He keeps tabs on me all the time. Please, please say you will help me.'

Ella felt truly sorry to put this on the shoulders of this total stranger, but she had so few options, and he presented himself as a possible saviour of her.

'I will, of course I will do all that I can.'

'Thank you. I will write down the address of my mailbox and give you the key.' As she did this, Ella told him, 'I'll also give you a promissory note to take to my bank. They will hand you the amount written on it. How much do you need?'

'Oh, um, five pounds, please. Thank you.'

'You lost as much as five pounds on a game of cards? Shame on you, Arnie. You certainly do need to mend your ways.' It was strange how she felt so at home with him, as if she had known him all her life.

'I know. I intend to, I promise. And I won't let you down. I can see that you have been through a lot and are in need of a friend. I will be that friend to you.'

There was a silence when their eyes met. Ella felt a deep connection to Arnie and thanked God for sending him to her. She wished she could ask him to stay a while and get to know him more, but she was already fearful of him being caught here. 'Hurry now, you must go. I'm afraid that my husband may return at any moment. I'll show you out of the back door. That is the best way to come to the house, but always check the front street first, to make sure his car isn't parked there; it is a dark-red Ford. If you do make a mistake and he is in, he will answer the door, so you will just have to repeat the story you told me and make no sign that you know me.' When they reached the door, Ella caught hold of Arnie's arm. 'I don't know how to thank you. But please be careful.'

Arnie smiled down at her. 'Smith-Palmer to the rescue, ma'am.'

'Call me Ella. My name is Ella.'

'What a lovely name for a lovely lady. I want to know all about you, Ella. Fate has brought us together, but somehow I think it was meant to be.'

Ella stood staring at the door after it had closed. She had the strangest feeling. Part of it was fear, but for the rest, she couldn't understand at all what had taken hold of her, and held her still. But suddenly fear took precedence over all other feelings, as the realization of what she'd done truly hit home. *What was I thinking? Oh God, what have I done? I've entrusted the only mailbox key I have – my connection with Rowena – to a complete stranger! And much more, I've told him I need to escape Shamus.*

After a million prayers of hers going unanswered, Ella prayed once more to God to help her. And it came to her to ask Him to keep Arnie safe, too.

Chapter Thirty-One

By the time Monday came round, Ella was in a state of nerves. Shamus had left the house early, and although she'd said she might take a walk, he'd warned her not to.

'If you're not here when I come back, that will be it. I've had enough, so I have. You're cold towards me, and it is that I feel like you are for hating me. Things have to change, Ella.'

'But I want to visit my son's grave. I haven't been in an age.' She daren't mention Paulo's, too, even though Shamus knew they were in the same plot. To mention Paulo was to ask for trouble.

To her surprise, Shamus softened. 'Aye, well, that's understandable. I'll be for taking you, come Sunday.'

Ella paced up and down when he'd gone. Wringing her hands, she tried to keep faith that Arnie would come, whilst praying that he did so when Shamus was out.

It was likely that he would be out for some time this morning, as he'd mentioned viewing some properties that he was interested in. A row of shops on the high street, which were coming up for auction. Most had tenants already in situ, and they came with good references from the selling landlord, as to the tenants keeping the properties in good order and paying their rent on time. Though whether they would be able to, if Shamus took over, was another matter. Already he'd scoffed at what they were paying and had said he'd need to double the rate. Ella had counselled him about this being a bad move, and he'd listened to her, but had still intimated that they would face a rise in what they paid.

The sound of the gate got Ella rushing to the back door. Through the kitchen window she saw Arnie coming up the path. Her heart stopped, then flickered and beat faster than normal. She tried to convince herself that it was because at last she would have news, but wondered at the mixture of feelings she experienced.

Opening the door, she was met with Arnie's huge smile. 'I have some letters for you, Ella. And all went well at the bank, too.'

'Thank you, thank you so much.'

'My pleasure. And may I say that you are looking much better, and very pretty.'

Ella blushed as if she were a schoolgirl. She could only manage a smile as she took the letters. 'Are you able to wait? I need to read them and act on them, and then ask you to kindly return them to my mailbox. I daren't keep them here.'

'I will of course. Is your husband not expected home yet?' Arnie's nervousness was apparent in his voice.

'No, not for a while. I'll be as quick as I can.'

'All right, only I have been hearing stories that have made me afraid for us both, if I'm caught here with you.'

'I'm sorry, I shouldn't have asked this of you, and I

wouldn't have, but for my desperate need to get away. I had no one else. It was like a miracle when you knocked on my door. I don't think Shamus will be home soon, but maybe it would be best if you stood in the shadows of the front-room window and kept an eye out, then you can make your escape out the back door if you see him coming along the street.'

Ella knew she was being reckless, but what choice did she have? Before Arnie had knocked on her door, she'd had no hope, and now she was filled with it. Opening the letter that was handwritten, she read with horror that Rowena had been visited, yet again, by Shamus:

We have to go soon, Missy Ella, we're all in agreement. Please make arrangements as soon as you can. I'll look for the post every day.
  Take care, honey child, Rowena x

Anguish filled Ella. Next she tore open the business-like envelope:

Dear Mrs Rennaise,
  We have put out tentative enquiries of an estate agent, and he is looking for the type of properties you were interested in, through his associates. There are some suitable houses – three, in all – coming up for auction very soon. Please advise as soon as you can if you wish to go ahead and bid for these. I can furnish you with information on the properties shortly.

The third envelope contained the information, and the houses sounded perfect. Although she really only needed two, the expected price that the three houses would fetch was as much as she thought she would have to pay for two. Maybe she could rent out the third one. Rowena could manage it for her. *Yes! Everything seems to be coming together.*

Scribbling as fast as she could, Ella penned letters to both Rowena and Mr Partridge. And then one to her bank, asking them to transfer funds to Mr Partridge – something she'd discussed with her bank manager, when she'd last visited the bank. And, lastly, another promissory note for a further five pounds for Arnie, along with instructions that they were to hand over twenty pounds to Rowena when she called at the bank, bringing a letter with her. Finally Ella penned a letter to Rowena giving her instructions to go to the bank with the enclosed note, and then to head at once to Birmingham and book themselves into temporary accommodation. All arrangements would be made for her, regarding the removal of her possessions to Birmingham, once everything was in place. Rowena was to write as soon as they were settled, with an address where she could be reached.

'Hurry, Ella. A car has just turned into the street. It could be him.'

'Oh God, here you are, Arnie. Please will you post all of the new letters for me, and place those you brought to me in my mailbox. And can you call again in a week's time to see if there is anything further for me? So sorry to put this on you, but you are my only hope.'

'Of course I will, and you don't have to pay me. Here, take this note back. And take care, Ella. I'll hold you in my heart until next week.'

A car door slamming got Arnie scampering for the back door. Ella stayed where she was for a moment, standing stiffly by the table, begging God to help her over these last hurdles. Just in time, she remembered to shove Arnie's promissory note into the pocket of her dress, screwing it into a ball with her hand as she did so.

The click of the back door happened simultaneously with the key turning in the front door. Ella looked up from where, a second before the front door opened, she'd sat down on the sofa.

'Did you win the auction? You weren't long.'

'I did that. And for a snip, as I was the only bidder. The fellow selling only just got his reserve, and I could tell by his face that it was as he was hoping for a lot more.'

'Oh, why was that? Is there something that other potential buyers found out, to put them off?'

Shamus turned from the table, where he was putting down various papers. 'What is it that they could know?'

'All sorts of things. That the properties are in the way of a new road scheme, for instance. The government is committed to a new programme of road-building, with the traffic getting heavier and heavier.'

A worried look crossed Shamus's face. 'And how is it that they would know these things, if indeed it was about to happen?'

Ella couldn't believe that Shamus didn't know such things. 'By searching the Land Registry, and for new works proposed. Usually a solicitor carries out this work for anyone thinking of buying a property.'

'If it is that you are so well informed, how is it you haven't told me before?'

'I assumed you did your business through a solicitor. I had no idea that you didn't.'

'No. It is that we deal in cash, as you see from the room in the attic with its strong boxes. And all our transactions are for being done the same way. We see, we like and we buy, in cash.'

Ella was glad of this distraction, and felt certain Arnie was well on his way, undiscovered. But to make sure, she continued counselling Shamus that this was no way to carry on his business. 'Have you never thought about if you have a fire here, and your boxes are burned to ash? All your money will be, too. And how can you protect yourself from being duped, if you don't have the proper searches done and do everything lawfully? I think it is time you sought advice on your affairs, Shamus. What was good enough for your mother, and generations of your family, may not be good enough for you today.'

'Will you help me with that? As I am seeing the powerful truth of it.'

Ella hadn't expected this. 'Of course I will. I can make an appointment at the bank on the high street and discuss your business with the manager, and I'll engage a solicitor to make sure all your transactions concerning your property holdings are in order.'

'And how much will all of that be costing me?'

'The bank will take charges and commission, and I will have to get quotes from the solicitor. But you can expect a hefty bill of a hundred pounds or more, in the first instance, as you have the deeds to so many properties that will need registering in your name. You may need a business name, too. And an accountant. Now don't look like that.'

Shamus's face looked as though it was going to explode.

'You should be running your business properly. You will be safe then and protected, and so will your assets.'

As she said this, his face changed as if a truth had dawned

on him. 'Come here, me little darling. Isn't it that I knew you would be useful to me one day, eh?'

Ella found herself smiling at this. Part of it was relief that she'd got away with Arnie having visited, and part of it was a genuine feeling of amusement at the childlike nature of Shamus at times. She went willingly into his arms.

'Now, that is for doing me heart good, to have you come to me in a way that tells me you want to.'

'Well, it isn't often you give me the respect you did just now. And if you go ahead with my suggestion, then I will be of use and can get outside the house, which feels like my prison.'

'Ah, so the truth comes to light. Well, if that is all you are doing it for, you can forget it.'

'Shamus, you are being ridiculous.' But something in Ella clicked, and she could see now that she had played him the wrong way. She needed to change that. She needed to make him believe in her. 'I'm your wife. Of course I have an interest in your business, and in you. I see you struggling to run everything on your own. Oh, I know you have your cronies, but I don't want anything to do with that side of your business. But look how I made the books balance for you, on the day of your mother's wake. And I have the advantage of an education that would be useful to you. You could come with me, if you didn't trust me out on my own. But, Shamus.' At this point she made herself look up at him, and put a kindness and a fondness that she didn't feel into her eyes. 'I want us to get on a better footing. I want to be different. I've realized what you have given me. If it wasn't for you, I would be in a workhouse.'

A genuine feeling came over her at that point. It was prompted by the thought of the workhouse, and what her

319

fate would have been, and she leaned into Shamus and reached up to kiss his cheek.

'Oh, Ella. Me Ella. If I was having the time, I'd take you to our bed, so I would.'

Hating herself, Ella whispered, 'Can you not make the time, for me?' Again she kissed his face and then snuggled into his body.

His voice held a deep-throated sound as he said her name and took her hand. 'That this day should come, me little Ella. Come on, then. Let's take the stairs to heaven.'

Ella fought the tight knot in her stomach. She had to be willing; she had to try to be how she'd been with Paulo. *That's it. I'll imagine it is Paulo making love to me. Forgive me, Paulo. I have to do this, I have to get Shamus eating out of my hand, then my plan to escape and reclaim our little Paulo may have a chance of succeeding.*

With her imagination showing her Paulo, Ella gave her all to the love-making with Shamus: eagerly helping him to undress, caressing him as he did so, and willingly accepting his caresses as he undressed her. To her surprise, she began to enjoy the experience, to want more . . . and more. Until she begged Shamus to take her. *This is it! This is what I needed, to be made love to, by my Paulo.*

When Shamus entered her, everything burst into the most sensational feelings that she'd not felt since Paulo. Gasping, Ella had to force herself not to cry out Paulo's name, because to her, this was him making love to her, kissing every part of her, caressing the very heart of her woman-hood, and giving her such pleasure that she wanted to holler out to the world. When finally she came down, and Shamus lay with her, the tears began to flow.

Shamus moved gently inside her. 'Are those tears of joy,

my Ella, for isn't it that I am weeping the same tears with you.'

Though she was now back in the real world, Ella kept up her subterfuge. 'Yes, yes, Shamus. You have given me so much joy, so much.'

With this, his movements quickened and within seconds he was hollering out his own release. And Ella accepted this final quelling of the fire that had burned inside her.

Shamus lay close to her, his head on her breast, wetting her with his tears. 'It is that this is the best day of me life, Ella. From now on, everything will change. And I'm hoping, now that you are willing, that you'll soon be presenting me with me first son, to be me heir.'

This thought shocked Ella. *Oh no. That's the last thing I need. Why haven't I thought of that before? And more so, why hasn't it happened before now? Shamus has hardly let a day go by, but for my monthly days, when he hasn't taken me – and sometimes twice, straight after each other – and always he comes inside me.*

Glad that it was so, that no pregnancy had occurred, Ella did begin to wonder if it would make a difference that she'd now been willing, and yes, had enjoyed the experience and been so aware of receiving his seed this time. *I hope, with all my soul, that it doesn't.*

And as the prayer died, she knew there might be many more times when it could, because the awful truth dawned on her that she wouldn't be resisting Shamus again. Her body had awoken once more to the joys of coupling with a man, and she knew it wouldn't let her go back into the cold, frigid shell it had been in.

This thought brought its own guilt – the guilt of betrayal – as she had given away to another man a precious part of herself that had belonged to Paulo; and with Paulo in his grave for less than twelve months.

'That was a powerful shudder – are you for being all right, me darling?'

She couldn't go back on her plan with Rowena. And it would be easier to carry it through with Shamus being amiable towards her. She had the key to that now. She had to play up to his obsession with her, and not fight it. 'Yes, it is just a reaction after your love-making to me.' And another lie, to give this one credence: 'I have never experienced feelings like that before, Shamus.'

Shamus didn't speak, but a small groan came from him and he held her tighter. Ella allowed his caressing of her and felt hatred for herself and what she was capable of as, once more, Shamus became aroused, and she didn't resist, or want to.

Chapter Thirty-Two

Three weeks had passed, in which Ella had made peace within herself as she focused on what the ultimate outcome would be, rather than the means by which she was planning to achieve it. At times she felt she was prostituting herself, but then would justify this with how much more in command she was of her destiny, and of Rowena's.

A letter had arrived that had eased her mind and paved the way for her to leave, in the not-too-distant future. She just needed to finalize everything, and get Rowena properly settled. The letter, delivered from her mailbox by Arnie, had told of the family moving to Birmingham. And Rowena had written of her joy, because at last her Tobias was going to retire:

> With the younger men in our family not having to pay rent, they are going to pool the money they earn and take care of us. They went to Birmingham a week before us and found good digs for us.
>
> My menfolk are in work already, and working on the railways and labouring in the building trade, and one

is working as a cleaner in the car factory. Them's all
happy, and making more money than they did here.
And they say they are treated better. Not as equals, but
with more respect. So, Missy Ella, it is a good thing that
you do for us.

And we went to see them houses you have in mind for
us, and them's lovely. There are some of our countrymen
living nearby and they are real friendly. It's like the
community we have, back home.

We have all our things with us, as we packed them all
up and the boys took them on the train with them. They
had to sit in the guard's van, but they said that was
comfortable, as they sat on the bags of my cushions.

None of the furniture is mine, it all belongs to Flora.
I have written to her and told her everything, and have
given her your address, at your mailbox. I enclose my
address.

Take care, Missy Ella x

Ella put Rowena's address in a coded form in her notebook, using numbers for letters.

Arnie had also brought a letter from her solicitor, telling
her that he had received the money and that everything was
set in motion to buy the houses. It seemed that the houses
were part of a slum-clearance scheme. Because of the intense
industrial nature of Birmingham, which had mushroomed
over the last century to a level that required a lot of housing,
many people lived in back-to-back terraces. Even the middle
class, although their houses were bigger and had better sani-
tation. It was three of these houses that were up for auction.
Previously owned by a button-making business, they had
housed the administration staff of the factory.

Now a massive building project was under way to provide better and less-crowded housing, but this row of houses was to survive and had come up for auction. Ella liked what she read about them and felt at ease that Rowena was safe, and that her family would be together, and happy.

It was a relief to her, too, that Arnie no longer needed to come to her home. On his last visit to her he had brought her another key to her mailbox, having had a second one cut. They'd come to this arrangement so that she could take over collecting her mail, and yet keep in touch with Arnie, by leaving him notes in the mailbox, and him leaving them for her, too.

Arnie's relief at not having to come to her home had compounded Ella's guilt about the danger she had put him in. But she rejoiced that they were still going to keep in contact and would meet up occasionally.

And now that possibility would soon become a reality, as Shamus was trusting her more and more. She'd already had one meeting with the bank and with a solicitor, on his behalf, and he had accompanied her to meet the accountant. He'd shifted most of his money into a bank account and grumbled about the prospect of having to pay taxes, which was not something he'd been used to, and was why he kept one strong box still stuffed with money. She hadn't objected to this. Shamus's dealings, more often than not, required cash. Those he dealt with didn't understand the concept of cheques and bank guarantees, as a lot of their business was underhand. But she could see a more confident Shamus emerging, as he lapped up the respect that these people, who he thought belonged to a different world, gave him. He stood now, dressed in his new suit, ready to go for yet another long meeting with his solicitor, because making all his holdings legally binding in his name was taking a lot of time.

Adjusting his neckerchief, she told him, 'There, you look the proper businessman. That suit we bought you is perfect, and you look very handsome.'

His hand smacked her bottom, then tightened on her bottom cheek. 'It's all down to you, me little Ella. You've lifted me place in the world, so you have. Ha! Me bank manager shook me hand yesterday.'

'Did he now.' Ella loved how proud Shamus was of these little things, which were commonplace to most other businessmen.

'Aye, it was like I'd been greeted by the King, so it was. I was as proud as a peacock.' He planted a kiss on the top of her head, then pulled her into his huge body. 'I love you, me Ella. And I long for the day you tell me you love me. It is that you act now as if you do, but you never say the words, and that keeps me heart sore.'

Taking a deep breath and mentally crossing herself, something she had been taught as a child – she could hear the words now: *If you are forced to tell a white lie, then cross yourself first, to show the Lord that's what it is, and that you have to do it* – Ella looked up into Shamus's eyes and said, 'I am coming to love you. And if things continue how they are between us, with you beginning to trust me and give me more freedom, then I think my feelings will deepen for you.'

'That will be a good day, so it will. But isn't me love-making helping? Sure it is that you're for telling me I take you to places you'd never dreamed of, and you're loving it.'

Ella's face coloured, as much from the truth of what he said as from embarrassment. Coupling with him was something her body betrayed her on, as she longed for it to happen and wallowed in the sensations he gave her. This weakness was the deepest source of the guilt that she harboured inside herself.

'Ha! Is that you blushing, me wee one? Isn't it that you are looking prettier than ever when you blush, and you make a man feel the need of you. But I'm having to go, so I am. All these newfangled things you have me involved in are for taking me from what I really want to be doing.' His voice had deepened and his hand had cupped her breast. 'Oh, Ella, have I time enough?'

'No, you haven't.' She playfully slapped his hand away. 'Behave yourself. As much as I fancy you, in your best bib and tucker, you have a business to run.'

Shamus laughed. 'Aye, and you have some shopping to do. I've been for neglecting you, so I have. Have you got the money I gave you in your purse?'

'I have, and I've already got a new outfit in mind. I saw it in the window of Marigold's Gowns when I last went to your bank, so you can drop me off there, as that will be my starting point.'

'Sure I cannot wait to see you in it. And it is that you and I, Mrs McMahon, will go up west and have the night of our lives. I might even book us into one of those fancy hotels. Yes, I will that. For we've not had a honeymoon, and that can be it.'

'That's a few weeks away, as I will have my outfit made and there will be fittings to have, but I will look forward to it. Thank you.'

Once they were settled in the car, the idea of the trip had really taken hold of her. 'Shamus, have you ever been to a show in the West End?'

'No, them places are not for the likes of me.'

'Of course they are, you are a rich and successful businessman. You are exactly the type of man who goes to the theatre.'

'But I'm not sure I will be liking it. Sure, I like the craic and used to enjoy a sing-song down the local Irish pub, but a show is out of me depths.'

'Well then, we'll have to do that: go for a sing-song. I love to hear your voice when you sing in the bath, and the songs you sing are sometimes very funny, and at other times nostalgic. We should have more fun.'

What had prompted this from her, Ella didn't know. She was used to everything she said to Shamus, and did with him, being part of her ultimate plan, but saying this had been spontaneous, as if they really were a couple. That was the wrong path to go down. She'd have to be more careful.

Shamus took up her idea and talked of nothing else, even singing her one of his funny Irish songs, 'Paddy McGinty's Goat'. Ella laughed out loud at the lyrics and especially at the last line, which spoke of an angel with a beard being Paddy McGinty's goat!

'Oh, Shamus, you Irish are so funny.'

'Ah, but that's not a song that came from Ireland. It was written a few years ago, by a pair of Englishmen who call themselves "The Two Bobs".'

This really creased Ella. 'Bob' was a term for a shilling, and the thought of two composers calling themselves that, on top of hearing the words of the hilarious song, undid her.

'I love your laugh, so I do, me Ella.' Shamus's voice became serious then. 'It is that I did wrong by you, and I'm heart-sorry, so I am. I was used to taking what I want, whether or not I was entitled to it. I was for looking at you when you came to see to me mammy, and I knew you were the one for me. There can be no one else. But sure it is that I did a terrible thing, kidnapping you – and you just having lost your husband.'

Ella didn't know what to say. She sat staring out of the window. For Shamus to apologize in this way was a huge thing for him, and showed how far he'd come as a man since she'd changed her ways with him.

'And, Ella, it is that I did an even worse thing, making you give your child away, when you had already lost a babby in the past. Can you find it in yourself to forgive me, Ella?'

She cringed against the feeling inside her that wanted to claw and scream at him that she could never forgive him. The moment gave her clarity. For somehow she'd slipped into the comfortable place she'd made for herself with her deceit, and had begun to let some feeling for Shamus creep into her. But now he had reminded her of the hateful things he was capable of, and she was back in her own skin. She knew for certain that she still hated this man.

'Ella, is it that my meaning to make things right has upset you again? I wasn't for meaning to do that. I'm wanting to clear the air between us, so I am.'

Inside her a voice yelled, *You can never do that!* But she swallowed hard and said, 'The memory of it all is still raw. I – I thank you for apologizing, but I can't yet forgive and forget. I'm just trying to live with it all. You being sorry will help that.'

Not a word of this was meant, but Ella knew she mustn't damage all that she'd worked towards.

Shamus's hand touched her leg. 'How can I make it up to you, for it is that I am a different man from the beast that did that to you. What if I went to Poland with me boys and we snatched your child back? Would that help? I would love him like those sons you are going to give me, and work for him as I do for me own.'

This shocked Ella. How much a man could change. Was it really possible? Could it be so?

Her heart thudded. Could she sacrifice her own plans to get her child back? Yes, she could. 'Would you really do that for me, Shamus?'

'I would, me darling. I'm in a state inside me as to what I did to you. I've thought about it this good while, so I have.'

She had to take up this offer, she had to. Yes, it would mean her life would be shackled to Shamus, but as things were, that wouldn't be a bad thing, and she could keep improving them little by little, couldn't she? And having her Paulo with her would fill any emotional gaps that remained inside her.

'If you do that for me, then I will love you forever, and will be the wife that you dream me to be.'

Shamus pulled into a lay-by and turned to her. 'Oh, Ella, me little darling, I've been a fool, so I have. Tell me that you can forgive, and can come to love me as I love you.'

'I can, Shamus. I truly can. Without my son, I am only half a person, unable to give of my whole self. You will make me complete by reuniting us. I will have my child, my memories of my loved ones, and a good husband to care for me and our future children. That is all that I can ask for in life.'

'I want to kiss you, Ella. Lean yourself towards me, me darling – come into me arms.'

Ella did as he bade and found an answering emotion in herself. As they came out of the kiss – and in complete contrast to what her feelings had been a few minutes earlier – she told him, 'I love you, Shamus.'

His eyes filled with tears.

As they drove the rest of the way in silence, Shamus with one hand over hers, Ella knew that she could live her life out with Shamus, and be happy, as her heart sang with the joy of soon having her child back in her arms.

On reaching her mailbox, Ella was nonplussed to find a note from Arnie, saying that he was missing her and wanted to meet up with her as soon as possible. If she was to make her future with Shamus work, then she had to put Arnie out of her life. She would have to meet him to tell him that, as he had been so kind to her.

There were three more letters for her. One was from Rowena, distinguishable by the scrawl that almost covered the envelope. Reading the letter gave Ella a good feeling. Her friend was safe and happy, but wanted to know when she could move into her house.

Then there was a welcome letter from Mr Partridge, saying that the sale had gone through and the houses were now hers, but Ella would need to sign a number of papers. Could she make an appointment, at her earliest convenience? It appeared that the houses were sold to her at half what she had expected to pay.

At last. Now she could relax, and stay if she wanted to, or leave. She was free.

The third letter was from Flora, who expressed her worry about all that Rowena had told her, and pleaded with Ella to contact her soon:

I understand that you had to get Rowena out of my house, but I am very upset by it, as I had given her the house for the rest of her and Tobias's days. However, I

331

know that you will look after her, and my heart goes out to you, my dear Ella. I cannot wait for the time when you come to me. It will be so wonderful to have you here.

We are faring well, but have had a setback, which Rowena tells me she explained to you.

I do have something to tell you. Please don't think badly of me, but I found out something very shocking, just before we came to France. I won't tell you in this letter, as it is something I need to tell you when we are together. And that won't be long, now that you have Rowena safe and sound.

My house is to be let. Cyrus has contacted our solicitor there, and he is seeing to it immediately.

My thoughts and prayers are with you, my dear friend. Remember all that we went through in Brussels, and in Dieppe. We got through that, so you can get through this.

Cyrus sends his love.

I am your loving friend, Flors x

Confusion held Ella still for a moment. Her future had looked set an hour ago, but with this letter, she wasn't so sure. And what was it that Flors needed to tell her? A deep sigh left her body as she walked over to the counter, where a space was made for customers to write. There was some paper and a pen to hand.

Ella wrote quickly to her solicitor, telling him that she would come to see him in two days' time, thinking that surely now Shamus would trust her to go on an errand on her own. She would tell him that she had a fitting for the outfits she intended to buy today.

In the letter she asked that Mr Partridge contact the agent

who had dealt with the sale of the houses to her, and get him to arrange for a furniture store in Birmingham to allow Rowena to buy what she needed, and to send the bill to her, at Mr Partridge's address. And then for him to settle the bill and his own costs out of the amount she had transferred to him, before transferring the rest back to her account.

After that, a note to Arnie to meet her in Kensington on the same day:

There is a tea shop just around the corner of Westbourne Grove and Kensington Park Road. I will meet you there on the afternoon of Thursday, 25th October.

The letter to Rowena was very short, telling her the information regarding the agent, and where she could pick up the keys. She was to pick whichever house they each wanted, and then the agent would give her the address of a furniture shop where she could buy all she needed.

With this done, and all safely in her mailbox, Ella decided she would delay writing to Flors, as she really didn't know what she was going to do. She would wait until she had a more definite plan in her mind.

Sipping tea in the cafe where she and Shamus were to meet, Ella felt pleased with how the day had gone. She had ordered three elegant dresses and a costume. Being so small, she had to have each one made for her, but this pleased her, as she would have plenty of excuses to go out alone.

Sitting back, she gazed out of the window at the shoppers traipsing the high street, and wondered what it would be like to be truly free. Had she ever been? It seemed a long, long time since her decisions were based entirely on what she wanted to do. In the Red Cross she had to obey orders; and then in her marriage to Paulo, everything relied on and was planned around his health – a shackle she would gladly take on again, if she could. And now? Yes, for all her joyful thoughts, and for all it looked as if everything was going to get better, she was still a prisoner.

Shamus's hold over me now is the possible return to me of little Paulo. Oh, what a worthy sacrifice. But what will happen if I do get him back? Yes, what then? Will I still want to leave Shamus? With a sigh, Ella had to concede that she didn't know the answer.

Chapter Thirty-Three

There was excitement in Ella as she boarded the Underground to take her to Kensington. She hoped Arnie had picked up her note and was able to meet her. But she had to admit that a lot of what was making her feel excited was the freedom she'd gained.

As she'd hoped, Shamus hadn't objected to her going out to have a fitting for her dress, and she'd even persuaded him to allow her to take time to shop for shoes, gloves and handbag, as well as a new coat. He was looking forward to taking her away for their honeymoon, and said he was planning to fetch her child back in time for Christmas, as that would be his present to her.

Not being a well-travelled man, he wanted Ella to go with him to Poland, plus the two men he intended to take along. This made sense, as she spoke the language, and it would mean that she would be able to care for her child on the return trip. It worried her that what they were proposing to do was illegal, and posed risks for them all, let alone her child; but her need to have Paulo with her was so strong that she was willing to do whatever it took.

And she could benefit from the need to shop for her child, as it would mean she'd have an excuse to make even more trips out of the house. All in all, there was a lot for Ella to look forward to now, and all the despair she had suffered had left her and been replaced by hope.

Turning the corner into Westbourne Grove, Ella saw Arnie sitting in the window. He looked so handsome that for a moment she caught her breath. Seeing her, he waved and smiled, and then stood up as she entered the cafe.

'Ella! So lovely to see you, and in a place where we needn't be afraid and can relax and get to know one another.'

Ella smiled. But under the smile was sadness that they could never get to know one another, and that their friendship had to end.

Their talk was of nothing in particular, both asking questions, both showing shyness about their situation, until Arnie asked, 'Have you something on your mind, Ella, or are you still feeling afraid?'

'I'm sorry, Arnie. Yes, there is something. Since we last met, a lot has changed . . .' When she'd finished telling him how much kinder to her Shamus was being, she said, 'And that isn't all. You see, I have a child.'

Arnie was quiet as she told him about her life, from marrying her beloved Paulo to losing him.

'My poor Ella. That is appalling. How have you borne such loss? And then Shamus McMahon kidnapped you! And how terrible that he made you give your child away. How could he have such a hold over you that you went through with it all?'

'I can't tell you that, but believe me, giving my child away was my only option. Yes, I accepted money from my relatives, but that was to get me out of the threat that held me to Shamus and motivated my actions. But, like I say, everything has changed. Shamus has changed, and I believe that if I can get my baby back, I could make a life with him.'

'No! I mean, please don't, Ella. You have heard that a leopard never changes its spots, haven't you? And people as evil as Shamus do not change. Yes, he can be nice at times, but if you cross him, then—'

'But don't you see? That is what I am trying not to do, by asking you not to see me in the future. I will always remain grateful to you, and you will have a special place in my heart, but we must stop seeing each other – we must.'

'Ella, I don't know if I can. I am . . . well, I am more than fond of you. I'm sorry, I shouldn't have said that. Oh, I don't know, maybe I should. Didn't the war teach us all not to rest on our laurels, but to grab all the chances that came our way? If anything at all came out of that carnage, it was that surely? And you don't need Shamus in order to get your baby back; in fact it might be disastrous to have him do so. I have heard some really bad things about him, which even include murder! What if things get out of hand, and your sister or her husband – or, God forbid, your child – gets hurt? From what I have heard about it all so far, there is a legal route you can go down.'

'I know all that you are saying, but, Arnie, English law won't stand in Poland. And I am fearful that something could go wrong with what Shamus proposes to do, but it is my only way. I have to do this.'

'At least keep our friendship going, Ella. I won't be able to bear it, not knowing how you are and what is happening. We will be careful. I can't imagine that Shamus's dealings bring him to this part of London, so how is he ever going to find out?'

'Oh, I don't know. I don't want to end it. You have done so much for me. You'll never know how much, but I'm afraid for you as well as for me.'

'You are worth a little danger, Ella. And something tells me that you may need a friend in the future. I will always be that to you. And, in my heart, much more, but I will never pressurize you or ask more of you than you are willing to give.'

A hot flush burned Ella's cheeks. Her mind went to Paulo, as it did so often. It seemed such a short time since she had lost him. And her grieving for him had to be done while she was going through what she'd never dreamed she would have to do. It had been a lonely and lost time. Her heart still ached for Paulo, and yet here she was, forming new friendships and going willingly to the man who'd violated her. Would Paulo hate her for it all?

She looked up at Arnie and saw love for her in his eyes – not a taking kind of love, but a giving and unselfish love, and she knew in that moment that Paulo would have wanted this for her, and would want her to take hold of it and nurture it and keep it safe, for when she might need it.

'Thank you, I accept what you are offering me. I will keep in touch through the mail box, and will let you know what is happening in my life, and I want to hear what is happening in yours. More than that, I can't promise; not at the moment I can't.'

Arnie's hand reached out and took hers. The touch sent a nice feeling trembling through her, as if it was meant to be. But then she came to her senses and told him, 'I have to go now, Arnie. Take care. You are a special friend to me.'

His face held disappointment, but then lit up in a grin. 'Until the next time, for as sure as the world is round, there will be another time when we will meet.'

'I hope so. I really do.'

With this, Ella left. But she knew she wasn't the same Ella who had gone into the cafe, determined to end the friendship; something had happened between herself and Arnie that would last a lifetime. She wouldn't put a name to it, she couldn't, as that would mean letting him into her heart. She would just know it for now.

That evening, while she and Shamus sat eating their dinner – Shamus had taken well to eating their main meal in the evening, after all his life having his dinner at midday and then supper later on – they discussed further the ways in which they could get Ella's child home.

'It is that you have to admit, me darling, that the only way is for me and me two men to snatch him. You show us how to get to the street where they live, and then we will take it in turns to watch the activity of the household. That way, we can be making a plan and then, on the fourth day of being there, we put it into action. We'll have a carriage waiting for us and will get straight back to you at the lodgings. You must be ready, as we'll have to be going straight to the train station to begin our journey home. Timing will be the thing, so it will. Everything must be done at a time that will see us able to get away as fast as we can.'

'But what do we do about my baby's papers? We will need his certification of birth. Oh, it all sounds impossible, and yet we must find a way – we must.'

'Have you any idea what the papers they issue in your country look like?'

'Yes, I have my own, and my nanny's. But how can that help?'

'Everything can be copied. I have a tenant in a small workshop who earns his living from printing material, and he is an artist, too. If I can take your papers to him, sure he can produce like for like, with a few alterations. You write down all the details of the child's birth, and everything that will need changing on your papers to make a set for the child.'

'Oh, Shamus, I really feel we can do it. My baby is really coming home.'

'He is that. And the more I think of it, the more I'm getting used to it, and getting myself to a place where I am ready to welcome him, for your sake.'

'Thank you, Shamus. I can't believe how you've changed. I'm seeing a different side to you, though I still hate the way you conduct your business.'

'Business is business. Do you think it is that I would get a return on me investments if I was soft-handed with me tenants, and those that borrow money from me? No, they'd twist me out of every penny I have.'

Ella didn't like to think about the tactics Shamus used to frighten, or even hurt, those who couldn't pay their dues. She didn't think she would ever change that, but she hoped to gradually make him see that he put too high a demand on people, and that if he lessened their burden he would still get his money; it would just take longer. 'You won't use violence when you snatch little Paulo, will you, Shamus? You mustn't hurt anyone. You have to promise me that.'

'I will do me best, but if it is that we are challenged and there is a scuffle, then I'll have to be defending meself, so I will.'

Ella worried about this, but had to accept that her child wasn't simply going to be handed over.

'You make the arrangements when you are ready; you know the days that I am committed elsewhere, and the days that me activities can be more flexible.'

'I'll need to be prepared. We will need to have a nursery ready for him. I thought to use the room next to our bedroom for that purpose.'

'Me mammy's room? Sure, it is too soon to be clearing her out. No, it will have to be the spare room opposite ours. There's nothing much to move out of that one, just a chest of drawers and a bedstead. I'll get that done for you tomorrow.'

Shopping for her son gave Ella so much pleasure, and by the end of the week she had the spare room just how she wanted it. Luckily it was in good order, so it hadn't needed redecorating, only some fresh curtains and a large rug to cover the brown linoleum on the floor. A wooden cot was now in situ, and she'd kept the chest of drawers, which Shamus had been going to move out. It was one of the better pieces of furniture in the house. Made of light oak, each drawer had a row of roses carved into it, and its legs were curved and looked as if they had shoes on, as they ended in a ballshape. The washstand had been brought in from Shamus's mother's room, and the nursing chair that Ella had purchased stood next to this, under the window.

Looking at the room filled Ella with a warm feeling, though she dared not hope too much.

Buying clothes was a little bit more difficult, because not knowing how big her baby had grown, she was unsure. In the end she decided on a dozen nappies and two dresses, one white and the other blue, and matching cardigans, bootees, mittens and bonnets. Then there was the purchase of feeding bottles, and a magazine that had an article about the ten best things for your baby. This she had devoured, because although she had experience of nursing her darling Christophe, that wasn't how it would be this time, and she needed to learn things like the age it was safe to sit a child up rather than keep them lying down; how to swaddle them; and how to move from mother's milk to diluted condensed milk – not that she could take steps in doing this, but at least she knew what to take with her to feed her child. And, at six months old, little Paulo could surely have some of what they ate, as long as it was finely mashed for him.

Standing on the deck of the ferry sailing towards Calais two weeks later, Ella pulled her fur coat tightly around her, trying to warm her body against the icy-cold winds. The sea was choppy, but the sky was a clear winter-blue.

Memories assailed her of her time in Dieppe, and her thoughts were of Flora and Mags, and then turned to Paddy. It took her a while, but eventually she let in memories of Paulo. These hurt her the most, but talking to him helped. Lifting her face to the sky, she told him of her mission and asked him to help her.

Spray from the waves wet her face, hiding the tears that streamed down her cheeks. Shaking herself mentally, she told herself that this should be a time of happy anticipation, and she must not spoil it by dwelling on the past. She must turn her thoughts towards the future and the times she would enjoy with her son.

The rest of the journey went smoothly. Left mostly to herself, even to having a single-berth cabin, she lost herself in E. M. Forster's *Howards End*, a book that she'd found in the tiny bookshop on the high street, which she loved to browse through. The book had been highly acclaimed, and to Ella it was a wonderful find, eleven years after its publication.

At last they arrived in Poland.

'Me little Ella, it is lovely to hear you using your native tongue. Ireland has its own language, but I have never spoken it. You must really feel that you have come home.'

Shamus couldn't have uttered a more meaningful phrase, because unlike the last time she came here, Ella did feel she was at home amongst her own, and a lot of that was to do with the fact that she was treading the same soil as her son.

The next few days were nerve-racking. Just entering the street where her sister lived assailed her with emotions, but waiting for and then seeing her sister leave the house with a uniformed nanny, and a huge pram, seared her with pain.

With the right people identified, the waiting game began, as Shamus and his men took it in turns to watch the comings and goings of people who lived in the apartment building.

Ella spent hours walking around Krakow, looking in shop windows, drinking coffee in the square and walking along the banks of the Vistula. Always nervous of the possibility of bumping into her half-sister.

At last Shamus said he was ready. He sat on the end of the bed in their hotel room and told her how he intended to carry out his mission. 'It is that the nanny takes the child for a walk every afternoon at three o'clock. And, that at that time, the streets are empty of folk.'

'Yes, many have a lie-down in the afternoon, and there seems to be a natural quiet time.'

'The nanny walks to the end of the street and meets with another nanny. They then walk together for a while, their attention taken up with their conversation. Their walk follows the same path, and there is part of it that takes them away from the houses and down a lane where there are only a scattering of properties. It is here that we will strike.'

'How will you do it? You won't hurt the girls, will you? Promise me that.'

'It is that they shouldn't be hurt. We have identified where we can hide and jump out at them. We will gag them and tie their hands and feet and then take the baby.'

'But what of the other child? It'll be left helpless.'

'I need you to write a note, telling where the child and the nanny are. And I need you to hire a cab for me, and tell the cabby that he will have to wait for us at the top of the lane. Tell him that he will be paid a year's wages: half when he delivers us back here, and a quarter when he delivers the note to your sister. Patrick will go with him to do that. And to be making sure that the cabby doesn't raise the alarm before we can get away, he is then to take us to the station, where he will receive the balance. So now it is that I need you to go to the bank and exchange the money we require.'

Ella rose from the chair she had been sitting on and walked to the window. Outside, snowflakes danced in the breeze and a Christmas scene unfolded, with horses and carriages slowly negotiating the wide snow-covered street below. On the other side of the street, pine trees dressed in white, as if ready for a wedding, glistened in the weak winter sunshine. Without turning, she asked, 'Isn't that a lot of money, Shamus? And how will we find out how much it is that the cabbies are paid?'

'I'm guessing it isn't anywhere near what I earn in a week.

344

This country is on its knees. There are beggars lining the streets. As to finding out the amount, we will go to dinner in a cab tonight and you will make conversation with the driver. If you think he is the one to do the job, then you are to book him to pick us up tomorrow afternoon and, at the same time, find out what amount he will need.'

Ella's nerves jangled. It was really going to happen. She clasped her hands together.

'Sure it is that you look a picture, me little Ella: your cheeks are flushed, and I can see the excitement that's in you. Come over and lie with me, and let me be calming you.'

Ella hated herself for the feelings that took her at this. Feelings she couldn't deny. She went willingly into Shamus's waiting arms and gave herself up to the pleasure that she knew awaited her there.

In the early afternoon of the next day, with everything in place, Ella watched through the window of the hotel as Shamus and his men boarded the cab that she'd arranged for them. *Oh God, please let everything go smoothly, and don't . . . please don't let anyone be hurt.*

The hours passed slowly, but at last it was three o'clock and time for her to prepare for their departure. Summoning a porter to transport their cases down to the lobby, she took hold of the bag that carried everything Paulo would need. She'd checked and rechecked it. And a dozen things had gone through her head, concerning him. How would she know when he was last fed, or what he liked and didn't like? Did he lie on his side or on his back to sleep? Was he well, was he teething? Everything that, as his mother, she should know and didn't.

Her conscience had visited places that she didn't want to go and had asked her: what of Calek and Abram? This was going to be very painful for them, for although they might guess that she had something to do with their baby's kidnap, they wouldn't know for certain. And how frightening the experience was going to be for the nannies. And oh, how she worried about the other baby. How long would it be left with no one to attend to it?

At times she hated herself for what she was doing, and had to remind herself that although she was grateful to Shamus, and had come to be able to live reasonably happily with him, all of this was his fault. His vile threats to Rowena and her family, his not wanting Ella's child in the first place – all of it had led to this day.

But going over these things was only serving to make her feel wretched and wasn't helping anything. Her path was set, and she had to walk it the best way she could. At least she knew she had enough money to care for her baby and herself, if the need should arise, and that Rowena was safe. This knowledge lifted her, and gave her the courage she needed to continue.

At last the carriage drew up outside the hotel. Ella ran out to greet them. Shamus opened the door and stepped out. 'I'm sorry, me wee Ella. But it wasn't for going how we planned it.'

'My baby?'

'No, we haven't got him. The girls didn't appear as normal. We were for waiting and waiting, but nothing. But don't you fret. We'll not go home without your child, so we won't.'

'Oh, Shamus, how can this be? Every day they did the same thing, so why not today?'

'It is that we should have watched for a full week maybe. It could be that on some days the routine is different. I'm not for knowing. I only know they didn't show today.'

Ella had the feeling in her stomach that she was going to be sick.

'Don't go to pieces, me little Ella. We've to go about this a different way, that's all. Tell the driver to come back tonight, at around one a.m. We have checked the residence and found that entry to it is not going to be difficult. We're going to have to break in during the night and take your child that way.'

'No, Shamus, it is too dangerous. Let's try our original plan tomorrow. It may just have been the cold and the snow that prevented them going out today. I know it has been cold since we got here, but today was exceptionally so.'

'No, we go tonight. I have plans for my time at home, and it is already that I will be late for that. Besides, people are beginning to notice us and know that we are not from around here. One person even approached us today, on the pretence of asking for a light for his cigarette, and then tried to engage us in conversation. They look afraid of us. So if one of them alerts the local police, we will be done for.'

Ella was shocked at this. 'It could be that they think you are Russians. Were you followed here?'

'No, we made sure of that. Now, make the arrangements with the driver and we will talk inside. Try not to make him suspicious, although the thought of the pay packet he is to receive will probably do the trick.'

Ella walked over to the cab. Shamus had given her some money to give to the cabby, but how was she to convince him that what they were doing wasn't anything to be alarmed about?

347

'We are not going to the station, driver, not yet. My husband was expecting to meet someone today, who is an important business associate, but he didn't make the rendez-vous.' Suddenly she had the idea to use the man who had asked for a light. 'He sent a messenger that he was delayed, and so we are not yet finished with your services.'

'Are you trying to get out of paying what you promised? I don't like this. Why should I have to wait for a long time, and not talk about anything that I see? And when I do so, I am not to be paid what I was told I would be paid. Are you spies?'

'No. Please wait a moment. I do have a good pay packet for you here, but I have to speak with my husband.'

Going inside the hotel, she told Shamus how the driver was getting suspicious and wanted his money for the job he'd done.

Shamus was quiet for a moment. Ella waited, fearful of this change of events and for their safety, if people began to suspect them. Her country was in turmoil, and no one trusted anyone else.

'I can only think that we must abandon our plans and go home, Ella.'

'No. Please, no. Let's talk about it. Shamus, will you pay out more to get my child back? You know it is what our future hangs on.'

'What are you thinking?'

'Pay the cabby what we promised, then tell him that he can have the same again, if he picks us up later.'

'It is that you ask a lot of me, Ella, but yes. I just want us home and to begin the new life we've promised each other.'

Ella took the whole of the payment to the driver. For a

moment he was hesitant about returning. But the promise of extra money swayed him.

As Ella returned to Shamus, he asked her to book them into the hotel for a further night. 'We're safe here; no one suspects us as you do all the talking, and we have been careful not to make ourselves noticed.'

Once back in their room, Ella asked about the plan Shamus had, and said again that she wasn't happy about them having to enter her sister's home.

'Ella, if we are to get your wee one back for you, it has to be done tonight, and we have to be on the road as soon as we have got the child. And it is that you will have to come with us. We will need you to be telling your sister what it is that we want, unless it is that they speak English?'

Ella never thought she would have to get involved, but simply accept her child back and take him home. But now she could see that she must. 'No, they don't speak a word of English.' *Thank goodness. It would be disastrous if Shamus could understand them, as then he would surely find out about the money they paid me!* 'But they are not easy or reasonable people; they could match you, when it comes to being ruthless. They won't be frightened into giving up my Paulo.'

'What hold is it that they have over him, that we have to go to all this trouble?'

'I – I'm not saying they have a hold over him. It is just that I gave him to them willingly, and they will have been treating him like their own son. They wanted nothing to do with me when I turned up; they were only interested in me giving up my child to them.'

'And for that they gave you nothing?'

Ella could see that, although it had taken him a while to

349

think this through, suspicions were beginning to seep into him.

She had to use the old tactic of attacking, not defending. 'No, they gave me nothing. After all, I had been forced to take him to them, if you remember? I had no bargaining power. Vile threats hung over me, if I returned home with my baby.'

'Aye, well, that is the truth of it, and I've been for saying that I'm sorry.'

'Sorry isn't enough, if you are still going to make veiled accusations towards me about everything that occurs to you not being how it should be. My sister is ruthless. You know that she took my inheritance and gave me nothing. You know that she took my baby and gave me nothing. She will not give up what she wants. This won't be a matter of me telling her that I have come for my child, and that is that.'

Shamus stared at her. His eyes betrayed his temper. When he spoke, it was a relief to Ella to find that it wasn't directed at her.

'In that case, the child still has to be snatched. But we have to be in and out of there very quickly. For that, we will still need you, as you know the layout of the apartment, and even which one it is, when we manage to get inside.'

'How will you get inside? The main door is huge and heavy and has many locks.'

'To be sure there's not a door in the world that my man, Michael, cannot get through, so that isn't a worry. And if, in this instance, he can't, then he can scale the drainpipe and get in through a window. I imagine that the one above the door is over the stairs and doesn't lead directly into anyone's apartment?'

'Yes, I think that is so, as the stairs that lead to each apartment are facing the door.'

'Well then, it is as I say: getting in isn't a problem. Any lock that Michael cannot pick from the outside, he can pick from the inside. We will go in, once we know that the house has settled and the occupants are all likely to be asleep. Only you and I will go in. Michael, once he has done his job, will re-join Patrick, and they will keep an eye out along the street.'

'What about the cab driver? Won't he be even more suspicious than he must already be?'

'He can do as he has been doing – waiting at the top of the street. I think it is that we have him in our palms once more. Money has spoken to him.'

Ella sighed. There was no going back; she'd come to get her child and no matter what she had to do to achieve that, she was going to go through with it. She only hoped it all went smoothly, and they could get Paulo and leave without anyone being the wiser until the morning.

Chapter Thirty-Four

Ella couldn't believe that she was once more inside her sister's apartment when, hours later, and finding the apartment block in darkness, they were let in through the door by Michael. It seemed that no locked door could keep him out, because getting through the main door had taken him no time at all, even though he'd had to scale the drainpipe and climb through the window. He'd soon been on the other side, tackling the locks and bolts. And getting through the door that led to the apartment hadn't given him any problems at all.

Once inside, the hall was in darkness. Ella, with Shamus close on her heels, had to feel her way around until her eyes adjusted and her vision became clearer. Leading Shamus to the nursery, she couldn't believe how simple this was turning out to be. Soon she was leaning over her sleeping baby boy. Her heart jolted with pain that was mixed with joy. Paulo seemed so huge, compared to the tiny mite she had given birth to.

Lifting him gently, Ella held Paulo to her, whilst taking a soft toy that lay beside him and the blanket that had been tucked around him. Carefully she wrapped this round him and snuggled his toy close to him. She hoped that, with these familiar things, he wouldn't detect anything different and would sleep through them taking him out of the apartment.

A voice had Ella standing ridged with fear.

'Where are you going, darling?'

'Nowhere – I'm just wanting the loo. I will look in on Heniek on my way back.'

'You're too fussy for a father. Leave him to sleep; you may disturb him by opening the door and letting the light in.'

'I won't.'

Ella's whole body trembled as she saw Shamus dash to stand behind the door. From the pocket of his coat he took what looked like a truncheon.

'No, Shamus! I said that no one was to get hurt.' Ella's whisper sounded to her as if she had shouted at the top of her voice. Her blood ran cold in her veins. She clung on to her child.

A flickering light showed under the door, and the handle moved downwards. From being icy cold, Ella broke out in a sweat.

'Abram, please don't go into the nursery. Let our child sleep!'

He let out a huge sigh. 'But I heard something.'

'No, you didn't. If you wake him, I will not forgive you. He has been fractious all day. He needs his sleep.'

Abram stood for a moment, with the door ajar. Ella prayed he would do as Calek said. She closed her eyes.

The door shut. Ella listened to the sounds of Abram going across the landing and then of a door closing. Just as she was letting relief in, a noise could be heard from the other side of the connecting door – the one that she knew led to the nanny's room. Once more Ella froze, waiting to be caught out. But nothing happened. After a few moments Shamus gestured to her to follow him.

On shaky legs that she didn't think would support her, Ella kept close behind Shamus, carrying Paulo carefully. Soon they were outside and running up the street towards the cab. Once settled inside, Shamus bade her tell the driver to go as fast as he could to the station. The horse's hooves sounded like a million drummers beating their doom. No one spoke, and her little Paulo didn't open his eyes.

When they reached the station, the bitter December wind whipped Ella as she opened the taxi door. 'Wherever the next train is going, we must get on it. We have to get away from here – as far away as we can.'

'Don't panic, me little darling. You have what is rightly yours. Now pay the driver and don't let him know anything about our onward journey.'

The driver wasn't easily satisfied. 'How do you come to have a baby now? I don't like this, it is all very strange.'

'You are being paid to deliver us where we need to be, not to ask questions. Here is your money.'

'I think I am worth more. I can go straight to the police and tell them what I have seen.'

'I'll have to ask my husband. Please wait.'

Shamus listened to what Ella had to say, his face deepening with anger with each word. 'So it is that he thinks he can double-cross us, eh? Get yourself and the child away onto the station. I'll see to him.'

Ella started to protest, but Shamus was having none of it. 'We've got what you want, and it is that we've done your bidding in this, but I'm not about to take my chances on going to prison in a foreign country because of it. You'll be doing as I say, Ella.'

His attitude brooked no argument. Ella knew that she was powerless; she had little Paulo to think of, and they weren't safe yet. If only the driver hadn't been so greedy. She could understand him being suspicious of their activities, but having taken on the job and been paid what amounted to two years' wages, why couldn't he just have kept his mouth shut and gone on his way?

With tears rolling down her face, Ella walked through the doorway of the station into the lobby and waited. Her body shook with fear at what might happen to the driver and she wanted to run outside and help him, but knew it would be useless to do so, as she had no way of guaranteeing that the driver wouldn't betray them.

The three days that it took them to get back to London had been draining. Paulo had been fractious from the moment he woke, and Ella was worn out and feeling desolate. Her confidence was shaken, as she asked herself if she had done the right thing by her son. What if he never settled? What if he pined so much for those he had come to look upon as his parents that he became ill? And yes, part of her anguish was for Calek and Abram. How were they going to feel, when they found their child gone?

They would know that it was Ella who had done this to them. But then, she thought, maybe they deserved to feel a taste of the agony of losing a child they loved.

A picture came to her of what had happened: how Calek had stopped Abram from checking on his child. And Calek's reasoning that he shouldn't disturb Paulo. Was that her real reason? Or was she of the same jealous nature as her mother, and hated the attention that Abram wanted to give Paulo? After all, Paulo had shown that he wasn't easily disturbed; he'd slept right through being taken and hadn't woken until they were on the train.

These thoughts settled her, because if she was right, then Calek's jealousy would only have grown, and might have manifested itself in her coming to hate Paulo. And then what would his life have become? Having come to this conclusion, Ella's mind eased, and she set about working out a routine for Paulo. Her heart was full of love for him, and as the days went on, she saw a response in him towards her, as they bonded in the way that only a mother and her child can.

But between herself and Shamus, all was not well. The incident of the driver's fate hung between them. Ella feared the worst, because when they had thought her asleep, Shamus and his two men had joked about how Shamus had got all of his money back. Ella feared this could only mean one thing: that the driver was dead.

This hung heavily over her and, where Shamus was concerned, put a cold barrier around her. As they lay in bed together, Ella kept herself as far away from him as she could and lay stiffly, afraid that he might touch her.

'How is it that I get you your deepest desire, and am willing to be a father to your child, and yet you revert to being cold with me? I'm not for having it, Ella. You promised that all would be better than it was. And we had found a happy place together.'

'You murdered that poor driver.'

'Ella, it is that I had no choice. Wouldn't you and I be languishing in jail in Poland, if I hadn't have sorted him? He was for being to blame.'

'But it is knowing what you are capable of – I cannot

condone it. He was a husband and father. Why didn't you just take him along with us until we were safely on the boat, and then let him make his own way back?'

'Oh, it is that you can come up with solutions now, then? I didn't hear you make any protest at the time. Besides, can you imagine the cabby sitting with us and being quite happy to be taken to France, and not to try to escape or call out for help? You are for being impractical. Put it out of your wee head, me little Ella, and let us get back to how we were. It is that you should be very pleased with how I went to a strange country and snatched your baby for you.'

Ella knew he was right, and yet so very wrong. Her own confusion didn't help her.

Shamus pulled her into his arms. 'Come here, me little darling – let Shamus make you happy.' As he said this he curled his leg around her body. And she could feel his need.

Against all that she wished to feel, a spark of reaction started up inside her and she wanted to yield to him, to have Shamus make love to her and take her to a place where there was no doubt in her. Part of her was disgusted with herself that it only took his caressing to make this happen.

As Shamus lay snoring gently, having set her alight and having quelled her desire, Ella stared into the darkness. What had she become? How could the desires of her body overrule her instincts? This man lying beside her, who had a hold over her, was a wicked, evil man, she knew that, so why did she give her all to him? When Paulo was alive, there were few times they could make love, and she had accepted that. She hadn't longed for it to happen, but had been in heaven when it did. Shamus had awoken a more animal instinct in her, a passion that she couldn't deny and that she hungered for. And yes, she hated herself for it.

357

Watching him sleeping as if he hadn't a care in the world, she knew that he was a complex man. A very handsome man, and one who knew how to treat a woman and bring out the raw desire that lay in her; and one who could be very loving and caring. But in all this, she had to remember that Shamus was ruthless, if crossed. And she had to remember all the vile things he'd done. Was she really prepared to spend the rest of her life with such a man? To have her son brought up by him?

A realization hit her as if lightning had struck. *No. No! No! I have to get away from him. What has happened to me, that I could ever think I could be happy with Shamus? His threats kept me imprisoned, but I have negated them. Rowena is safe, and now I must get away, too. I have to get my baby to safety. We will go to Flors in France, as I had always planned to.*

For a moment, Ella pondered how she was going to do this. Arnie came into her mind. He would help her. Tomorrow she would leave him a note.

PART SIX
London, 1921–22

~

Ella and Arnie
A Price to Pay

Chapter Thirty-Five

Ella's nerves were on edge as she waited for Arnie to appear. Her heart longed for him to do so, but she was afraid, too, as their meeting place was a lot nearer home than when they had met before, due to her not being able to travel such a distance with the pram.

Arnie had picked up her note and had left her one saying he would do his best, but that lectures were becoming more and more important now as he neared his final exam, which would be in March.

All Ella's hopes were pinned on Arnie being able to help her get away. It was what had occupied most of her thoughts over the last two weeks since she'd finally made up her mind to leave. The fact that it was now only just over a week until Christmas had helped Ella get the freedom to leave home often to visit the shops, as Shamus could see the urgency in having to get what they needed.

The enjoyment that she should have felt hadn't been present as she'd ordered a Christmas tree, and the decorations for it, to be delivered. And then she had bought a wooden train for Paulo, and a set of painted wooden soldiers. These she'd tucked into the bottom of Paulo's pram. The huge sides to the pram and the hood served to keep him warm. He'd sat up, happily enjoying all that passed by him, but was now sleepy and leaning back against his pillow. His little face reminded Ella so much of Christophe that it hurt at times, but at others it gave her great joy that it should be so.

Finding a Christmas present for Shamus hadn't been difficult. He was becoming more and more the businessman now, and had ordered work to be done on one of the small cottages that he owned, to turn it into an office for himself. Most often he went out in a suit, rather than dressed as if ready to evict someone – or, worse, beat them up. And so she had bought him a pocket-watch for his present. On the back, she'd had her name engraved. She hadn't been able to bring herself to put anything about love on it. That would have been too hypocritical, because now that she was thinking straight again, she knew that deep down she loathed Shamus and all he stood for.

Seeing Arnie walking towards the cafe caused Ella's heart to jolt. Not painfully, but in a way that gave her the knowledge of how much he had come to mean to her. It seemed a true saying that absence makes the heart grow fonder.

'Ella! It is so good to see you. How are you? You look tired. And is this who I think it is?'

'Yes, this is my son, Paulo. I'm so happy to have him home, and yet achieving that has also brought me extreme grief and made me come to a decision. One that I am feeling the strain of.'

'I hope this decision is that you are going to leave that thug! Let's order. Tea?'

Once they were settled with their tea and cakes, and Arnie

had gently introduced himself to a smiling Paulo, Ella confirmed that what Arnie had hoped for was what she planned.

'At last – thank God for that.'

'I cannot do it alone, Arnie. I need your help.'

'Of course. I will do anything that I can. What have you in mind, and where will you go?'

Ella told him where she planned to go and then added, 'I will need so many things for Paulo, but getting them out of the house all in one go will be impossible. I wondered if we could meet on a regular basis, and each time I could give you something that I will need, and you could store it for me until I am ready to go. When that time comes, I will leave the house as if I am going on a shopping trip, but I will never go back. I will make sure that I have my train and boat tickets all ready and will just take off.'

'Oh, Ella, I am so pleased you have made this decision, as it is the right one. But how will you manage? You say that your friends live in the South of France? That's a massive journey on your own. Look, how soon can you go?'

'I hope to go in January. Maybe towards the end, that will give me time to get everything ready.'

'And time to change your mind, too. Listen, I have attended my last lecture and have six weeks off from college. I am due to begin an apprenticeship with my father's solicitor at the end of January, and then return to college to sit my final exams. I'll come with you, but we need to leave as soon as we can get on a boat. That will give me time to get there and return, in readiness to take up my position. Not that I'm looking forward to it, as I have been having second thoughts about my future. I just feel so unsettled, since the war.'

'I know. I think we all are. It is three years since it ended, and yet so many people are still displaced, and those that aren't are restless and finding it hard to settle back into the life they had mapped out for themselves.'

'That's exactly it! To be truthful, I no longer want to be a boring old solicitor. I want adventure. I want to . . . Yes, I want to sail away with you, and live my life in the South of France with you. We could set up our own wine business and— You're laughing at me!'

'No. Not at you – with you. I was caught up in your dreams.' They were silent for a moment, a time when they held each other's gaze.

'Would you live my dream with me?'

Arnie's low tone sent a shiver of delight through Ella. It was as if someone had switched on a light. And she knew that was what she wanted.

He reached out and took her free hand. 'Ella, I love you. I want to care for you.'

She couldn't speak for a moment. Her eyes filled with tears. To her, Arnie was her Paulo. It was as if Paulo was living inside him. But then she realized that no, Paulo was gone, but he'd sent someone in his place. Someone to love and care for her.

'I never thought it would be possible for me to feel as I do, so soon after my Paulo left me, but I love you too, Arnie.'

Arnie's eyes shone. 'My darling, it will be all right. You are delicate still, from the loss of your first love. And you haven't had the time to grieve for him properly. And you need time to heal from what Shamus has done to you. That beast ripped you from the life you had known. You have been lost, but now I promise you are found. I will give you time to heal, and will be with you every step of the way. We will go through it together, whatever it takes to bring you that healing, before we embark on our own relationship. I promise.'

Ella's tears spilled over and tumbled down her face.

'It's all right, my darling, that is just the process beginning. But you will have to overcome it for now. You need to be strong.'

'I don't know what to do, Arnie. I know that you're right, and I thank you for promising me time. I do need that. But you say we should leave now? What about the things I will need for Paulo? His feed, his change of nappies – oh, it won't work. I come burdened with too much for someone like you to take on.'

'You don't. No one can ask more of me than I was asked to give during the war; but if you did ask, I would give it. Let's plan to go in three days' time. I will book our passage, and you must concentrate on putting all you will need until we reach France into the bottom of your pram. Does it have a storage compartment under the mattress?'

'Yes, it does. The bottom lifts out and there's quite a big space underneath. I can get enough in there to tide little Paulo over until we have crossed the sea. But will there be a boat over the Christmas period?'

'I'll make enquiries and let you know. On the day, double up on what you wear. That is all we can take, because you are going to have to leave your home on an ordinary shopping trip and then meet me at the station. I'll make sure you have the times of the trains, but there is usually an overnight one, so we may meet around three p.m. How would that be?'

'Yes, I can do that. Oh, Arnie, can we really pull it off?'

'We can do anything we choose. We just have to be careful.'

'But what about you? Your career? Your family?'

'I will try to get back in time to begin my apprenticeship, but if I'm not back, I will assure my parents that I will return for my finals. I'll tell them that I am going on an extended holiday, and that I need a break. They will understand. My mother is always saying that I haven't had a let-up since my return from the trenches. She will be in my corner.'

'You will return here?'

'Yes. I owe that much to my parents, who have made sacrifices to put me through my law degree. And then we shall see. By then I will know whether it's simply a pipe-dream to live in France or something I really want to do with my life.'

'Whatever you decide, I will back you, my love.'

Arnie squeezed her hand a little tighter. 'You called me "my love"?'

Shyness came over Ella at this. 'I did, and you are.'

'Thank you, my darling. Thank you. Oh, if only this wasn't a public place. I so want to kiss you. I—'

'You just fucking try it!'

'Shamus!' Ella screamed as Arnie landed on his back from Shamus's punch.

'Yes, your husband – is it that you forgot that? You fucking whore!' Shamus's hand lifted in the air again and Ella cringed against the blow, as the slap knocked her onto the floor.

'Now then, now then – none of that in me tearoom.' The woman who had served them came towards them with a rolling pin in her hand and swiped out at Shamus. His yelp as the rolling pin caught his arm turned into a tirade of abuse as he shoved the woman, and then kicked out at Arnie, who was trying to get to his feet.

Ella reached for her screaming child. Her body was in shock, her mind in despair, but Paulo's wails had given her courage to rise from the floor and make sure he was safe and comforted. Holding him close, she stared in horror as Shamus lifted a chair. 'No, Shamus. Noooo!'

The woman had recovered and lunged her bulk at Shamus, toppling him and stopping him from crashing the chair down onto Arnie.

'Get out! Get out, the pair of you, while he's down. Go! Go!'

Arnie was up on his feet and grabbed Ella's arm. She felt herself compelled to run with him. Once out in the street, luck was with them as a taxi came towards them. Hailing it, they jumped in. 'Take us to two-one-five Hartford Place, please. And as quickly as you can, driver.'

Ella caught hold of Arnie's sleeve and whispered, 'Is that your home? Oh, Arnie, Shamus will follow us. Don't let him know where you live. You don't know what he is capable of.'

Arnie patted her hand. The gesture was meant to reassure, but Ella could see the fear in his face. 'Sorry, Driver, a change of direction. Can you take us to a boarding house, please, one that is not well known? We are in a hurry.' Arnie looked at Ella. In his eyes she saw a plea. He whispered, 'Sorry, needs must.' And to the driver he said, 'We have been caught red-handed by an irate husband, I'm afraid.'

'I don't want any trouble, mate.'

'No. Nor do we, so if you see a dark-red Ford motor car come up behind us, can you try to lose it? I'll pay handsomely for your trouble.'

'Who d'yer think I am – the Keystone Cops? I'm pulling

up 'ere, mate, I know that car and who it belongs to, and if that's who you're running from, I want nothing to do with it. You and your floozy can get out of me cab. Though that'll be a tanner before you do.'

Arnie paid the driver his sixpence and helped Ella out. They both glanced along the high street, but couldn't see Shamus's car. 'That cafe owner must have kept him from leaving; she was like an army all rolled into one.'

Ella gave a deep sigh. 'Thank God for her.'

'Are you hurt, Ella?'

'A bit bruised, but never mind that; we have to get out of sight. Oh, Arnie, what are we going to do?'

He pulled her into a nearby alley and then held her close, his arms around her and her child. 'My darling, I will look after you. Don't be afraid. It is what we wanted, it is just sooner than we wished for it. We'll rest for a moment out of sight. Shamus will be looking to find the taxi we jumped into. So in a way, the driver dumping us may have done us a favour.'

Although Arnie's words were brave, Ella could detect a tremor in his voice. 'Oh, Arnie, I'm so scared. He will kill us. What have I done? I should have known it was too dangerous to meet so near where I live.'

'It's done now. And as I see it, with a pram in tow, you had no choice. You couldn't lug that onto a train, or down the Underground. Let's not waste time in recriminations, as we have to think of a solution. Maybe we can start by walking to the end of the alley. We have time on our side – come on.'

Feeling tired and afraid to the very heart of her, Ella followed Arnie. The alley smelt of urine and grime. A dumping ground, it was littered with rubbish, and every step was a hazard. At the end, they found a quieter street, but neither of them had any idea which way they should go.

A man walked towards them, his head down, whistling a tuneless song. Ella froze. He had the look of Michael, one of Shamus's cronies. She turned and looked the other way. To her horror, Patrick was walking towards them from the other direction. 'Run, Arnie, run! Go! Oh God!'

'What is it?'

'Shamus's men . . . Run into that alley, and run for all you are worth, please. Please. They will kill you!'

Alerted now, the men began to run towards them. Ella felt trapped. Her whole body shook with terror.

'Please, Arnie, you're younger than them, and it is your only chance.'

'But you—'

'Leave me. Get help for me. It's the only way.'

The men were within yards of them now. Arnie began to run, telling Ella that he would get assistance to her. 'I can't bear to leave you, but we do need help. Hang on, darling. I promise you, I will come for you.'

Ella held her breath as Arnie crossed over the road and ran down the alley facing the one they'd just come from. Patrick shouted, 'I'll be after chasing him; you grab the whore, Michael!'

His words had hardly died when Ella felt her arm gripped in a painful hold that bruised her, but her fear wasn't for herself, it was for Arnie. *Please God. Please, please take care of him.*

Chapter Thirty-Six

With her wrists and hands bound, Ella was distraught not to be able to help her crying, distressed son. Nor could she soothe him by talking to him, as her mouth was bound tightly with a cloth that tasted of filth. The van she'd been dragged to and bundled into jolted her, bruising her, as its movements threw her around. She was like a bead in a baby's rattle, powerless to stop her body tumbling from side to side; and helpless to stop the same thing happening to her child, who now lay on the van floor, his blanket no longer wrapped around him, exposed to the bitter cold.

At last the van stopped. Within minutes the doors were flung open. 'So, we have her. That's good, so it is. For now she'll learn that no one crosses Shamus McMahon.'

Ella looked up into Shamus's face and saw a different man from the one she'd almost allowed herself to love. Now he wore a mask of pure evil, as his hand grabbed her hair. Agony shot through her. Tears sprang to her eyes with the intensity of it. Trying to get a grip with her feet, Ella was desperate to take the pressure off her hair, but she couldn't. Shamus dragged her limp body by it, heading towards what looked like a barn. The excruciating pain in her head prevented Ella from speaking. But she felt dread to settle in her. Where was this? *How will Arnie find me? How?*

Inside, the barn smelt of horses. Ella's feet slid in their excrement, and the stinking dung clung to her frock. At last Shamus let go of her hair. She slumped in a heap as sobs racked her body. Snot ran from her nose. Gasping in air through her mouth, Ella looked around her. She was in a stable, but whether it was still in use, she didn't know. There was no sound of any horses, and the straw strewn on the ground looked dirty and scant. The dung that she had slid on, she could now see, was crusted over.

Shamus turned from her. 'Michael, I want you to be taking the babby to the nuns now. You will get there by morning. Tell them it was as you found him abandoned and you thought to bring him to them.'

Ella wanted to scream out 'No!' but all she could do was frantically shake her head.

'Oh yes. It is to be so, me wee whore. For when I am finished with you, you'll never be fit again to take a babby to your breast. As it is that you will have no more of them.' Shamus let out a laugh that cackled with malicious glee. 'Get yourself away, Michael. For sure, that babby's howling is getting on me nerves. Maybe the cold of him will quieten him, or maybe it will be that he may not survive the journey. But that is God's will, so it is.'

To Ella's horror, it sounded as though Shamus was instructing Michael to kill her child. His look showed the pleasure that she knew he felt, aware that he was inflicting the greatest possible pain on her.

Never had Ella felt so desolate; not even when she lost Christophe, as then she'd had the comfort of Paulo; and when she lost Paulo, her grief had held slight relief that he no longer suffered. Now she was helpless and unable to stop the cruelty that Shamus was inflicting on her. Unable to help her son.

As Michael left with her screaming child, Ella's despair was compounded. She no longer cared what happened to her. If she died, then so be it. Without little Paulo, and Arnie – whom she knew she loved just as deeply as she had her Paulo – there was nothing to live for. Slumping back down, she gave up fighting.

'Oh no, me little whore, you're not giving up that easily. I'm going to be having me revenge on you first. You're going to suffer as you have made me suffer.' Shamus swiped her face, sending her head rolling on her neck.

Ella didn't care. She lay, limp and unfeeling.

Taking her by the shoulders, he shook her. Her head wobbled on her neck, and slobber dripped from her mouth. 'Open your eyes, you whore – open them!'

Her body hit the ground with a thud. Pain ricocheted through her, but still Ella didn't care. No moan came from her. No more tears came from her eyes.

Shamus stared down at her. His head shook. 'Why? Why is it you did that to me? You said it was that you loved me, and we were just settling down. Didn't I risk me liberty to get your child back for you? And this is the way you return me love for you. By . . . by . . . Oh, Jesus!'

Shamus sank to his knees. He buried his head in his hands and wept. In his weeping he showed despair, something Ella had never thought to see.

'Why? Why? Why?' With each time of saying it, his despair turned to anger that came from deep within him and surfaced almost on a scream, as he asked for the last time. With that, his body lunged on top of hers. His hands grabbed Ella's hair on each side of her head. Still the word 'why' came from him, as he banged her head repeatedly on the ground.

The room began to swirl around Ella. She could hardly breathe, as her nose was blocked by the swelling of her nostrils and her mouth was bound tightly, between her teeth. She prayed for death to take her. As she did so, the swirling turned to blackness and she sank into the blessed relief it offered.

When she came to, her body was shivering with shock and cold. Turning her head, she couldn't see Shamus through the haze that clouded her vision. Nothing about the shapes around her suggested that he was in the barn with her.

Every part of her hurt, but her head felt as though it had swollen to twice its normal size. Pain zinged through it, as if lightning was striking her brain. Lights hovered in front of her eyes. She was going to be sick!

With an effort that took her through immense pain, Ella managed to roll onto her side, just as her body ejected the vomit from her. Spitting and choking, she fought for breath while her stomach heaved involuntarily. It was then she realized that the cloth had been taken from her mouth. Had Shamus been afraid that she would suffocate? Did he really want her alive? But what for? So that he could punish her forever? Yes, that was something she could see him doing.

A movement caught her eye. A figure stepped out of the shadows.

'Who – who's there?'

'Me name's Tilly, Missus. I'm to watch over you. I'll fetch a bucket of water to swill that mess away.'

The water splashed on Ella's face, but she didn't try to move, as the tingling, cold sensation soothed her. Looking up at Tilly, she saw that she was a pretty girl, with dark curly hair that looked as though it was a long time since it had been washed, or seen a comb for that matter. She had big brown eyes, which showed no zest for life; and there was a weariness about her, for her young age, which Ella guessed was no more than sixteen. Her whole appearance, from her lank hair to her ragged brown dress, was unkempt.

Through swollen lips she asked Tilly, 'Would you be kind enough to swill my face for me, and give me a drink of water, please?'

'Yeah, there you go.' Tilly's hand felt rough as she washed it over Ella's face.

After sipping the water from a dipping jug that Tilly had fetched for her, Ella asked, 'Am I on a farm, Tilly?'

'No. These are the old stables where some of the cabbies used to keep their horses at night, before them motors took over. Me dad used to own them, but Shamus does now, as me dad got into debt once the horses stopped coming. Are you hurt bad, Missus?'

'My name's Ella. And thank you for your kindness.' Although the water had been soothing, the sores on her face began to smart as it dried slowly. She winced. 'Yes, Shamus beat me. I'm badly bruised, but the worst thing is that he . . . he took my son away from me. He . . .'

'Aye, I know the ways of him. He made me his mistress when I was only twelve, and still rapes me, when he thinks fit. He thinks I'm grateful, but I hate him. I had a boyfriend once. Ronnie, his name were, but Shamus beat him up, so Ronnie went off and I ain't seen or heard of him since.'

This shocked Ella. She lay still, unable to think what to

say. *Shamus rapes this girl, even though he's married to me?* For some reason this knowledge hurt her pride, but then a deep sorrow for the girl replaced this feeling. 'I'm so sorry. Can't you get away? Go somewhere where he can't find you?'

'I can't leave me dad. Me mam died a few years back. I reckon as Shamus were to blame for that, as I heard a few things when he visited. And me mam went downhill fast after he started messing with her; she were a good-looking woman, and a kind one.' Ella heard the girl's voice catch with emotion and her loathing of Shamus deepened. As did her shame at ever thinking good of him and going along with him.

'Me dad couldn't keep up the payments on his debt to Shamus, and ended up having to sign the stables over to him and still having to make payments. He's a saddle-maker, me dad, as well as a blacksmith – his whole life has been lived around horses. There's not much work for him now. Not that he can do much, as he's riddled with the rheumatics.'

Ella's heart bled for the girl. 'I'm so sorry. I wish that I could help you.'

'Folk say that you're as bad as him. That you were married to a sick bloke and nursed Shamus's mother, then the minute your man died, you moved in with Shamus and have been living the life of a lady ever since. Shamus boasts about his posh wife, and allus says that folk have to pay up their debts quicker now, as he has you to keep in the style as you're accustomed to.'

'That's not right, Tilly. Shamus kidnapped me. I had no choice but to stay with him.' Ella told the girl how it was that she came to be forced to stay with Shamus, although, not being sure of Tilly yet, Ella didn't tell her that the threat that had hung over her – to hurt her beloved Rowena, if she didn't comply with Shamus's wishes – no longer applied.

'Well, I'm sorry for your plight, Ella. Shamus is a beast. He rules around here, and everyone is afraid of him. Oh, aye, lately he's took to acting the businessman, but his cronies still do his dirty work for him.'

Ella felt her cheeks burn at this. She had been the one to get Shamus to look more respectable, but she'd thought he was being more lenient with his clients as a result. But a little hope entered her as she detected that she might have a friend in the girl, now that she knew her story. 'Tilly, will you help me?'

'Don't ask that of me. I want to, but it would be more than me life's worth. I can't. I'm sorry.'

'What if I gave you enough money to pay off the debt to Shamus and get you and your dad away from here?'

'You have that much? I mean, it would take a lot, as we'd need to set up in the country somewhere, where they still rely on horses, and me and me dad could do some work. Cos I know a lot about horses – I were brought up caring for them. I can even shoe them, and lately I have been doing some of the cutting of the leather for a saddle, which me dad can't manage.'

'Yes, I could give you enough for that.'

'But, Shamus – he'd kill me.'

'All I want you to do is take a message to someone. Can I trust you, Tilly?'

'Aye, you can, but I can't leave you. Shamus said I've to stay and watch over you until he gets back.'

Ella leaned her head back down. Dizziness sent the roof swirling once more, and the sick feeling came back. Her training told her that she might have concussion, and might black out again at any moment. Cold seeped into her bones. It all seemed hopeless, and she felt that death was her only salvage.

'Here, I'll put this horse blanket over you, or you'll end up with pneumonia. It's a bit smelly, but it will keep you warm.'

The blanket stank of stale animal bodies, but Ella welcomed the warmth of it.

'Have you really got that amount of money then, Ella? Only I reckon as me dad could get a cabby to deliver the message. I can get to him through that door. It leads into a yard opposite our cottage. He knows all the cabbies. A lot of them used to have horses, before they got their motors. They often call in to have a chat with him and to bring him stuff. There's bound to be a couple will do that tonight, and they'd do anything for me dad.'

The hope that had died was rekindled in Ella. Yes, she had doubts about trusting these strangers, but what else could she do? And what would it matter anyway? Nothing could worsen the plight she was in.

'Thank you, Tilly. Ask your dad to send a message to a Mr Arnold Smith-Palmer.' Ella gave her the address. Tilly assured her that she would remember it. 'Tell him to let Arnold know where I am.'

'Oh, I'm not sure about that, Ella. It could bring big trouble down on us.'

'Tilly, this isn't about saving me. Shamus has to be stopped. Arnold will bring the police, Shamus will be arrested and, with all the people who have evidence on him, he'll be put away for a long time – maybe even hanged. Arnold is a solicitor and he knows that the local police are in Arnold's pay, so he will go to another area, and get help that way. I promise you that you won't suffer from this, but will only benefit.'

'I'll see what me dad says.' With this, Tilly disappeared through the door.

When she came back, Tilly was about to say something, when the door to the stables opened and Shamus stood there. Ella cringed.

'So, cosying up, are we, me two whores?'

'No, Shamus, only she were cold and I thought she were going to die. And I knew you wouldn't want that, so I covered her with a blanket, that's all.'

'It is that I like that: one of me whores helping the other. You do know, Ella, that Tilly here is for being very obliging at such times as you can't accommodate me? And why *is* that? You've proved you can be having bairns, but you're still at your monthly bleeding, when it is that you should be pregnant long before now.'

Seeing a way to insult him, Ella looked directly at him. 'That can only mean one thing, Shamus, seeing as though Tilly has never become pregnant, either: the fault lies with you. You are not man enough to get either of us with child.'

Ella felt immediate remorse, mixed with satisfaction, as Shamus turned red in the face and kicked her viciously in her thigh. But then the remorse won, as Tilly giggled and Shamus seized her by her hair. 'Are you for thinking that was funny, eh? Well, let's see if you think this funny.'

He aimed a blow at Tilly, but the girl wriggled out of his grip and ran towards the door that led to her cottage. Shamus was left holding a clump of her hair. After a moment of surprise, he ran and grabbed her. But Tilly fought like a cat, until Shamus finally got her trapped in his bear-like arms. 'You'll pay for this, Tilly, and it is that I have a mind to make you do so right now.' Bending Tilly over one of the bales of hay, he lifted her skirt.

'No, Shamus, don't. Don't, please.'

'Ah, to have me wife beg me not to shag another woman. Is there any greater pleasure? Just you be watching me – me little whore of a wife – and see how it is that I give it to Tilly, and the reason she's not with child.'

Horror gripped Ella. Neither her cries, nor the pitiful cries of Tilly, made any difference. Shamus tore Tilly's clothing until she was naked from the waist down, all the while hitting her every time she struggled and tried to rise. And then he forced himself into her from the back.

Tilly's screams, as the sickening assault went on and on, cut Ella in two and racked deep sobs from her and cries of 'Stop, please stop.' But Shamus was like a man possessed and hollered his pleasure as he thrust hard at poor Tilly. The agony of it took Ella to depths so low, she thought she was visiting hell, as she cried out to God to help them, but no such help came.

At last Shamus made the sound that she was so familiar with, an animal-like, uncontrolled moan. For a moment he lay slumped on top of Tilly, making Ella fear that he would crush the girl to death. But then he slid to his knees and stood up, as he did up his fly buttons.

'There, was you enjoying that, me Ella? Eh? Did you see the way I took me second whore? Well, when I've recovered you'll be having some of the same, for it is that after that experience, I'll not want to take me pleasure on you as I have been doing. It doesn't compare, so it doesn't.'

Having visited the very depths Ella thought any human could descend to, she felt no fear any more. 'I hate you, Shamus. I hate you so much that it doesn't matter what you do to me any longer. You're depraved. You are not a man, but an animal, and what you've just done proves that. One day someone will stop you.'

'Well, it is that it won't be you. Now, shall I be starting me carving up of your body, or shall I wait until I'm ready to have me way with you? As you know, feeling those breasts of yours gives us both pleasure, so it would be a pity if they'd been cut off before the last time I give it to you, so it would.'

Shamus was near her now, and gazing down at her. His face was unreadable, until he gathered the spittle in his mouth and spat down on her. 'So, you've been carrying on behind me back. Who with? Who was that weed of a man that you held hands with, eh?'

'A better man than you.'

His kick creased Ella in two. The pain in her leg felt as if it was broken. But that was nothing to his next kick, which landed in her ribs. Ella heard the crack as the excruciating agony pierced her. Trying to draw in breath, her last thought, before sinking back into unconsciousness, was that a broken rib could have pierced her lung.

Chapter Thirty-Seven

The whiteness surrounding her, when Ella opened her eyes, made her wonder if she had died. But then the pain seared through her and she cried out, until a beloved voice came through the misty cloud that hung over her.

'Ella darling, it's okay, you are in hospital.'

'Arnie?'

'Yes, Ella, it is me. Lie still.'

Another male voice that she recognized spoke then. 'Nurses are not good patients, I'm afraid.'

'Daniel?'

'Yes. Good to see you, Ella, though I wish it had been under better circumstances. We have been worried sick about you. Why didn't you keep in touch with Alan and Connie? They have been out of their minds with worry. Even the Red Cross could no longer trace you, but said that you just vanished.'

'It's a long, long story, Daniel. Why am I here? I mean, you are a neurosurgeon?'

'Yes, and you were badly in need of one. A cracked skull and several broken ribs, one of which had pierced your lung.

And yes, I do know most of what has happened to you. I'm so sorry – it all beggars belief. But you are safe now, and maybe could have been a long time ago, if you had kept those who love you informed of what was going on.' Daniel sounded different. The shy, retiring man that she'd known in France was now a confident surgeon, unafraid to speak his mind.

'I'm sorry. In the beginning it was pride that stopped me, and then it was impossible for me to contact anyone. Am I going to be all right?'

'Yes, you're on the mend, though it may not feel like it. You also had a femur injury, so we have put a splint on that. We will be putting a cast on it later today, but you have been through an operation on both your head and your chest. So you will feel pretty grim for a few days.'

Her questions piled up, but Daniel quietened her.

'I will leave Arnold to tell you all that has happened. I have to tend to other patients, but I will be back later to check on you. Now, Arnold, don't tire her. Yes, she's needs to know, but be careful not to upset her too much.'

As Daniel left her side, Ella asked, 'My baby? My little Paulo?'

'I'm sorry, Ella, my love, but he hasn't been located yet. The police are questioning the men; they will find him.'

Ella closed her eyes against the pain of this.

'You have to call on all the resources that you used as a nurse, Ella. All that strength and courage. Daniel has told me a bit about what you coped with. Now you have to be as strong as you were then. The police will find Paulo, they will.'

Taking a deep breath, which caused her to moan with the

intensity of the hurt it caused, Ella asked, 'How long have I been here? And what happened – what about Tilly?'

'One at a time, darling. You have been here for two days. A cab driver called at my house with the message that you sent. I went to the solicitor I told you about, the one I was going to work with; it was after his office hours, but he didn't baulk at helping me. He knew people – policemen and detectives, people he could talk to about everything, off the record at first. When they arrived at the stables, you were unconscious. The other girl was not as bad as you, but she was taken to the local hospital. Anyway, Shamus was arrested, and they have since rounded up his cronies. The local police have been cleared out; it seems all but three of them, including their sergeant, were in the pay of Shamus. They have been replaced. The other three are doing the rounds, gathering evidence with which to convict Shamus and his men. I have it, from my solicitor friend, that some of the evidence concerns eye-witnesses to murders that Shamus has carried out. It is likely that he will hang, and possibly his cronies, too. So you are safe, my darling. You're safe.' This last came out on a sob.

'Hold my hand, Arnie. Hold me and stop me from falling. Don't let me let go, or I will never come round again.'

'What are you saying, my darling, what's happening?'

'I am losing the will to live. To face it all. Many people die that way, when they have lost hope. I have lost hope of ever seeing my little Paulo again.'

'Don't, please don't. The police have a lot of negotiating power. My solicitor friend told me they will use it against the one who took your child away. It seems Tilly was able to say which man it was, and it also seems that he hasn't as much hanging over him as the others. But apparently the police will tell him that unless he trades information about where he took your son, he will be charged with everything that the others are charged with.'

'Will it work?'

'I think so. So far he can be done for intimidation and assault, but as I understand it, most people are saying that he was not as bad as the others, and only used bullying tactics when the others were around. Some even had a good word for him. So he won't want a conviction of murder – and possibly hanging – for a crime he didn't commit; or even one of accessory to murder, which is still a very serious offence. The game is up for Shamus, and therefore the man who took Paulo has nothing to gain by keeping quiet, and everything to lose.'

Hope – a feeling that she'd had so little of – seeped into Ella. *But two days? Why haven't they any knowledge of where my Paulo is, by now?*

The ward was in darkness when Ella woke again. Daniel was sitting by her side.

'Aren't you off-duty yet?'

'Yes, I am, but I needed to talk to you. Are you up to it?'

'You're the doctor. But first, is there any news?'

'Yes. Your Arnold came to the hospital about an hour ago. He was going with the police to a woman's house in Brighton. It appears she is the sister of the man who took your child away in the van. Arnold has gone there because the child has seen him before, and it may help him to see a familiar face.'

'Oh, thank God. Thank God!'

'Don't get upset, Ella, it won't help your recovery.'

'These are tears of relief and joy, Daniel. Now, what did you want to talk to me about?'

Daniel cleared his throat. 'I don't know if I should, because I have just told you that I don't want you upset. But I have never forgotten the young man that we helped to die.'

'No, I haven't, either. But I remember him with a peace in me, as you and I were brave enough not to let him suffer any longer. We helped him to a peaceful end. I sense that you are feeling guilty about it, but please don't.'

'I can't help it. What we did was against all medical ethics. I want to confess to it.'

'No, you must not. With all the war trials and recriminations going on, you could be done for murder, and me as an accessory, when all we did was speed up what would have happened anyway. Daniel, you are a brilliant surgeon; you have saved countless lives since, and will save many more. You pioneer treatment. Many will die needlessly if you are lost to the world of medicine.'

'I know, but I cannot reconcile what we did.'

'Daniel, I have paid. I have paid any guilt that you think is attributed to me, a million times over. Don't make me suffer any more. Please, don't. I beg of you. What we did was the right thing. We treated a patient – a dying patient – to the best of our ability. No more or less could have been asked of us.'

Ella felt a different desperation settle in her, at Daniel's demeanour. She could see that he was suffering, and had suffered, mentally from their action, and didn't know how to stop him destroying them both. Gasping for breath, she pleaded with him one more time. 'Talk to someone . . . s – someone you trust. A priest, anyone. P – please, Daniel.'

'Oh, Ella, what have I done? You're sweating. Oh, my dear, I've done the very thing I didn't want to happen.

Forgive me.' Returning to the doctor he was, Daniel began to administer to her: clearing her airways, with a tube that almost choked her; injecting her with something that made her woozy; and talking in a soothing voice. 'Don't worry, dear Ella, I will talk to someone. I'll seek help from someone that I can trust not to report us. I will sort it out. I'm so sorry.'

Ella left him then and sank into the mercy that the drug gave her.

It was the sound of a baby gurgling that Ella woke to the next morning. Sitting next to her was Arnie, holding little Paulo. Never had she seen a more beautiful sight. 'Oh, Arnie. Paulo, my boys, my darlings.'

Arnie's kiss was the first she'd ever had from him. He placed Paulo on her legs and leaned over her. His lips touched hers for a brief moment, but a moment that she knew would be engraved in her memory forever. When he pulled away, his eyes were full of tears.

'You are part of me, Ella; you *are* me. How this happened so quickly to me, I do not know, but what I said before still stands. I will give you time. I want you to grieve properly for Paulo, and to come to terms with all that has happened to you.' As she put her hand on her baby's face and stroked it, Arnie asked, 'Do you still want to go to France?'

'Yes. Yes, more than anything.'

'Well. As soon as we can, we will go. But you do know there is a trial to get through first, and that you are the chief witness? The police have already enquired as to whether you are able to answer any questions yet or not.'

'Yes, I understand that. But, Arnie, there is something else pressing on my mind.' Ella told Arnie how she and

Daniel had administered a strong dose of morphine to a dying soldier, knowing that it would kill him, and how Daniel was still troubled by it.

'A mercy killing?'

'Yes. The boy was in agony and had an hour at the most to live.'

'I understand. A soldier friend and I did much the same. We were trapped in a dugout, three of us, and our mate was shot in the stomach as he went to leave and get help. We were trying to cover him. It was bad, really bad. I can still hear his cries of agony; him begging us to shoot him. My friend looked at me after about an hour of this, and I knew what he wanted to do, and I nodded. His shot echoed around what was by then a still and dark field. Someone shouted in German that it was an attack. I speak German, and I heard another voice say, "No. A mercy killing. Quieten down." And all went silent. My mate and I crawled out of the hole to no resistance, and made it back to the trench.'

'Oh, Arnie, it was a terrible time.'

'It was, and all of us took actions that we wouldn't normally take.'

'Does your friend's death bother you?'

'No. I'm just glad we had the courage to help him, and I know that to this day he is grateful to us. This is how Daniel should think of it.'

'I know, but Daniel has always been different, very deep. A thinking man, who over-thinks things.'

'I have, haven't I?'

'Daniel! Oh, I'm sorry. I know I promised never to discuss what happened, but—'

'No, it's all right. I instigated this and left you with no choice. I'm sorry. I did as you said and went to see the hospital chaplain. He guessed I had something serious on my mind and granted me the status of confession, and told me that whatever I said – no matter how bad – it would never be repeated or acted upon.'

'And?'

'He had a story similar to what I have just heard Arnold tell you. And as a priest, although he could not give me details, he said that he had counselled many doctors who had done the same – both during the war and since. "So, you see," he said, "if you did wrong, so did all of them." And besides, he said that we had done the work God put us on earth to do. To treat and make well those we could, and to help those we couldn't pass on to Him, with as little pain and discomfort as possible.'

'And do you agree? Is your mind at rest?'

'It is, Ella. It is. I feel as though that man lifted a huge weight from me; and not only from me, but from my soul.'

'Oh, Daniel, I am so glad. Come and meet my son. Little Paulo.'

Daniel lifted Paulo up into the air. 'You're a fine boy, and do you know, my wife is expecting a child, and I hope that it is a boy, just like you.'

'Your wife!'

'Yes, I know what you all thought; but I'm not a man who likes men, I'm just a bit on the delicate side.' His laughter made Paulo jump and Daniel giggled with him, and so did Ella.

'Oh, Daniel, you knew that?'

'Yes, and you weren't the only ones to think it. I have been teased all my life. But my wife says it is my gentle, caring side, and is nothing to be ashamed of.'

'It isn't, and you are a special person, Daniel.'

'Thank you, Ella. I would say the same about you.'

With that, he placed Paulo in Arnie's arms, gave a huge smile and turned and left the room.

'Well, you'll have to tell me what that was all about another time, darling. I need to prepare you. The police are coming to question you. I'll be with you, so don't worry, just tell them honestly all the answers they want to know.'

The ordeal with the police wasn't as bad as Ella had thought it would be. At the moment they were simply concerned with what happened on the night Shamus took her to the stables. 'We need something concrete to charge them all with, in these initial stages, and to enable us to keep them in prison without granting them bail. As you might expect, with all Shamus McMahon's money, he has been able to engage a good lawyer and is proving tricky to pin down. But what you have given us is borne out by Tilly Manton and her father, so we have enough now, and plenty more information coming in. Don't you worry, Miss. You are rid of Shamus for good, I promise you that. And I'm sorry for what you have been through.'

Somehow Ella couldn't relax at these words. His previous comment had a greater impact on her and put fear into her: *Shamus has a good lawyer.*

Chapter Thirty-Eight

'M'Lord, gentlemen of the jury. This witness has been presented to you by the prosecution as a woman of courage – and no one doubts that; after all, she was awarded the Albert Medal for bravery during the Great War. She is also a woman who has known great sorrow – yes, to lose a beloved husband and a child, that is sorrow. And finally, she is presented as a woman wronged by my client, Shamus McMahon. It is this that I will bring into question. I will present to you a very different woman and one who is not, in my opinion, a credible witness.'

Ella's heart thudded against her chest and her mouth dried. Yes, she had been warned that the defence would try and discredit her, but what tactic would they use? What did he mean? *Why am I not credible?*

'Mrs McMahon, did you not coerce my client to go to Poland with you to steal your sister's child?'

A gasp could be heard rippling around the court. The prosecution lawyer, who had been very gentle with her, had a look of horror and disbelief on his face. Ella hadn't mentioned anything about her child to him – at least not what she'd been through, or what she had done to get him back.

'He is my child!'

'Can you show us his birth certificate?'

Ella stared at the defence lawyer, a man in his forties, short and dumpy-looking, with a shock of red hair; he had a spiteful look about him, and was always ready to pounce and wound.

'Well, Mrs McMahon?'

'No. My child was born in Poland.'

'And is it not true that the papers you do have for him are false?'

Ella couldn't swallow. Her tongue felt like sandpaper. 'Yes, but—'

'There are no "buts", Mrs McMahon. The child you have in your possession, and whom you coerced my client into snatching from his mother and father, is your sister's child. I have a copy of the original and correct birth registration, given to me by your very distraught sister – my Exhibit A for this witness, M'Lord. There is also a translation document included with the exhibit.'

'Paulo is *my* baby. I went to Poland to give birth to him. I was forced to hand him over to my half-sister. I had to snatch him back!'

'If he is your child, can you tell us the name of the doctor in attendance on you during your pregnancy?'

'No. I – I couldn't afford to go to a doctor. I am a nurse, and I looked after myself. But nearly every witness who has spoken today saw me when I was pregnant.'

'They saw you pregnant, or at least you *told* many people that you were pregnant, but they all say you didn't look far gone. They will also tell this court that they didn't see the

391

end result of that pregnancy. They will say that you suddenly disappeared after your husband died, and the next thing they knew, you were married to Mr McMahon and living the life of a lady. I put it to you, Mrs McMahon, that you miscarried the child you were carrying, and understandably were distraught. You had been through so much. Then to hear that your sister had given birth to a healthy child set your mind, which was unhinged at the time, due to the tragedy you had experienced, on having your sister's child as your own.'

'No!'

'I think *yes*. Because that wouldn't just satisfy your need for a child, but would also give you the revenge you sought.'

'Objection, M'Lord. This witness is not on trial.'

'M'Lord, I am trying to establish that the witness is not credible. That she is a liar. A baby-snatcher, who used my client for her own ends. Who flirted with him while her own husband was dying, and who moved in with him very soon after he did die. And finally, when she did get revenge, she wanted to get out of the marriage, and so she began an affair with another man. Which led to the events that my client stands accused of.'

'Your client stands accused of much more than the events that Mrs McMahon is witness to. But yes, I will allow the questioning, as it seems another crime may have been committed here.'

'M'Lord, I strongly object and ask for an adjournment.'

'On what grounds?'

'M'Lord, I was not informed about this line of questioning. My witness has not discussed her child with me. I need a chance to bring counter-evidence and be able to prove that my client is telling the truth, and that all her actions at the time were driven by the terrible threat of what might happen to her friend, whose testimony you heard earlier.'

'A black woman, M'Lord. We heard the testimony of a black woman.' This drawl from the defence lawyer lit up the court with mutterings, and it seemed everyone had something to say. Ella glanced up at Rowena, who was sitting in the public gallery. Her head was lowered. Ella wanted to scream out that Rowena was the kindest, most honest person she had ever met, but at this moment she herself looked like a criminal – a baby-snatcher – and nothing she said would have any bearing on anyone or anything.

The judge banged his gavel on the counter in front of him. 'Silence. Silence in court! I will not have my court disrupted! We will adjourn. The court will reconvene tomorrow at nine a.m. Warden, take the prisoner down, and present him once more at that time.'

'All rise.'

As the judge left, Ella felt all eyes on her. It was as if she was the accused now. *How am I to convince everyone? I have no proof. That lawyer must have been in touch with Calek, to have been able to present the birth-registration document. God knows what she told him.* Sinking down on the bench behind her, Ella felt fear reverberate through her body. *What if I am prosecuted? Oh God!*

The prosecution lawyer, a tall man with dark hair greying at the temples and a long angular face, stared at her across his desk. 'Everything you say sounds true, but it will need verifying in some way. And if we manage that, it still does not put you in a good light. You will be seen as a woman who sold her child, settled down with her new husband and didn't seem to have a care in the world. Who then coerced that husband into snatching her baby back. Yes, there was the threat against your friend, which might excuse some of your actions; but you didn't give your baby away for his own safety, you used him as a bargaining tool to get money. I understand that you needed that money to get your friend to safety, but your actions after that, concerning snatching the baby back, well . . . And then we do have to face the fact that the only other witness to the threat is an immigrant woman.'

'Why should that make Rowena any different from any other witness? She is a good, kind, Christian woman and would never lie under oath.'

'I agree. And I hate the implication that my learned friend threw into the proceedings, but we have to be realistic: most people are prejudiced against black people. In their minds, they are not to be trusted. It is appalling, but it's a fact. We have to face it, Mrs McMahon: you have been discredited; and further to that, you may face losing your child and being prosecuted for kidnapping.'

Ella began to shake. Her whole body trembled uncontrollably.

Arnie took her hand. 'There must be a way, sir, of making Ella's sister testify and tell the truth.'

'If there is, I don't know of it. A Polish national cannot be subpoenaed under British law. You should know that. Haven't you just taken your finals in law?'

'I have, and yes, I do know. I was speaking out of desperation. I know Ella is telling the truth, and I'm feeling the frustration of not being able to prove it.'

'That is a frustration you will have many times in your career, Arnold. So often you will know a truth, but be unable to prove it. You will even see clients go to the gallows when you know them to be innocent. In that, you and I differ, as I often have the duty to prove that the apparently innocent are guilty. We do our jobs. We fight for justice. Never work for the prosecution unless you are one hundred per cent certain of the guilt of the accused. That's the only advice I can give you.'

Arnie didn't answer. His head was down, his demeanour that of a defeated man. It was a feeling that reflected what Ella was feeling, as her mind sought for answers – for anything that would prove she was telling the truth. But she could think of nothing.

'You have to leave, Ella. You have to go tonight. I can't bear you to be prosecuted.'

Ella sat across from Arnie, in the lovely living room of his parents' house, where she had been staying with little Paulo for the last four months.

Eve and Reginald Smith-Palmer were a loving couple who adored their son. They hadn't questioned that the woman he loved should move in with them so that Arnie could look after her, and had taken to Paulo as if he was their grandson. To Ella, it felt as though she had landed in heaven.

A large house, Arnie's family home didn't feel crowded with her presence. Of the eight bedrooms, she had been given the nursery and what had once been Arnie's nanny's adjoining room, for her sole use. And she had been treated like a daughter as she slowly recovered from her ordeal.

But now that ordeal had grown to enormous proportions, and instead of Shamus being the one on trial, it seemed that she was.

'Ella, please listen to me. You have to get away. They can't touch you and Paulo while you are in France. If you stay here, you risk losing Paulo and going to jail. I am so worried about you. Please, Ella.'

'Yes. I can see that I will be saved by leaving, but what of Shamus? He will get away scot-free.'

'On the charge of kidnapping and assaulting you, yes. But there are a lot more charges that he faces. Charges that you will not have any influence over, as you are not a witness to them, except for Shamus's final assault and rape of Tilly; but there are many witnesses to what he put Tilly through, who can speak for her. You can have no bearing on the murders, extortion and many other crimes, and he won't get off all of them. He can't. There are so many witnesses willing to come forward, and so much solid evidence that the police have unearthed. You have to save yourself and Paulo. Shamus is trying to take you down with him. Don't let him, please, darling – don't let him.'

'Yes, you are right. I can never clear my name. Calek and Abram won't ever admit the truth or stand up for me.'

'Thank goodness you have seen the sense of leaving now. I wish I could come with you, but I haven't been called as a witness yet, so I cannot. I am one witness Tilly will need. I can't run out on her.'

'Oh, Arnie, I am so sorry for putting you through all this.'

'You haven't. I am involved because of my love for you and Paulo. All the blame is on Shamus's shoulders.'

Ella knew that whilst most of this was true, she was to blame, too. She'd sought Arnie's help and had involved him.

'Now we must spend the time getting everything sorted for your trip. You will need money.'

'I have plenty. And the banks are still open. I can draw out up to one hundred pounds in cash and can have the rest put on an international money order, which will enable me to open an account in France.'

'Let's go immediately then. Mother will take care of Paulo. You go and get your coat, while I explain to my parents what is happening. They won't object, as we have already spoken about this while you were seeing to Paulo. I'll ask Mother to pack up all of your things. Have you got the papers for Paulo?'

'Yes, I always keep them in my handbag.'

'Be as quick as you can then, darling, as time is getting on.'

Once her business at the bank was done, Ella knew there was one more thing for her to do before she left these shores. 'Arnie, I need to go to the cemetery. I – I . . .'

'Of course, we will go there right now. That is, if you want me to come with you?'

'Yes, I do. It is always an ordeal for me, so I would be grateful for your support.'

They didn't speak on the way and, when they arrived, Arnie told Ella he would wait for her, and to take all the time she needed.

Walking towards the grave that held a life she'd known that was so different from the one she had now, Ella felt the shame of all that had happened. The two beloved people buried beneath the earth were from a time that was pure. A time when *she* was pure. Now she was tainted by lies and the deceit perpetrated against her, and by her own actions. For she had carried out some actions that she wasn't proud of. Yes, they were motivated by fear, but could she have done things differently? Falling to her knees, she cried, 'Oh, Paulo, I am not worthy to say your name. I'm tainted. I gave what was yours to another man, for my own gain. How can you ever forgive me – how?'

Sobs racked her body. They weakened her so that she had to lean forward on her hands and, in this position, she implored Paulo and Christophe to forgive her, over and over again. Never once did she offer excuses for her behaviour, but when she was drained, she offered a promise. 'Paulo, I will protect our son. I will bring him up to be a proud Frenchman, as you were, my darling. I'll instil in him the values that I know you held dear. And he will be a shining example of all that you stood for.'

Calming a little, Ella wiped her tears.

'Paulo, being you, and a typical Frenchman, I know you won't deny me going forward and finding love. You always said that you never wanted me to be alone. Well, I have found that love, my darling. His name is Arnie. He is a gentleman, like you, and has many of your ways. And he is kind. He is prepared to give me the time that was snatched from me, to grieve for our parting, and for our son. I need that. I need to heal. When I have, I will marry Arnie. I know you would approve of that. And we will make our life in your country. Look after little Christophe, my darling. I love you both, and always will.'

Finding the strength coming back into her, Ella stood up. Blowing two kisses, she walked back to the car and to Arnie.

Saying goodbye to Arnie, as they stood on the station, tore at Ella's heart.

'I will be with you soon, my darling. My mind is made up that I, too, will make my life in France. I cannot live without you, and you cannot live in England until such time as you are exonerated. But it won't be an encumbrance upon me, as I have told you that part of me has always wanted to live a freer life than my chosen career would allow. I am excited about being in France, with you. We will find a place for ourselves, and a lifestyle that we both enjoy. I cannot wait.'

EPILOGUE
France, 1924

~

Ella and Flora

A Friendship Renewed – A Love Freed

Chapter Thirty-Nine

Although the spring sun warmed her as she sat in the garden of her home in the South of France, which stood on the edge of the vineyard owned by her dear friends, Flora and Cyrus, Ella's body was stiff and cold. She shuddered as, in the distance, the church clock struck one p.m. In England, due to the way the countries changed their clocks back and forth, it was twelve noon – the time when Shamus was to hang.

He'd won reprieve after reprieve, but would he truly die this time? Part of Ella, a very small part, didn't want him to. The part that held her caring side and honoured the preservation of life. But the largest part of her wanted it over. For him, and for herself.

His crimes were heinous and had devastated so many lives: murder being the most serious, with three victims in all. Then the raping of women, with his cronies holding their husbands and forcing them to watch; and his treatment of Tilly, poor Tilly. She had suffered so much at Shamus's hands. And all done to gain wealth and extort money from those who had so little.

When Ella thought about it all, she wanted him to suffer the agony of walking towards his own death, and felt her shame at having been taken in by him and even thinking she could grow to love him. But even a demon such as Shamus could show a compassionate side; and, yes, the loving and passion that she had experienced.

Two months ago he had done something for her which, she knew, in his mind, would seem to make up for all he'd put her through in the past – he'd finally given a statement admitting that he had lied about Paulo. Shamus doing so had been down to Arnie. Oh, how she missed Arnie, and yet she had needed this time away from him.

Arnie had stayed in England and had worked tirelessly to clear her name. He'd even travelled to Poland and had confronted Calek with the statement Shamus had made, and had somehow persuaded her to give a statement, too, in which she admitted everything. Even to being a party to knowing that her mother had committed fraud. It appeared that Calek's mother had had power of attorney for Ella's father in his last two years, a time when his health was very poor and his mind wandered back in time. As he lost the ability to know what was happening around him, she gradually put everything in her own name.

Like mother, like daughter, because the only truthful thing Calek said was that she didn't then know about Ella – just that there was a reason that drove her mother to do what she did; a reason her mother never shared with Calek, but which Calek now realized was that her mother wanted to eradicate her husband's former life and see all his wealth go to the child she had borne him.

What had brought about this change of heart in Calek, Ella discovered, was that a miracle had happened, and Calek

– despite what she'd been told – had fallen pregnant. It appeared that a pioneering doctor who worked in the field of gynaecology had been able to sort out whatever problem she had. Ella was happy for her and had forgiven Calek, but didn't know if she would ever form a relationship with her in the future.

'Are you all right, Ella?'

A hand reached out to her and held hers. Flors, her beloved friend, sat next to her. The years since they had parted hadn't changed her. She was what Ella would term a beautiful person, inside and out. Her long, dark hair shone in the sunlight, and her dark eyes held kindness. Nothing about her delicate features spoke of what Flors had been through in the past, at the hands of her family. It had all horrified Ella when, just after she arrived here in the South of France nearly two years ago, Flora had opened up to her. Ella still couldn't take in the fact that Flora's adored husband, Cyrus, had turned out to be her half-brother. How brave they were to have gone against convention and moved to where no one knew them, so that they could be together.

A squeal of delight caught Ella's attention. Flora's four lovely children ran around happily, playing with and laughing at the antics of Paulo.

Squeezing Flora's hand, Ella nodded. 'Yes. I am. Do you think this time it will finally happen?'

'Arnie seems to think so. Didn't he say in his letter that Shamus has now accepted his guilt?'

'Yes, he did. And that Shamus sent for a priest so that he could make a full confession.'

'Well then, if that is so, no one will be working to get a reprieve for him.'

'Can God forgive someone like Shamus, Flors?'

'According to everything we have been taught, He can. But I have had many times in my life when I have doubted those teachings.'

'I think everyone who was involved in the war, as we were, must doubt. I do myself.'

'How do you see those years now, Ella? As you look back at them, I mean. Do they haunt you?'

'No, Flors, why should they? We did our best. Do you have nightmares about them then?'

'Sometimes. And a feeling of guilt that I was weak, and didn't carry on nursing when Freddy died. I still grieve for him; he was the loveliest of brothers, and a gentle soul. A gifted musician who should never have gone to war.'

'He was one of life's lovely souls. We saw so many like him.'

'We did.'

'And it is easy, now that the emotions of the time have faded, to have recriminations. To think we should have done this or that. But the actions we took were driven by the situation we were in. We were such young women, tasked with trying to save lives whilst living in a bloodbath of hell. We all did our best. And but for you, Flors, we – Mags, you and I – would never have got out of Brussels alive. Nor would many of those French soldiers have survived. The way you took charge of that hospital, even though you weren't a qualified nurse, and the way you led us to safety was amazing.'

'We were so young, as you say. I remember when we arrived in Brussels in 1914, on that first posting, how we were all eager and ready to give our all. Then Germany invaded and reality soon hit us.'

'Yes. How did we get through it?'

They were silent for a moment. Memories assailed Ella: the appalling conditions, becoming stranded behind enemy lines and then finding themselves alone, short of food and without guidance. Then the fear of what they had experienced during their escape visited her once more, as she thought of how they had stared down the barrel of a guard's gun on the border of Holland. A shudder went through her.

'I will never forget what we endured together, Flors. It bound us like sisters. And you are one of life's unsung heroes. Your bravery should have been officially recognized.'

Flors didn't answer. Ella saw a tear seep out of the corner of her eye and knew that, deep within her, Flors still suffered from all that had happened. How come they – two innocent young girls at the time – should have had to face so much? Ella squeezed her hand.

'I wished Mags would write. I worry about her, and haven't heard anything from her. Do you ever wonder about Mags, Ella?'

'Yes. And as I told you when I first came here, I feel guilty about never having contacted her.'

'My brother Harold is a beast. I've wished a million times that I hadn't introduced him to Mags. She had everything he wanted – wealth, and the prospect of even more, when eventually she was left her father's cotton mill. He pursued Mags relentlessly, making her believe he loved her.'

'I know, but you must not take all of that on yourself. We were such close friends; it was bound to happen that we would meet each other's families. At least your own family and Mags's. I didn't know if I had any family back then.'

'Harold thought he had Mags right where he wanted her, but you know – I never told you before – she defied him once, when he wouldn't help me. Cyrus and I were destitute and my little Alice needed medical care. And Mags went against Harold's orders and helped me. She was with me through my little Alice's passing, and I still feel that she is with me, even though she doesn't contact me.'

'We will make it our mission to find her in the future, I promise. I just need to sort my own life out first. And go forward from the past. It is terrible to say it, but if at this moment Shamus is dead, then I can begin to do that.'

'You have never spoken of your plans, Ella. And I haven't liked to push you to. Have you made any?'

'Yes. Arnie tells me that I will inherit everything Shamus had. It will amount to a fortune. I intend to set up a trust fund that will help all those he wronged. Especially Tilly, the girl I told you about, although I have helped her already, and her letters speak of her happiness and how she is doing so well. She has met a man she has fallen in love with. He was a reporter at the court during Shamus's trial, so he knows all she has been through. She tells me they will marry later this year. I'll make Tilly's home and stables back over to her. And I'll fund her wish to turn the stables into a shop that sells clothing for horse-riding and home-made saddles, besides other equipment for those who go hunting or ride for pleasure.'

'That sounds wonderful. When you told me of Tilly, my heart went out to her. It's so nice to hear of a happy ending.'

'Yes, and to think that she and her father will see the day when they get back all – and more – of what Shamus took from them. I've other plans, too. I'll make a generous dona-tion to the Red Cross, as a thank-you and a tribute to Miss Embury's work; and to the Salvation Army, which I will stipulate must be used specifically for those soldiers who returned so badly wounded that they have been unable to work and ended up on the street. This donation will be a salve to my conscience, as I always intended to volunteer my services to them, but life got in the way. And it will make me feel better about the way I treated Miss Embury, after all her kindness to me. It hurt her that I didn't turn to her when I needed help. My stupid pride stopped me. And then with the rest of the money, I will secure my own, Paulo's and Arnie's future. Shamus owes me that much.'

'Oh, Ella. Are you finally ready to let Arnie fully into your life?'

'I am. I have loved him from the start, though I didn't realize it at first, but I wasn't ready. And Arnie has been generous in his love for me, and has given me the time I needed. This time I have spent here with you, and in this lovely house that I have bought, has given me that healing, but I couldn't take the final step. Shamus wouldn't divorce me, so I have been shackled. Arnie didn't deserve to live like that, with a woman he couldn't make his wife. I have missed him so much. His letters have been a salve to me. Through them, our knowledge of each other and our love has developed and grown. And, Flors, I am ready, really ready, not only to receive Arnie, but also to let go of my beloved Paulo. He will always have a place in my heart, but there is a large part of it that is vacant, and Arnie will fill that.'

'And Shamus?'

'Yes, I am ready to let go of him and all he did to me. I can only do that in forgiveness. And I realize now, that can happen. Shamus has repented and has made my life better; he has made his peace with God. And I now know that I want him to find peace, and that he would want me to distribute his fortune in the way I have described. I just need that telegram to arrive and for it to say that he and I are free.'

'Is there some tea, for a soul who is dying of thirst? Or are you two honey childs of mine going to sit and talk right through the afternoon?'

'Ha, sorry, Rowena.' Ella rose and ran to Rowena and into her open arms, where she received a hug and a kiss planted on her cheek.

'I knows what it is you're going through, Missy Ella, and I'm sorry I dropped off to sleep and missed sitting with you through it.'

'No, don't be. You need your naps.'

Letting go of Ella and hugging Flors, Rowena smiled through her tears. She was always emotional these days, and a simple show of affection could set her crying.

Not long after the trial ended, her husband Tobias had suffered a heart attack and died. Rowena's world had all but ended. Flors had travelled to England to bring her to France for what was meant to be a break, staying with Ella. But Rowena had settled so well and had made such a niche for herself – looking after the children, when needed, and helping Flors with the household chores in her huge chateau – that neither she nor they wanted her to return to England. Not that Rowena had a job as such, or was in any way a servant to them; she just did what she wanted to do and what kept her happy. And to Ella and Flors's delight, happiness had seeped back into Rowena, and her jolly countenance kept them all going.

'You two go and sit in the sun and I'll fetch tea for us, and some refreshment for the children.'

'No, Missy Ella, you gonna have to stop looking after me.

410

I'll help. I ain't too old yet, even if this bulk of mine needs more shut-eye than a newborn.'

Ella laughed out loud, 'Come on then, Bossy-boots.'

Rowena held her hands together under her huge bosom and let out a laugh that warmed Ella right through. There was no tonic like the one Rowena's jolly and loving nature could bestow, and suddenly Ella felt that no matter what had happened at twelve noon, she would cope. She had Rowena and Flors by her side, and she knew, too, that it was time to let Arnie fully into her life.

Ella had mixed emotions when two telegrams arrived the next day. Shamus had gone to his death in a brave manner, with a priest by his side. His last words had been, 'Tell Ella that I am sorry. Ask her to make right all the wrong that I did.' Looking across at the gentle hills that led to the azure sea, Ella had let her tears flow.

It was over.

As she wiped away the tears that had given her relief, the fields lining the slopes came into view. They housed rows and rows of grape vines that Cyrus and his men had planted. To Ella, they represented the future. A future full of hope. A future spent with her Arnie and the family they would build together.

The second telegram said that Arnie had given notice of terminating his job:

My life is yours now, Ella. We will go forward together. It is our time. And I want that time to be spent in France. In three weeks we will be reunited, and soon we will be married. I love you beyond words, my darling.

411

Ella allowed the smile that played around her lips to develop into a giggle and then a full belly laugh, as she raised her hands in the air and looked heavenwards. 'I'm free! Free!'

Twirling her body, she let the joy that she felt cleanse her of the final remnants of the past. Then she stood still and allowed her heart to long for the day when Arnie arrived and she would give herself completely to him. Life from now on was going to be beautiful. Beautiful. No more ripples, no more losing those she loved.

She had her son; and her lovely friend, Flors, was back in her life; and dear Rowena, and soon, very soon, her life would be complete. Her love – her Arnie – was coming to make her his wife.

Letter to Readers

Dear Reader,

Thank you for taking this journey with me, I hope very much that you enjoyed Ella's story – the second in The Girls Who Went to War series.

My research for the series took many turns. I visited the Somme and Dieppe, where I trod the path of many of the theatres of war, and the huge cemeteries tore at my heart, as did coming across many small but unforgotten ones, holding the men who were buried where they fell. All are beautifully kept, with the lines of gravestones giving you a sense of the enormity of the suffering that prevailed. Most were inscribed with the names and very young ages of those who had fallen, but some simply read: *Soldier known only to God*. These gave me a deeper sadness.

But whilst we will be forever grateful to the millions of young men who gave their lives, we also celebrate the courage of the young women, too: many took on the work at home that men were used to doing, and others showed extreme bravery as they went abroad to nurse the fallen and give comfort to the dying.

For my research into the work of these nurses and the lives of the Voluntary Aid Deployment workers, I found a wealth of information in the book *Women in the War Zone* by Anne Powell, which I purchased in the Musée Somme 1916 in Albert (pronounced 'Albear'). The book is a wonderful true account of many of the nurses and young doctors who served in World War I.

I also trawled the internet and there I found a story that gave me the beginning of the series: the diary of Miss Esmee Sartorius, a nurse who took the journey to Brussels that Flora, Mags and Ella take. It can be found at http://www.firstworldwar.com/diaries/august1914.htm and is a story that fills you with admiration. Esmee's experiences are also published in *Everyman at War* by Charles Benjamin Purdom (1930) – a book I have promised myself for Christmas.

The first book in the series, *The Forgotten Daughter*, tells the story of Flora, Ella and Mags: how they met and formed a deep friendship; their extreme bravery when trapped in Brussels behind enemy lines; how they coped with running a hospital that had been abandoned; and how they made their daring escape when all the patients had been despatched. It then goes on to tell Flora's story as Ella goes to France to continue nursing and Mags, the most damaged of the three girls, goes home to her family. Flora's story is a love story with a difference as she is banished from her home and her fortunes wane, leaving her to face betrayal, incest and the deaths of some of those she loves most. If you missed this one, don't worry as all of the books stand alone. You can purchase a copy at any good bookshop or online.

The third in the series, *The Wronged Daughter*, tells Mags's story. It begins from her parting with Flora and takes us on her journey through changes in her life that have far-reaching consequences. The only child of a mill owner in Blackburn and Darwen, Mags is treated more like a son. She is taken into the family business and loves everything about the cotton industry, showing great talent and business acumen. However, for a woman of her time, life isn't easy, especially when she falls in love with Flora's ambitious, ruthless brother Harold. But Mags has a friend in Betsy, a salt-of-the-earth northern girl who, despite her own troubles, refuses to let Mags fall. This is a story of betrayal and hardship, but also of friendship and ultimate happiness. It is due to be published in Winter 2019.

However, the girls' story doesn't end there, as the tragedy of the first half of the twentieth century saw the world flare into another conflict, far greater in its impact on the lives and infrastructure of the home front of Great Britain.

A follow-on book, with a working title of *The Courageous Daughters*, is planned. This is the time of the sons and daughters of Flora, Mags and Ella, a war that will pit sibling against sibling and break hearts and lives as Flora's and Ella's children, brought up in what is to become Vichy – the so-called free France – and Mags's child, brought up in Blackburn, England, take different sides in the conflict. It is set to be published in Spring 2020.

If you enjoyed this book, do keep the others in mind for future reading, but also visit my website to learn more about my books and me: www.authormarywood.com.

And/or, join me on Facebook. My page www.facebook.com/HistoricalNovels is a lively interaction with my readers, with laughter and love in abundance, as well as all the latest book news, competitions and guest authors. I would love to see you there.

Much love to all, Mary x

Acknowledgements

An author is nothing without her editors and I am blessed to have the wonderful Wayne Brookes and his team, and Alex Saunders and his team, at Pan Macmillan publishers taking care of me and my work. Along with freelance editor Victoria Hughes Williams, they take my creation and make it sing off the page. Thank you.

And, besides editors, others within the Pan Macmillan team work very hard on my behalf – Kate Green, publicist, and her team tirelessly arrange book signings, press releases and blog tours, and make sure I am taken care of while carrying out these events. And the sales team, who work so hard to get my book shelf-space. Thank you.

And thank you to my son, James Wood, who reads my work before I release it to anyone, making suggestions as he picks up on areas that may be a little flat or need to have more dramatic impact. Thank you. After your advice I feel confident to send my work on its journey to the publishers.

And thank you, too, to my agent Judith Murdoch, who is always there for me and always encouraging, as her signature words 'Onwards and Upwards' testify. Judith, you are simply The Best.

To my darling husband, Roy, for his love and support. And our children, Christine Martin, Julie Bowling, Rachel Gradwell and James Wood, their partners and the beautiful grandchildren, great-grandchildren and added family they have given me. And to my Olley and Wood families. All of you give me support, encouragement and above all, love. You all enrich my life. Thank you.

And to those who saw me to this point with their editing and book designing skills in my self-publishing days. You are never forgotten; without you I wouldn't have made it this far: Rebecca Keys, Julie Hitchin, the late Stanley Living-stone, and Patrick Fox. Thank you.

But no acknowledgement is ever complete without giving my thanks to my very special readers. Especially to those who follow me on Facebook. Each and every one of you brings so much to me. Your eagerness for every book is such an encouragement, seeing me through many hours of writing. Your help with promoting me and my books is invaluable too. I wish I could name you all. Without each and every one of you, there would be no 'Author Mary Wood'. You help me to achieve my dream. Thank you.

My love to you all x

If you enjoyed

The Abandoned Daughter

then you'll love

The Forgotten Daughter

by Mary Wood

From a tender age, Flora felt unloved and unwanted by her parents, but she finds safety in the arms of caring Nanny Pru. But when Pru is cast out of the family home, under a shadow of secrets and with a baby boy of her own on the way, it shatters little Flora.

Over the years, however, Flora and Pru meet in secret – unbeknown to Flora's parents. Pru becomes the mother she never had, and Flora grows into a fine young woman. When she signs up as a volunteer with St John Ambulance, she begins to shape her life. But the drum of war beats loudly and her world is turned upside down when she receives a letter asking her to join the Red Cross in Belgium.

With the fate of the country in the balance, it is a time for bravery. Flora's determined to be the strong woman she was destined to be. But with horror, loss and heartache on her horizon, there's a lot for young Flora to learn . . .

Available now

The Street Orphans

by Mary Wood

Outcast and alone –
can they ever reunite their family?

Born with a club foot in a remote village in the Pennines, Ruth is feared and ridiculed by the superstitious neighbours who see her affliction as a sign of witchcraft. When her father is killed in an accident and her family evicted from their cottage, she hopes to leave her old life behind, to start afresh in the Blackburn cotton mills. But tragedy strikes once again, setting in motion a chain of events that will unravel her family's lives.

Their fate is in the hands of the Earl of Harrogate, and his betrothed, Lady Katrina. But more sinister is the scheming Marcia, Lady Katrina's jealous sister. Impossible dreams beset Ruth from the moment she meets the Earl. Dreams that lead her to hope that he will save her from the terrible fate that awaits those accused of witchcraft. Dreams that one day her destiny and the Earl's will be entwined . . .

'Wood is a born storyteller'
Lancashire Evening Post

Available now

Brighter Days Ahead

by Mary Wood

War pulled them apart, but can it bring them back together?

Molly lives with her repugnant father, who has betrayed her many times. From a young age, living on the streets of London's East End, she has seen the harsh realities of life. When she's kidnapped by a gang and forced into their underworld, her future seems bleak.

Flo spent her early years in an orphanage and is about to turn her hand to teacher training. When a kindly teacher at her school approaches her about a job at Bletchley Park, it could turn out to be everything she never realized she wanted.

Will the girls' friendship be enough to weather the hard times ahead?

Available now

Tomorrow Brings Sorrow

by Mary Wood

You can't choose your family

Megan and her husband Jack have finally found stability in their lives. But the threat of Megan's troubled son Billy is never far from their minds. Billy's release from the local asylum is imminent and it should be a time for celebration. Sadly, Megan and Jack know all too well what Billy is capable of . . .

Can you choose who you love?

Sarah and Billy were inseparable as children, before Billy committed a devastating crime. While Billy has been shut away from the world, he has fixated on one thing: Sarah. Sarah knows there's only one way she can keep her family safe and it means forsaking true love.

Sometimes love is dangerous

Twins Theresa and Terence Crompton are used to getting their own way. But with the threat of war looming, the tides of fortune are turning. Forces are at work to unearth a secret that will shake the very roots of the tight-knit community . . .

Available now

All I Have to Give

by Mary Wood

When all is lost, can she find the strength to start again?

It is 1916 and Edith Mellor is one of the few female surgeons in Britain. Compelled to use her skills for the war effort, she travels to the Somme, where she is confronted with the horrors at the Front. Yet amongst the bloodshed on the battlefield, there is a ray of light in the form of the working-class Albert, a corporal from the East End of London. Despite being worlds apart, Edith and Albert can't deny their attraction to each other. But as the brutality of war reveals itself to Albert, he makes a drastic decision that will change both Edith and Albert's lives forever.

In the north of England, strong-minded Ada is left heart-broken when her only remaining son Jimmy heads off to fight in the war. Desperate to rebuild her shattered life, Ada takes up a position in the munition factory. But life deals her a further blow when she discovers that her mentally unstable sister Beryl is pregnant with her husband Paddy's child. Soon, even the love of the gentle Joe, a supervisor at the factory, can't erase Ada's pain. An encounter with Edith's cousin, Lady Eloise, brings Edith into her life. Together, they realize, they may be able to turn their lives around . . .

Available now

Proud of You

by Mary Wood

A heartfelt historical saga with a compelling mystery at its heart.

Alice, an upper-class Londoner, is recruited into the Special Operations Executive and sent to Paris where she meets Gertrude, an ex-prostitute working for the Resistance Movement. Together they discover that they have a connection to the same man, Ralph D'Olivier, and vow to unravel the mystery of his death.

After narrowly escaping capture by the Germans, Alice is lifted out of France and taken to a hospital for wounded officers where she meets Lil, a working-class northern girl employed as a nurse. Though worlds apart, Alice and Lil form a friendship, and Alice discovers Lil is also linked to Ralph D'Olivier.

Soon, the war irrevocably changes each of these women and they are thrust into a world of heartache and strife beyond anything they have had to endure before. Can they clear Ralph's name and find lasting love and happiness for themselves?

Available now